Rex's hand is around my hip and I'm floating. Dreaming. I must be dreaming. Sleepwalking. I must be about to fall flat on my face. But the strength of Rex's hand holding me up, the light grip of his fingers pushing into my skin, the tingles moving up and down my left side and through my body, tell me I'm not. Tell me this is real, just like I thought.

"Hi," he says, in a low voice, his smiling eyes wandering across my face.

"Hi," I say in return.

LIARA TAMANI

ALL THE THINGS WE NEVER KNEW

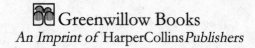

Greenwillow Books
An Imprint of HarperCollins Publishers

The lines quoted on page 351 are by Tracy K. Smith, excerpted from "Everything That Ever Was" from *Life on Mars*. Copyright © 2011 by Tracy K. Smith. Reprinted with the permission of The Permissions Company, LLC, on behalf of Graywolf Press, Minneapolis, Minnesota. www.graywolfpress.org

The text of this book is set in Garamond. Book design by Sylvie Le Floc'h

Library of Congress Cataloging-in-Publication Data

Names: Tamani, Liara, author.
Title: All the things we never knew / Liara Tamani.
Description: First edition. | New York, NY : Greenwillow Books, an imprint of HarperCollinsPublishers, [2020] | Audience: Ages 13 up. | Audience: Grades 10-12. | Summary: "Carli and Rex have an immediate connection, an understanding that must mean first love, but family secrets, disappointments—and basketball, which holds center stage in both their lives—all create complications"—Provided by publisher.
Identifiers: LCCN 2019060207 | ISBN 9780062656926 (pbk ed.)
Subjects: CYAC: Dating (Social customs)—Fiction. | Basketball—Fiction. | Family life—Texas—Fiction. | African Americans—Fiction. | Texas—Fiction.
Classification: LCC PZ7.1.T355 All 2020 | DDC [Fic]—dc23
    LC record available at https://lccn.loc.gov/2019060207

21 22 23 24 25 PC/LSCH 10 9 8 7 6 5 4 3 2 1

First Edition

 Greenwillow Books

For anyone who's ever wanted love from someone in pain

"Love is never any better than the lover."
—Toni Morrison, *The Bluest Eye*

CONTENTS

THE
VERY
FIRST
KISSES

CARLI

Nobody ever warned me about love. Nobody ever warned me that when the greatest thing in the world hits you too hard, too fast, the blast can crush the organs in your belly, send heat flying up the right side of your face, and make your heart forget how to beat normally.

I'm trying to stay in my body, on the sidelines of the gym, but the pain in my belly is making the sound of the bouncing basketball grow fainter. The fluorescent lights keep giving way to darkness.

The boy is the only one who can see the pain. The boy at the free-throw line in his high socks with his high-top fade and his inverted triangle face, drenched with tenderness. The boy who just came out of nowhere, blowing me a kiss in the middle of his game. Who even blows kisses these days? But it wasn't corny like you'd think. It came from somewhere deep, like all of his years and hurts and hopes were attached to it—his whole history.

And now our histories are mixing.

Pain on high, feeling like I'm about to die, an old fact flickers at the front of my mind:

> *The very first kisses were blown in Mesopotamia as a way to get in good with the gods.*

Tacked that up on my bedroom wall after Bradley Dixon blew me a kiss in the fifth grade. The next day he told everyone the kiss wasn't meant for me.

The boy drops the basketball at the free-throw line and runs toward me, just off the court.

Darkness briefly takes me, but the sharp sound of a whistle blown scares the darkness away. I bite some skin peeling on my bottom lip and try to stay in the gym. Keep my focus on him.

He's wearing number twelve—ten less than the number on the jersey underneath my warm-ups. I need to take off these stupid polyester pants, this jacket. I'm burning up, drenched in sweat. Zipper. Where's the zipper? My fingers fumble to find it, but the pain . . . the darkness . . . I can't fight it anymore. I'm losing myself to it . . . falling.

His arms around me, and my insides light up with his down-slanted, hooded eyes. It feels so good the way they're staring into mine. For a second I've never felt so alive. Then I'm gone.

● REX ●

I miss a shot. An easy shot. My mid-range jumper always drops. Always. But man, I can't stop thinking about that girl. About how she passed out in my arms. How, for a second, I thought she might've been dead, and it was somehow my fault.

I was so scared I started crying. I didn't even stop when I saw her chest rising. Rising and falling, again and again, underneath her royal-blue warm-ups. It took four whole breaths for my eyes to convince my head of what my heart was afraid to trust. Good thing my back was to everyone else.

"Carli!" her team's trainer called out, running onto the court. She was a tiny woman, five feet at best. "Lay her down flat on the floor," she ordered with a steady downward motion of her right arm.

I did what I was told.

"Carli!" she shouted again, and lifted Carli's legs up about twenty degrees.

Kneeling beside Carli, I leaned in close and said her name for the first time, feeling the *ar* wobble in my throat.

"Back up, back up," the trainer yelled at me. "Give her some space!"

She could hang that up. I wasn't going anywhere. I reached down and scraped Carli's big, sweaty hair off the sides of her face. Even in a ponytail, it was everywhere. I was about to say her name again—

"I said back up!" the trainer yelled, like I can only imagine a mama would after she's repeated herself for the last time and you'd better listen this time if you know what's good for you.

I stood, backed up, and Carli's eyelashes fluttered like she didn't want me to leave. But the rest of her team immediately crowded me out. I stayed close, though, looking over the tops of their heads, watching her eyes tremble and go still.

The trainer waved something under her nose that made her eyes open wide, but only for a second. Then the paramedics came and rolled her out on a stretcher.

I hope she's okay. She has to be okay, right? They wouldn't let us keep playing if she wasn't okay. Right?

"Hustle back! Hustle back!" Coach Bell shouts, running up the sideline, swinging his short arm in a wide circle.

Twenty-eight seconds left in the game and it's tied 71–71. *Focus, Rex,* I tell myself, and sprint back. We can't lose to Gaines and let them get their confidence up. They'll be our biggest competition at the state championship, only five weeks out. We gotta shut these boys down now.

I'm coming up behind their point guard, Russell Price. Can't stand this dude. He thinks he's so much better than he actually is. He dribbles the ball between his legs—once . . . twice . . . three times—trying to look cool. Then he tries to pass to his shooting guard, but the pass is lazy and slow.

Thanks, I'll take that. I steal the ball and sprint back up the left side of court. Out of the corner of my eye, I see Russell coming up behind me on my right. *You ain't slick.* I switch the ball to my left hand so he can't steal it back. The crowd is chanting, "Rex! Rex! Rex!" Nearing the basket, I cross back to my right, leap, and cock the ball back for a nasty dunk. But Russell tackles me hard to the ground.

"Number-one player my ass," he says, still on top of me.

With the back of my head and tailbone throbbing, I

quickly shove Russell off of me. All I want to do is get up and knock this fool out. I can almost feel my fist meeting his sweaty cheek, see his head whipping back over his right shoulder before he falls limp to the ground. But the referee blows his whistle and wakes me from my rage. Then he holds his fist in the air and signals for two regular foul shots.

"What?" I shout, and quickly hop up to protest the call. "It should've been a flagrant!"

Coach Bell agrees. He's on the sideline yelling, "Flagrant!" and banging his forearms together in an X above his head.

The crowd is booing in agreement, too.

"If that wasn't a flagrant foul, I don't know what is!" I shout, walking behind the ref. "This ain't football. You can't tackle somebody like that."

But the ref ignores me.

"Man, this is some bullshit!" I yell at the back of the ref's balding head.

The ref immediately makes a hard T with his hands to signal a technical foul.

"Are you serious?" I shout, throwing up both of my arms.

Danny, our point guard, grabs me and pulls me away from the ref before I get another tech.

At the free-throw line, I calm down. This is exactly where Carli caught the kiss usually meant for Mom.

Wait, before you try to play me, blowing a kiss has been a part of my free-throw routine since I was eight and discovered Jason Kidd on YouTube. I figured if a ten-time NBA All-Star and two-time Olympic Gold Medal winner could blow kisses as part of his game and not be lame, then so could I.

Every time he went to the free-throw line, he blew a kiss, took one dribble, and shot. To tell his wife and kids he loved them. Every time I go to the line, I blow a kiss, take three dribbles, and shoot. To tell Mom I'm sorry.

But today, Carli was there instead. And I swear it was like she was a gift straight from Mom. See, I pray to Mom every day. Figure she should have some clout, hanging with the celestial bodies and all.

And for the longest, I've been praying she'd send someone my way who could really see me. Not like these girls out here flashing cute smiles, trying to get at me because of how I ball. Or even the genuine ones I can't make myself feel anything for.

The way Carli looked at me was like she could feel the deepest parts of me. The soft parts. The parts that nobody sees. Man, her look pushed up against me so hard that something inside me shook loose and started falling. I was scared. But the way Carli's dark brown eyes stared into mine told me something inside her was falling, too. I'm telling you nothing has ever felt so good.

Focus, Rex. With everyone lined up around the key, the ref passes me the ball. I blow a kiss, dribble three times, and shoot, like always. But I can't help looking beyond the rim, remembering Carli's eyes dimming, her long body going limp.

The ball misses everything.

Damn.

And to make matters worse, the crowd starts chanting, "Air ball . . . air ball."

Another chance, another kiss, another three dribbles, another air ball, and another stupid chant from the crowd.

From half-court, I watch Russell Price shoot the technical fouls. And make them. *Great, just great.*

Fifteen seconds left. Gaines gets the ball back. Their point guard inbounds to Russell. *Can't let this dude score on top of everything else.* I get in my best defensive stance—legs and arms wide and ready. He fakes left and tries to drive to the basket, but I stay in front of him and stop him. He pulls up to shoot, but I put a hand in his face, and he misses. I block him out, grab the rebound, and dribble up the court.

Five seconds. Two points down.

I fake right and go left past two defenders. I'm at

the three-point line, within shooting range.

Three seconds.

A couple more steps to get a higher probability shot.

One second.

With Russell's hands in my face, trying to block the ball, I shoot.

Looks like it's going in, but the ball hits the inside of the rim—*fall, please fall*—and bounces out.

The whole Gaines team and their fans descend upon center court, jumping and cheering.

We just lost the tournament. To Matthew Gaines High. And it's my fault. I should be pissed. I should feel like taking the basketball and drop-kicking it across the gym. But instead, I'm standing here thinking about Carli . . . remembering her face . . . hoping she's okay.

CARLI

The hospital room door flies open and my brother Cole rushes in with way too much excitement.

"Dude! Do you know who that was?"

I stare at him wide-eyed, like he's gone crazy—my default expression for watching his fits of excitement. Boy is prone to having at least one a day.

"Rex Carrington! You managed to pass out in the arms of *the* Rex Carrington!"

The name sounds familiar, but I can't place it. "Okaaay."

"Do you really not know who Rex Carrington is? He only holds the record for the most points scored in a Texas high school basketball game. Ever. Like, in the history of the world. And he's only a junior! He's ESPN's high school player of the year, for Christ's sake!"

"Wait, are you talking about that boy Daddy calls the next LeBron? I thought he went to Yates."

"Yes, him! He moved to Woodside this year. And look! I found a video of him catching you," he says, and pulls his iPhone from his pocket.

Of course, Cole thinks he's king of the Internet. But do I thank the king and kindly ask him to hurry up because I'm about to lose my mind in anticipation of seeing the boy's face again?

No.

Do I obey the urge surging through my body to squeal with glee?

Absolutely not.

The title of the YouTube video is "Rex Carrington to the Rescue!" Come on, could it get any cheesier? Cole presses Play and I stare at the screen, hoping to get a glimpse of the boy's face as he blew me a kiss. But the camera angle is behind him, and whoever made the video started late. So there's only me and my frizzy red hair, collapsing in his arms, looking all damsel-in-distress dramatic. "Uh, cut it off," I moan.

"What? It's brilliant!" Cole says.

"It doesn't even have the part where he blew me the kiss," I complain, and eye my dinner menu, still on the hospital tray beside the bland chicken, white rice, and pale, limp broccoli I picked at. On the back of it, I'd written:

The very first kisses were blown in Mesopotamia as a way to get in good with the gods.

Until I get home and unearth the original from my bedroom wall, it'll have to do. That fact, together with Rex's kiss, has to be a sign, right?

"Blew you a kiss?" Cole asks.

"Yeah, they didn't catch it on the video, but Rex blew me a kiss while he was standing at the free-throw line."

"No, that's part of his free-throw routine."

"The kiss?"

"Yeah, he blows a kiss every time he goes to the line," Cole says, and snaps a picture of me.

"Come on, Cole. You know I'm rough," I whine.

"You're beautiful," he says, and takes another pic—always his response.

"Anyway, I'm telling you, Rex blew *me* a kiss. I mean, he was looking dead at me."

"Oh, I see. You wanted him to blow you a kiss."

"No, I'm just stating the facts."

"Look, all I know is that he always blows a kiss before his free throws. It's, like, his thing. I think he does it for good luck or something. I don't know, but he's been doing it for years."

Everything I thought me and Rex had crumples into a hard ball. *I swear I'm so stupid.*

But it was so real. The way he looked at me. It was like he was offering himself up. His whole, tender self. And I wrapped myself in him, my heart bleeding color.

"Oh, snap. You like him, don't you?" Cole says, staring at me, every freckle on his face ready to bust out doing backflips. He doesn't have nearly as many as Daddy and me, but still.

I sit up a little straighter in the hospital bed, trying to

regain some of my dignity. "Boy, please. I don't even know that boy like that."

He eyes me down, hunting for the lie. I swear Cole is a romance junkie. Had what he calls his first serious relationship in the second grade. Had a two-year run with Alexis in the fourth and fifth grades. For the past five years, seems like he's had a new girl on his screensaver every month. And according to him, they've all been the real thing.

A few knocks on the open door, and a lady pushing a big, silver cart walks in. She has on way too much foundation, and it doesn't quite match the beige of her face. "Done with your food?" she asks.

I look down at the tray, thinking about the other side of the menu. About the first kisses fact. About the things I feel but won't admit. It doesn't seem right letting this lady with bad makeup roll it away.

She opens the door to the cart, exposing a stack of trays with half-eaten food.

Well, it's definitely not going in there. "Yeah, I'm done. Thanks," I say. And while Cole is busy getting out of the lady's way, I quickly grab the menu and tuck it underneath my right thigh. The kiss wasn't for me—fine!—but I still can't let the first sign of me and Rex's fate become hospital waste.

The lady slips the tray into an empty slot inside the cart and heads out.

Cole slides next to me and says, "So, back to you liking Rex."

"Whatever. Nobody's even thinking about that boy like that," I say, imagining the first kisses fact as a tattoo on the back of my thigh.

"Rex Carrington! His name is Rex Carrington!" he practically shouts.

"Give your sister a break, why don't you," Daddy tells Cole as he ducks under the doorframe. The doorframe actually looks taller than his reddish-brown fade by a few inches. But being six-foot-seven, he's had enough headbutting experiences to instinctively duck whenever it's a close call. He walks around to the other side of the bed and gives me a kiss on the cheek. His face, usually smooth, is rough with bright, patchy stubble. "How are you feeling, Angel-face?"

Angel-face? I haven't heard that name since I was, like, eight. Hospital or not, we are *not* about to revive *Angel-face.* "Not dying or anything," I answer. "Carli is still good."

"Got it," Daddy says, with a single nod of his head. "I spoke to the doctor in the hall. If we schedule the surgery soon, you could be back as early as two weeks."

Back home? I think. But the surgery isn't that serious.

Back to school? But that would be way too long. Then I realize he's talking about basketball. Of course, he's talking about basketball. He's always talking about basketball. "Yeah?" I reply, close my eyes, and pretend to be tired from all the drama of passing out.

I forgot to tell you about that. At the basketball tournament earlier today, I had a gallbladder attack. Yes, a gallbladder attack. Apparently, in rare cases, sixteen-year-olds can have them. Basically, the pain of a gall stone passing through my bile duct was so intense that it made me faint. And now the doctor says my gallbladder has to come out.

"Hey, Mom," Cole says.

I open my eyes and see Cole giving Mom a hug. Dang, he's so much taller than her now. I guess I'm taller than her, too—barely. Cole only passed her last year but has grown five inches since. Now he's almost catching Daddy. I swear the boy has gotten taller since dinner last night.

"Oh, did y'all win?" I ask Cole. He had a basketball tournament today, too. Caught up with all the gallbladder stuff, I'd forgotten to ask him about it. I try to be super supportive because he can get down on himself about still playing on JV. It's normal for sophomores to play on JV. Me making varsity three years ago as a freshman is not the norm.

Cole doesn't answer me. He's still hugging Mom. Cole

loves hugs—good-morning hugs . . . good-night hugs . . . happy-to-meet-you hugs . . . happy-to-see-you (even though I just saw you five minutes ago) hugs . . . sorry-you-had-to-spend-the-last-three-hours-detangling-your-hair hugs . . . sorry-you-spilled-water-all-over-your-magazine hugs. He lets go of Mom but still doesn't answer me. He's staring at her.

Mom walks over to me, and Daddy backs up toward the window. He doesn't speak to Mom and Mom doesn't speak to him. Mom's eyes are red and puffy, like she's been crying for a long time. Clearly, they've been fighting.

Mom pinches my big toe, poking up from underneath the thin hospital bedding, and briefly wiggles it around. Then she pats my left leg—shin, knee, thigh—as she walks closer to the head of the bed. "Gallbladder attack, huh?" she says. It's crazy; even with puffy eyes and no makeup, she's still beautiful.

"That's what they tell me," I say, staring at her. It's weird. She's my mom and I see her every day, but her beauty still strikes me all the time. She's tall and slim and has a teeny-weeny 'fro that makes her face, with its high cheekbones and thick lips and dark glowing skin, pop . . . even on what seems to be a sad, shitty day.

"Must be hereditary. I had to get mine removed in my late twenties."

"For real?" I say, and a forgotten memory of me running my fingers over a scar on her stomach rushes to the front of my brain. I was super young, probably like five.

"Yep, had a gallbladder attack when I was in New Orleans, furniture shopping for a client. Passed out in one of my favorite little antique shops. Had to get rushed to the hospital just like you, you know."

"No, we don't know. Why didn't you ever tell us about this?" Cole asks, but it sounds more like an accusation than a question. He's clearly still worried about Mom. The boy needs to relax.

Mom shrugs. "I don't know. Guess it never crossed my mind."

"While you're telling things, would you be so kind as to tell everyone what you decided today?" Daddy says in his lawyer voice. He goes from leaning on the windowsill to standing up straight, like he's readying himself to approach the witness. I hate when his lawyer side comes out . . . always acting like someone's on trial. But this is not the courtroom. We are not his clients. And Mom is not on the witness stand. He can save the drama for work.

Mom ignores him, not even turning around to look at him. When she's pissed, she doesn't curse or shout. She ignores.

And Daddy hates it. "Barbara, please answer the question." Now he's standing with his hands behind his back, in serious lawyer mode.

She turns around and gives him a look. "Derek, this is not the time or the place."

Cole walks around Mom and stands by the head of my bed. Mom and Daddy never fight like this in front of us. They save their fights for behind bedroom and car doors, mostly about Mom working so much.

I wonder if this is about her opening up that new boutique. It's going to be similar to the one already attached to her interior design offices, only bigger. It's been in the works for a while, but she's been waiting on the right time to tell Daddy. Cole doesn't know about it, either. Can't tell him anything unless you want the whole world to know.

"Barbara, you're the one who wants this. So go ahead and tell them." His emotions are starting to get the best of him and he's falling out of lawyer mode.

"For fuck's sake, can somebody please tell us what's going on," Cole exclaims, his voice super high and shaking all over the place.

No one corrects Cole about his language. Mom and Daddy are too busy staring each other down.

The door swings open. "Now that the whole gang is

here," Dr. Williams says, walking in, tossing her long gray locs over her shoulder. But she doesn't finish her sentence. She's noticing the tension in the room, and we're all noticing her notice the tension in the room. Can't get any more awkward. She looks down at her clipboard through her rectangular, red-framed glasses like she's reading something (she knows she's not reading anything) and looks back up.

Then she starts talking about the surgery. Yes, the surgery. That's what she's here to discuss—what the laparoscopic cholecystectomy (gallbladder removal surgery) will involve.

Four tiny incisions around my belly button.

A tiny video camera, which she will insert into my abdomen via one of the incisions.

A video monitor (not tiny), which will display the inside of my abdomen via the camera.

Surgical tools, which she will use to remove my gallbladder from my abdomen while watching the monitor.

Insane, right? But apparently it's no big deal. I should be able to leave the hospital a few hours after surgery. And I'll only take about two weeks to recover.

Daddy brings up the state championship, the fact that it's only five weeks away.

Mom and I trade glances.

Cole is staring at the TV, high up in the corner of the room, looking like he's about to cry.

Daddy wants to schedule the surgery for this Monday, as in the day after tomorrow.

The doctor brings up the necessary presurgery lab work.

Mom brings up school.

The surgery will be scheduled for this Friday.

I'm free to go. In the meantime, if I start feeling another attack coming on, I need to find somewhere to lie down so I don't hurt myself fainting. I was lucky this time.

 REX

First thing I do when I get on the bus is head straight to the back. Doubt anyone wants to sit next to me. But to be safe, I take the very last seat, toss my backpack in the one across from me, put my headphones on, and arrange my face to match the mood I should be in.

Not only did Coach give us (really me) a thirty-minute locker-room speech about the need to focus, he made everybody make ten free throws in a row before we could get on the bus to go home. Mind you, it's a Saturday night, i.e., date night, and it's still gonna take us another forty-five minutes to get all the way back out to the boonies. Phones have been blowing up. Nya has already texted me twice.

But I'm not worried about any of that. All I want is some private time with Carli. I want to sit back, with no eyes over my shoulders, and find her on IG to make sure she's okay. Scroll through her pictures and stare at her face.

Josh, our backup small forward, walks up the aisle and eyes the seat across from me that I've clearly already claimed with my backpack.

No music playing yet, but I slide the left side of my headphones above my ear. "Nah, that's me," I tell him.

"Well, you're sitting over there. So which one is it?" he asks, hate smeared across his round, red-cheeked face. Dude *stays* trying to start some shit. He can't stand me because I took his starting position when I moved out here this year.

It's too bad for Josh. Heard he's been praying for a letter from Michigan State. But graduating this year with the playing time he's been getting, he'll be lucky if he gets to play at the YMCA. Jokes, but he probably won't be playing D1.

But what am I supposed to do? I have goals, too. Lofty-ass goals at that. Your boy is trying to be one-and-done.

"Dude, you got *all* these seats," I say, floating my extended arm across the width of the rumbling bus. All I need to add is *presentiiiing*. Thirteen rows, twelve players, two coaches who always share the first row, and one trainer. Josh *was* the last one to get on the bus. He'd better find the trainer and double up with him.

"But what if I really want *that* seat?" Josh says with a hard, directed nod of his big head.

A few players look back to see what's going on.

"You wanna sit beside me that bad, huh?"

Josh shoves his short, curly bangs away from his face. "Not as bad as I wanna kick your ass."

All I can do is laugh. This fool must think that because he has the body of a linebacker and I'm on the lean side that he could take me. Clearly, he doesn't know me. He doesn't know about all the scraps I've gotten into roaming the streets as a kid in my old neighborhood.

Josh walks off, throwing a weak "asshole" over his shoulder, and settles into a row toward the middle of the bus. The lights lower and the grumbling bus starts rolling.

Finally. I slide my left headphone back on, find

Khalid in Spotify, and snuggle up with Carli.

Ten minutes later, thanks to her brother's IG, I know Carli Renée Alexander is more than okay. Man, let me tell you. She's perfect. And she's in the hospital—not dead. It's not like I really thought she was dead or anything, but it's good to know she's alive and well. *And* I'm playing a game at her school in a week! Doubt she'll be there with the surgery and everything, but her brother is on the JV team, which plays right before our game. So I can give my number to him.

Twenty minutes later and I'm still digging. I'm not one of those crazy stalker dudes or anything. I just can't stop looking for new pictures of her face. She has this cute little button nose, sprinkled with freckles, and these dark brown eyes that pop out of her pale brown skin and take hold of me.

Man, I can't even tell you what I feel when I look at her face. It's better than stepping into an empty gym before the sun comes up. Better than walking through the pines after it rains and having a stray drop land on my nose. Better than thumbing through Mom's old poetry books, finding words I can feel. Or listening to her old records. Or staring at her old beetle collection. Looking at Carli's face, it's like I get lost to some kind of force. Sounds stupid, I know, but

I've never felt anything like it before. Anything *close*.

I look up to grab a Snickers bar out of my duffel bag and notice most of the team crowded around someone's seat toward the middle of the bus. I slide my headphones off and hear people cracking up.

"It must've been that big-ass afro," someone says in a low voice.

"He likes big 'fros and he cannot lie," someone else says in the rhythm of that old Sir Mix-a-Lot song.

Everyone laughs.

I think about Carli's big red hair, about Nya's natural puff. A knot forms in my chest and I stand up.

"Oh my gosh, Becky, look at her 'fro. It is so big. She looks like one of Rex's girlfriends," someone continues in the Valley girl accent from the song.

Everybody busts out laughing again.

More knots, pounding harder. It's not like it's the first time I've overheard my new teammates talking about me. I usually ignore it. But them bringing Carli and Nya into it is different. It's like all the air around me, the engine rumbling beneath me, everything inside me is begging me to shut it down.

As I walk down the aisle, I see a light coming from a seat. Closer, and I peep over our shooting guard's shoulder and see Carli passing out in my arms on Josh's phone.

Illuminated faces all around and I swear I want to knock the laughs right out of their mouths. Our point guard, Danny, kneeling on the seat in front of Josh, is laughing so hard he's in tears. Out of everyone, I thought he could've been my friend.

Leo, our backup point guard, sees me and elbows Danny. Danny looks up at me guiltily, turns around, and sits down.

Josh (of course it's Josh) continues in his Valley girl voice. "I can't believe it's just so round . . . it's like out there. I mean gross. Look, she's just so . . . Black."

That does it. I reach over the back of the seat and snatch the phone out of his hand. "Say something else about my girl and your phone is as good as gone."

Someone says, "Oh shit," and everyone ducks off back to their seats.

Wait, did I just call Carli "my girl"?

The hard pounding in my chest answers with a thousand pissed-off yeses.

Josh stands up. "Give me back my phone!" he whines like he's five years old.

And my five-year-old self knows exactly how to

respond. "What phone?" I ask, and slide it into my right warm-up pocket.

"What's the big deal? I wasn't even talking about Nya. I was talking about that girl who passed out. It's not like you know that stupid girl."

The pounding in my chest shoots through the top of my head, and I can feel the last bit of my sense leaving me. I don't try to stop it. "So first you want to make fun of her hair and now you want to call her stupid?" I yell. "Oh, you gon' learn today!" I march back to my seat, feeling Josh close behind me. When I get there, I squeeze the latches on the window and pull it down—cold air rushing in.

"You better stop playing, Rex! Give me back my phone!"

The cold air slapping me in the face gives me a rare glimpse of my anger. He's like the homie from way-back-when who always has my back but chronically takes shit too far. But what am I supposed to do now? Back down from Josh? Nah. I grab his phone out of my pocket and hold it out of the window.

Everyone gasps. They're all turned around, kneeling on their seats, staring at who they think they see. The asshole who acts like he's too good to talk to anybody or hang with anybody. But it's not even like that. Not even close.

"What the hell is going on back there?" Coach Bell finally gets up and yells.

Everyone sits down and faces forward in their seats.

It takes a lot for Coach to intervene on the bus. It's the one place he completely removes himself. In the name of team bonding, the one place we get to make up our own rules, settle our own disputes.

"Rex is trying to throw my phone out of the window!" Josh answers, his five-year-old self back in full effect.

My five-year-old self wants to yell *Snitch!* But I don't let him, not in front of Coach.

"Have you lost your mind?" Coach shouts down the aisle. "Give Josh his phone back."

I pull my arm back in and toss the phone on the seat.

Josh grabs it and storms off.

"Rex, do I need to treat you like you're my child and make you come sit up here with me?" Coach yells.

A simple rhetorical question, but it shoots deep, pricking the place I'm always pushing further down inside of me. It's just that the words *my child* make me want to answer *yes*. I swear I'm so pathetic.

WHERE
IT
HURTS

CARLI

When I get home, Cole's in my room, sitting on my floor, still in his basketball warm-ups. He's leaning against my bed, surrounded by a ton of old photos. Him and Daddy left the hospital right after the doctor left the room. Mom and I had to wait over an hour for my discharge papers. Looks like Cole's been in here the whole time.

"Hey," I say.

"Hey," he replies, but doesn't look up from a photo he's holding.

I head to my desk, where I remember tacking up the fact about ancient kisses, and look for it underneath a magazine clipping of a guitarfish. Not there. A charcoal sketch of Mom doing a backbend. Nope. A card of a young girl—eyes closed, hugging a book to her chest, with castles and dinosaurs and ships and cities and birds and trees in her curly afro. Not there, either.

"We have to choose," Cole says.

I look over at him, and his eyes are red. He's definitely been crying. But Cole cries at least once every couple of weeks, so I'm not too worried. Still, I stop my search after one last look under a crayon picture of a dark sea.

Then I tiptoe around all of Cole's photos to the corner of the room where my bed is.

"We have to choose," he repeats, and hands me a picture as I climb onto my bed.

I cross my legs and look down at the photo. I've never seen it before but remember Cole taking it. We were on the suspension bridge at the Bayou Bend Gardens a few years ago. While Mom, Daddy, and I waited in the middle of the bridge, Cole pushed the timer on the camera he'd set up and ran to get in place.

"Cute," I say, looking at Daddy's long arm draped around Mom and my head in the crux of Cole's elbow, one leg up in the air like I'm about to fall over. Real smiles all around. I hand it back to him.

"Did you hear what I said? We have to choose." He rips

the photo in half—Mom and I on one side, him and Daddy on the other.

"Really, Cole?" I swear he can't get any more dramatic. "You might as well give it to me now." I scan my walls for the perfect place to fit the photo. *There,* I think, spotting the winged Greek goddess, Solange of Samothrace (I gave the Nike sculpture Solange's head, and in my mind, she thanked me), right above my closet. The Bayou Bend Gardens has a cool collection of Greek goddess statues. The picture will feel at home there.

"Listen," he says, and places the half of the picture with him and Daddy down beside his long, outstretched legs. "Dad's moving out."

The words come at me so straight it's hard to register them. "Wait. What?"

Then he places the half with Mom and me on the other side of his legs. "They're getting divorced."

"Huh?" I wish he would slow down. He's not making any sense.

Cole turns to face me. "Look, Mom and Dad are getting divorced, and we have to choose who we want to live with."

My insides start plummeting. I feel like a baby fish who just got dropped out of a plane. A baby fish who's flapping her fins in foreign air, trying to stay afloat, but keeps falling faster and faster. I read about it in *National Geographic* last night. About how some states repopulate their lakes by farming fish until they reach a certain age and then they release them into the wild by dropping them out of planes. After hitting the water, 90 percent of them survive. But I don't know if I'll survive. I can't take this new reality Cole is dumping me into. "Will you wait a second!"

But Cole's not listening. "If we choose Dad, we go to a new school. He's not sure where yet, but somewhere closer to his job." His voice is so even, so unemotional, like he's not even talking about our life, our parents, our family. "We'll get to see the parent we don't choose every other weekend."

"This is our life you're talking about!" I yell. Something breaks behind my eyes, and tears rage down my face. Strange, warm tears. It's been so long since I've felt them.

"I know," he says, without trying to give me a hug. He's still so calm. It's like we've switched places and I'm the emotional wreck and he's the chill one. What the hell's going on? I am *not* supposed to be like this. He is *not* supposed to be like this. This is *not* supposed to be happening.

I scoot fast to the edge of the bed, preparing myself to

run out of the room, to confront Mom and Daddy. Then I remember that Mom had to go to the office, and Daddy's key chain with his bazillion keys wasn't in the key bowl when I came in.

Cole picks up the pieces of the picture and turns to place them on my bed. "Here, you can have it."

"Why? Why are they splitting up? Why like this?" This *cannot* be about the boutique. Daddy would never take his issues with Mom's work this far. None of their arguments ever get this serious. Not to say that the residue of black-blue words hasn't hung around for a few days here and there—house cold and quiet. But eventually someone cracks a joke or cuddles up or cranks up some nineties R&B or breaks out Monopoly or burps really loud, and things go back to normal. It's like they've always known the limit of how far they could stress their love. But this is way over the limit.

"He wouldn't say."

"He didn't say anything about why? Like, nothing?"

"You know there's no getting real talk out of Dad. I'm surprised I got that much," Cole says, picking up a couple of the photos around him.

"Well, did they get in a fight this morning after I left?"

He grabs another photo. "No."

"Did you see anything weird between them?"

"Not really."

"Come on, Cole! Something had to have happened!" I yell.

He lets out a long, hard sigh and then shifts his tired, swollen face into a bright smile. It's almost scary. "It was a normal Saturday. Mom went to work before I got up. Then Dad drove me up to the school for my tournament."

He's speaking in a high-pitched tone with a slow cadence, like he's reading a fairy tale to a bunch of first graders. This boy is not my brother. My brother is never this rude. I want to tell whoever this boy is to kiss my ass, but I don't because I need to hear what happened.

"He seemed cool in the car. Talked about the strengths and weaknesses of a few forwards from other teams and how he wanted to see a better follow-through from me. He left after the first game. He usually stays, but I didn't think anything of it. Then he picked me up and filled me in on what was going on with you. Didn't say two words on the way to the hospital, but you know how Dad's always lost in his head.

"Is that enough for you? Or do you want me to remember what we were listening to on the radio or how many red lights we stopped at or exactly where we were when the clock struck six or which way the wind was blowing when we drove under the live oaks on Rice Boulevard? Or maybe you want to know how many times Dad cleared his throat or scratched his chin. Because I can try to recall all of that if you need me to," he says, face still fake with cheer.

The sting of how ridiculous he just made me sound won't let me respond. *Am I really that stupid for trying to keep an eye out for things that might clue me in on my future?* I can't even approach the answer. The question has only been here two seconds and it's already changed my shape. And now it's like I don't fit right inside of myself.

"Sorry, I'm just tired," Cole says. He stands, picking up the rest of the photos and putting them back in his black storage boxes. "Give me a second and I'll be out of your room."

What? He dumps me in this foreign place, turns me into this foreign shape, and now he wants to leave me? *No!* I grab his hand.

He looks over at me in surprise.

The thing is, I'm usually the one trying to kick Cole out of my room. He's *always* in here. Says he likes staring at my walls. At the sketches and writings torn from my notebooks, at the images I'm drawn to in magazines . . . the photos he lets me keep . . . my favorite pieces from art classes over the years . . . all the poems and notes and lists and cards and quotes and random facts I collect. I've always figured that if I'm constantly looking at things that call out to me, then the Universe would eventually *have* to tell me what I'm supposed to do with my life. But it hasn't happened yet.

Cole squeezes my hand, lets it go, and gets back to collecting his photos.

"And what? Daddy told you to pass all this information along to me?" I ask, trying to slow him down. It pisses me off that Daddy would tell him and not me.

He grabs a black box off a stack of magazines on my desk. "No, he probably thought Mom would tell you," he says, and slides three photos behind a tab in the box.

"Mom didn't say anything to me. We talked about—" I almost tell on myself, but don't. On the way to get my car, I talked to Mom about the gallbladder attack finally being *the* sign to quit basketball. She's the only one who knows I want to quit. Known since I was in seventh grade and told her that getting my period was a sign to quit. Known I've been afraid to quit because I don't have a better dream to replace it with.

Daddy would die if he knew the truth. He's had a

basketball in my hands since before I could walk. If Cole knew, he would die, too. He *loves* basketball. And we've been playing each other our whole lives . . . pushing each other . . . supporting each other . . . defending each other when Daddy's too hard on us. Sometimes I wonder if we'd be so close if I didn't play.

Cole hasn't even noticed I stopped mid-sentence. It's like he's in a trance, focused on picking up and organizing his photos. "Oh, and we have until March eighteenth. That's the date we'll have to sit down with the judge and state which parent we want to live with," he says. I swear it's like someone has steamrolled over his emotions. Flattened him right out.

"That's not even six weeks! What if we refuse?"

"Then they'll have to spend a whole lot of time and money fighting over us. Believe me, I've already asked Dad these questions. And a million more. We need to choose. And I think we should stay together. It's one thing for Mom and Dad to get a divorce, but it's a whole different thing to split from you, too."

There's my brother. There's my Cole. "Me, too," I say, feeling the agreement soothe the hurt a little.

"Right now, I'm thinking we should stay with Mom. I don't like the idea of her being in the house by herself at night. Plus, we wouldn't have to go through the trouble of switching schools."

What about Daddy? I think. *What about the way his eyes go sad when he's alone? The way he can look scared even when he's sitting on a barstool eating pancakes.* "But you know Daddy needs us around," I say. "Mom will be fine. She's always fine."

Cole stops stacking his black boxes of photos and looks at me. "Do you really want to switch schools?"

"No." I feel lost enough as it is. I couldn't imagine throwing the change of a new school into the mix. *But still . . . Daddy.*

I stand up and grab the photo box at my feet. "Look, I'm not arguing in favor of Daddy or anything." *In favor.* The words taste greasy and bitter in my mouth. I hate them. I hate everything about this situation.

"I'm tired and I stink. Can we talk about this later?" Cole asks, and stacks another box.

"Okay," I say, walking over to him. I place the last box on top of the six others. And before he reaches down to grab them, I reach out for a hug.

He hugs me longer than I usually let him. And when he tries to let go, I hold on to him and hide my face in the ripe funk of his basketball clothes, where I feel safe. Where I'm just a sister. Not the girl whose parents are suddenly splitting up. Not the girl who has to choose which one to live with. Not the girl who's thinking about quitting the team, throwing all of her scholarship opportunities away, giving up everything she's worked for her whole life, and having the whole team, her daddy, and her brother probably hate her for it. And for what? The girl doesn't have a clue what to do with her life. Not a single fucking clue. I'm not ready to be alone with this girl.

I'm not ready.

I'm not ready.

I'm not ready.

Tears flood my face and I'm a 100 percent sure the ill-fitting girl inside me is going to explode.

"Everything will be okay," Cole reassures me.

He says it three times, and I still don't believe him.

REX

The house is freezing when I get home. My father must be here. With this house being so big and him being such a reclusive neat freak, the temperature of the house is one of the only ways I can tell the man is in. I never see his car because he keeps it parked in the garage, which is too small for my pickup truck.

My phone rings and it's Nya.

"Hello," I answer, and sit down on the concrete bench in the mudroom.

"Hey, heard about the game. Sorry you lost," she says.

"Thanks," I reply, and take off my LeBrons. The cold stone floor shocks the bottoms of my feet, even through thick socks.

"Heard you still had thirty-six points, though."

Did I? I think. Carli made me forget all about my stats.

"It never feels good losing, but at least that's a positive," she says.

Nya's big on positives. I like that about her. "True," I say, and store my shoes in a cubicle beneath the bench.

"So, did Danny have an off night?"

"Nah, not really."

"Oh, Jason was ball hogging again?"

"No."

"Well, what happened, then?"

I usually like that Nya asks a lot of questions. Keeps the conversation flowing, which I'll admit, I'm not always the best at. But tonight, the only answer to her questions is Carli. How do I tell her that?

"Oh, well. Can't win 'em all," she says, letting me off the hook. "I figured since y'all lost, you wouldn't feel like going to the movies."

But I can tell by the hope in her voice that she still wants to go. Hope that's making me feel terrible because I'm wondering what it would be like to take Carli to the movies. What it would be like to see her again. I have to see her again. "Yeah, it's probably too late now."

"Well, there's actually a midnight showing if you want to make that?"

"Sorry, I'm too tired," I lie, and make my way to the kitchen. When I get there, I open the fridge. "Arepas! Angie must've come today."

"A-what-who?"

I take the Pyrex out of the fridge and put it on the counter. "Let me tell you, Angie's arepas go so hard."

"Who's Angie?" Nya asks with a hint of she-bet'-not-be-a-side-piece in her voice, which doesn't even make sense.

I've already told her that I don't have time to waste trying to keep up with multiple girls. And even if I did, what kind of fool would I be telling her about one of them? "My babysitter," I say, and get a plate out of the cabinet.

"Babysitter?" Now she sounds confused.

I start preparing a plate of Angie's arepas and rosemary chicken (also bomb). "Well, she was my babysitter growing up." Damn, I miss Angie. She was the only person I had to talk to around the house. She started looking after me when I was born and my father decided to become a heart surgeon. He took forever. Twelve years, to be exact. Twelve years of never being home and studying in his room whenever he *was* home. Finally finished his residency two years ago, but nothing's changed. He's still always gone or in his room. Only difference is that now we live in this big-ass house in the boonies and I have a team that hates me. I pop the plate in the microwave.

"Oh," she sighs. "So she still comes by sometimes to make . . . wait, what's it called?"

"Arepas. They're these little corn pancake things filled with cheese," I answer, thinking about how Angie used to come over every morning and make them for me. That is, until she had a kid of her own. I was about nine.

After that she'd come over two or three times a week to bring groceries, make meals, and take me to games. Man, I used to get so hyped the days I'd step off the bus and see her blue Corolla parked outside our house. Having her around lifted me out of my father's cold silence.

But there's no escaping it these days. Now that we live way out here in Woodside, I can drive, and Angie has three kids; she makes it when she can, which is usually once a month. And that's if I'm lucky.

"They sound good. Maybe when you finally let me come over, I can try some."

"Shi—oooot," I say, catching myself, "these are as good as gone."

"I heard that," Nya says in a stern-mama type tone. See, she has this thing with cursing. Probably comes from going to church every Sunday. She's always inviting me, but I like to spend my Sundays outside, taking in the glory of trees and sky. Anyway, every time I curse, I owe her a kiss (with tongue) in the hallway beside her locker at school.

"But I didn't curse, though."

"Yeah, whatever."

"I didn't!"

"You almost did."

"Almost doesn't count," I say. I mean it's cool that I've had someone to walk the halls with the last few months, but I'm still not down with all that PDA stuff. I take out the apple juice and drink it straight from the jar. The sweet, cold liquid feels good running down my throat.

"What are you drinking?"

"Juice," I answer, and pour myself a tall glass—straight up liquid gold.

"So first you want to curse, and now you're over there sippin' on gin and juice?"

I chuckle. It's almost funny. I like how Nya can almost be funny sometimes. But I shouldn't be laughing at all. Not when I have to tell her about Carli.

The microwave beeps, but I don't get my food out.

"I have something I need to tell you," I say.

"What?" she asks.

I don't know why this feels so hard. I mean, what sixteen-year-old hasn't left one person for another person or told someone *I can't do this anymore* or straight up ignored someone until they stopped calling.

But Nya is the closest thing I've had to a friend since I've moved out here. Because I'm kind of quiet and mostly keep to myself, people are always making up stuff about me. Me being an arrogant asshole is my new team's favorite.

The thing that people don't understand is that when you spend a lot of time by yourself, you get used to keeping how you feel and what you think on the inside. But most people aren't having that. They need words. Words to put them at ease. Words to validate them. Words to excite and entertain them. And when you're not coming with the words they need, they'll start trying to figure out what's wrong with you. And when they can't figure it out, they have no problem making stuff up.

Learned that early, when the kids in my hood started calling me Half-taco. They said I didn't talk (barely said anything back then) because I could only speak Mexican. Used to piss me off so bad. First of all, Mexican is not a language. Second of all, Angie was Colombian and spoke better English than Spanish. If they wanted to be racist, they could've at least gotten their facts straight. But no.

So I'd fight. And when I got tired of that, I'd keep to myself. Had to walk a mile and a half to the basketball court at Emancipation Park, where all anyone cared about was ball, just to have some normal interaction with people. And by the time I was old enough to play ball for the school, I was used to keeping to myself. Used to being the dude everybody saw but nobody really knew. It felt safer that way.

I mean, the last couple years got better. Years and years of balling with the same people, and they start to get to know you a little. But then I moved out to Woodside.

The point is, I feel safe with Nya, less lonely with Nya.

And it's hard to give that up. But Carli. Carli makes me feel . . . everything.

"Well?" Nya says, sounding frustrated.

And it's the kind of everything that's not going away.

"Hello! Earth to Rex! What is it that you gotta tell me?"

I take a deep breath and push out, "I met somebody else."

"Who?"

The question comes at me with lightning speed. I want to say, *This girl you don't know* to keep things vague, but the ache in my throat won't let me call Carli something so impersonal. "Carli."

"Carli?"

I can hear her face twisting up.

"Who's Carli?"

"You don't know her."

"Did you have sex with her?"

"Whoa! Hold up a second," I reply, trying to think of why she would ask that. I didn't even think sex was on her brain. We never even got past touching above the waist with our clothes on.

"Well, did you?"

"No."

"Did you kiss her?"

"No."

"How long have you been talking to her?"

"I haven't been talking to her. I—"

"Well, when did you meet her then?"

"Tonight."

"At the game?"

"Yeah."

"Wait, is it that girl from the video?"

"You saw that?"

"Of course I saw it. Everybody saw it. So, is it?"

"Yeah."

"So, what exactly happened?"

"I caught her and—"

"So you already knew her?"

"No."

"Sooooo . . . you caught her and what?"

"I felt something."

"You felt something?"

"Yeah."

"Felt what?"

"I don't know . . . something deep."

She cracks up laughing in a way I've never heard her laugh before—hard and high, like she has her head thrown all the way back. "You felt something deep? That's the stupidest shit I've ever heard. And for a girl you don't even know? Everybody said you were an asshole, but I didn't know I was dealing with a fool, too."

My ear throbs with that familiar word—*asshole*—with the unfamiliar brand-newness of Nya. It's like she just smacked me upside the head through the phone. This can't be Nya. I wish I could clap back and call her a fraud, but shock has dulled my anger.

"But what can I say? You are *the* Rex Carrington. At least I got to try you out for myself. If you would've waited another two weeks, I would've given you the goods. But too bad for you, boo-boo."

No anger at my back, a fresh wound starts to spread just beneath my skin. I push it down to the place with the million other hurts I don't have time to deal with and hang up. Then I grab my juice, my plate out of the microwave, and sit at the counter on one of our uncomfortable-ass barstools.

Every time I have to sit on one of these, it pisses me off. Who buys concrete chairs? I would sit at the table, but those chairs aren't any better. All the furniture in this house is uncomfortable. My father says it has to match the house's modern style. Man, he can get on somewhere with his modern style.

I have to give big ups to her little brother. Carli's social media is on lockdown, but Cole's is wide open. And he's a sharer, a big-time sharer. A big-time lover, too. Seems like every few weeks, a new girl takes over his feed. Not completely, though. Carli constantly gets play.

But tonight, Cole's posted a bazillion pics of their whole family together. Old vacation and family outing photos . . . things like that. And it's not even throwback Thursday. The gallbladder thing with Carli must really have him thinking about how much he loves his family. How perfect they are. What I would give to know that feeling for even one second.

After finishing my dishes, I head upstairs to my room. But before I reach the landing in the middle of the stairs, where my father's frame disappears from my line of vision, I turn around and look one more time.

Two minutes later I'm still standing here, staring at nothing.

This is stupid. I'll go knock on his door. If he doesn't answer, he doesn't answer. Wouldn't be the first time.

I walk back down the stairs and then down the hall that leads to his room. There's a slit of light underneath his door, and when I get closer I hear the faint sound of the TV. My knuckles are about to hit the door when I stop and think about how much he hates me.

Our old tiny house, with all of its worn upholstered furniture and wallpapered rooms and halls, where Mom had once walked and ate and slept and talked and been . . . where she'd been . . . was perfect if you ask me. But my father didn't ask me. He sold the house without—you know what, I'm not *even* about to start.

After a couple of bites, I look over at the opening to the hall that leads to my father's room. One look, that's all I'll allow myself. Sometimes, after I've been out here a while, he'll come out of his room and ask me about the game. And I'll ask him about the hearts he looked at that day and if he had a surgery. And we'll actually have something that resembles a conversation.

Okay, one more look, but that's it. The entry to the hall looks like an empty picture frame. The frame is modern (of course) with a wide, dark wood trim. And inside the frame, there's a white wall, illuminated by a small recessed light. Doesn't look like the frame is getting a picture tonight.

I eat my last bit of arepa, wash it down with juice, and carry my dishes to the sink. But before I rinse my dishes and put them in the dishwasher, I lean back against the counter and look at more pictures of Carli on her brother's IG feed. Her gentle face is the perfect antidote to tonight's roughness.

The thing about it is, I don't blame him for hating me. I don't blame him for never wanting to be around me or talk to me. I get it. If I had never been conceived, Mom would still be alive. It's my fault she's not here. I've always gotten it.

But right now I need to share Carli with someone who won't laugh. Even though we have no history of talking about girls, and I'm pretty sure the conversation will be awkward as hell, I want to sit on my father's bed, like one of his patients, and talk about what I feel in my heart.

The slit underneath his door turns black, and the TV silences.

I lower my fist. It's all good. I'll go out back, lie under the trees, and talk to Mom, like I always do.

 CARLI

I'm sitting in the gym after school on Wednesday, half reading a magazine and half watching my team run through plays. Even though I can't practice, Coach Hill still wants me here because I'm the captain, the leader of the team. I swear every time she reminds me of that, which is every chance she gets, an alarm goes off in my head. An alarm that's been sounding since Saturday. A reminder to tell her and the team that I don't want to play anymore. That I'm not coming back to play after the surgery tomorrow.

With my Spanish book open to hide my magazine tucked inside, I'm reading an article about how numbers can provide clues to your life's direction. The girl in the picture beside the article looks crazy-confident, like she knows exactly where her life is headed, and I'm trying to get a little bit of that.

Coach Hill blows her whistle, long and hard.

"Carli, watch out!" a few of my teammates shout.

I look up in time to miss a ball flying toward my head. It bangs loudly against the bleachers behind me.

"My bad," Vanessa, my backup, says with a way-too-sorry look on her face. I didn't see what happened, but I'm guessing she missed another one of Jordan's hard passes. It's really not her fault, though. Coach Hill plays me so much that Vanessa hardly ever touches the court. And now, with the playoffs so close, everyone's putting on the pressure for her to step up.

"Why don't you go ahead and take her out for the rest of the season?" Jordan, our point guard, yells at Vanessa.

The bestie can be a little overprotective. She's standing with her hands interlaced on top of her head—deep dimples in her milky brown cheeks even when she's mad.

If you only knew, I think before saying, "I'm fine," and get up to get the ball.

"Well, hurry up, then," Jordan says, and jokingly gives me the middle finger.

I smile, happy she's playing with me. We've been kind of distant this week. She's been complaining that I've been too quiet, that I've been keeping something from her. But there's no way I can tell her about quitting the team. And I can't tell her about my parents, either. Telling her would make it too real.

At least we've had Rex to talk about. She's convinced the kiss was at least partially for me. You see, he broke up with his girl hours after catching me.

Jordan knows because she has a cousin who has a best friend who has a boyfriend who plays basketball for Woodside who said that Rex broke up with his girl on the bus and everyone heard. Said she cursed Rex out so bad for leaving her that he had to hold his phone out of the window so he wouldn't have to listen to it all. Sounds crazy, I know. Why not just hang up in her face? Maybe because he's too sweet.

As I walk to get the ball, which bounced two rows down and rolled to the opposite side of the bleachers where the band always sits, I reach to touch the hospital menu in my back pocket, to make sure it's still there. I've been secretly carrying it everywhere with me since Saturday. Gonna write my number on the back and give it to Jordan to give it to Rex when he plays at our school Monday. I don't even have to tell you how bad I wish I could go (holding-my-pee-until-the-end-of-the-movie bad). But I'll be at home recovering from surgery.

After I retrieve the ball, I overhead pass it back to Jordan as hard as I can.

Jordan catches the ball and immediately drives down the lane for a layup, her tongue hanging out of the side of her mouth and the wristband on her left arm pulled up over her elbow.

"You ain't Michael!" I jokingly shout.

She makes the layup. "Oh, I'm not?" she asks, and walks the ball way out beyond the three-point line. She shoots and it drops.

"Oooooooo," the team says in unison. But I'm not even surprised.

Jordan has known since elementary school that she wanted to be the female version of Michael Jordan and has been pushing toward her dream ever since. I wonder if it has to do with her name.

I've been reading about this theory called normative determinism, which basically says that people's names can influence what they want to do with their lives. If Jordan is any indication, it's definitely true. Either way, I'm happy for her, I really am. But sometimes I get jealous that she has a dream and I don't.

"Okay, let's get back to work!" Coach shouts.

And back to the magazine. Here's what the article's telling me to do in order to get a clear look at my life's direction: write the numbers one to ten and beside them, list things that have happened the corresponding number of times this week.

Can't be trivial things, like how many Jelly Belly Buttered Popcorn candies I ate or how many times I've spotted Sabina Karlsson (this Black model with red hair and freckles like me) in a magazine. Although I *have* been seeing her everywhere lately. They have to be things with meaning. Things with weight (with the way my life has been going, I should have no problem there).

And after I make the list, signs are supposed to start popping up with more frequency. Signs. Yeah, only the things I've been following since the fifth grade when one saved my life.

It was a Sunday. Daddy was getting ready to visit his parents' grave. I wanted to go, but he always insisted on going alone. So I went outside to practice my ball-handling skills in the driveway, hoping that when Daddy came out to get in his car, he'd be so pleased that he'd take me with him.

The basketball rolled into the street, and I ran after it without looking. Then a giant swallowtail, the largest butterfly in North America, swooped in. I'd cut one out of the *Houston Chronicle* after reading about its six-inch wingspan the day before. Tacked the photo up on my wall.

And there it was, in all its majesty, flying right in front of my face. I stopped suddenly, and a car whizzed by me so close that it felt like death giving me a cold hug.

And now, when the world is coming at me faster than ever—and I have to decide which parent to live with and how to tell my team I want to quit basketball and what to do with my life—I'm supposed to up and stop looking for signs just because Cole made me feel stupid? Exactly. So here goes:

1. Number of shoes Daddy removed before going to sleep on the sofa Saturday night after the hospital. On Sunday I woke before

dawn and saw him asleep with his long legs hanging over the sofa's edge in the same clothes from the night before. I removed his other sneaker, covered him with a blanket, turned off SportsCenter, and went back to my room.

2. Number of Lucille Clifton poems I copied in my prettiest handwriting and placed on my wall while waiting to hear the kettle whistle from the kitchen on Sunday. Mom makes tea first thing every morning.

3. Number of words I said to Mom and Daddy when I walked into the living room. It. It. True. Cole was still asleep. Mom looked confused. Initially, Daddy looked scared, like a little kid who'd just gotten in big trouble, but his lawyer side came through.

4. Number of sips Mom took of her tea as lawyer Daddy summarized the same details Cole had given me the night before. As usual, Mom tried to keep her cool. But her right pinky finger wasn't having it. It was tapping the hell out of her mug. Her right pinky was pissed.

5. Number of minutes that elapsed between the end of the conversation and Daddy

leaving to buy boxes from U-Haul

6. Number of exchanges Mom and Daddy had before Daddy moved out. All averaging ten seconds and all about which thing belonged to who.

7. Number of times per hour I begged Mom to tell me the reason they were splitting up.

8. Number of times this morning I thought I heard a knock at my door and got up and checked, but no one was there. Cole hasn't been in my room since Saturday night. Four days.

9. Number of times Daddy called me last night. The Rockets were playing the Clippers and he wanted me to study the rhythm of James Harden's step back. Normally I'd be annoyed, but every time I saw *Daddy* flash across my iPhone's screen, I was five years old again, hearing his keys jangling at the door, telling me he's home.

10. (x a thousand) Number of times I've closed my eyes and seen Rex's face. His big down-slanted eyes staring into mine. If only he could see my pain and come hold me now.

✦ REX ✦

When a mother tree is dying, she passes on messages of wisdom to her baby seedlings. No lie. Suzanne Simard, this badass forest ecologist, has actually traced messages moving down a dying mother's tree trunk, through the fungus in the ground, and into her seedlings. Dying trees speak to their children.

Crazy, right? That's my favorite thing to think about when I'm out here in the pine forest behind our house. Makes me think Mom spoke to me when she was dying, too. Makes me think, in the thirty seconds she held me on her chest before her heart stopped beating, she somehow gave me a lifetime of lessons.

I just wish I knew what they were.

TELL
ME

CARLI

Cole came into my room this morning *and* I get to see Daddy today. That's all.

REX

Yo! Once again my boy Cole comes through. He started to fall off for a minute. Hadn't posted all week. But this morning, on my way to school, he's making up for it— plenty! At the red light, I look down at my phone again and see he's posted another picture of Carli. She's riding in the backseat of their old-school Land Rover in a pink T-shirt with a rainbow. Underneath the rainbow the words *Easy Like Sunday Morning* are in gold, glittery letters. Man, easy is right. I swear it's never been easier to look at someone's face. And she's smiling so big. I mean huge.

They're on their way to Carli's surgery and Cole gave up *all* the deets. Say *what!* It's like he was personally giving them to me.

There's only one problem. Well, actually four.

1. I'd have to skip school and I have a precalc test second period. Dude, I studied all night for that thing. I *could* make it up next week, but a weekend is a long time to forget things like:

$$(a+b)^n = \sum_{k=0}^{n} \binom{n}{k} a^{n-k} b^k$$

2. I'd miss gym period, which is the mini-practice before tonight's game. I need that time to make my 111 shots a day. Gotta keep the jump shot dropping! Plus, Coach Bell will wonder where I am. I don't want to disappoint him again.

3. Carli's surgery will be at Houston Methodist in the Medical Center, the same hospital where

my father practices. Last time my father caught me skipping school (eighth grade, to try and stop this OG oak tree in the neighborhood from being chopped down by a builder), he didn't say a single word to me for weeks.

4. I hate hospitals. Haven't stepped foot in one since I was born. Every time I even drive by one, the world plops its fat ass right down on my chest, making it almost impossible to breathe.

But really, all these problems don't have shit on the promise of Carli. All week she's been glinting off the shiny parts still tucked inside of me. The pure and happy and hopeful parts, the parts starving for love. I'm telling you, it would kill me to miss this chance to see her. No question, all my shiny parts would go dull.

CARLI

When we get to the hospital, Daddy's already in the waiting room. He's sitting in a chair, hugging his briefcase, staring at the ground. Even though he's in his lawyer clothes, his scared little-boy face is in full effect.

See, this is exactly what I was trying to tell Cole. I hate seeing Daddy like this. Whenever I catch him this way, everything inside me plunges toward the place he must've gone when he was eight after hearing both of his parents died in a car accident. An endless pit with no sound or light.

I hope Daddy hasn't been sitting around his rental house like this. The thought of it makes me want to tell him that I chose him. Makes me want to tell him that I'm going to his place after surgery today.

When he sees us, he wipes himself clean of the little boy and stands up.

Without thinking, I run to him.

As I slam into his chest, he hugs me tight, lifting my feet off the floor. "Hey, Angel-face," he says.

"Hey, Daddy," I say, and as my feet touch the ground, my stomach growls super loud, like it's saying *Hi,* too.

"Hungry, huh?" Daddy says, and laughs. "Yeah, I remember when I tore my ACL in college and couldn't eat the night or morning before surgery. It was awful."

I've heard about his ACL a million times. Everybody has. He tore it mid-season of his senior year at Kentucky.

Left knee. Says it's what ruined his chances of going to the league. But right now I can hear about his ligament all day. Every word he speaks is filling up the massive hole his absence is digging inside me.

I want to tell him how strange it's been not having him home. How I've been missing his morning pancakes, the smell of his aftershave, the sight of his socks on barstools and sofas and tables, and his keys, especially his keys. But nothing comes out.

"Hey, Dad," Cole says, right behind me.

Dang, already? I feel like the girls on *The Bachelor* when someone interrupts their one-on-one time too soon. But I act like the bigger person and step aside.

Mom doesn't come into the waiting room. She's in the lobby, talking to the reception lady behind the large, circular desk. Mom must feel my eyes on her because she glances in my direction through her oversized shades before pointing toward a hallway. The reception lady nods, and Mom turns away and waves at us to follow her.

Walking down the hall, Mom's ahead with Cole and I'm lagging back with Daddy.

"How's the new place?" I ask Daddy, hoping it's full of those manila folders and flip-top boxes he's always bringing home from work. Better to be working than sitting around sad.

"It's nice. You'll have to come stay for a weekend as soon as you've healed up. I only signed a six-month lease because I plan to buy a house this summer, but I still want it to feel like home for you and Cole."

Way too much of the new reality rushes in at once, and I can't think of anything else to say.

Daddy ducks under a doorway. "You can do that thing you do to your walls, and I can help you transfer it all when we move. I've already helped you start. Hung a life-sized poster of Candace Parker in your room yesterday."

Astonishment helps me break my silence. "Really?" I say, but I want to be like, *Seriously, Daddy? Have you seen my walls?* Candace Parker can ball and all, but I don't have a single picture of a basketball player in my room. My walls are full of random things I love.

Maybe they haven't told me what I want to do with my life *yet*. But one thing's for certain: staring at a life-sized basketball player will tell me zero things about my future. I don't know how I'm going to take it down without hurting Daddy's feelings, but best believe it's coming down.

As I approach the elevator, Mom says, "The gastro-intestinal surgery department is on the sixteenth floor and you're sixteen!" Guess my feelings about that poster were still all over my face becase Mom only points out potential signs when she catches me with a sad or sideways look. It usually perks me up, but today it makes my mood worse.

You see, Mom doesn't believe in all my sign stuff. She's never said so, but she's not exactly big on believing in general. Well, believing in yourself, in your dreams, in love—those types of things—sure. But with everything else, she's always preached that questioning and studying is more important that believing. And every time she's asked me how my signs work, I've never had a good answer for her.

All I know is that I can't afford to miss them. What if the one time they clearly point me in the direction of what I'm meant to do with my life, I'm not even paying attention? What then?

I step onto the elevator, she pushes the circle with the sixteen, and it lights up. Sixteen years and the signs still haven't told me what I need to know most. I finally have the chance to quit basketball, but I still don't have a clue what to replace it with.

Mom's always telling me to be patient, to keep listening to myself and it will come. Yeah, easy for her to say. She's known she wanted to be an interior designer since she was a little girl, like Cole has known he wants to be a photographer or Jordan has known she wants to play basketball.

Sometimes I think about being a magazine editor, but then I think being a poet or writer would be cool, or maybe some type of visual artist, or a historian, or even an astrologist or a thrift shop owner. But I could also see myself as a professor. Or even an astronomer. It would be amazing studying stars, moons, planets . . . the whole universe. I don't know. At any given moment, I could have a million ideas about who I'm meant to be floating through my head. So what exactly am I supposed to be listening to?

Cole must see the angst on my face because he reaches for one of his hugs. I let him pull me in, and watch Daddy walk past us to the back corner of the elevator, as far away as he can get from Mom.

REX

I turn off the car. Check my phone again. Cole's posted a new pic of Carli walking into her hospital room with the caption "The strongest girl I know." She's looking back over her shoulder, scared.

"You're okay," I whisper, tracing the curve of her face with my finger. But her expression doesn't change.

My heart slumps and I'm out of my truck, hitting the lock button. I have a plan. I'm going to move as fast as I can. So fast I can't think about where I am.

Full-speed through the parking lot. I mean, my legs are moving so fast in these stiff jeans, I'm sweating. I swear February doesn't mean shit in Houston.

A minute later my red-and-black Air Jordan 1s hit the curb to the hospital entrance (like what!), and I'm walking toward the doors. Almost there. So close that the sliding glass doors part for me.

Then *bam*! Here comes the world's fat ass—thirteen million billion billion pounds—trying to sit down on my chest.

I turn around, walk away from the doors, and slide my right hand down the back of my neck, trying to get rid of the weight. But this hospital is extra heavy. Air is ripping in and out of the very top of my lungs—in-and-out and in-and-out and in-and-out so fast it burns. Feels worse than the final minute of a game I've played all thirty-two minutes of, when I'm sure my lungs are about to say, *I'm done*.

Come on, Rex. Hands interlaced on the top of my head,

I place one foot in front of the other until I make a wide circle around the porte cochère. Two wide circles and I'm breathing a little easier.

Turning back toward the doors, I nearly bump into a tall, brown-skinned man wearing a white coat over scrubs. My insides jump. He looks about ten years younger than my father, though. False alarm.

Back to the plan. *Let's go!*

This time I run (damn near fly!) through the doors and down the waxy hospital floors toward the elevators. Shoes squeaking, I pass a man walking in Wranglers and a cowboy hat like he's standing still.

In the elevator I close my eyes and see Carli's face in front of 1604. I push sixteen and it lights up. I can't believe I'm about to see her again. A mixture of ease and excitement wash over me. Then the metal doors slide closed, and I'm staring at my reflection.

My chest tightens.

I swear anytime I catch my reflection, it's looking at me funny. Thick brows (like my father's) tense like they wish I *would* step to them. Big lips (like my father's) perfectly still like they have nothing to say to me and never will. All my moles like tiny unforgiveable sins.

See, this is exactly why I don't keep a mirror in my

bathroom. Instead I keep a sticky note that says *You're good.* The only time I intentionally look in the mirror is once a week in the chair at the barbershop. Gotta make sure the high-top fade is on point.

And it is. Sponged the top this morning. Don't need to do much else but let the barber keep the lineup fresh. And I went yesterday, so I'm cool. With my fingertips, I brush the edge where my hair meets my forehead and tell myself, *You're good.*

But my reflection tells me that's a lie. *Dude, what are you doing? I don't remember anybody inviting you.*

And he's right. The only reason I know about Carli's surgery is because I've been stalking her brother's IG. What if she thinks I'm crazy when I show up? The red number above the elevator doors blinks to eleven, and I push buttons twelve through fifteen to buy more time.

When the doors open on twelve, two buff-looking dudes in blue scrubs walk on. "Thirteen plea—" the blond one starts before he sees it's already lit up. The dark-haired one stands behind him, talking about a lady over-waxing his eyebrows. Then a man rolling a pregnant lady in a wheelchair gets on and stands right beside me.

Really? I close my eyes and brace myself for the weight.

But it doesn't come.

We all start rising, and I actually feel the opposite of weight. It's the feeling I get sometimes when I'm sitting under the trees, when the wind is blowing just right and the sun is glinting down through the leaves. Like everything is okay. Like I'm right where I'm supposed to be.

CARLI

In the pre-op room, when I get Mom alone (Cole and Dad went to get a snack from the vending machine. Yes, they actually announced it in front of me like I'm not lying here starving), I try to take my mind off the surgery by asking her the same question for the millionth time:

What happened between you and Dad?

She's sitting beside me in a puke-pink pleather chair. Her sunglasses are off, and her eyes are definitely looking better than they did this morning. They've been in a perpetual state of red puffiness since last Saturday, but first thing in the morning, they're always the worst.

"I'll be fine," she says, looking up from a design budget. I guess she felt me eyeing her. She's had *I'll be fine* on repeat all week, mostly for Cole. She doesn't need to say it to me. I believe her. Mom always finds her way back to happy.

Found her way back after her first design business failed and she had to close her studio and start working from home again. We were in elementary school. Found her way back after her mom died from breast cancer four years ago. Grandma Rosemary was cool.

And it's not that fake, always smiling kind of happy. With Mom, it's like no matter what happens, big or small, she finds her way back to enjoying her work, her family (well, that's obviously complicated right now), her music, her books, her art, her random dance sessions, her tea, her candles, her long baths, her wine, her million trinkets around the house—her life. It's a kind of enjoyment that gets all up in your face, but in a good way. I swear if she didn't enjoy her life so damn much, I'd probably still be planning to ball. But I see her happiness and want it for myself.

"I know," I say, voice cracking. *Wait, where did that come from?* I'm not worried about Mom. I'm really not. But she has been crying a lot. The most I've seen since her mom died.

"Carli," Mom says, and puts her paperwork down. She has a look of concern in her big, Diana Ross–looking eyes. "Sometimes life hits you with things, but you have to keep going, you know."

Wait, what? I see what she's doing. She's trying to flip this conversation from her sadness to mine. But you know what, if she wants to do that, I'm going to use it. I reach down (don't have to reach very far) and pull out the sadness I've been feeling all week—about our family, Daddy, this whole situation—and I say, "It would help if I knew what happened." Tears pool at the base of my throat, and I gently guide them up behind my eyes and let them fall.

"Carli," Mom says, and picks up the Styrofoam cup from the nightstand. She takes a sip. There's a Lipton tea tag hanging by a string on the outside of the cup. Mom is bougie about her tea. No way she's enjoying that Lipton. "You want me to get you some ice chips?" she asks.

"Are you serious? I cry and all you offer me are ice chips?" I sit up in the bed and feel the chill from the cold room hit my bare back through the sparse ties of the hospital gown. "Forget ice chips! I want to know what happened between you and Daddy," I say, tears gone. Pretending gone. Patience gone.

I swear all fifty-two million times I've asked her about why she and Daddy are getting divorced, she acts shady, which is not like her at all. She never shies away from the truth. It's one of my favorite things about her. My whole life, I've always been able to ask her about anything. And I mean *anything*—sex, drama at school, drugs, alcohol, religion, masturbation. Yes, masturbation! But she can't talk about what happened between her and Daddy? Makes no freaking sense.

"You'll have to ask your dad, Carli."

"Seriously?" It's so irritating the way she keeps suggesting this like it's possible. I mean, I can ask Daddy about impersonal stuff, like how to craft the best arguments for my teachers to give me extra credit for all the random things I read. Or what I should use to get all my hair out of the drain. Or why we don't have one-person-one-vote if we live in a democracy.

But whenever I try to talk to Daddy about life outside the very practical or intellectual—basically anything dealing with feelings—he always gets that look in his eyes, that look that makes me stop pressing. After twenty years together, she might be immune to the look, but I'm not.

"Well, I can't talk about it, Carli. I wish I could, but I can't."

"You're the one always talking about questioning everything! And now I'm asking something that you have all the answers to, but you refuse to give them to me?"

"Look, Carli," she says. "I wish I could. I really do. But your dad has to be ready to talk to you about it, you know, or it won't do you any good."

"I'll take my chances."

"No, Carli."

"Seriously, if it doesn't do me any good, it'll be on me. I asked for it."

"I said no."

Cole and Daddy walk back in before I can get an answer out of Mom.

Dr. Williams is with them. "It's time," she says, two nurses right behind her. One comes over and releases the brakes on my bed, and the two of them together begin to steer me out of the room. Daddy, Mom, and Cole are right behind them.

I guess this is it. It all seems to be happening so fast. The nurses are wheeling me to a room where the doctors are about to take out a part of me . . . a part I've lived with my whole life . . . a part I might miss. What if I never wake up?

My bed clears the room and I'm moving down the hall, staring up at harsh, fluorescent lights.

When we come to a set of double doors, Dr. Williams presses a large red button on the wall, they swing open, and we all pass through, Daddy ducking. "The waiting room is just up there to the left," Dr. Williams says, and points to a space ahead with more puke-pink chairs arranged in a square.

The nurses turn me toward a long hall with more double doors.

Let my family come with me! I want to beg.

Cole grabs my hand.

"We'll be close, Angel-face," Daddy says, standing on my right.

Mom puts her hand on my left leg and says, "Just down the hall."

I look up at my family, all together, wanting so much I can't have. Wanting to wail like a baby, but instead I close my eyes.

 REX

I make it just in time to catch Carli in the hall upstairs. When I see her, my heart starts floating in my chest. At least that's how it feels. Like there's nothing attached to it, like it might just go overboard and decide to float off somewhere. And that's without even seeing her face. Through the large glass windows on the double doors in the hallway, all I can see is her big red hair peeking up over the back of the hospital bed.

On one side of her, a beautiful tall woman with short natural hair is patting her leg. Must be her mom. And on her other side, her brother is holding her hand. Her dad (clearly where Cole and Carli get most of their height from) reaches down to give her a kiss on the forehead. Damn, she's lucky! Makes me want to push the red button and rush through the doors so I can join in on the love, too.

The nurses start to wheel Carli off, and I see her face. Hold up, she's scared. Her eyes are wide open, and her small, round nostrils are flared. Carli pushes up onto her elbow and turns back to look at her family. But walking away, her dad is looking down, her mom is gazing out a window, and Cole is busy with his phone.

Two fat tears fall down Carli's cheeks, and I'm sick. I hate seeing her like this. I wish I could rush in and hold her hand . . . rush in and tell her everything will be okay.

I press my forehead to the window of the door and mouth:

You're okay.
You're okay.
You're okay.

Over and over again. And before the nurses wheel her out of view, our eyes meet, her face rearranges itself to resemble something like peace, and I feel like I'm back in the gym, catching her again.

VERY
IMPORTANT
THINGS

CARLI

It's four thirty p.m. on Monday. Cole's at his game. Mom's back at work after taking the weekend off. And I'm sitting on the orange velvet sofa in the living room with my legs stretched out. I'm alternating between cutting very important things out of magazines and staring at a blank page in my notebook.

No more boys in my notebooks.

And definitely no more boys on my walls.

Instituted those rules after I kissed my first boy (Patrick) behind the bathroom stalls at basketball camp when I was twelve. After I got home, I must've written his name down in every color marker, crayon, and ink pen I owned. Then I waited for him to call, waited for him to ask me to be his girl, waited to put bursts of colors—bright, intoxicating colors—all over my walls.

None of it happened.

After Patrick, I might've been tempted to write a few more boys' names down, thinking they were true. But between side chicks, ego-tripping, dudes trying to get all big and bad, dudes thinking they could tell me what to wear or how to do my hair, dudes not doing what they said they would do, dudes being all sweet one second and not even texting me back the next, dudes trying to pressure me into sex, or dudes plain working my nerves, they were all false alarms.

But nothing about Rex feels false. I know this is going to sound crazy, but in the hospital, he came to me in a vision. There he was, on the other side of my operating room doors, same face drenched with the same tenderness.

It felt like déjà vu, as if it was the same moment I first saw him on the basketball court wrapped in different skin. Instead of burning up, I was freezing cold. Instead of catching me with his arms, he caught me with his words.

And now all I want to do is write down his name. And around and in between his name, I want to paste the things I just cut out of my magazine: a tree with blush-pink leaves, a luna moth with lime-green wings, a boy standing on a double helix reaching for purple stars. Signs I'm hoping will somehow find him in his dreams and let him know my heart.

But my rules.

Feel so small compared to what I feel for Rex. The smallest specks of dust in a gleaming stain-glassed cathedral.

I sit down in a pew, allow my long, skinny fingers to pull the royal blue Pigma pen from the crevice between open pages and write:

Rex Carrington

Rex Carrington

Rex Carrington

Rex Carrington

Rex Carrington

Rex Carrington

Rex Carrington

Over and over again until I'm beaming with a thousand colors. Then I scribble tiny hearts around his names in the shape of a giant heart. Does it look like the work of a first grader? Sure, but ask me if I care.

Outside, the yellow school bus stops in front of our house. Through the window above the sofa, I see Cole hop off.

"Let's go!" Cole shouts as soon as he's in the house. A few fast and squeaky footsteps across the wooden floor, and now he's standing in the entrance of the living room in his basketball warm-ups, out of breath. He's not supposed to be here. His game starts at five. His team is shooting around, like, right now.

"Go where?" I ask, alarmed, my mind sprinting off to the worst fear it can find. Car accident. Mom and Daddy. I quickly lift my legs and turn around so that my feet are on the ground. *Ouch!*

"Rex is playing at our school tonight, and I've decided that you're coming."

I let out a sigh. "You seriously came all the way home for that? What's wrong with you?" I yell. "You know I can't go anywhere."

"What's wrong with me? Really? I don't get you, Carli," he says, face going bright red like he's about to explode from exasperation. "You know . . . you're always worried about what this random thing means and what that completely arbitrary thing means. But when something simple is staring you right in the face, it's like you don't see it. I should be at my game, right now, but I'm standing here ready to take you to see Rex. And you're really telling me *no*?"

I want to get defensive, but the bright sun swinging inside my chest won't let me. I can't believe I've never considered going to the game. Maybe because my stomach hurts like hell. Or because the doctor ordered me to stay home until Wednesday. Or because a teacher or coach or any of my teammates could spot me. But they're even smaller than the smallest specks of dust—not *even* about to stop me from seeing Rex.

REX

Carli. Is. In. The. Building. Can you believe it? I mean, I dreamed of her coming, but there's no way I thought she'd be here this soon after surgery.

I'm sitting high up in the stands, a couple rows above my team. The JV game is about to start. Carli's walking along the sidelines with Cole, who's suited up for the game. A few of his teammates, standing in a huddle around their coach, look back at him like, *What the fuck?* But he doesn't pay them any mind. His attention is on Carli, his arm around her for support. And judging by how slow they're moving, she needs every bit of it.

I stand up, ready to run to her and relieve him so he can get on the court.

But the first horn on the game clock sounds, and I sit back down.

Coach is sitting in the bleachers above me, so he can keep a good eye on the team. He likes us to stay put during the JV games, stay focused. I mean, we can run to the bathroom or go get a bag of chips from the vending machines if we want, but if he catches anybody wandering around trying to holla at girls, he benches them for the game.

But man, this feeling inside me right now has me thinking crazy. Has me thinking this moment is bigger than a game on the bench. Has my whole body feeling like it's about to explode into some rainbows and shit. I'm telling you, another minute of trying to contain it, and people are gonna be picking me up as Lucky Charms scattered around the gym.

The second horn sounds. Game time. *Man, forget this.* I run down the bleachers and sidelines until I'm standing in front of Carli, looking straight into her brown eyes, taking in their surprise, their delight.

I wrap my arm around her other side. "I got her," I tell Cole, and he flashes me a giant smile before letting go.

CARLI

Rex's hand is around my hip and I'm floating. Dreaming. I must be dreaming. Sleepwalking. I must be about to fall flat on my face. But the strength of Rex's hand holding me up, the light grip of his fingers pushing into my skin, the tingles moving up and down my left side and through my body, tell me I'm not. Tell me this is real, just like I thought.

"Hi," he says, in a low voice, his smiling eyes wandering across my face.

"Hi," I say in return, and let my eyes travel, too. From the tight, spiraling curls in his high-top . . . to his thick brows . . . to his hooded eyes . . . to the mole on the right side of his nose . . . to his big, curvy lips. I can't help but pause there for a bit. They look so soft.

"Is here good?" he asks, and points to the opening on the first row we're standing in front of.

"Perfect," I say, thinking about how I'm going to get my butt all the way down to the wooden bench without ripping my stomach open. He must read my mind because as we turn to sit down, he pulls my body closer to his until he's taken almost all of my weight and our bodies are sitting down as one.

After we sit down, we hold hands, interlocking our

fingers. It's automatic. Like we've done it a million times.

My hand is on top—his long, brown fingers reaching over my knuckles showing his short, shiny nails. Not just-got-them-buffed shiny, more like really clean shiny.

Looking over my left shoulder, I take in more of him—the way his strong neck eases down into his collarbones, the way his chest bulges underneath his dark green uniform, the way he smells like a pine forest. It's making me want to lean in, put my nose right up to the crook of his neck, and take a sniff. Or maybe even kiss his chin or bite his cheek or eat him up or have him eat me up or bury myself forever inside his earthy-sweet-smelling uniform. Clearly, I'm losing my mind being this close to him.

REX

My nervousness makes me start bursting with words, spitting them out right and left. "It's crazy you're here. Man, that surgery had to be no joke. How are you feeling? I can't believe you're actually here . . . sitting next to me. Sorry, you'll have to excuse me . . . it's just that I've been dreaming . . .

nah . . . never mind. You healing okay, though? Cole said you've been feeling better every day." This is not me. This is not how I talk. It's like some whack, diarrhea-of-the-mouth dude has invaded my body and won't shut up.

"Cole, my brother?" Carli asks, sparse eyebrows scrunched together.

Damn, I just told on myself, didn't I? Now how am I supposed to explain knowing her brother's name? I guess I could make up a different Cole. But what other Cole would know how she's been? Even if I *could* get my mouth to slow down and be cool long enough to formulate a lie, that one wouldn't even make sense.

She lets go of my hand and grabs a round, gold pendant hanging from her necklace. She slides it back and forth slowly along her chain, eyeing me curiously.

Sweat rolls from under my arm, down my side, and I unzip the jacket to my warm-ups. "Yeah, your brother," I say, pushing the words past the knot at the back of my throat screaming, *Don't mess this up!*

"You know him?" she says, looking confused—pale, bare lips clasped tight, every freckle sprinkled on and around her nose giving me the eye.

"No, I started following him on IG after you passed out a few weeks ago. Wait, it wasn't a few weeks. Feels like it, though. Feels like forever. When was it, again?"

"Saturday before last," she says, studying my face.

"Saturday before last, yeah . . . after you passed out," I repeat like a bumbling fool and look down, feeling my face go long and soft. If Carli's still reading me, she can definitely see how scared I am.

"So, you're basically telling me you've been stalking me on my brother's Instagram?"

Shit. I will every muscle in my face to go stiff. Now she probably thinks I'm pissed, but it's better than her seeing how many hours I've spent staring at her face on the Internet. I can't have her thinking I'm some type of weirdo. I can't lose her like this. I swear I can't. Just thinking about it is making my throat swell up, making my insides turn black.

My face accidentally slips into softness again, and I can feel her eyes—a warm glow—looking around inside of me.

CARLI

Everything in me wants to kiss him. Not because his lips look about as delicious as delicious gets (and they do!), but because everything I've been feeling for him, I can see he's been feeling for me, too.

Plus, his nervousness is about the cutest, most kissable thing in the world. He'd better be glad I'm not selfish. If I was, I wouldn't even think about putting him at ease. "Kidding . . . kidding. You wanted to check on me?" I say, letting go of my necklace. "That's sweet."

He lets out a long sigh. "Yeah, I wanted to make sure you were okay," he says, looking up, his wide mouth cracking a small smile. But the rest of his face is still long, like it hasn't gotten over me playing around.

Dang, now I feel bad. I hope I didn't hurt him. "Trust me, if you had anything besides highlight clips on your Instagram, I would've been stalking you, too."

His face brightens way up. "Oh, you looked?"

A strange lightness rushes to the center of my forehead. I can't ever remember making a boy so happy. It feels so reassuring, so good. "Of course. Had to do my background research."

"Is that right?" he says, grinning, and tilts his head to the side. His nose is crooked, like maybe it's been broken a few times. I wish I could kiss that, too.

"Not that it gave up any goods on you. You don't have any real pics on there. No friends. No ex-girls. Nothing but basketball stuff. And nobody has time to be sitting around watching you dunk and drain threes all day," I say.

He smiles big, like I'm making his day.

But I'm greedy. I want to make his year, his life. So I gently reach for the menu in my back pocket. The one I wrote the fact about kisses on before I even knew how he felt about me. The one I carried around in my back pocket for over a week— steady stream of hope coming from my right butt cheek. Rex is about to flip when he sees it. But it's not there. "Damn," I mumble, remembering the menu is with Jordan and she's not coming until the end of Rex's game.

"Oh, is it your stomach?" Rex asks, thick eyebrows raised in concern.

"No, I'm okay."

"What is it then?"

"Nothing."

"You can tell me."

"Don't worry about it. I'll tell you later."

"Why can't you tell me now?" he says.

I'm a little surprised by his persistence, but it feels kinda nice. Like we've skipped right over the beginning phase of our relationship, when people hold back trying to say and do all the right things. Like we're already in this thing deep. "Because," I say.

"Because what?"

"*Because* it'll be better later," I explain. For the full effect, I want to give him the menu in person. Telling him about it wouldn't be the same.

"I hate when people do that."

"Do what?"

"Tell you there's a secret without telling you the secret."

"Secret? There is no secret," I say, now wondering if we're having our first argument.

"Yeah, you just told me there was something to tell and simultaneously told me you can't tell me what it is."

"No, I said *damn*, and then you got nosy."

"Well, if you weren't going to tell me, why not keep the *damn* to yourself?"

I could be cool and say, *It slipped out*, but I decide to push back and ask, "Why you gettin' mad?" He actually sounds more worked up than mad, but the question itself usually makes people mad, and I'm kind of curious what he'd be like mad.

Don't get me wrong, I'm not trying to start something for the sake of starting something, but he's already taken it this far. And if he's the type who grits his teeth or clenches his fists over stupid shit, the type I could see yelling and name-calling and trying to humiliate, the type who makes my insides either want to curl up into a tight ball or grow sharp teeth, I need to know now. Because no matter what the signs say or how many fuchsia flowers he has blooming in my chest, I'm not *even* about to deal with that.

But his face grows long and soft before he lowers his head again. When he got like this earlier, I thought it was nerves. But now I see it's something else . . . something deeper that hurts. And he's sitting up here showing it to me in a way no other boy has before.

The pain inside me peeks its head out, eyeing a friend. And now it's like his hurt and my pain are hiding under the bleachers together, holding hands.

● REX ●

I swear I hate myself. "Sorry, I didn't mean to," I say, and look up. Her pale face has blurred. A thin layer of tears coats my eyes. Lots of blinks, really fast, and it's better. But what does it matter? She's not gonna want me. She's already seen how messed up I am.

"Hey, it's okay," she says, and interlaces her long, soft fingers with mine.

"No, it's not!" I say, harder than I want to. *What the hell is wrong with me? Oh, yeah, this is the way to show Carli how I feel about her. I swear I'm so stupid. This is exactly why I usually keep my mouth shut.*

She looks down at her high-top burgundy Nike Blazers, but doesn't take her hand away from mine.

I slowly slide my thumb back and forth over hers, gently squeeze her hand, and rub my thumb back and forth again, hoping my hand will speak for me.

She briefly looks up at me but looks back down. My hand is not gonna cut it.

"Sorry, I'm not usually like this," I start to explain, but I stop because my eyes are glazing over again. *What the hell?* I swear it's like everything inside of me, everything I usually try to keep on lock, has up and decided it wants to come out and lay bare at Carli's feet. But can it hold up a second?

She looks back at my thumb, sliding back and forth over hers.

"I'm usually quiet," I start again. "But I don't know what's happening to me. It's like I don't know what to do with everything I'm feeling right now . . . where to put it all. And it's coming out in weird ways."

Her eyes meet mine, then start wandering around my face.

"Not to say, I don't get hype. I mean, when it comes to basketball, I'm like a different person. Or if somebody steps to me, now that's a whole different story. I mean, I let a lot of shit slide, but some shit—" *Damn, Rex. Go ahead and curse up a storm, why don't you.*

Her eyes return to mine, like she's waiting for what else I have to say.

"I'm just finding it really hard to act normal around you."

She bites the inside corner of her bottom lip, like she's thinking, but she doesn't say anything.

"But in a way, talking like this is making me feel more normal than I've ever felt," I continue, words pushing up and out of me like, *we got this.* I sure hope they know what they're doing. "It's weird being quiet all the time. Keeping everything inside. It's like nobody ever really gets to know me. I'm not gon' lie, letting it all out feels weird, too. So weird. Man, I feel crazy-exposed. But in a way, it feels good. I want you to know me, Carli. Like, straight up. And I'm really sorry for things coming out wrong earlier. It's just that this saying-how-I-feel thing is new to me. So new. Like, you don't even understand."

"I can't even imagine you being quiet," she says, her eyes searching me again.

"I know. It's weird," I say, happy she's not done with me yet.

"I see you like the word *weird*."

"What do you mean?"

"You just said it, like, five times."

"Did I?"

"Yeah, back in the day-day-day it used to mean *destiny*, you know?"

"Really?"

"Yeah, it used to be spelled with a *y*, like *w-y-r-d*, but it got all messed up when Shakespeare— Wait, are you sure you want to hear about this?"

"Yeah."

"Don't say *yeah* just to be saying *yeah*. Because I don't want to be sitting up here wasting all my breath if you're really not that interested," she says, and reaches into the right pocket of her jean jacket with her free hand.

"I'm one hundred percent interested," I assure her. How could I not be? She's trying to teach me something I don't know.

She lets go of my hand. "Well, there were these three Weird Sisters, right," she explains, opening what looks like a tiny box of movie popcorn. She taps the box against her palm and three light-yellow jelly beans roll out. "Want some?"

"No, thanks," I say. I'm more of a chocolate person, but mostly I want her to get back to the story.

She pops the jelly beans into her mouth, closes the box, and puts it back in her pocket. "Wait, I guess for all of this to make sense, we have to take it back to Greek mythology. Okay, there were these three weaving goddesses called the Fates, right."

I nod.

"I forget their names, but one spun the thread of human fate, one gave it out, and one cut the thread, basically deciding when people died. Talk about girl power. Doesn't get more powerful than deciding people's destinies. Even their daddy Zeus couldn't tell them what to do," she says, smacking and then swallows.

"Anyway, the three sisters had that staying power, too. They kept going strong through Roman mythology, with name changes here and there, and then made it all the way to *Holinshed's Chronicles* as the Weird Sisters. Holinshed was ones of the guys in charge of writing this book about the UK's history back in the sixteenth century. Apparently Shakespeare, like a lot of writers of his day, was really into the *Chronicles* and used it a lot in his plays."

She pauses, shifts her bottom jaw to the right, and slides her tongue back and forth under her cheek. Must be some jelly bean stuck to her teeth. Don't ask me why but seeing her trying to get it out is making her look cuter than ever.

"Got it?" I ask, smiling.

"Yeah," she says, and looks down for a second, like she's embarrassed.

"Continue . . . continue."

"Okay, so where was I?"

"*Holinshed's Chronicles*. Shakespeare liked using it for his plays."

"That's right," she says, tilting her head back and to the side.

"Don't act surprised. I told you I was interested."

"All right, then," she says, smiling. "So, when Holinshed and his people wrote about the Weird Sisters, they described them as these beautiful nymphs and fairies, right? As these goddesses of destiny. But when Shakespeare wrote about the three sisters—well, remember the Weird Sisters in *Macbeth*?"

"No," I answer, feeling stupid. We just read that play in English last year, but I have no idea. And I thought I was smart. I mean, your boy *has* gotten straight As since the first grade. But Carli's more than good-grades smart. She's that nonrequired-reading kind of smart.

"No? Okay, well, they were these strange-looking witches with beards who foretold Macbeth was gonna murder that dude Duncan. Anyway, Shakespeare knew exactly what he was doing by making the sisters witches. At the time people were losing their minds over witchcraft. Blaming it for everything bad. So by turning the Weird Sisters into these strange witches, Shakespeare gave his play that extra hype. Got everybody all scared and fascinated and whatnot. And basically changed the word *weird* forever."

"Word?" I say, staring at Carli in amazement. "Why didn't I know that?"

"Well, it's not exactly like they teach it in school. But wouldn't it be cool if they did? Or at least if they gave some bonus points for knowing random things? It's crazy, it's like every school wants to teach everybody the same exact things, like those are the only important things in life to learn about. But there are sooooo many things in this world to know. Who decides what's most important, anyway? And why do they get to decide?"

CARLI

Usually when I run my mouth this long around a boy, I start feeling stupid, like I need to superglue my lips shut. But the way Rex is looking at me—eyes wide and glazed over with gleam, like he's staring at something sparkling—is making me feel like there's some kind of hidden jewel inside me.

"So, I'm taking it that you're the question-authority type," Rex says, reaching for my hand again.

I interlace my fingers with his. "Never really thought about it like that, but I guess my mom does always say to question everything."

"Your mom sounds cool."

A wave of irritation rushes up inside of me at the thought of Mom. At the fact that her eyes haven't been red and puffy for the last two days, and she seems to be getting back to normal (not that I wanted her to cry forever, but this fast?). At the fact that she still hasn't told me what happened between her and Daddy. "Yeah, but having so many questions leaves me with a lot of stuff unanswered."

"You mean Google doesn't have all the answers?"

"I wish!" I say, and laugh. Then I ask, "What's your sign?" I'm thinking he has to be an Aries. He has way too much honesty, even when he's trying to be funny, to be anything else.

"My sign?"

"Yeah, like, when were you born?"

"August second," he says, briefly looking down.

"Oh, a Leo. I can see that, too. Your passion. Not to mention how bold you are."

"Bold?"

"Well, you *did* come down here putting your arm around me like you knew me and thangs," I say with a playful attitude.

"Well, you *are* sitting here holding my hand like you know me and thangs," he mimics me in a high voice, then laughs low and deep.

"That's not how I talk," I say, cheesing, and bang my knee against his.

"I know," he says, his voice turning serious. "I'm not gonna lie, though. I *do* already feel like I know you. Not know-you-know-you, obviously, because I just met you. But it's like somehow, I've always known you. Like it took me seeing you to remember. Wait, that doesn't even make sense. It's hard to explain. It's like . . . man, I don't know."

"I know what you mean."

"You do?"

"Yeah," I say, "it's just this feeling."

"Exactly . . . this feeling," he says, sliding this thumb gently back and forth across my thumb. "And it didn't waste no time. I swear it started the first moment I saw you on the court."

"Same here. It's like I didn't even know what was happening to me. I literally thought you, or what I was feeling for you, was why my body was freaking out."

"No you didn't," he says, and laughs.

I laugh, too. "Yes I did! And then it was crazy because I had this . . . No, never mind."

"Had what?"

"I've been thinking about you a lot, that's all," I say, not wanting to spoil the vision of him. How real it felt.

"That's not what you were about to say."

No denying that, I look down. But the soft whirling in my chest makes me look back up. "I had a vision of you."

"Word?" he says, still sliding his strong thumb gently across my thumb. "What did you see?"

"Well, you were at the hospital that day I had surgery. It was crazy how real it felt."

His face lights up. With all seriousness, if the power in the gym were to go out right now, there would be a beam of light coming from right beside me. "It wasn't a vision. I was there," he says.

"What? But how?"

"Cole posted where the surgery was going to be that morning, and I had to go . . . had to see you. I don't usually do things like that. But you got me . . . man, I don't know. I've never felt like this before."

His words make me feel beyond good. It's like every cell in my body is twerking and cartwheeling and high-kicking all over the place. *I don't usually do things like this, either. . . .*

REX

Carli is kissing me. And it's warm and soft and wet and sweet. Her lips sandwich my bottom lip and then my top . . . bottom, top, bottom, top, her tongue sliding over mine in between. A final press into both of my lips, and she pulls away far enough to look at me.

But the way her eyes are moving around my face feels like she's still kissing me. "One . . . two . . . three," she counts.

"Three what?" I ask, smiling, and reach up to touch her hair. A risk. Trust, even before Solange's song "Don't Touch My Hair," I received the memo. But Carli just kissed me, so I figure I get a pass. Plus, I've never seen hair so big and long and red and brown and kinky and coily on one person's head at the same time. It's soft and smells like jasmine.

"Four . . . five . . . six. Oh, that one's nice," she says, and turns to touch my face with her free hand. She grimaces and straightens out a little. "But I think I like this one best," she says, and rubs her pointer finger in a tiny circle on the side bridge of my nose before bringing her arm back down.

She must be talking about my moles. I hate my moles. Hardly ever have to see them since I avoid mirrors. But hearing her talk about them is almost making me want to break out my phone and look at myself. *Almost.* Instead, I bend down and press my lips to her hand. Then I lift her hand—slightly, gently—and hold it between my hands. "Thank you," I say.

"Sure thing," she says, and nods.

"No, not about the moles."

"So, what are you thanking me for then? Kissing you?" she asks, head cocked to the side, cute and confident as can be.

"No," I say, and laugh, trying to think of a good way to

put it. But I can't. Man, it's like one day I'm getting through life alone, hanging on to any kind of happiness I can find. I mean, I'm doing pretty good, despite the circumstances.

But then—*bam!*—here Carli comes, and it's like a whole new world. A world where I don't have to feel so damn lonely anymore. "A whole new wooorrld," I'm singing before I can even stop myself. Man, this girl has me acting corny as hell!

She laughs the cutest laugh, high-pitched and throaty, with her button nose pinching along the bridge and her straight white teeth showing.

I'll be a cornball all day every day if this is the reward.

"*Aladdin?* You are not singing the *Aladdin* song right now!"

And then a different voice, a much deeper voice, from behind, "Rex!"

A whistle blows. Sneakers squeak against the gym floor. People around us chant "Defense!" as our JV team takes the ball up the court. Two girls, a bench up behind Carli, are snickering and looking at us. Trying to reorient myself to the world outside of Carli is making me dizzy. Everything's rushing at me all at once.

"Rex!" I hear again, closer.

Carli looks up, over my right shoulder, and the residue of laughter wipes clean off her face.

CARLI

"Rex!" A short, muscly man walking up behind Rex shouts. He looks pissed, eyebrows pulled down over his small eyes. He needs to stop, lift those brows back up. His hairline-forehead combo is unfortunate enough. It's like they can't stand to be around each other—forehead jutting forward and hairline running back—far, far away.

Rex lets go of my hand and stands up.

The man walks past us and makes a strong wave motion for Rex to follow. The man is wearing khakis and a dark green vest over a white polo shirt, which is way too tight around his biceps. Dark green and white, same colors as Rex's warm-ups. That's got to be his coach.

Rex follows him to the side of the bleachers, near the entrance, where the man snatches Rex by the elbow. Rex doesn't pull away. Then with his other hand, the man starts waving his pointer finger in Rex's face.

Look, I get chastising players for not being where they're supposed to be . . . not sitting with the team. Coach Hill does it, too. Makes us run suicides the next day after school. But is all this finger-waving and elbow-grabbing business really necessary? This man is being extra.

And Rex is standing there taking it. He's more than a foot taller than the man, but by the way he's standing with his head all down and his shoulders all hunched over, you can barely tell. It's like he's leaning into the verbal beating. I hate it.

Doesn't Rex know who he is? He's Rex Carrington! He's ESPN's high school player of the year, for Christ's sake! And I wish I could remember all the other things Cole told me, but it's a lot. Way too much to be standing there taking that man's shit.

Rex wipes his face.

And then I realize he's crying.

And this familiar feeling shoots through me. It's the same deep-throated darkness I feel when I see Daddy sad. Everything in me wants to go to Rex. Wants to tell that man to fuck off. But I'd only get him into more trouble.

Head hanging, Rex exits the gym without looking back. When his coach walks past me, I catch him giving me a once-over.

Fifteen minutes later Rex comes back through the gym's double doors in street clothes—gray T, black Nike joggers, and some Jordans 1s. Damn, I can't believe his coach is benching him for the game. Because of me.

Along the sidelines Rex walks toward me but won't look at me. Won't even look in my direction.

My eyes are on his eyes, pleading with them to connect, but he looks straight ahead, gaze cold. Everything in me freezes with the fear that this thing between us that only just began is already over.

He's three strides away from me, and my eyes are practically on their knees begging him to look at me, but he won't even give me a glance. Two strides and still nothing. One stride, and all the color inside me starts to drain. He's passing me and it's over.

But when I hang my head, I see a small, folded note in my lap.

THE
SUM
COLOR

REX

I'm sitting at my desk trying to figure out how many four-digit numbers there are with at least one repeating digit, but I can't even concentrate. It's almost midnight, and Carli still hasn't called.

What if she didn't get the paper with my number inside? My shot *has* been off lately. It could've missed her lap and landed on the floor. Or what if she got it and decided not to call? Man, I felt like such the asshole walking right past her and not saying anything. But I couldn't get into any more trouble.

I'm no closer to solving the problem when my phone rings. My heart leaps, but it's only Nya. She's been calling and texting with weak apologies since last Sunday—she didn't know what she was saying . . . it was the devil . . . please take her back. Straight to voice mail, where I've been sending her. She calls again. Straight to voice mail. And again. You already know.

Another five minutes and my phone rings with a number I don't recognize. It could be Nya calling from a friend's phone. Plenty of girls have gotten me with that trick. But what if it's Carli? I can't take the risk. "Hello," I answer.

"Hey, it's Carli."

"Hey," I say, relieved.

"Hope I'm not calling too late. Just got off the phone with my dad."

"It's all good. You gave me some more time to try to figure out this math problem for a little extra credit."

"Did you figure it out?"

"Nah."

"You want me to let you go?"

"Nah, never. I mean, nah. Just plain nah. Not *never*. *Never* would be weird." *Really, Rex?* I stand up, trying to rid myself of these damn nerves. I thought they'd gotten used to Carli at the gym, but a few hours of separation and they don't know how to act again.

"I swear your nervousness is the cutest thing ever,"

Carli says, and hits me with a little high-pitched laugh that calms me down a bit.

I walk over to my bed, pick up the three T-shirts that lost in the what-to-wear battle this morning, and toss them onto my desk chair. "I have all week to figure it out, though. Mrs. Johnson only gave us the problem today."

"Dang, you must love you some math."

"Yeah, it's cool," I say, and lay back on my bed. I want to tell her that it's mostly a means to an end. That one day, after basketball takes me however far it will take me, I want to be a landscape architect. I want to design dope spaces that will bring people closer to trees. And my math needs to be on point for that. But just thinking about saying so many words right now is making my nerves act up again.

"What's your favorite number?"

"I don't know. I guess if I could name the largest number at any given moment, that would be my favorite."

"Really? Why?"

"I don't know. There's something reassuring about the fact that numbers never run out . . . that they keep getting higher and higher, forever and ever. It's like numbers never really die."

"Oooo, I like that," she says, in a voice that takes my

mind back to kissing her. "But I thought you would've said twelve."

Her shadowy lips pull away from mine, and I'm back to staring at my white ceiling. "Yeah, I guess twelve is my lucky number. It was on the very first practice jersey I wore. Picked it out of a bag at my first basketball camp when I was seven, and I've kept it ever since."

"The number twelve is super connected to the cosmic bodies, you know."

"Oooo, I like that," I say, mimicking her again. Partly because it made her laugh when I did it earlier at the game, but mostly because it feels good having the sound of her in my mouth.

"Yeah? Well, I have more where that came from. Did you know that the moon moves twelve degrees around its orbit every day?"

"Nope."

"Well, it does. And you know there's twelve months in a year because they chopped up the number of days it takes the Earth to rotate around the sun by the number of days it takes the moon to rotate around the Earth, right?"

"Yeah, I think I knew that," I answer, although I'm pretty sure I didn't.

"And there are twelve zodiac signs."

"You're really into that kind of stuff, huh?

"Yeah, *that* kind of stuff is interesting to me," she says defensively.

"Sorry, I didn't mean it like that. It does sound interesting," I try to assure her.

But she doesn't respond.

I bring my hand up to my forehead, trying to think back to what I said and how I said it and how it might have hurt her, but I can't find my crime. Doesn't matter, I'm clearly guilty. I want to apologize and tell her I didn't mean it, but I've already said that. Seconds of silence pass, and they feel like forever. "Sorry about earlier at the game. I would've stopped and said good-bye, but my coach."

"It's okay. I hope I didn't get you into too much trouble," she says, sounding like she's already forgiven me.

I relax my arm back down by my side.

"I can't believe your coach made you sit out the game. He seems like a real asshole."

Her criticism of Coach stings, but I say, "Nah, he's cool. Just trying to make sure I stay focused, that's all." I don't tell her that Coach comes up to the school every morning at five thirty a.m. to open the gym for me. I don't tell her that he's always studying my game so he can help pinpoint areas that need improvement. I definitely don't tell her that he believes in me. Or that his belief in me often makes me wish that I was his son.

Meanwhile, I haven't seen my real father since last week. I literally have not seen him or any evidence of him. The house hasn't even been cold. But telling her that my coaches have always been the closest thing I've had to a dad is out of the question.

"But he was all up in your face. I mean, was it that serious? Your game wasn't even close to starting."

I roll over on my side and stare out of my sliding-glass doors. The moon is bright in the sky and lights up the tops of the pine trees. "Nah, it's only that the playoffs are so close. And he knows how many scouts will be there."

"So what's your top school?"

"Man, I don't even know. I just wanna go somewhere I can shine for a year. I'm trying to be one-and-done."

"Dang, big baller!" she says, her voice smiling at me hard through the phone, making me feel like I've already made it. "When you get to the NBA, you better not start acting brand-new!"

"First of all, brand-new? Nah, never that. And secondly, the statistical chances of me going to the league at all is about .03 percent, like three in every ten thousand dudes. So I'm not bettin' on it or anything," I tell Carli. But really,

I'm all *but* bettin' on it. I already know what team I want to play for. And no, it's not Los Angeles. I'm thinking San Antonio. Gregg Popovich's teams always seem like a family.

"Boy, don't play modest with me. You are not the average player. And you still have another year."

She's making me feel so good it's embarrassing. "But what about you? Don't you have dreams of playing in the league one day?" I ask to get the attention off of me. "I bet the top schools are already sending you letters. And you know they'll all be coming to the playoffs to see you in a few weeks, big baller!"

Carli goes quiet.

Damn, I forgot about the surgery. What if she won't be back in time for the playoffs? Great, just great. Here I am the asshole again.

 CARLI

The stupid playoffs. I don't tell him I could care less about which scouts will be there because I don't want to play basketball anymore. I don't tell him that I'm more concerned with which color Le Pen to pull from my Pamela

Barsky canvas pencil pouch than being able to run up and down a court. He sounds way too excited, and I'm not ready to burst his bubble. I'm not ready to tell him that I don't love the game like he does.

"My bad. I wasn't even thinking about the surgery. What's the doctor saying about your chances of being ready for the playoffs?" he asks.

Periwinkle, I decide. I'm lying in my bed with my notebook, filling in the white space around *Rex Carrington* with the words *Numbers never really die* in multicolored columns. "Don't know. I have an appointment next week. Supposed to tell me then."

A text comes in from Jordan: **I'll get it back from him tomorrow. I swear**

You better, I text back. I can't believe this girl has lost the menu with the first kisses fact on the back. And I still can't find the original fact on my walls anywhere, so it's even more crucial for Jordan to find it. And no, I can't just write it again like she suggested. It wouldn't be the same. **For real, Jordan**

Ok . . . ok

Earlier, Jordan's mom said she couldn't go to the game because she needed to study. So Jordan gave the menu to her brother to give to Cole to give to me. The problem is, her brother never gave it to Cole. When Cole didn't show up for shootaround, he gave it to Chico—this dude I used to date on Cole's team. Now, everybody and their mama know I dumped Chico over a month ago, but I guess Jordan's brother didn't get the memo.

So now the first sign on me and Rex's path is in the hands of a dude who doesn't know the difference between *they're,* *their,* and *there,* but who had the nerve to call me stupid for saying that crossing the train tracks on Westheimer at the exact same time it started pouring down hail (it was only pea-sized, but still!) was a sign that we should take a break.

"I'm sure you'll be good to go."

"What?"

"You know, good for the playoffs."

"I guess we'll see," I say. And then add, "But when can I see you, though?" to get on to more important things.

"When do you want to see me?" he says, putting some extra smooth sweetness in his voice, like he's spreading a layer of Nutella over his words. I can't even lie. . . . It's sexy.

"Like now. Like right now," I say, and laugh. "But I guess I could settle for this weekend."

"Look, I'll drive out there this second if you want me to."

"Yeah, whatever."

"No, I'm serious," he says.

My heart lights up at the possibility of seeing him. "You wouldn't get in trouble? You can sneak out this late without your parents noticing?"

"I wouldn't have to sneak. It's only my father and me, and he doesn't really care what I do," he answers in a voice that tells me he doesn't feel lucky to have so much freedom.

The hurt on his face earlier today jumps to the front of my mind, and I want to ask why his father doesn't care and where his mom is. But thinking about turning the conversation toward parents is making my own pain feel naked. A dark cloud swoops in, covers it, and I say, "Well, I'd definitely get in trouble. What about Friday?"

"I have a game on Friday. What about Saturday?" he asks.

"That works."

"Okay, text me your address."

My address. Dang, that's what Daddy called about earlier. Cole and I will be staying at his new rental house this weekend. But how can somewhere I've never been, somewhere Daddy doesn't belong, be my address?

Daddy's supposed to be lying on the sofa in our living room right now, watching SportsCenter. He's supposed to be standing in front of the stove tomorrow morning, whisking pancake mix in his big plastic bowl (the only plastic bowl in the house . . . Mom's tea is not the only thing she's bougie about). I swear sometimes I can still hear him shouting at the TV. I can smell his aftershave when I walk past the stove. But he's never there to reach out and hug me.

The cloud grows larger, but it's still not big enough to cover the pain. I put down my notebook and pen and gently reach for the lamp on my nightstand—cover myself in pitch darkness.

"I mean, not right now or anything. I can get it from you later."

"Huh?"

"Your address. No rush. We have all week," Rex explains.

"Yeah," I say, struggling for more words. Lying in bed with Rex on the other end of my phone should feel like heaven. But the darkness all around me, inside me, won't let me feel anything good. "I'm about to go to bed."

"Okay, talk tomorrow?"

"Yeah."

"And the day after that?"

"Yeah."

"And the day after that?"

A tiny sun peeks up from behind the cloud inside of me and I answer, "Yeah," smiling a little.

"And the day after that?"

More suns, rising higher. "Yeah, and the day after that," I say, and add a brief "bye" before hanging up, holding on to the good.

● REX ●

Carli's street has a dope canopy of trees. Getting out of my pickup truck, I can't help but look up at the bright February sun peeking through the leaves of the large oak at the end of her driveway. Through the leaves of the oak beside it. And the one beside that, leaves wilding out in the wind. The sidewalk is lined with live oaks on both sides.

But walking up her driveway, I stop when I notice a sick magnolia tree alone in the middle of her yard. It makes me think about how trees like to grow close to each other. How they depend on each other. Sure, aboveground they may throw a few 'bows to get the most sun. But underground, they share—water, nitrogen, and nutrients—especially when one of them is suffering.

Even the strong trees, like the oak at the bottom of her driveway with the huge trunk and the mature crown stretching across the street, go through things. Even the strong ones do better when they're not alone.

CARLI

It's half past noon, and I'm sitting on the sofa in the living room of Daddy's rental house, which is way out in Woodside, closer to his job. Closer to Rex, too, who's supposed to be here any minute.

I should be happy that I'm here with Daddy, that I'm about to see Rex. But it feels weird having Rex come *here* to pick me up for the first time. To this foreign house, where he'll look at these foreign walls, walk on this foreign carpet, and sit on this foreign couch. And as if all this foreignness wasn't bad enough, everything is beige. It's like whoever decorated this house had a motto: *If it ain't beige, I ain't buying it.*

But apparently beige is the color of the universe. Yes, all the color of all the light of all the galaxies amounts to what scientists call *cosmic latte*—basically beige. Wouldn't think it, would you? Just found that fact on Google. I needed to find one good thing about this sad color around me, about this sad situation that led us to this sad house where Mom will never be. This bland house with no memories.

I write down the cosmic latte fact in my notebook with my brown Le Pen, cursive letters taking up most of the page, and draw small messy stars all around them, hoping they'll help light the way forward in this new house. Then I crease the paper around all four sides, folding it back and forth, and run my nail along the creases to make sure the paper tears clean.

Now that's a good rhombus! And I already know exactly where it needs to hang. I push myself off the sofa. Hard. Even harder because it's one of those sofas that tries to swallow you whole. Good thing my stomach is feeling better. No way I could've done this last week.

My new room is bare except for a bed underneath a large multipaned window, two cherry nightstands with iron scroll lamps, a matching dresser, and that life-sized poster of Candace Parker. I know, I know. I said she was coming down. But I didn't have the heart. Daddy was too proud of her. But you know what I *will* do? I'll pin this cosmic latte fact over the orange-and-white Spalding she's dribbling up the court.

Much better. Candace's yellow Los Angeles Sparks uniform will be next. Then her black knee braces, then her orange high-tops, and finally her black socks. Her face can stay. It would be a shame to cover such a determined face. Oooo, maybe I'll add a little speech bubble next to her mouth with a quote about those ancient penguins who grew to be almost seven feet tall.

The doorbell rings. Rex. If only I had the hospital menu to give to him today. But Chico claims he gave it to Cole, who claims he never got anything from Chico. So who knows where it's at now?

"I'll get it!" Cole shouts from the kitchen. He's been in there making snacks for Rex for the last hour.

Dang, can I be the one to answer the door? Rex *is* my date.

"Oh, is Rex here?" Daddy yells from his bedroom.

"Yeah," Cole shouts back. And by the time I walk out of my room, Cole is already whizzing past me to answer the door. I swear, Daddy and Cole have been entirely too excited about Rex coming today.

Cole swings opens the front door. "What up!" he says, and reaches to give Rex a hug.

REX

Cole hugs me, and it feels like love. Carli, standing right behind him, smiles at me, and it feels like love. Carli's dad comes around a corner, filling out the hallway frame with his tall body, and it feels like love.

Hold up. I'm not used to this. My father doesn't give two shits about me—fact. No need to sugarcoat it. And sure, Angie checks for me. But at first, she was paid to. And she has the people she's never been paid to care for waiting for her at home. Also fact. And no girl has ever truly cared about me. Maybe the basketball me, but never the real me.

And now it's like a few people are showing me a little love and I'm losing it. Filling up with way too many feelings, way too fast. I cannot, will not, start crying again. Crying in front of Carli once was enough. Twice in less than a week *and* in front of her family? Nah, dawg, I'm not *even* going out like that.

"Derek," her dad says, sidestepping Carli for a handshake—weaker than what I expected coming from a man even taller than I am.

Carli rolls her eyes, only a little bit but I still catch it.

She's standing behind him, sliding her small, gold medallion back and forth across its chain.

Her dad continues, "Carli tells me you live close. Hope it wasn't too hard to find."

"Nah, not at all." I say.

Carli playfully throws up her hands and says, "Dang, is it my turn now?"

Man, does she look good. She's wearing this faded black 2Pac T-shirt under a pale purple cardigan, some ripped jeans, and her burgundy Blazers. Doesn't even look like she has on makeup. Not that she needs any.

I take advantage of her open arms to get up in there for a hug. I don't want to hug her too tight now. Not with her surgery. And not with Cole and her dad standing right here watching, either. But her hair. I forgot how good it smells. It's like putting my face in a hedge of jasmine. I take two deep breaths, forgetting all about the audience.

Carli lets go of me. "Come," she says, and takes my hand.

We sit on the sofa, situated in front of three large windows, and I sink into its softness. I'd almost forgotten what it feels like to sit on a comfortable couch. It feels like home.

Without telling us to pose, Cole snaps a pic of Carli

and me with his phone and then says, "Made some fresh guacamole and lemonade. Want some?"

"Do I?" I say, smiling. Love me some guacamole. Makes all of the frozen taquitos and burritos I eat feel like a real meal. And I must say, my guacamole goes hard. Cole better come with it.

"Hope you can take a little heat. I make mine spicy."

"Trust, I can take the heat. I make mine with jalapeño *and* serrano," I respond.

"All right, then," Cole says, and disappears into the kitchen.

"Hope you can take all this attention," Carli says, and widens her eyes, "because *damn!*"

"I have something I want to show y'all," Carli's dad says excitedly, like he has big news. He's standing up in front of the TV with two remotes in hand. Once he gets Apple TV up on the screen, he settles into the love seat beside a big fake tree.

Can somebody please tell me the point of fake trees? They don't give oxygen. They don't clean the air. They're frauds. Who wants to be looking at a fraud every day? But I try not to let the fake tree bother me. This house is only temporary anyway. Carli said her mom and dad are just taking a breather. A little space for a few months, then her dad is gonna move back in this summer.

Carli is up on the screen. Ah, man. Look at her. Can't be more than six or seven with a million twists, and she's dribbling a basketball. Even that young, the girl had handles.

"Daddy!" Carli protests. "Really?"

"It's not too long, I promise," her dad says, staring at the screen, eyes wide and full of pride.

Carli rolls hers, but I don't know why. I can't imagine my father looking at me the way her dad looks at her. I can't imagine my father taking the time to do something this special for me.

The montage of videos and photos moves from year to year, uniform to uniform, and hairstyle to hairstyle with Carli dribbling, shooting, stealing balls, breaking away for layups, headlining newspapers, accepting awards, and— wait. That's me.

At a basketball camp hosted by the Houston Rockets when I was eight. How did he find that picture? I've never even seen it. And me again, winning my first AAU championship when I was, like, ten. Angie took that same pic from a different angle. Newspaper clippings, team photos, and online articles from over the years. The times I made the highlight reel on ESPN.

I can't believe he did all of this for me. He doesn't even know me. Damn, here it comes again. This feeling of love, filling me up, trying to spill over. I blink it back.

Cole walks in with a tray of guacamole, chips, and lemonade, and I'm over the brim. A tear falls down my right cheek, and I wipe it quick. But not before Carli sees. I let go of her hand and stand up.

"Excuse me for a minute," I say, trying to hold my voice steady and get up out of there.

CARLI

"Not cool," I say, and stand up. "Rex is my date. *Mine.* Y'all around here trippin' over him so hard that y'all scared him off." I walk over to the front door. "I swear if y'all have messed this up for me—" I can't think of anything to complete the threat, so I repeat, "I swear," and walk out, annoyed I'm not dramatic enough to slam the door behind me.

Outside it's bright and cool. Rex is standing near the big tree in the center of the yard.

"Your magnolia has scale," he says.

"Yeah?" I say, not really knowing what he's talking about. I walk onto the freshly cut grass, crunching beneath my Blazers, to be with him.

"The infestation is pretty bad. It needs to be sprayed." He runs his fingers along the branch of the tree and starts picking off some gross-looking white stuff.

It's a pretty tree, I'll admit, with its huge, waxy leaves and white flowers. But this is not my tree or my house. "We're not going to be living here that long."

"I know, but if the tree doesn't get treatment, it'll die," he says like it's a big problem. Like it's my big problem.

"Okaaaay." Look, I don't want the tree to die, I really don't. But I also don't have time to be worried about a random tree right now. "Why you so worried about a tree?"

● REX ●

I really don't want to be this dude. This crying-ass dude. Where did he come from? I've been going through life *cool*. Sure, I have a father who hates me and a dead mom, but that's been the case from day one. And I've been *cool*.

But it seems like ever since I met Carli, this dude keeps creepin' up on me. I came out here to get away from him. Started telling Carli about the scale on the tree to *keep* away from him. But here he comes again.

"Trees make me feel close to my mom," I say, truth pouring out of me. I pick at the scale on a small limb, trying to keep the crying-ass dude away.

"Where is she?" Carli asks, and interlaces her fingers with mine. She starts to walk.

I let go of the limb and walk with her, off the grass and onto the sidewalk. "She died," I say.

"I'm so sorry," she says, looks over at me, and squeezes my hand.

I want to kiss her. Yeah, the timing might seem a little weird, but I need something to help me kick this dude to the curb. It's time for him to go.

But before I can stop and lean in, Carli says, "Can I ask how she died? How old were you?"

I start to overflow. I mean, I'm crying hard. Right in front of Carli.

Carli stops walking and turns toward me. "It's okay," she says, and brushes my cheeks with her thumbs.

But it's not okay. Not only is it ridiculously embarrassing

to be crying like this, I've never talked about what happened to Mom to anyone. Not even Angie. Sure, we've talked about her, but never what happened to her.

Carli grabs my hand and starts walking again.

I look down at my blurred, black-and-red Jordans—one in front of the other, in front of the other, on white concrete. I am dude and dude is me. There's no getting away from him or the answer to Carli's questions. It's banging around inside me like it wants to be free. Like it's been waiting to come out since the day I figured out what I'd done.

I was four and Angie was showing me a stack of old pictures she'd found. Mom pregnant at the park. Mom pregnant at a museum. Mom pregnant in the living room. Mom pregnant at the hospital. And then the pictures ran out.

But do I really have to admit out loud to killing Mom? I admit it to myself every day. I tell Mom I'm sorry every morning when I wake up and every night before I go to sleep. I ask her for forgiveness every time I go to the free-throw line. I hate myself for it. Isn't that enough? But the banging is getting stronger, blurred J after blurred J, and then looking into Carli's teary eyes.

"She died giving birth to me," I admit to her. "Yeah, I'm the asshole who killed his own mom."

"Don't say that. You're not an asshole," I tell him. But the tight squeeze of his closed eyes and the low hang of his long jaw tells me he doesn't believe me. I wrap my arms around his waist and bury my head in the crook of his neck, hoping to drive some of his pain away.

He hugs me back and cries into my hair.

"It's not your fault," I tell him. "You were a newborn."

He lets out a low moan, and it vibrates through my body—baby explosions of pain. They make me feel like I'm dying.

Oh my God. Is this what Rex feels like? I can't even imagine. My pain doesn't even come close to his. At least both of my parents are still alive. Just thinking about it makes me feel grateful. And for half a second, I half forget about Rex's pain and feel happy.

Seriously, Carli? How could I possibly feel anything good when Rex is feeling so bad?

Oh no! Panic rings through my body like a three a.m. burglar alarm. What if Rex just felt my happiness like I could feel his pain? How could I even begin to explain?

But it wasn't me. It was gratitude.

The truth never sounded so stupid.

Part of me waits for him to push me away, but he pulls me in even closer. And I'm so relieved I could cry. But the relief doesn't last long in the swarming guilt, under the crushing weight, where it's a strain to find my next breath.

We can't stay here.

I take in a slow, deep breath—my belly pressing against Rex's trembling belly—and let it out. Again. And again, until the trembling stops. Until his belly finally pushes firmly into mine and falls away. Until his breath picks up the pace of my own—now warm and moist on my face.

I lift my head out of the hot crook of his neck toward the bright blue sky. So cool and sweet I have to close my eyes. When I open them, Rex is looking up, too. I take it as a sign that he's okay and start walking again.

At the corner I guide us left. Daddy says there's a park up here. Figure it'll be a nice to sit on some swings and chill out for a little while.

"Y'all got a court over here?" Rex exclaims, face lit up like a kid on Christmas. He reclaims his arm from around my shoulder and picks up the pace.

I look for a basketball court but can't see it. Then, just above a thick hedge ahead, I spot a slither of orange hoop. How did he even see that?

We cross the street, Rex with extra pep in his step. It's crazy how much spotting the court lifted his mood. It's like the whole breakdown over his mom never even happened. Who knew basketball was out here working miracles like this?

"Man, I've been looking for a court out here for the *longest*," he says excitedly. "They got this joint hidden! You know white people don't like basketball courts in their neighborhoods . . . attracts too many of us," Rex says, and rubs the top of his brown hand with his pointer finger. He's walking so fast I can barely keep up. "Well, guess what? We found the secret court and we're tellin' *all* our friends!" He laughs. "Wait, I don't really have any friends," he says, and turns back toward me. "But now at least I have you."

We walk through a small opening in the thick hedge.

"No friends?" I ask, looking around the secret park. No swings. Just the court to the left and an open field in the back. Leave it to Daddy to find the only public basketball court in Woodside.

"Nah, not really." He walks ahead of me, then turns around so that he's walking backward, facing me. He brings his hands up to eye level, about body-width apart, and moves them in sync—right to left, left to right, right to left—like windshield wipers or something. It's strange. "I guess there's Dante and Paul, two of the dudes I used to ball with at the court close to my old neighborhood. But once I moved out here, I haven't seen them. Same with Craig and James, two of my old teammates who were pretty cool."

He pushes his arms toward the sky, flicks his right wrist, and I see it. The follow-through. The invisible basketball. I don't know why I didn't see it sooner. Jordon's always playing with hers.

"And forget about any of my new teammates."

"So, who do you hang with then?" I ask, hoping he's had somebody before me. Everybody needs somebody.

But his feet have already hit the court. A huge smile flashes across his face before he turns around and takes off running, dribbling his invisible ball. Approaching the goal, he crosses over left, dribbles between his legs, and goes up for a windmill dunk—head almost hitting the rim. When he lands, he shouts, "What! These fools can't hold me . . . they can't stop me!"

REX

Carli's walking up to the three-point line, looking at me like I'm half-crazy. Okay, maybe the yelling was a little much.

But when it comes to basketball, I go straight beast mode. I can't help myself.

"Carli Alexander has the ball," I say in my commentator voice, trying to take the attention off me, and chest pass her the invisible ball.

Her arms stay by her sides. She doesn't even try to catch it.

"Oh, so you're not playing with me?" I ask, standing underneath the rim, dramatically throwing up my hands.

She cracks a small smile, playfully rolls her eyes, runs to get the ball, and dribbles it back toward me. "Happy now?"

"Yes," I answer, mostly because it's good to see her run. I knew she was feeling better, but not that much better.

She bounce passes the ball back to me.

"That's all you got?"

"Yep."

"What about that behind-the-back move you did with all those ponytails? Man, that was sick." I bounce pass the ball back to her.

She catches it. "Ugh, I'd almost forgotten about that. I can't believe my dad. I'm so sorry. He's a bit of a basketball freak and he's—"

"Are you kidding me? I loved it!" I say, walking toward her. "Seeing you ball way back in the day and the old footage of me was everything. I swear your dad is the best. My father would never." And I stop right there. Not about to give her two sob stories in one day.

She dribbles toward me. "Seriously? My dad makes videos like that all the time. *So* annoying. But I must admit, I liked seeing you when you were little. Too cute." She backs into me, still dribbling.

Behind her, I swipe like I'm trying to steal the ball.

"I can send you the video if you want," she says before dribbling left.

I was hoping she'd offer. "That'd be cool," I say, arms extended wide in my defensive stance. She goes up for a layup and I put both of my arms straight up in the air. Nobody gets an easy shot. Not even just-had-surgery Carli. Yeah, I'm savage like that.

"Oh, it's like that?" she asks, getting up in my face after she makes her layup.

I step closer to her. So close our bodies are touching and I'm getting lost in the patch of freckles around her nose, in her smiling brown eyes. "Yeah, it's like that."

CARLI

The way Rex is looking at me . . . it's like he knows everything about me. Everything that ever was. Everything that will ever be.

Looking straight into his dark, tender eyes, all I want to do is lose myself to the infinite parts of me that he sees and forget about what's actually going on in my life. But the way he just opened up and poured out all his pain makes me feel bad for keeping so many secrets.

But it's too late, I think. I've already lied, omitted so much truth. He can't know I could lie to him. He needs someone to trust, someone to be his friend, someone to help heal his hurts. *I can be all of that,* I tell myself. *I can be his everything.*

"What?" he asks.

"Nothing," I say, and kiss him. Pressing my lips into his big, soft lips is way easier than admitting my parents are getting a divorce and I have to decide which one to live with. And rolling my tongue over and around his tongue is way better than letting him know I plan to quit basketball.

He pulls me in closer, his strong hand pressing into my back, making me feel things in low places. Low places that want to explode. Then he pulls away and looks me in the eyes. "I'm so happy I met you," he says.

"Me, too," I say, head tilted back, looking at his face. It's radiating with adoration—for me. I take in as much of it as I can, whole skies of it, hoping it will stay with me forever.

He briefly kisses me again. "Seriously, my life is so much better with you in it."

"Mine, too."

"Carli," he says, looking straight into my eyes.

Words cannot even touch the happiness I feel . . . here . . . with him . . . under the light of the winter sun. Happiness in a way I've never felt before. "Yes," I answer.

"Who's recruiting you?"

Hold up a second. How did we get on basketball?

"I know Texas probably is. UConn, Stanford, Vanderbilt, Duke? You're probably getting recruited by the top schools in the country. Tell me I'm wrong."

I don't, because he's not.

"I know I'm getting way ahead of myself. Waaaaay. It's a whole year out. But wouldn't it be cool if we lived in the same city after we graduated? At least the same state. Trust, you'd have front-row seats to every game you could make. And you'd better have some seats with my name on them, too. I could even visit you at your dorm. Kick your roommate to the curb for a little bit," he says, and laughs.

"Yeah," I say, feeling his words flying around inside me with no place to land. Most of the schools recruiting me will be off the table if I don't play basketball. Who knows where I'll end up?

College applications are due next January. I need to start working on them this fall, but which ones? If I want to study astronomy, Vassar and Vanderbilt have cool observatories. If I want to be some type of artist or designer, RISD or Parsons would be good choices. If I want to be a writer, Northwestern and Brown have good creative writing programs. If I want to be some type of historian, UCLA would be a good option. It's not like I haven't done the research. The signs just haven't spoken yet. *But what exactly am I supposed to do about that? I've done everything I can!* I want to yell from the top of my lungs. I want to tell him everything.

But I don't. And it feels miserable. It's like all of Rex's pain got to go outside and play in the rain—with everything we feel, with his dreams—until the sun came out. But all of my pain is still stuck inside, staring through rain-streaked windows at everyone playing.

BUBBLES
OF
HOPE

CARLI

Mom pulls into the lot behind her design studio. We just got back from my two-week checkup, where I got the worst news. Dr. Williams advised easing back into playing over the next day or so but said that I should be able to go full force for the first round of the playoffs next Saturday.

"So that's it? You just want me to show up for practice on Monday and start playing again?" I say, rubbing my hands together in front of the vents of her old Land Rover Discovery. I swear it took the whole drive over here for the heat to kick in. I've *been* telling Mom she needs a new car. She's had this thing since before I was born but refuses to give it up. Says she likes the old body style. I'd take good heat and not having to stop at a gas station every three seconds, but that's me.

"Well, you know, Dr. Williams *did* clear you to play," she says, and starts wrapping an oversized mustard-yellow scarf around her neck.

"Maybe she doesn't know what she's talking about. I could go back to play too soon and rip my stomach apart," I say, annoyed at my own high-pitched, whiny voice.

Mom grabs her phone and keys out of one of the cupholders in the center console and says, "Okay." But it's not a you're-right okay. It's more like a you're-being-ridiculous okay. Doesn't she know I can hear the difference?

"I'm serious, Mom! I bet you won't be so nonchalant when my stomach rips open." Then I remember Mom and me getting down to old-school Ciara this morning in the kitchen before she took me to the doctor. I had the nerve to drop down into the splits. Yes, the splits! With ease, like I never even had surgery. I'm telling you, technology has gotten too advanced for its own damn good.

"Not sure how that's gonna happen. The puncture wounds were so tiny you didn't even need stitches."

Oooo, I hate when Mom calmly throws out facts when all I'm trying to do is pitch a fit.

"And honestly, Carli," Mom says, reaching into the backseat for her neon-yellow Cambridge satchel, "I don't see any reason you shouldn't finish the season if you're physically able." She throws her phone and keys into the bag.

"But you know I hate basketball!"

"Yes, but the championship game is only . . . what? Two weeks away. And that's if your team keeps winning. Either way, it will all be over soon. After that, you can choose a different direction. You have a lot to think about, you know." She lifts her portable tea infuser from the cupholder closest to her and takes a sip.

"Yeah, how can I forget?"

"Come on," she says, and opens the car door, cold air blasting my face. Late February, and winter finally decides to show up in Houston. It's freaking thirty-one degrees. I swear everything wants to be on my nerves today.

We walk through the back door and down a hall lined with tiny, glass-front offices. It's been forever since I've been in here. I don't recognize any of the girls behind their white, modern desks, staring at their large Mac screens. But their white, pushpin walls, covered by all things interior design, are just as cool as I remember.

One office rushes at me with color and patterns—a photo of a cobalt-blue sofa below a turquoise chandelier; a sample of a hot pink, orange, and gold rug; and swatches of diamond-patterned fabrics. I stop walking and look inside. On the back wall there are photos of beautifully tiled Moroccan arches and columns. *This house is gonna be dope,* I think, before the Emma Watson–looking girl behind the desk, with a brown pixie cut and dark red lips, looks up. She sees Mom, grabs a folder off her desk, springs out of her chair, and quickly tiptoes around the intricately carved cream tile organized on the concrete floor.

She swings her glass door open, says "Hey, Carli," like she knows me, and runs to catch up with Mom.

"Mrs. Alexander!" calls a different girl, from somewhere behind me.

I turn around like she's calling me, like I'm the boss. And for a second, my neck gets long, my shoulders roll back, and I'm feeling myself. Like I'm doing it big and I have life all worked out. Then she runs past me to secure her position on the other side of Mom and bursts my little bubble.

The front of the store opens up to the retail shop with its teal-framed floor-to-ceiling windows enticing everyone passing by on Westheimer Road to come on in. Oh my God, it smells so good in here. And I see why. There's a long rectangular table full of candles. I pick up one with two small crystals sitting on either side of its wick.

"That's the moon batch candle, hand poured only during full moons," says the guy behind the hammered gold checkout desk. He's a young Black dude wearing a multicolored, silky, patched jacket. Sounds ugly, but it's super cute. There's a huge yellow *G* on the front, left side of the jacket above a patch that reads *Men at Work*. And the right sleeve is full of bright blue stars of all different sizes.

"Cool, I'll take one," I say, and then add, "Cute jacket."

"Thanks, made it myself," he replies.

I can't believe how much the shop has changed. Mom used to sell only home accessories, but now there are kimono robes, leather totes, woven pouches, handmade jewelry, fancy chocolate, notebooks, gold engraved pencils, and wait— There's a whole wall of greeting cards. I walk closer to see what they're talking about.

You have the trying-to-be-cool section with sayings like *Yaas Queen* and *Birthday Squad* printed over graphic images. Then you have the legitimately beautiful section with intricate designs and lots of gold leaf. There's even a whole collage section. A sympathy card with cut-out footprints in the sand. A congratulations card with cut-out champagne flutes. Come on, now. I could do better than that.

The best one is a printed collage of a girl standing in a long T-shirt holding a bouquet of peach flowers over her face. In the background are planets, stars, a dog on its hind legs wearing a party hat, and the words *dance to your own music . . . it's your birthday*. My birthday is not until November, but this card absolutely belongs on my walls next to the watercolor I did in art class last year. A bouquet of balloons high in the sky carrying a baby elephant—the only other mammal that knows how to dance.

At the checkout desk, the guy with the cute jacket asks, "Are you adding this to your mom's account?"

I guess everyone in here knows who I am. "No, that's okay," I say. Mom and Daddy always stress the importance of me and Cole budgeting for what we want. Plus, I have plenty of money in my checking account. We've both had accounts since we were ten. That's where Mom and Daddy deposit our allowance. And I like to see my money stack. I mean, I spend money on magazines and the occasional cute top or jumpsuit or whatever I find in thrift shops. But that's it.

"You sure?" he asks, his bright blue-lined eyes looking confused.

"Yeah, I'm good." I reply, and pull my phone out of my back pocket for Apple Pay. There's a missed text from Rex asking how the doctor's appointment went. I don't *even* feel like thinking about that.

And there's a missed group text from Daddy asking to stop by tonight. Mom has already responded with *OK*. Cole responded with 👍 💜 🙂 My heart lifts and twirls in my chest at the thought of the whole family being together again. I can't help but think it's a sign that there's still hope.

● REX ●

Sitting in my pickup truck in the parking lot after school, heat on blast trying to warm up, I check my phone again. Still no response from my father. Took me all week to work up the nerve to send him that video Carli's dad made. Each time I'd load the video into our conversation—where my last message, **1st game of season tonight at 7 if you wanna come**, still sat unanswered—I'd delete it.

But this morning, I loaded it, typed, **What I've been up to all these years**, and quickly pressed Send.

When I checked my phone at lunch and he hadn't replied, I added, **Oh that's my new girlfriend. She can ball too**.

And after fifth period, when he still hadn't replied, I texted, **And she's dope in a million other ways**.

Now that school's over and he still hasn't replied, I type, **Not that you care**. But something inside me won't let me press Send. Something stupid and weak and still hopeful. You'd think that after all these years, I'd be all out of hope. Nope, not my dumb ass.

I ring Carli. She still hasn't texted me back from earlier. I want to know how her doctor's appointment went, but she doesn't pick up. *Damn, did the doctor tell her she couldn't play?*

Coach gave us a rare day off—no practice, no game, no team meeting, nothing. Said we needed rest before the playoffs. But it's hard to rest when I don't know what's up with my girl.

When I get back to the crib, my father's Tesla is parked in the driveway. His sneakers and messenger bag are haphazardly tossed by the front door. The house is toasty. And I can hear the TV playing in the living room. It feels like home. So much so that I want to drop my backpack and yell, "Dad, I'm home!" like people do in the movies. But my mouth acts like it doesn't know how to move.

And my body isn't doing any better. Instead of heading to the living room, I'm standing frozen in the foyer with my arms folded across my chest, feeling like . . . It's hard to explain.

Man, do you know how many times I've hoped to come home to my father sitting in the living room? How many times I've psyched myself into thinking, *Today is the day*. The day he'll be chillin' on the sofa when I get home and I'll join him, and we'll chop it up and maybe even bust out a bag of potato chips. Now today really could be that day. It definitely feels like that day. But what if it isn't?

Well, it wouldn't be anything new. I don't have anything to lose, I convince myself, and take off my coat and shoes and put them away in the mudroom. Then I take as much air as I can into my lungs and blow it out slow before walking down the hall and turning the corner.

I don't see my father, but he must be around here somewhere. A clip from my freshman year is playing on our ridiculously large flat-screen. Not one from the video Carli's dad made. Must be YouTube or something. And I'm right on time to see my younger self cock the ball back and posterize somebody.

"Damn, your boy is cold!" I say, out loud to myself. In case you haven't noticed, your boy is prone to referring to himself in third person. Makes talking to himself more fun.

But this time there's a response. "You really are," my father says in his soft voice, and sits up on the sofa. He looks back at me, eyes red and puffy, like he's been crying. Actually, he's still crying.

And once again I can't move or speak. This moment

should feel good, right? In my head, my father watching me play, giving me praise, and shedding tears for me is like heaven.

But standing ten feet from the man who ignored me all these years and actually hearing his words and seeing his tears is different. It's all kinds of shock and hope and sadness and love and hurt and anger and hate—yes, hate—pushing up inside me all at once, trying to get out.

I don't know whether I want to run to him or away from him. Whether I want to punch him in the face or hug him. I just don't know.

"Why did I buy this sofa?" he asks, and reaches around to rub his back. "They shouldn't even be able to call this thing a sofa."

Of *all* things for him to say. It's weird. I think if he would've said, *Sorry*, or something like that, my hate would've come raging out. But I could feel him on the sofa tip—deeply. "Man! I. Don't. Know," I reply. "That sofa is trash. All the seating in this house is trash."

"It really is. We need new furniture, stat. I want to be out here—"

"Word," I interrupt, "like yesterday." I'm not ready for everything he has to say. Not yet. I walk a few steps closer but don't go sit down.

"Let's do it. This time you can pick it out. Clearly I don't know what I'm doing."

"Bet! Carli's mom is a designer. I'm sure she could hook the house up," I say before realizing he doesn't know who Carli is. "Carli's my girlfriend."

"Figured that," he says, and guiltily shifts his eyes away from me. "The one from the video you sent?"

"Yeah," I say, trying to pretend that our everything-is-cool bubble just didn't crack, trying to pretend that him not knowing Carli's name or not really knowing who I am or never seeing me ball or him refusing to love me all these years doesn't hurt, doesn't piss me off.

I walk over to the kitchen to get myself some apple juice. "Want some juice?" I call out to my father to try to repair the crack. I'm good with the everything-is-cool bubble for now. Nah, I *need* the bubble right now.

"Yes, please," my father says. "And can you heat up a couple of those arepas?"

"Arepas! Angie was here again?"

"Yep."

"Man, Angie's arepas go so hard."

"Don't they?"

And just like that, we're back in there.

CARLI

When we pull up to the house, Daddy's Tahoe is parked in the middle of the driveway.

"Now, why would he do that?" Mom says, and parks on the street.

"Probably wasn't thinking." I defend Daddy, even though I'm mad we'll have to walk in the cold instead of going straight into the house from the garage. But right now, it's not about me. If Mom and Daddy have any chance of reconciling today, she can't start off with an attitude. "You need help carrying anything?" I ask Mom to try to help better her mood.

"Yeah, can you grab those plans off the backseat? Thanks."

I turn around, get on my knees, and grab two giant rolls of architectural plans. *Barbara A*, the name of Mom's interior design business (her first name and middle initial), is stamped in red on the outside. "Are these for the new boutique?"

"Sure are," she says, smiling. "We start the build-out next month."

Inside, Daddy's keys are in the singing bowl on the side table near the front door. I stop and smile at them for a second before going into the breakfast room where he and Cole are at the table playing chess on our vintage chessboard. Well, actually, Daddy looks like he's trying to decide his next move and Cole is taking pictures. Not even with his iPhone; he brought out the Nikon—the big dog. He's probably thinking the same thing I am—*There's hope!*

"Hey," Cole says, and comes to give me a hug. But he has on entirely too much cologne. Don't know what girl he was trying to impress, but he's not about to have me smelling like that.

I duck his arms. "Dang, bathe in cologne much?"

Cole pinches his shirt as if poppin' his collar. "Don't hate. Appreciate," he says, and laughs.

"Brought some Ethiopian food," Daddy says, and stands up out of the deep-seated bench flanking the window.

Behind him the wind whips through the big tree in the backyard, making the antique brass bells hanging from its branches softly ring out.

"It's in there on the island," he adds.

He knows Ethiopian is Mom's favorite. *There's definitely hope.*

Mom looks over at the white plastic bags sitting on the kitchen island—teal with a butcher-block countertop. "Thanks, just give me a minute to put all this down," she says, referring to the stack of catalogs she's carrying.

"I'll get 'em," Cole says, offering to take them from her.

"No, it's fine," she says, and walks past the kitchen and down the hall to her office.

Before I hug Daddy, I place the plans down on the table next to the chessboard. Man-oh-man-oh-man, does it feel good to be hugging him in our house.

"What are these?" Daddy says, and lets go of me. He reaches down for one.

Oh shit! He's not supposed to know about the new boutique. "Oh, just some old plans," I lie, hoping it ends there.

But it doesn't. He slides the green rubber band off one of the rolls and takes a look.

"Why you being so nosy?" I ask, trying to play it off.

Daddy spreads the plans out on the table.

Cole walks over to take a look, too. "Oh, what's this going to be?" he asks excitedly. "A bar? A restaurant?" Mom has designed several of those. Cole gets closer. "Big rounders . . . tiny squares . . . small rounders . . . rectangles everywhere. Oh, I see. It's a boutique. It's cool the way it's set up," he says, running his fingers along the blue lines. He's always been able to easily read plans. But he's terrible at reading the room. Can't he see Daddy standing here fuming?

"Yeah, looks like your mom is opening another shop," Daddy says.

"Oh, cool. I didn't even know. Expanding! Go, Mom!" Cole says, still clueless.

Daddy sits back on the bench, crosses his arms, and starts

biting the inside of his cheek near his bottom lip. He's pissed.

Cole finally notices that something is up, and his face drains of excitement.

Mom walks into the kitchen and gets four plates down from the cabinet. She hasn't even looked at Daddy.

I go help, taking four sets of silverware out of the drawer near the dishwasher. We are soooo close to having a family dinner. All of us together, sitting around the table, talking and sharing.

"You know what?" Daddy starts, and stands up. The crease above the bridge of his nose is deep, his eyebrows low, and his nostrils are flared.

Mom looks up at him. She's holding two glass tumblers that she just got down from the cabinet.

"I came over here to apologize. For everything. For creating this whole mess. But then I see this. You want to talk about my secrets, but you have yours, too, *Barbara A.*" Daddy's voice is loud and harsh, and the emphasis on Mom's business name is nasty.

Cole and I exchange glances. He already looks ready to cry. But I'm sitting up here wondering about secrets. I mean, I know all about Mom's secret. And yeah, she should have told Daddy about the new boutique, but Daddy *stays* trippin' about how much she works. It's not like he was about to be supportive. But what are Daddy's secrets?

Mom doesn't say anything. She places the two glasses on the counter and reaches to get one more (there goes our family dinner). I wish she would at least say something.

"Okay, okay," Daddy continues, his face red. "You want to sit up here and ignore me? Well, I'm filing for sole custody. Let's see how well you can ignore that."

"That's absurd," Mom says, like it's a fact, and starts unpacking the Ethiopian food.

"I have grounds," Daddy says, turning on his lawyer voice. "With the new store, you'll never be home. Hell, you were never home before. You can visit the kids at my house if you want."

"Visit? My kids?" Mom responds, her voice going uncharacteristically high. Daddy's last comments definitely got her attention. "I think it's time for you to leave," she says, her voice returning to normal. "I hope you're not serious."

"Oh, I'm dead serious," Daddy says, walking toward the door. "And by the way," he says, turning back and directing his attention toward me and Cole, "I found a house in the same neighborhood where the rental house is. So, if y'all come live with me, y'all can go to Woodside High."

"With Rex?" Cole asks, as if that makes everything better.

"Rex! Who cares about Rex right now!" I yell, and run to my room.

● REX ●

It's freezing and I've been standing outside of Carli's heavily studded, powder-blue front door for entirely too long. I lift the ring on the large metal knocker. *I shouldn't be here,* I think for the hundredth time.

See, Carli didn't exactly invite me over. Actually, she didn't invite me at all and still hasn't returned any of my calls. And she's never told me where her mom's house is. Cole's photo tags on IG helped me find the street—quiet and tree-lined in South Hampton near Rice University. And their mom's old-school Discovery parked outside helped me pinpoint the house. It consistently appears in Cole's feed.

Yo, this is waaay too stalkerish. What am I thinking? I gently set the knocker back down without making a sound and put my hands in my coat pockets to warm them up.

"Ugh." I sigh, frustrated with myself, and a cloud of my breath hits the door. I swear it's braver than I am.

But I'm not getting back in my pickup truck without seeing Carli, you can bet on that. I need to make sure she's okay. Assure her that missing the playoffs is not the end of the world. Plus, this crazy good day with my father won't be the same if I don't share it with her.

The door starts making unlocking sounds from the inside. Shit! I want to run, but there's no time! I look for somewhere to hide on the long porch, but there's only the hanging swing and two large pots with unhappy succulents. It's too cold for them to be outside.

The door opens. The same tall woman with short hair from the hospital is about to walk out of the house with a thick blanket wrapped around her. But when she sees me, she stops and narrows the opening in the door. She looks at me—alarmed.

Oh, wait. She doesn't know me. "Hi, I'm Rex," I hurry up and say.

"So *you're* Rex," she says, like she's been hearing things about me.

"Yes, ma'am."

"No need for *ma'am*s," she says, and widens the door. "Why don't you come in."

"Thanks," I say, and step in, feeling my body relax into the warmth. I swear, the insides of a house have never felt or smelt so good. It's like the toffee candy Angie used to make mixed with her morning coffee with a little bit of Christmas and a dash of lavender. Don't forget about the vanilla. It's like the scents never end.

Carli's mom closes the door and says, "I'm Barbara,"

extending her hand out from underneath the blanket to shake mine.

"A pleasure to meet you," I say as politely as I can.

"Carli!" she shouts over her shoulder, "Rex is here!" Then she turns back to me and asks, "So, you go to school with Carli?"

"No, I go to Woodside High."

"I see," she says, and nods.

Carli comes walking down the hall in a long NASA T-shirt hiding everything underneath. What exactly? My eyes are begging to know. They look closer and I tell them to stop, but they're like hardheaded kids. They've never seen so much of her skin. The strong curve of her calves, the light spots dotting her right shin and knee (I wonder what those are), the dark bruise on her left thigh (I wonder how she got that), the way her thighs get paler and thicker, much thicker, as they reach higher toward the shirt. My eyes turn things over to my head and I wonder what her thighs look like higher, even higher—*hot damn*.

"It's so cold," Carli says, hugging herself as she nears the doorway. She looks confused, like she's wondering what I'm doing here, and her usual brightness is strained behind sad eyes.

Damn, I feel awful. I'm standing here eyeing her up, not even thinking about the whole reason I came over in the first place. I can't imagine having to sit out the rest of the season and missing the playoffs. I wish I could wrap my arms around her and tell her it's going to be okay. But I don't want to do all that in front of her mom, so I say, "Yeah, it is."

"Well, maybe you should go put some clothes on," her mom says, and gives her a look.

Carli rolls her eyes. "I have clothes on," she says, and raises her shirt to show some small drawstring shorts.

"Barely," her mom replies.

"Really, Mom?" Carli whines, widening her eyes.

"Fine, I'm going out to put the Rover in the garage."

"Okaaay," Carli says in a way that sounds like, *Why you telling me?*

I'm so embarrassed I could disappear. Sad or not, that was rude as hell.

Her mom tilts her head, shifts her neck back, and gives Carli a look. I don't need a mom to know that look. When a woman starts using neck action, shit is real.

"Sorry," Carli says, and softens her eyes. "It's just—"

"I know," her mom interrupts, returning the soft look, and adds, "It's okay," before hitting the unlock button on a car key, tightening the blanket around herself, and dashing outside.

I scoop Carli up in my arms.

She hugs my neck and sighs, breath hot and sticky with hurt.

"It's okay. Everything is going to be okay," I say, holding her.

She sighs again and slides her long body down mine. "What are you doing here? How'd you even know where I live?"

But before I can come up with an answer, she gently takes my hand and leads me farther into the warm house with its old wooden floors and colorful rugs and clusters of sweet-smelling candles burning on every table. Past paintings and masks and maps and mirrors and framed photos hanging on white walls. Past the living room with its velvet burnt-orange sofa and floor-to-ceiling books on recessed shelves. (Man, I would kill to live in this house.) And down the hall to her room.

CARLI

I close the door to my room, lean back against it, and grab Rex's hands—still cold. I bring him closer to me, rub my nose against the tip of his nose—even colder. Rub my left cheek against his, back and forth, until his warms.

"Damn, how long were you standing out there?" I say, and give him a kiss.

"A *minute*," he says, "a long minute."

"Sorry, I didn't know you were coming. What are you even doing here?"

He's looking around at my walls. "Well, Cole—"

"Oh my gosh. I'm so stupid. Of course it was Cole," I say, feeling my upper lip hike up. If Cole thinks inviting Rex over tonight is about to make me peace out Mom, he has another thing coming.

"No, no. I just wanted to make sure you were okay. Tried calling and texting but hadn't heard from you," Rex says, and lowers the black hoodie off his head, his face holding space for everything good and sweet.

I kiss him again. Regardless of Cole's motivation for inviting him over, Rex being here feels like a thick, cool layer of salve on tonight's new wounds.

Rex interlocks his fingers with mine, presses his palms into mine, and brings our hands up to frame our faces.

I press back, hard, even harder, and he takes a step back. Ha! He wasn't ready for that.

"Oh, so first you want to ignore me and now you want to push me around," he says, grinning.

I keep pushing, and he keeps stepping backward until he's up against my bed and then lying back with his feet on the floor. "Sorry, I didn't have the best day," I say, standing between his legs.

"Yeah, I figured the doctor didn't give you the okay for the playoffs. I'm so sorry."

I wish. But sadly, that's not it. How can I tell him that I'm pissed about having to play? That I would be absolutely fine with never touching another basketball the rest of my life. It seems impossible.

And it's not exactly going to be easy telling him that Daddy is trying to use him to bribe me and Cole to leave our mother, either. I'm glad he's occupying himself with looking around at my walls while I come up with the right words.

He looks back up at me and says, "It's okay. You have next year. Senior year is what really counts."

"The doctor actually gave me the okay today," I blurt out, and all my secrets dart off to dark corners inside me, hoping they're not next. I lie down next to Rex on my bed and look at the ceiling, the only blank space in my room.

"Yeah?" he asks, and out of the corner of my eye, I see him turn his head toward me.

I stare straight ahead. I can't have this conversation looking into his eyes when all my secrets are being so shy. I grab his hand, trying to let my secrets know that Rex is okay. Then I take a deep breath and say, "Basketball is not why I had a bad day. I know I said that my parents were just taking a break, but they're not. They're getting a divorce. Like, there's no hope. It's really happening."

"So you can play?" Rex asks.

Not, *Sorry about your parents.*

Not, *Sorry about your family breaking apart.*

Not, *Are you okay?*

Not even, *So what's all this stuff on your walls?*

So you can play? That's all he has to say.

REX

Carli snatches her hand away from mine and places it on her belly. "Can I play? Is that all you care about? I swear, everything with you is always about basketball."

Wait! What? Hand aching with abandonment, I answer, "No, of course not."

"Well, I sure as hell can't tell."

Hold up a second. Did Carli just curse at me? Cursing in general and cursing *at* somebody are two different things. But I tell myself to be cool and roll over on my side to face her, hoping she'll face me, too.

She gives me a hard glance before staring back up at the ceiling.

Be cool, Rex. Be cool. "I knew you were going to the doctor today. When I didn't hear back from you, I was worried that you were going to have to sit out the rest of the season. Can you blame me for that?"

No answer. She rolls her eyes and starts fiddling with her necklace without even bothering to look in my direction.

Be cool, Rex. Be cool. "I mean, I drove all the way over here just to make sure you were okay."

She glares at me, says, "Nobody asked you to come over here," and looks back at the ceiling.

Okay. Clearly I have Carli confused. And it's my fault. I've texted her sixteen times today. And called her three. And then brought my ass all the way over here in the freezing cold to check on her. But you see, I'm not that dude. That dude that's going to be sweating her. That dude she can ignore and treat however bad she wants. That dude she can push around. Clearly she thinks I'm that dude. But he is not I.

And I get it, her parents are breaking up. But it's kinda old news, isn't it? It's not like they just plopped it on her today like, *Surprise!* They're not even living together.

Don't get me wrong, I'm sure the whole situation is still sad. But if she didn't feel like talking (even after she got the great news from her doctor), she could've at least sent a text telling me she'd hit me up tomorrow or something. But no. Nothing. And now instead of apologizing, she wants to treat me like shit? Naw, dawg. I'm not even going out like that.

I sit up in the bed and look over at her, and she actually has the nerve to look up at me with an attitude. Like I'm the one in the wrong.

"Don't worry. I won't be poppin' up over your house again," I say.

"Good" is all she says and closes her eyes.

A hurt deep inside me hurls its voice up through a dark sky. "Good? Really, Carli?"

She ignores me.

Another hurt, another hurl, but my throat closes over its voice. *How could you do me like this? After everything we've shared. And now it's like I'm nothing to you. Like I'm nobody,* I scream inside myself.

I swallow my hurt back down. "It's getting late," I say, and stand up.

Cole walks in. "So, I was thinking," he says before he sees me. And then after, "Rex!" and gives me a giant hug. I don't think a hug has ever been more on time.

"Not now, Cole," Carli says, and sits up on the bed, face scrunched up.

Cole turns to me. "Did Carli tell you that we may be going to your—"

"Are you out of your fucking mind?" Carli screams, and stands up. "Out! Get out! Now!"

Hurt welling up in his eyes, he turns to walk out.

"What's going on in here?" their mom asks, appearing in the doorway behind him.

No one speaks. Everyone's looking at Carli. Her fists are balled up, her jaw is clenched, and her nostrils are flared like she wants to give us all a serious beatdown.

Part of me wants to go to her, hug her, and make her relax. But the other part, the part that's been working overtime my whole life to hold myself together, demands that I stay back.

THAT'S
ALL
SHE
WROTE

CARLI

Monday after school and I'm at basketball practice, where I'm supposed to be learning new defensive plays. But I can't stop running the scene of Rex leaving my room through my head. How he looked at me like he didn't know me. How I looked back at him, with all the anger I felt about my parents' divorce, their custody battle, basketball, my life. How Mom put her hand on his back and said, "I'll walk you out," and I let her, without even telling him good-bye.

"Jordan, if Shannon gets the ball at the top of the left key, go and help Carli trap her," Coach says, and points to the left corner of the free-throw line. Jordan walks down to the corner from right outside the three-point line, smacking on gum.

I haven't told Jordan about the breakup. Rex and I haven't officially said we were over, but what we had definitely feels broken. No more rise-and-shine texts from him every morning. No more staying up late talking to him on the phone every night. No contact at all since he left my house on Friday.

"Carli, get your head out of the clouds and come up here to trap!" Coach yells. The whole team's eyes widen in surprise. Jordan's mouth is literally hanging open.

Coach never yells at me. Everybody else, yes, but never me.

"Shannon cost us the championship last year, and I'll be damned if I let her take it away from us again this year," Coach continues.

Shannon is this sophomore from Langham High. Yeah, she can ball, but she ain't all that. Plus, she's always looking at me funny and trying to copy my style. Been on varsity since she was a freshman, like me. Tall, six-foot-one to be exact, like me. Okay, maybe she can't help either of those two things, but she wears number twenty-two. Now, everybody and their mama know that's my number. And one time she slipped me a note after a game that said, "Hey." *Hey?* Like, she couldn't have opened her mouth to say that? I swear I can't figure out if the girl likes me or wants to be me. But either way, I can't stand her.

"You good?" Jordan whispers after I get to the corner.

"Rex and I broke up," I whisper back.

"Okay," Coach says, "now if Shannon gets the ball on the right key, Carli, you drop back down to the block. Jordan, you slide over. And Meagan, you come up to help Jordan."

"Are you serious?" Jordan asks as we switch positions.

After practice Jordan and I go to Baskin-Robbins in Rice Village. Once we get our ice cream, we sit outside at a hot pink bistro table, backs against the red brick building. It's eighty degrees. Houston sure knows how to flip the switch on the weather, but nobody's mad at it today. Everybody and their mama are out walking and shopping and eating in the sun.

Cold sweetness dissolving on my tongue, I explain, "It would be everything spending senior year with Rex, but leave my mom? I can't do that." Oh, I had to tell Jordan about the whole thing with my parents because the whole thing with Rex wouldn't make any sense otherwise. Plus, I'm tired of keeping so many secrets.

"Not only that, you can't leave the team your senior

year! It's crazy your dad is even asking you to. What is he thinking?" Jordan asks, and tucks in her outstretched legs to make room for a woman walking by on the sidewalk with a stroller.

I'm leaving the team either way, I think but don't dare say. Jordan will never forgive me. Like, our friendship will be over. I stay silent and scoop out another spoonful of my Cannoli Be With You ice cream—mascarpone, pistachios, crunchy cannoli shell pieces, and chocolate chips. Some goodness I need right about now.

"So, you think you'll be ready for Shannon?" Jordan asks, and eats a scoop of her Pink Bubblegum ice cream with sprinkles, chocolate chips, Butterfinger pieces, and cherries. Leave it up to Jordan to mess up ice cream.

"I guess," is all I say, hoping she'll drop the basketball talk.

"She gave us some serious problems last year, and that's when she was a freshman. No telling what she's gonna be coming with this year."

When Jordan says *us*, she means me. Shannon plays *my* position. *I'm* the one who has to guard her. And I'm not sure how I'm supposed to do that when I don't even want to play.

"I need to say something to Rex," I say, trying to change the subject. "But I don't know what."

"*I'm sorry* sounds like it will do just fine."

"But what about the fact that all he wanted to do was talk about basketball even after I told him about my parents?" I don't know why I just bothered to ask Jordan that. It's all she ever wants to talk about, too.

"Well, you didn't even tell him the real deal. It's not like he knows you and Cole have to decide which parent to live with. He's not a mind reader, Carli. Plus, it *is* a big deal that you'll be back for the playoffs. No way we could handle Shannon without you."

"Couldn't handle her with me. So, what's the difference?"

"Girl, stop. You are Carli Alexander and you are about to shut Shannon down," she says, and reaches her spoon for my bowl. I swear Jordan's always trying to steal somebody's food.

I move my bowl over and shield it with my hand. "Eww, I don't want all that nastiness mixed up with all this goodness."

She sucks her spoon clean and tries again.

Disgusting, but I let her. Hoping that she'll remember this. Hoping that this will somehow count when I have to tell her the truth about basketball.

REX

I'm running down the court, trying to get back on D, when I spot them. Light-blue scrubs walking up the stands. A tall, slim man with dark skin and a low-cut fade. Halfway up, the man in scrubs sits down, and I see his face. My father. For the first time ever, my father is at my game.

The dude I'm supposed to be guarding shoots a three. *Swish.*

Shit.

"Take that, Mr. Rex Carrington," dude says, shooting hand still hanging in the air. He's wearing yellow wristbands on both wrists to match his uniform.

"Man, get on somewhere. That's your first three the whole game," I reply, and give him a light bump while running back up the court.

The ref blows her whistle and a jolt of fear rushes through my body. *Not another technical!* But she holds up her hand to signal a time-out.

"Hustle up! Hustle up!" Coach Bell shouts, waving his right arm in a big circle. As I approach the huddle, he gives me a water bottle and asks, "You all right? You didn't even have a hand in his face."

"I'm good. I'm good." I take the water bottle, hold it up, and squeeze, giving myself the cold smack in the face I need. When I look back at my father, he's staring straight at me.

"Listen!" Coach Bell says, crouched down in the middle of the huddle. "We only have three minutes left and we're down six. We need everybody's head in the game right now." He looks up at me. "If we lose tonight, it's over. No going to San Antonio to play for the championship. And we've worked too hard and come too far for that. We can do this. We have to do this!" He stands up and puts his hand out. The whole team piles their hands on. "'Hustle hard' on three. One. Two. Three."

"Hustle hard!" And we lift our hands and run back to our positions.

Danny brings the ball up the court and passes to me just outside the three-point line on the left.

Dude guarding me is moving back and forth with his hands outstretched and his sweaty brown hair stuck to his forehead, saying, "Whatchu got? Whatchu got?"

Does this cornball really think he can hold me? He probably does because my shot has been off all night. But that has nothing to do with him. I've been thinking about Carli. I swear that girl is always throwing me off my game some kind of way. I pass it back to Danny, and he swings it around to our shooting guard, Tommy.

Tommy gives his defender a little head fake, dribbles past him, and passes the ball to Josh at the top of the key. Coach has been playing us both lately when he wants to go with more of a small-ball lineup.

Next thing you know, Josh is passing the ball to me. Wasn't expecting that! And neither was dude guarding me. I gather my legs underneath me and release, feeling my father watching me.

Swish!

The crowd erupts in cheers, and my father is on his feet, clapping. And I swear each time his hands come together, I hear a thousand claps. All the claps from all the games he's ever missed. Every *Good job, son* or *I'm so proud of you* that I've always wanted to hear. And I'm taking all of it in.

"Let's go!" I yell, slap the court with both hands, and sprint to get back on defense.

Danny swipes the ball off the other team's point guard. And I'm running full speed back toward our basket. Corny dude is running alongside me, but he can't stop what's about to go down. As I approach the basket, I leap, catch Danny's perfectly thrown alley-oop, and do a 360 midair before *boom*—that's all she wrote!

The whole gym goes crazy, and the other team calls a time-out. We're still one point down, but the momentum has already shifted in our direction. Ain't no way we're about to let these fools beat us now.

CARLI

Clearly Rex isn't feeling my *I'm sorry*. Texted him over three hours ago and still haven't heard back. Now I'm in my room, sitting at my desk, making him a card. The first card I've ever made for anybody. Hopefully something he can feel.

The front has no words. Only our bodies from that picture Cole took of us sitting on Daddy's swallow-you-whole sofa. It's not a great picture of me—mostly hair with a little bit of profile looking at Rex.

But Rex's face is everything. In it, I can feel what he sees in me. I swear it's like walking to the center of his heart and seeing my own reflection. A bright, glorious, confident girl. Nothing like how I see myself.

I cut us away from the background and paste us on

gold linen card stock. Then I break out all the LePens I own and draw a big, swirly sun behind us. Arrange a coral peony cut from a magazine to look like I'm handing it to him. And paste four tissue-papered lavender rays straight from my heart to his. Hoping he'll feel how sorry I am. Hoping he'll feel what I see in him. A fiercely tender boy. A million streaks of softness, cutting through all the dark clouds.

I push down the peony, smoothing the thin, glossy paper over the glue. The card actually looks pretty cool. Better than most of the cards in Mom's shop, I'll tell you that.

"I've decided," Cole says, walking into my room. Didn't need to break out an *I'm sorry* for Cole. Friday night seemed to slip right off him.

"Please tell me the blue one," I say, turning around in my chair. He was in here five minutes ago holding up a basic blue T-shirt and a red silky shirt that looked like it came straight out of a nineties R&B video, asking which one he should wear on his date. After school tomorrow he's taking this senior from his photography class to the Cockrell Butterfly Center. Or I should say, she's taking him. She's the one with a license, so she'll be picking him up.

"No, I mean I'm going to live with Dad next year."

"What!" I stand up from my chair so fast that it nearly falls over. "I thought we said we'd decide together?"

"Shh. Can you be any louder? Mom is home." He extends his long arm and pushes the door to my bedroom closed.

"Yeah, and you want to leave her, your own mom, just so you can go to school with Rex," I whisper hard, and walk away from him to my bed.

After I sit down, I glimpse Cole's pink ice cream cone–patterned socks, and an image of the light pink house shoe in the middle of the road on the way to school this morning pops in my head. It was on the white separating line, still fresh and fluffy, like it hadn't been run over yet. At the time I took it as a sign that me and Rex still had a chance.

But now I'm thinking the abandoned house shoe was trying to tell me not to leave Mom. Even in its fresh fluffiness, it still looked forgotten and sad. How could I even think about leaving Mom alone like that? Not that I planned to. But I'd be lying if I said I haven't imagined spending my last year with Rex—kissing between classes, walking down the hall holding hands, throwing our caps in the air together on the day the rest of our lives begin.

"No, Woodside High has a better boys' basketball program and one of the best photography teachers in the state," Cole says, and walks over to sit beside me. "She's always doing celebrity portraits for *Texas Monthly* and food photography for *PaperCity Magazine* and *Houston Press*. She even has credits in *National Geographic* and *Travel and Leisure*." He looks around at my walls. "There may even be something of hers in here."

"Oh, my bad. So, it's Rex, basketball, and a teacher you don't even know you'll have over Mom," I say, and scoot away from him, trying to make myself feel superior for only thinking of leaving Mom and never saying it aloud.

"Look, it's not like Dad can stop me from seeing Mom. I'll see her whenever I want. I could go by her shop or stop over for dinner or come spend weekends with y'all whenever. We're not little kids anymore, Carli. Our parents are still our parents, yeah, but they can't control us like they used to."

"What are you talking about?" I say, and stand up. "Of course they can control us! Didn't you hear Daddy? He's filing for sole custody!"

"I'm almost positive Dad was just pissed when he said all that stuff. Divorce gets ugly like that," he says in a calm voice, grabs my hand, and tries to get me to sit back down.

I snatch my hand away. "Oh, you're such the adult. You have all the fucking answers."

Cole doesn't reply. He looks up like he's surprised by me. Then like he's sorry for me and disappointed in me.

I don't know who he thinks he is, looking at me like that. He's the one talking about leaving Mom on the side of the road. I should be the one giving him the disappointed looks. But I can barely meet his eyes.

He's still looking at me, but his face isn't saying anything anymore. It's just as silent as his mouth.

I can't take this silence. The stillness of it. The way it's making me look back at this messed-up, pissed-off girl who has no problem pushing her own brother away. Not to mention the first boy who's ever given her a glimpse of a higher version of herself. I can't stand her right now.

"Sorry," I say, and sit back down. The apology is meant for tonight and Friday, but I don't say all that.

Pretty sure Cole gets it, though, because he puts his arm around me. "I still want us to stick together, I do. I just thought you should know where I stand. After this year you'll only have one year of high school left, but I'll have two. It's a bigger decision for me."

Is this boy really trying to minimize the impact this decision is going to have on my life? But I stay cuddled up under his arm, tell myself to calm down. "I'm not saying I won't go live with Daddy, but we still have two weeks. Let's use our time to think it all through."

"You're right . . . we should," Cole says, and squeezes me.

"And promise we'll talk about this again before we make our final decision, before you tell anyone?"

"Promise," he says. "This stays between us."

REX

There's no reason I should still be awake. It's after midnight, and I'm lying in bed with the lights out. The house is wonderfully warm. My belly is comfortably full. And the frame, the entrance to the hall that leads to my father's room, got a great picture tonight.

After my father and I ate Thai takeout and watched a

little late-night TV, he filled up the frame for over an hour, talking about my game.

We won, just like I thought. And I hit the winning shot—a three from the baseline. The whole team tackled me in joy. Josh even rubbed my head. And Danny actually texted me tonight after the 360 alley-oop dunk made ESPN's high school highlight reel. I should be sleeping like a baby.

But I can't stop thinking about Carli. About that text she sent—*Sorry*. That's it. No elaboration. What am I supposed to say back to that? *It's okay?* No, because it's not. *I forgive you?* No, because I don't. I need more words. An explanation of why she was acting like that. A promise to never treat me that way again.

My phone lights up and I quickly grab it off my nightstand. Another text from Carli saying the same thing: **Sorry**

I don't respond.

The next day, fourth period, honors chemistry: **I'm sorry**

Oooo, she added the word *I'm*. All the words that usually roll off her tongue and this is the best she can come up with? I don't respond.

Wednesday after basketball practice, grabbing my

precalculus book out of my locker to take home:

I

M

S

O

R

R

Y

She's getting a little creative with it. Won't lie, makes me smile, but I don't respond. You see, she ignored sixteen of my texts last Friday and three of my calls (yep, I still remember). I've only ignored one-fourth that amount, and she hasn't even bothered to call. I have to make it to eight, so she at least knows half of how I felt. Yes, petty, but sometimes it beez like that.

Thursday, at 6:47 a.m., same time I used to give her a wake-up text: **I'm sorry, Rex**

Damn, she gets me with this one. I know it's only one added word, but it's my name and I can hear her saying it. I type, **I'm sorry too . . . for ignoring you. I miss you**. But I decide that once again I'm doing way too much and erase everything.

After school on Friday: **What's your address? I have something to send you**

I wonder what it is. Did she buy me an apology present?

Maybe some new Js. Did she make a donation to plant some trees in my name? Yo, what if she wrote me a poem and kissed it with glossy lips? Hahaha, I'm being stupid. But really, what if she did? I want to ask her. I want to joke and play with her. I want to talk to her and see her and hug her and kiss her.

But this is only her sixth text. So, I only respond with my address—no *hello* or *how are you doing*. She better be glad I'm even texting her back.

SECRET
SPOTS

CARLI

Nineteen East Shady Trail is this huge, white, futuristic house surrounded by a pine forest. It has a sloped roof that juts out from the rest of the house, toward the sky, and is perched on concrete piers. As I walk up the steel staircase on the side of the house that leads to the front door, trying to think of the words that will make Rex forgive me, it feels like I'm boarding a giant spaceship. Like maybe, just maybe, Rex will open the door and we'll blast off to the stars, leaving all our earthly problems behind.

REX

I open the door and it's Carli. At my house. Standing on my porch. Wearing some button-fly cutoffs and a vintage *Jaws* T-shirt. In front of the setting sun. Damn, she couldn't be more perfect. So perfect I have to stop myself from picking her up, twirling her around, and carrying her into the house— honeymoon style.

Yeah, Rex. Forget about how she ignored you. How bad she treated you when you drove all the way over to her house in the freezing cold. And that look she gave you. Dawg, it was like she didn't give a shit about you. Yeah, go ahead and let all that slide.

"Look who's the stalker now," I say playfully. I mean, somebody had to say something. The silence was getting weird.

"No, you gave me your address."

"You said you were sending me something," I say. "Not coming over."

"Well, I lied!" Carli says, tilting her head and widening her eyes.

We both crack up laughing.

Call me a sucker, but damn being mad. I grab her hands, pull her into the house, and tell her, "I've missed you so much."

Carli closes her eyes, almost like it hurts, and puts her head down. She looks like she's about to cry. I pull her into me, and she buries her face in my shoulder. Warm tears soak through my T-shirt and she's shaking.

What the hell just happened? I'm so confused. She was just laughing. *Wait, did I do this? I swear to God I hate myself for ignoring her like that.*

"I'm sorry," I say softly. "I'm so, so sorry," I repeat, holding her tight and rubbing her back in slow circles, the way Angie used to rub mine as a child.

CARLI

"There's so much I need to tell you," I say under my breath, voice squeaking and trembling all over the place. I don't expect him to understand me. I mean, I can barely understand myself. One minute I'm acting like a raging lunatic, the next minute I'm laughing up a storm, and the next I'm crying uncontrollably. I swear I don't know who I am anymore.

"You can tell me anything. You know that, right?" Rex

says, separates from me a little, and kisses my forehead with soft, wet lips. "I want you to tell me . . . everything. I want to know all of you."

I don't lift my head. Thick mucus is running down the slope below my nose and hanging over my top lip. *Can you say gross?* Oh, my gosh; I got it all over the shoulder of his white T-shirt.

"I have a lot to tell you, too," he says, lifts my chin, and looks me in the eyes.

I quickly turn my head to wipe the snot on my shoulder. And now it's smeared all over my right cheek. *Great, just great.* But it's weird . . . I don't feel embarrassed. The fact that Rex can see me like this and not run away . . . see me like this and still look at me like I'm his everything makes me feel safe . . . and free . . . like I'm home.

"There's snot all over your shirt," I say.

"Yeah, it's all over your cheek, too."

"I know. I can feel it crusting up on my skin."

"Damn, you nasty," Rex says, and gives me a smack on the lips. The kiss is quick, but his lips do indeed touch mine. Yes, where the snot just was. This boy must be into me, like, for-real-for-real.

● REX ●

After a quick stop in the bathroom, I give Carli a tour of the house. Trust, not my idea. But she seems to really be into its design. She's talking about its clean lines . . . its floor-to-ceiling windows . . . its lack of trim around the doors . . . its sloped ceiling . . . its linear air vents . . . its unadorned walls . . . its minimalism this . . . and modern that . . . and on and on and on.

"I'm glad you like it, but I sure as hell don't," I tell her, walking up the stairs.

"Seriously? How could you not? Look at it. There's so much empty space. Even these floating stairs. I mean, it's everywhere. I don't know . . . it makes me feel light and airy. Free in a way."

"You get all of that from a whole bunch of blank walls and hard-ass furniture?" I ask, stepping off the top step and heading to my room.

"I guess my house is the exact opposite. There's stuff everywhere you look. And you've seen my room, my walls. Looking at so much stuff can get exhausting. Don't get me wrong; I love my mom's decorating style and I love everything I put up on my walls. But right now my mind feels so full. I'm just saying some emptiness would be nice."

I open the door to my room. "Well, you're not about to get it in here."

CARLI

Rex wasn't kidding. Everywhere I look there's something new for my eyes to land on. Other than the wall straight ahead with the sliding-glass door leading outside, there's stuff everywhere.

"I'll grab us some snot-free tees," Rex says, and laughs.

"You're never going to let me forget about that, are you?"

"Nope," he says, and disappears into his walk-in closet to the left.

"I can't wait until you slip up and do something embarrassing," I say loudly, walking toward the wall-to-wall shelving unit to the right.

"Yeah, yeah, yeah."

On the top shelf, there's a display box with a collection of pinned beetles between an old encyclopedia set and a framed pencil sketch of someone hugging a huge tree. On the shelves below, there are two globes, various art history books, a record player, a big stack of records, four African female busts wearing Rex's baseball caps, a small green lamp sitting on a gold tray, and a ceramic red-and-blue clock. On his nightstand there's a miniature rocking chair holding a silver watch on a stack of worn novels.

"Who knew you had such eclectic taste? I like . . . I like," I say.

"Huh?" Rex shouts from the closet.

"Oh, nothing," I mumble under my breath and walk over to his desk in the corner near his closet. His desk is actually an old wooden drafting table with a brass-and-steel file cabinet underneath it for drawers. On it there's a silver vintage pencil sharpener and five neatly sharpened number-two pencils beside an opened precalculus book. *Dang, this boy loves him some math.* Above his desk there's a roughly sketched portrait of a woman with two french braids.

I want to ask, *Is that your mom?* But I'm not ready to feel anymore sadness. Instead, I divert my eyes to the glass dome paperweight sitting on the upper right corner of his desk on top of a small notepad from Hotel Locarno Roma.

"Cool! You and your dad have been to Rome?" I shout, picking up the paperweight. There's an abstract purple-and-blue watercolor painting inside.

Rex's muffled voice comes from the closet. "Ha! Real funny. I seriously have so much to tell you."

I'm tired of shouting. So I put the paperweight down and follow his voice into the closet, where he's bent over looking inside his bottom built-in drawer along the left wall. When he sees me, he stands up with a shirt in his hand.

But there's not one on his body.

REX

Carli is looking at me like I'm a straight-up snack. Like if she could, she would fold me in half, slap some peanut butter on me, and chomp away. I'm not gon' even lie, she has your boy feeling a little shy up in here. I bite my lip to ease the embarrassment.

CARLI

Oh my goodness. He did not just bite his bottom lip. Is he trying to make me lose my mind? In this small space with his smooth, brown skin . . . his hard chest . . . his six-pack. And don't even let me get me started on his dips. You know those creases that start at his hips and angle down toward his . . .

REX

"This is the smallest shirt I could find," I say, trying to take some of the attention off me, and hold out a long-sleeved black-and-navy striped tee.

CARLI

Did he just invite me to come closer? Is that what he did? Okay, if he says so.

The first thing I do when I get to him is rub my hands down his chest and abs—hard and moisturized. I usually behave a little better than that, but I can't help myself.

Then I start taking off my shirt. I mean, I'm looking at

him so it's only fair for him to be looking at me, right?

Rex must agree because he's helping me get it over my shoulders and head.

He grabs my bare waist with both hands and I swear . . .

REX

If I could run off into my future with Carli right now, I would. No lie. But for now, I pull her body into mine. We're so close I can see the faint tear streaks on her cheeks, so close I can feel her heat. Like it's seeping into my chest, taking over me.

I gently dig my fingers into her waist, and she parts her mouth and reaches her lips toward mine. Her lip over my bottom lip, her tongue over my tongue, her breath mixing with my breath. Soft and wet. And hard.

CARLI

I'm feeling Rex like I've never felt another boy, and I want to feel more. I press into him and kiss him harder. Faster. It's like my mouth, my body, can't get enough.

His hands are underneath my ribs and I'm up on the dresser.

My lips race toward the closest part of his face, his forehead, and then down to the mole on the side of his nose, back to his mouth. My hands wrap around his neck, and his travel up over my bra.

He pulls away, his big black eyes asking me if it's okay.

Yes! And I let out a moan as his fingers touch the tips of my nipples. Again as his wet tongue moves in circles, as his mouth sucks.

His hands on my thighs. His fingers up the outsides of my jean shorts.

But I want them on the inside.

REX

Carli's moving her waist in circles. Somebody, help. Please. We cannot have sex in this closet. Don't get me wrong, we could very well have sex in this closet. Dude, if we don't stop with all this kissing and touching and circling, we will definitely have sex in this closet. And it would be amazing. I've waited forever and a day to make love. But I don't have condoms. And what I wouldn't love is having a baby right now.

CARLI

Rex takes his mouth off me and slides his hands down to my knees.

"Will your dad be home soon?" I ask.

"Nah, he'll probably be at the hospital all night," he says, and brings one of his hands back up. I will it to my breasts, but he reaches higher and runs his fingers along my collarbone underneath my thin, gold chain. Balancing my medallion on his middle finger, he says, "I've never really taken a good look at this before. It's dope."

"Thanks," I say, lean down, and grab his bottom lips with my lips.

He pulls away. "I don't have any condoms."

"Oh," I say, feeling heat start to escape. There's nothing sexy about the thought of getting pregnant right now. I might not know what I want to do with my life, but I do know I want options.

He hands me his shirt and I put it on. It smells like him, a mixture of pine trees and sweat. "You must've not washed this after you wore it last."

"Don't know. Here, you want another one?" he asks, bending down to look in his drawer.

"No, I love the way your funk smells."

"Okay, you're officially nasty," he says, laughing, and slides on a black long-sleeved T-shirt.

"And you love it."

REX

Back in my room, I'm sitting on my bed and Carli is walking

around looking at everything. Touching everything. She picks up a small gold-and-pearl turtle off my nightstand and lifts its shell. "Where do you get all this stuff?" she asks. "Do you go antiquing?"

"Antiquing? Man, nah. I found it all in some boxes marked for donation during our move. It all belonged to my mom."

She can't put down the turtle fast enough. "Why would your dad want to give your mom's stuff away? It's all so cool."

"I don't know. When we moved, it seemed like he wanted to leave everything behind, including my mom." The words feel so right coming out. Like they needed to be said. They've been floating around in my head since we moved out here last summer.

"Your dad doesn't care that you kept it all and have it up here?"

"He doesn't know."

"What do you mean he doesn't know?"

"Well, he's never been up here. So—"

"Wait. Your dad has never been in your room?"

"I told you I had a lot to tell you."

Carli's standing beside my bed with her hands clasped in front of her—hush-mouthed. She clearly doesn't know what to say about my father. And she hasn't picked up anything else. Don't know if she thinks I would care or Mom would care, but either way, it's starting to feel way too heavy in here. "I have something I want to show you," I say, get up, and grab my backpack from the corner beside the sliding door. "Come on."

CARLI

Rex is leading me across his backyard by the hand. When the lawn ends and the forest begins, he doesn't pause. But it's dark. And who knows what's in there.

I stop. "Umm, where are we going?" I ask, and fold my arms across my chest like it's cold, even though it's pretty warm.

"Come on. You'll see. Trust me."

I don't move. I feel like I'm the star of a scary movie and the audience is screaming, *Girl, don't do it.*

"I come back here all the time. You'll love it," he promises.

The audience is still screaming, *Don't listen to him, girl. Not unless you want to die!* And to their point, what good can come out of walking into a dark forest at night?

Rex reaches into his backpack, takes out a big flashlight,

and shines it into the woods. "See, just trees." He lights the ground. "And dead leaves and shrubs and fungus. No boogeyman."

"What about snakes and raccoons and whatever else lives in there."

"We'll be fine," Rex says, and shines the light at our feet.

In protest, I take a deep breath and let it out slow and loud. But when he grabs my hand, I start walking again.

After a few minutes, we reach a clearing with a wooden picnic table. "You brought this out here?" I ask.

"Yeah, it used to be in the backyard at my old house," he says, and takes out a long, red lighter, like Daddy uses to light the barbeque pit. He hands me the flashlight and lights two tin citronella candles sitting on the benches, one on each side of the table. Then he takes a blanket out of his backpack and arranges it on top of the picnic table.

"This is actually pretty cool," I say, admiring the setup.

"You better listen to your boy," Rex says, smiling, and climbs up on the table.

I climb up, too.

And now we're lying on top of the table with our pinky fingers linked, looking up at the crowns of tall pines reaching for a patch of star-sprinkled sky.

● REX ●

This has always been my secret spot. Even at my old house, when there was just a tiny backyard with two cedar elm trees. This table, the trees, the stars, this stillness—they've always been there for me. And now Carli is here, and it's like I've introduced her to my best friends and they're vibin'. And it's making me feel closer to her than I've ever felt. Like even if we were butt-naked having sex, I doubt I'd feel closer.

"Crazy that there are more trees on Earth than stars in the Milky Way, isn't it?" Carli says, her voice soft beside me.

I was already looking up at the stars, but I look closer. At all the bright spots peeking out from the darkness. At the giant pines stretching toward them. "Are there really?" I ask, wondering why I've never come across that fact.

"Yeah, there's something like three trillion trees on the planet. But scientists estimate there are somewhere between one hundred and four hundred billion stars in the galaxy."

"Word? I never would've guessed that. Especially since fifteen billion trees are chopped down every year. Did you know that almost fifty percent of the trees on the planet have either been cut down or died some kind of way since humans have been around?" I ask, offering up my own facts.

"Really? I knew all the Amazon boxes had to come from somewhere, but fifteen billion? Dang, at this rate, our stars are going to start catching up to our trees."

"I know, right?" I say, feeling my insides grin because I'm sitting in my favorite place talking to my favorite person about one of my favorite things. I didn't even think Carli was into trees like that. She acted like she barely cared about the magnolia dying outside of her dad's house. "Who knew you were into trees?"

"I'm not," she says, bursting my little bubble.

"So, you're into stars then?"

"Well, kinda. But I'm more into random facts. I like collecting ones I find interesting and putting them up on my walls."

"Yeah, I saw all the stuff in your room. It's dope. You must not let Cole take pictures in there because I've never seen your walls on his feed."

"Cole and his Instagram," she says, like she's rolling her eyes. "Yeah, no pictures of my walls allowed."

"Why not?"

"I don't know. I guess I'm afraid of them losing their magic."

"Magic?"

"Yeah, I've always found magic in small, random things . . . in thinking about them . . . in piecing them together . . . in seeing what they may have to say about big, important things."

"What do they say?"

"A lot. But nothing, really. I don't know. I mean, my walls still have a lot to tell me. And I can't have them out there speaking to everyone else before they even let me know what's up," she says, and laughs a little.

I love talking to Carli like this. It's like I'm inside her mind, hearing how it works. "So what are you waiting on them to tell you?" I ask.

"Everything," she says.

"Everything like what?" I ask, remembering her necklace. It looked magical. I sit up on my elbow and reach for it. Rub my thumb along the curved left edge, where the raised crescent moon sits cradling a sun in the form of a cut-out circle. From the circle I slide my thumb along the engraved rays that reach toward tiny raised stars on the other side. It's like she has the whole universe dangling from her neck.

"I don't know. Just everything."

"Everything is a lot."

"I know."

It feels like she's kicked me out of her mind. I want back in, but I don't know which words will get me there. So I lie back down. Don't say anything.

And neither does she.

For a long minute.

Then she shifts around on the table. "I can't see you," she whispers. Her words—after our long, dark silence—feel like a spark.

I roll on my side to face her like she's facing me. "I can't see you, either," I say into the blackness. There's only a sliver of a moon tonight. And I'm not sure when, but our candles went out.

"But I'm here," she responds.

It's weird. In the darkness, it's almost like we don't have bodies. Like we're spirits in the night. "You know I come out here to feel closer to my mom," I say, imagining Mom's spirit floating around us through the trees.

"I can see that. Out here, it's like we're closer to God or the Universe or whatever you want to call the mystery of all there is. And I guess your mom is a part of all that now."

"Yeah, I guess she is," I say, thinking about Mom's soul leaving the Earth, traveling out of our solar system, out of our galaxy, and on and on through the stars forever.

Carli puts the palm of her hand against my chest.

"My father blames me for her death, you know," I say, surprised at how easy the words glide out of my mouth. "I mean, he's never said it, but he's pretty much ignored me my whole life. And I always knew why. Then he went off and sold our old house. The house my mom lived in, my biggest connection to her, without even telling me first."

"Oh my gosh. That's awful. I'm so sorry," she says.

"It's okay. We're cool, now," I try to reassure her. "Actually, you know that video your dad made?"

"Yeah."

"Well, I sent it to my father, and afterward he came to my game. Like, for the first time in my life. And we've been talking more. And he's been out of his room more. He used to stay in there all the time when he was home. I rarely saw him. But now we've even chilled on the sofa a few times. Oh, I forgot to tell you. We want to hire your mom to help us make the house more of a home."

"Wait . . . wait," Carli says. "You mean your father basically ignored you your whole life and sold your mom's old house, but now, just like that, everything is cool?"

In the darkness, her words almost feel like my own. The ones I've been shoving back down inside myself every time they try to rise up. But out here, I can't push them around. "No. I mean, it's surface cool, but that's it. We haven't really talked or gotten deep about anything, yet. And to be honest, I'm kind of afraid to. Afraid of everything that might come up. You don't even want to know. Let's just say I've felt a lot of bad things over the years."

"I'm sure you have." Her hand leaves my chest, and I feel its warm softness on my cheek.

We lie in silence for a minute, and I imagine her feeling everything I've felt—the confusion, the loneliness, the disappointment, the sadness, the hurt, the rage.

"Thanks for sharing all this with me," she says. "This place. All the stuff about your dad. I know it can't be easy to talk about."

"But it kinda is with you," I say. "Especially out here. I don't know. I wasn't lying when I said I'm trying to share everything with you. You saw what happened when we were keeping things to ourselves. I was trying to act all hard and not answer your calls, but that shit sucked ass!"

She laughs. "That's what you get for ignoring me."

"What about you ignoring me? What was that about?"

Carli removes her hand from my cheek and goes quiet.

"No more secrets," I say.

"No more secrets," she repeats.

"Nah, don't say it if you don't mean it."

"No, I do . . . I promise. On everything."

CARLI

"I hate basketball," I say, feeling a huge swell of relief.

"I know it's gotta be hard," Rex says, and his hand—cool—finds my waist underneath his T-shirt.

Okay, I'm 200 percent sure that he's not taking me seriously. "I'm not speaking in hyperbole, here. I, Carli Alexander, can't stand basketball. Like, if you put one in front of me right now, I'd find something to stab it with. And as it deflated, I'd have a huge smile on my face. I'm grinning just thinking about it."

Crickets. The calls of two birds.

Rex laughs that awkward I-don't-get-the-joke laugh and gently squeezes my waist. "Sorry, what? I'm confused. I thought you loved basketball. You're a beast."

"Well, you thought wrong. There's a difference between being good at something and actually liking it. I'm only good because my dad has been coaching me since birth. I haven't been able to stand basketball since middle school."

"Middle school? Damn, so you're telling me that you've hated basketball the whole time you've been in high school?"

"Yep."

"Even the times you made the All-American team?"

"Yep."

"Even when y'all won the championship?"

"Yep."

"Even with—"

"Yes. The answer is gonna be *yes*," I say, getting a little annoyed.

"Sorry," he says, his voice going soft. "It's just hard to believe. If you've hated it for so long, why haven't you just quit?"

"It's not like I have anything better to do," I say, feeling myself sulk like a six-year-old who just got put in time-out.

"What do mean? You're interested in plenty of things."

"Yeah, but I don't have anything big to focus on."

"Big?"

"Yeah, like a . . . a," I say, the last word out of reach. It's always felt so much greater than me, so far away. And lately it's been worse, like it's running from me as fast as it can. Like maybe I'll never catch it.

Rex gently squeezes my waist, bringing me back into my body. And the shadowy trees behind him, the soft stream of light falling on their crowns, their limbs, the calls of invisible birds and insects, all seem to be telling me I'm wrong.

"A dream," I say, feeling some of my panic around the word soften.

"So. At least if you're doing something you like, you'd be getting closer to it. Don't get me wrong, it blows my mind that you don't want to ball. You're so damn good. But if you don't love it, you don't love it. Life is too short not to do what you love. Or at least what you like until you find what you love."

"You say that like it's easy. Like it would be cake to stop playing basketball and disappoint everyone I know. Well, besides my mom. She knows I hate basketball. But nobody else does. Not even Jordan, my best friend. She's our point guard. If we both win our games this week, you'll meet her at the championship next weekend."

"Wait. So, you're gonna play?"

"Yeah, started back playing this week. Figure the playoffs is not the best time to spring the news on my team. I'm going to tell them this summer."

More crickets and birds. Guess he's processing. And rubbing my ribs with his thumb. He can process all he wants as long as he keeps doing that.

"Wanna know another secret?" I ask, done with talking about basketball.

"You know I do."

"The very first kisses were blown in Mesopotamia as

a way to get in good with the gods."

"Huh?"

"Remember that secret I didn't tell you when we were sitting up in the stands after my surgery and you started getting mad?"

"I wasn't getting mad."

"Yes, you were. But anyway, when you blew a kiss that day on the court, the fact popped in my head."

"Wait, what is it again?"

"The very first kisses were blown in Mesopotamia as a way to get in good with the gods."

His thumb goes still on my ribs. "Where'd that come from?"

"I put it up on my wall after this boy blew me a kiss in, like, the fifth grade. The next day he tried to front like he blew it to somebody else, but I left the fact up there anyway. Didn't really think about it again until you blew me that kiss on the court. Well, at least blew it in my direction.

"Then the fact about kisses came rushing back to me, which I took as a sign that we were totally meant to be. So much so that while I was in the hospital that night, I rewrote the fact on the back of my dinner menu—even though I had *no idea* how you felt about me—and I saved it to give to you. Carried it around in my back pocket for almost a week. But then . . . well, it's a long story. But the bottom line is: it got lost. I was waiting to tell you about it until I could give it to you in person, so it would be special. But it looks like that's not gonna happen, so there you go."

"No. I mean, what's the story behind the fact? How exactly did blowing kisses allow people to get in good with the gods?" Rex asks, totally ignoring my whole romantic story.

"I don't know. That's all I wrote down," I say, disappointed.

He repeats the fact four times, like he wants to remember it forever.

"Yep, that's it," I finally say.

"Crazy I've never heard of that. You know I blow a kiss every time I go to the free-throw line, right?"

"So I've heard."

"I blow them to my mom," he says.

And here I am worried about my stupid romantic story. "Really?" I say.

"Yeah, every time I blow a kiss, I ask her for forgiveness."

A heavy weight drops down on my chest, "Oh Rex," I say, and reach for his cheek again.

His hand leaves my waist and lands on my hand. Then he interlaces his fingers with mine and brings our hands down to rest in the space between us.

"No, no, it's cool. This is actually really good," he says

cheerfully. "You see, your fact means that my kisses have probably been working. It's like all that stuff we were talking about earlier with my mom being a part of Everything. If she's a part of Everything, that means I've been getting in good with her every time I blow a kiss. I don't know if she's forgiven me yet, but if I keep blowing kisses, she'll definitely have to forgive me one day."

His happiness is so sad, I don't know where to begin.

I want to tell him that he doesn't need to be forgiven, that it's not his fault. But I've already told him that, and I'm starting to think that even if I tell him again, and again and again, we'd only go around and around in the same circle.

I want to cry for him. But what good would that really do?

I want to ask him where the bottom of his pain is. Like how many kisses will he have to blow to know he's forgiven? But it's clear he doesn't know that.

I want to shake him, maybe slap him, tell him that he needs to move on. But I'm afraid of how he'd turn on me.

I don't know what to do. How can I be his everything when so much of it has nothing to do with me?

It feels terrible, but I decide there's not much I can do about his pain and try to get out from under it by changing the subject. "Oh, and another secret: Cole and I have to decide which parent we want to live with. In what? Like, a week and a half."

"What! That's nuts! You told me your parents were getting divorced, but you didn't tell me y'all had to decide who to live with."

"Yeah, it's complicated."

"So how's that even going to work? Like, where would y'all go to school?" he asks, a hint of hope in his eyes.

I wish my eyes hadn't adjusted to the dark so I wouldn't have had to see that. Maybe I could've told him the truth. I swear on a stack of a thousand notebooks I don't want to lie to him. But what am I supposed to say? *I have the option to spend senior year with you, but I'm probably gonna pass?* I glance away from him and say, "Staying put. Cole and I have already agreed that switching schools on top of everything else would be too much."

Rex pulls me close to him. "Well, at least you don't have to deal with that."

REX

Fuzzy hair on my face before I feel her lips.

CARLI

I kiss him a thousand times. Until I exhaust my guilt about ditching his pain. My guilt about lying. Until there is only me and Rex. And the urgent pleasure of our lips. And my insides turning colors. Brilliant colors.

REX

I open my eyes. Pull my lips away from hers. Push her hair back away from her face. My hands are shaking.

I need her to know what she's given me.

Shaking so bad it feels like I'm taking off.

What I've always wanted . . . my whole life.

Like I'm blasting through dark clouds.

More than anything else.

CARLI

"I love you, Rex," I tell him. And I feel his trembling hands go still on the crown of my head. See his tender face burst open. Hear a hundred tiny bells toll in my heart. No false alarms.

REX

"I love you, too," I say, looking at her, looking at me. Feeling her, feeling me. "So much. You don't even know."

I kiss her.

After a while she pulls away and stares at me.

She kisses me.

After a while I pull away and stare at her.

And it's like we're two trees secretly sharing nutrients underground, two stars orbiting around all the things there's no language for.

TWO
AND
TWO

CARLI

It's official. Shannon wants to be me.

"Do you see this chick?" I ask Jordan. We're walking toward the middle of the Alamodome court for the jump ball. The whole first level of the arena is packed out. Forty-five thousand people, Cole told me before the start of the game, in San Antonio to see us ball.

"How could I not? Girl got issues," Jordan says, and ties her new twists—royal blue to match our uniforms—up in a ponytail.

"Yeah, *Single Black Female*-type issues," I say, catching a shot of Jordan and me above on the jumbotron.

"I don't know. Maybe she's doing it to mess with you."

"Mess with me?"

"Yeah, maybe this is her version of the Lance Stephenson ear-blowing move. It sure did mess up LeBron. Don't let her throw you off your game, Carli," Jordan says before lightly elbowing me and walking to her position on the other side of the circle.

I'm in the middle of the circle, under what feels like a million bright lights, facing Shannon—that forward from Langham who gave us problems last year. The one who wears my number, twenty-two. Yeah, her.

Home chick has decided to dye her hair the same color as mine. Not a fiery red or a burgundy red or a violet red, which could all pass as reasonable ways to switch it up from her old black hair. Oh no, she chose a born-with-it red. A brownish, golden red. Ain't too many Black ginger girls in this world, and I guess she *just* so happened to decide to become one of us.

"I like your hair," I tell her.

"Thanks," she replies, and shyly smiles—the corners of her pale lips, almost the same color of her pale skin, barely curving up. She clearly doesn't get the intended sarcasm. I need her to get it, but now the ref is here about to toss up the ball.

"Okay, ladies. We all know what's on the line. But let's keep it clean. Good luck," the spiky-haired man says, and steadies the ball in his right palm.

I place my right foot down so that it almost touches the center court line and bend down, ready to leap. Shannon does the same. I give her the hardest look I can muster—eyes squinted, nostrils flared, upper lip raised up. But her face stays calm, like she's unfazed. So, when the ref makes the toss, I take it back to first grade and shout, "Copycat!"

When I tap the ball to Jordan, Shannon's hand is nowhere in sight.

After I land, the ref gives me a cautionary look, but doesn't blow his whistle.

"Let's go!" I shout, and run back to get on the block. Time to teach this Shannon girl that she could never be me. Not even the girl I no longer want to be.

● REX ●

Carli has been on fire the whole game. Jump shots, hook shots, bank shots—all dropping. She even had the nerve to drain two threes. Dang, and another one! I stand up and shout, "That's my girl! That's my girl right there!"

The rest of my team is looking at me like I'm lame, but

I don't give a damn. It's the fourth quarter, and Allen High is twelve points up. Carli is about to take home the state championship! And as soon as she wraps up her game, your boy is about to snatch his championship up, too. We're out here doing it like Jay-Z and Beyoncé!

Cole sits down beside me. He's been rotating between me, his dad, and his mom the whole game. We're all spread out in the arena behind Allen's bench. "Did you see that?" he asks.

"Hell yeah, I saw it! I mean, I knew your sister could ball but damn. Threes? I didn't know she could shoot like that."

"Oh yeah. Carli can do it all," Cole says. Then he stands up and joins the cheerleaders clapping their hands and chanting, "*D-E-F-E-N-S-E*, go defense!"

The girl Carli's guarding, also sporting number twenty-two, misses another turnaround jumper. Carli snags the rebound, makes an overhead throw to Jordan, and sprints up the court. Jordan passes it back to her near the basket. Another two points for Carli, and the other team calls a time-out with six minutes and twenty-one seconds on the clock.

"That's what I'm talking about!" Cole shouts before sitting back down.

Man, I love having Cole around. He stays coming with the good vibes. "You know you're like the little brother I never had," I say, and put my arm around him.

In total Cole-fashion, he gently bangs his right fist on his chest a few times. "Dude, you don't even know what that means to me. I've looked up to you since as long as I can remember. I seriously can't wait to ball with you next year. It's going to be a dream," he says excitedly. Then he leans forward, looks over to my team, and shouts, "Woodside High here I come!" None of them pay him attention.

Wait, I'm confused. How is he talking about coming to Woodside when Carli told me last week that they were staying at Allen? Did things change? And if so, why didn't she tell me?

Well, maybe something changed today. "Yeah, it's going to be sick," I say, fronting like I know what's up. Can't be out here looking like my girl doesn't keep me in the loop. "Me, you, and Carli at the same school? What! They ain't ready," I say, half believing the words coming out of my mouth.

"Oh, has Carli been talking about living with Dad, too?" Cole asks, looking surprised. "Awesome! She's been talking like she wants to stay with Mom and go to Allen. I thought I'd have to put in work to bring her around, but it looks like you beat me to it. Thanks, bro!"

I'm too stunned to bother correcting him.

The time-out buzzer sounds, and Cole is back on his feet. "If I don't catch you before your game, good luck! Not that you'll need it. I know you're about to stomp them Matthew Gaines boys."

"Thanks," I say through a thin, forced smile. I swear to God, I'm a complete fucking fool. Not because she's choosing to stay at her school instead of coming to mine. (That's a huge decision dealing with family stuff that's way bigger than me.) But because I believed there was no way she would she lie to me. After all we shared? No way. In my sacred place? No way. When she promised no more secrets on everything? Nah, man. But she fixed her lips to tell me a lie anyway.

CARLI

After the time-out, I'm back in Shannon's ear. "Fine, if you wanna be my impersonator, go ahead." We're running up the court. I've been hitting her with copycat lines all game. I'll admit, they're getting kind of stale. But hey, if it ain't broke. . . .

"I'm not trying to be you," Shannon responds, breathing heavily, and gets in position on the block. It's the first time she's responded the whole game.

Standing behind her, I give her a little shove in the back to let her know how much of a liar I think she is. Nothing the refs will notice, though.

She whips her head around, glares at me, and then calls for the ball. The two guard with the brown bob whips her a chest pass, and Shannon turns to face me.

"Oh, look. It's me on me," I say.

She pulls up to shoot, and I'm off my feet ready to block, ready to knock her shot into next week.

But she doesn't shoot. And I'm still in the air. And now she's around me scoring an easy two. *Damn.*

"I've had red hair all my life," Shannon says, catching the ball after it falls through the net. "I only started dying it black when I started playing you." She shoves the ball into my solar plexus on the sly.

All my breath rushes out at once. Everything in me wants to bend over, to wrap itself around the hurt. But I stay upright and pass the ball to the ref. "Why you so worried about me?" I manage to push out in a normal voice.

"You really don't know, do you?"

I take off running up the court and she runs right beside

me. Like, literally her shoulder touching my shoulder. "I know you have an obsession with me. That's what I know." Jordan holds up a four, and I run to the free-throw line. She passes me a quick overhead pass.

"Sure, I'm curious. How could I not be? You're my sister," Shannon says, and gives me a little shove in the back. I throw myself forward, like she's just pushed me hard, but the refs don't buy it.

I square up to face Shannon and laugh. Then I pivot while holding the ball with my elbows wide to create some space. "Sister? You officially need help." I try to drive right, toward the basket, but she stays in front of me and cuts off my driving lane.

"Have you ever wondered where your dad goes every Sunday?" she says, hands way up.

Not that it's any of her business, but Daddy drives out to Waller to visit his parents' graves every Sunday. I look to shoot, but I can't get a shot off with her crowding my space. I've already picked up the ball, so I can't put it down again without double dribbling. I look to pass, but no one is open.

The ref blows the whistle and points three fingers toward Langham's goal. *Shit, three-seconds.*

"Come on, Carli!" Jordan yells at me with her face scrunched up.

Copycat!" Super trite at this point, but it's the only thing I have time to think of. Doesn't work. Her three drops.

Coach Hill calls a time-out.

"Shame you have to make up such elaborate lies to get a shot off," I say before walking toward the bench.

"Ask your mom," she replies. "She knows. My mom finally called her and told her about a month ago."

About a month ago, I think. That's when all this drama started going down with the divorce. Well, five weeks, but still.

"Hustle up, Carli!" Coach yells. When I get close, she hands me a bottle of water. I squeeze it all over my face, hoping to wash Shannon's words away. Coach leans in close to me, so close I can smell the spearmint gum in her mouth. "We're almost there, Carli. But you have to give it your all these last few minutes. Do you hear me?"

I nod my head yes.

"Are you tired? Do you need to rest?"

I shake my head no.

"Well, I need you to get your head in the game. They're closing our lead," she says, and turns to speak to the whole team huddled around her.

I look up at Daddy, sitting in the third row, halfway between our bench and Langham's bench, but he's not

"My bad, my bad," I reply, and look at the scoreb[...]
Eighty-seven to seventy-seven with five minutes left o[...]
clock.

"It's not your fault you don't know," Shannon [...]
running back toward her goal. "I only found out a c[...]
years ago when I saw you play in the All-American gam[...]
TV. Saw Daddy cheering for you in the stands—"

"Daddy?" I interrupt, and give her a hard shove. [...]
girl has really lost her mind. She thinks she's me. Like, [...]
need security after the game.

She shoves me back. "Yeah, at first I wondered w[...]
was there. But it wasn't hard putting two and two tog[...]
with me and you looking so much alike. He denied it a[...]
But when I pressed, he admitted it . . . made me pr[...]
to never tell or he would stop coming to see me," she [...]
straight faced, standing out beyond the three-point li[...]

I know she's only trying to distract me, but I wish [...]
shut up. I've never seen her make a three, so I play o[...]
a little and try to ignore all the nonsense she's talking. [...]
probably trying to clear the way for their point guard t[...]
a pick and roll with their post. And after my last mess[...]
want to be ready to help.

Their point guard passes to Shannon, and Sha[...]
readies herself to shoot. I throw up my hand and [...]

looking at me. I follow his eyes over to Shannon. She's standing over her team drawing on the clipboard like she's the coach or something. I swear I hate that girl.

But Daddy looks like . . . like he's proud of her. I know that face—soft and bright, mouth stretched wide over a concealed smile. *Wait, she's not wearing my number. She's wearing his old number.* I look down at the twenty-two on my own jersey and remember him telling me as a kid that he'd be honored if I continued the Alexander legacy.

"Carli!" Coach Hill shouts. "Have you heard anything I said. What the hell is wrong with you? The championship game is on the line and you're over here daydreaming? Vanessa, go check in. Carli, take a seat."

I don't even protest.

I sit here and watch as Shannon takes it to Vanessa. Back dooring her, posting her up, and taking every rebound. I sit here and watch as we go from being up seven to five to two to none.

With less than a minute left on the clock, Coach Hill looks down the bench at me, ready to put me back in the game, ready for me to save the day. But I slump down in my chair and look away.

REX

Right, left, and jump. A simple-ass layup. But here I am spelling it out to myself, trying to keep my mind on the court and off Carli.

Head fake, crossover, pull up, and shoot. I miss. Halfway into my pregame warm-up, and I haven't seen her yet. After her team won (thanks to a last-minute three by Jordan) and everybody's family and friends rushed the court to celebrate the new champions, she wasn't there.

I was there. Even though I was still mad about her lying, I was in the middle of the court, wading the crowd, looking for her face. Waiting to pick her up and twirl her around—ready to celebrate. Cole, her mom, and her dad were looking for her, too.

You know what, forget seeing Carli. Good that she's off pouting somewhere just because she didn't get to play the last few minutes of the game.

Girls in royal blue warm-ups walk down the sidelines toward the stands. My eyes can't help but scan the line for big red hair. No Carli, so I sit down toward center court to stretch and look again. I hate myself for needing to see her. Why can't I get her out of my head!

"You ready to take this ass-whooping?" a voice beside me asks. I already know who it is before I look: Russell Price. I didn't even see him stretching before I sat down.

I don't have time for this dude right now. Carli's team is taking their seats low in the stands. I scan them again for her face, but don't see her.

Did she leave? I think. No way. They save the joint trophy ceremony until the very end, so I know she's still in the building. Plus, her mom and dad are still up in the stands. Cole just left their dad and is walking toward their mom. He catches me looking at him, pumps his fist in the air, and yells something I can't hear. Something encouraging, I'd bet from his big grin.

I smile and give him a thumbs-up.

My father and Angie, sitting right below where Cole is walking, must think the thumbs-up is for them because they start to wave.

I wave back right before the game clock sounds.

"Shame you're about to disappoint your fans," Russell says, standing.

"At least I have fans," I say, get up, and scan the crowd one more time. Wait! There she is! Up in the middle of the stands. But why is she sitting with Langham? Damn, not her. Just that girl she was guarding who looks like her.

Same height. Same nose. Same pale skin with freckles. Same red hair.

Every Sunday for as long as I can remember.

Daddy.

She called him Daddy.

Suddenly and swiftly crumbling the vision of my own.

I can't go out there. I can't look at that man who's lied to me my whole life. That man who hid a whole sister from me.

This shower stall isn't hiding anything. I'm sitting balled up in a corner with my tears, snot, and iPhone between an empty bottle of Dove bodywash and a rusty Venus razor. A nest of brown hair covers the drain. The moldy bottom edge of the beige shower curtain almost hides a used tampon, but it's not long enough. All signs of my shitty life.

So many years of hiding her in plain sight. I wipe my nose with the sleeve of my warm-ups.

According to Facebook, Shannon Alexander Jackson was born November eighth—about a year and a half after me and two months after Cole. A throwback Thursday post shows a baby photo of her at the hospital in her mom's arms. In the background there's a man ducking underneath the doorway, leaving the room.

How am I ever going to leave this stall? As nasty as it is, I wish it would swallow me whole, keep my life on pause.

What am I even going to say when I have to see him?

Should I ask him about all the times I asked to go with him on Sunday? All the times he said he needed to be alone.

Should I ask him why he had to cheat on Mom? While she was pregnant, at that.

Why he had to hide his other child? Man up, for God's sake!

How could he live with himself?

How could he sit in the stands and watch us slam into each other? Watch us use all the things he's taught us against each other.

Should I ask him who he was cheering for?

Does he call Shannon Angel-face, too?

Forget it, he can call her Angel-face all he wants. And she can call him Daddy. I don't want him anymore.

MAKE
IT
STOP

● REX ●

I can't even be bothered with giving the play-by-play. We lose. Terribly. Russell Price scores thirty-seven. I score twelve. Couldn't get anything to drop. Couldn't get Carli out of my head. And now I want to erase her. Straight up. I want to find and destroy every little bit of her inside of me. Make it like I never caught her. Never kissed her. Never felt her. Never loved her. Like we were never anything.

CARLI

"Carli!" A locker bangs shut. "You need to bring your ass, Carli! I know you're in here. I see all your stuff." It's Jordan. Sounds like she's in the changing area. "Yo, we need to go! Everybody's waiting on us." And she's getting closer.

I squeeze my eyes shut like it's going to magically make me disappear. Stupid, I know, but I can't go out there.

More banging as she kicks the bathroom doors open one by one. The screech of metal rings sliding on metal bars as she flings back the shower curtains.

Now she's standing over me. "Get up!" she says, hands on her hips like she's somebody's mama. "You're not about to miss the award ceremony just because you didn't play the last few minutes of the game."

Is that why she thinks I'm in here? But I can't correct her. What am I going to say? *Oh, Shannon is actually my sister. My dad fucked her mom and hid her from us all these years.*

"What kind of sick shit is this?" she says, stepping over the used tampon. She grabs my arm. "I'm not playing, Carli. You need to get up."

But there's no way she can make me move. I'm way bigger than her.

"Okay, fine, then," she says, picks up the razor, throws it into the shower stall across the aisle, and sits down. "If you're missing it, I'm missing it."

"Jordan, no. Go," I say.

"I'm not going anywhere until you get up."

"You're being stupid. Go." Basketball means everything to her. No way she's going to miss the championship award ceremony because of me. And I know she's going to get the MVP.

"Me? I'm being stupid? I'm not the reason we're in here."

"Just go, Jordan. Please. Leave me alone," I say, feeling an onslaught of tears rush down my face. There's no way to stop them. All I want to do is stay in here. I'm not ready to face the truth, the lies, that man I used to call Daddy.

"It's not that serious, Carli," Jordan says, and puts her arm around me. She's never this affectionate. But I guess I've never been sitting in a nasty shower stall crying, either. "We won," she continues. "So what if that weird *Single Black Female* girl got the best of you for a few plays. Nobody's game is perfect."

I don't know what I'm supposed to think about Jordan talking about Shannon like that. Am I supposed to defend her like a good big sister? Am I supposed to join in trashing her because I can't stand her, because she just tore my world apart? Trying to decide how to feel is making my head hurt, my heart hurt, my everything hurt. I squeeze my eyes shut.

"Come on, Carli," she says, and puts her head on my shoulder. "I really don't want to miss this."

"I really don't want you to miss it, either," I say, sounding like some kind of whimpering dog.

She stands up, pulling me along with her, and I let her, thinking of the ways my body can be out there while my mind stays in here. On pause.

REX

About damn time. Carli is walking across the gym with Jordan. The captains of the other three teams have been standing in the center of the court for over ten minutes waiting on them. Russell Price and his point guard up on a winning platform posing for pics and shit, and me down here with the losers.

It's bad enough Carli made everybody wait on her, but this girl has the nerve to still be pouting. Her head is down so far I can't even see her face. Only hair.

She's coming up beside me, walking so close behind Jordan, I keep thinking she's going to step on a heel and pull off one of her sneakers. I swear to God, she better not say anything to me because I'm not hearing it. *Nah, baby girl. Not this time. No more letting you do me wrong while I'm over here giving 110 percent. You got me messed up.*

Now she's in front of me. So close that strands of her hair practically tickle my nose. A part of me wants to lean into it, put my face in it. Nah, fuck her good-smelling hair. I hold my breath, stop taking her in, and she passes me without even looking in my direction.

"Let's all give a big round of applause for all the championship teams," Jim Morrison, chairman of the Texas High School Basketball Association since forever, says as Carli and Jordan walk up the platform stairs. White dude has to be pushing ninety.

Most of the arena has emptied out. But the people left, mostly friends and family of the teams, give us their best— clapping, yelling, and stomping on the bleachers. My father and Angie are both clapping with their hands above their heads.

It almost makes me smile before I remember how terrible I played. How bad we lost. How much I embarrassed myself in front of everybody, including the college scouts. The look on Coach Bell's face. I've never seen a coach so disappointed in me.

Jim recognizes the sponsors and moves on to the trophies. He starts with the small ones, for the losers. "Langham High," he says, and picks up a small gold basketball with a wooden base off the folding table behind him.

The Langham team stands up off the visiting bench to the left. And the red-headed Langham girl, to my right, walks up on the platform to accept to the trophy.

"You all played a great game," Jim says to the whole team. Then he hands the trophy to the girl and says, "I'm looking forward to seeing big things from you in the years to come, young lady."

Meanwhile, Carli's head is *all* the way down. She could at least look up and be a good sport. Shake the girl's hand like Jordan and say something generic like *Good game*. Doesn't matter if she means it or not. That's what good athletes are supposed to do. But she's standing there playing with the zipper on her warm-ups. So damn self-centered.

"And Woodside High," Jim says.

I guess it's my turn. I wait for the Langham girl to come down.

"Being runner-up at this level is no small feat. It takes a fierce dedication to your sport and a strong commitment to excellence," Jim continues as I walk up the steps.

As I'm accepting the small-ass, loser-ass trophy, Carli, who's standing to the left of Jim, looks up at me. I look back at her, wanting something from her I wish I didn't want. I don't even know what. Maybe a look that says, *I'm sorry you lost* . . . or *I'm sorry I wasn't there for you* . . . or *Are you okay?*

But it's like she's looking right through me. Like I'm not even here. Like I don't even matter. Man, I'm so fucking stupid. I don't know when I'm going to get it through my thick head that this girl could care less about me. I look away and try to brush it off. But the hurt isn't going anywhere.

Russell Price, standing to Jim's right, reaches out to shake my hand and says, "It was close."

I swear to God I want to pop this dude in the mouth, but I shake his hand and say, "It won't be, next year."

"Yeah, we'll see about that," Russell says, and takes a step toward me.

Is this dude serious? He wins and all of a sudden he thinks he can step to me? "We sure will," I say, and stand an inch away from his face.

"And here we have the winning champion and MVP

of the Texas Boys State Championship," Jim says, overly cheery. He grabs Russell's arm and raises it toward the bright lights overhead. Yeah, Jim knows what's up. Knows he needs to save Russell from getting beat down.

But I still have to walk off the stage with the little-ass trophy.

CARLI

The winning trophy, a big gold basketball going through a gold hoop, is lighter than the one from freshman year. Looks the same, but they must've ordered it from a different company. Somewhere cheaper. And there's a huge scratch running along the top of it.

"Let me see it," Jordan says.

I reluctantly hand it to her. That's what I get for criticizing it, but I needed something to occupy my eyes. I can't look up. I can't risk seeing Shannon or her daddy and losing it up here in front of everyone.

Jordan lifts the trophy above her head, the crowd erupts in cheers, and our whole team rushes the stage.

"Yeah, that's right. Get up here and get your hands on this trophy!" Jim shouts over all the commotion. "You've earned it."

I take a step back. And back and back and back, letting my team pile in front of me, grateful for the opportunity to fade away.

"Carli Alexander," Jim says loudly into the microphone. I can't even see him with everybody on stage. "Get back up here, Carli."

Why? I think and hide myself behind Vanessa.

"Now, here we have a young girl," Jim says, and all of a sudden, his cold, bony arm is around my arm, leading me back to the front. "A young girl who's led her team to not one but two championships. A girl who's averaged a double-double her whole high school career, and in this game alone scored thirty-three points."

Did I? I think, looking high up in the arena where no one's sitting. Better than staring at the zipper, especially with all eyes on me.

"And she's only a junior. So I'm sure we'll see her back here next year, trying to lead her team to victory again. And that's why I'm so proud to award Carli Alexander with the MVP of the Texas Girls' Basketball Championship."

What? Jordan was supposed to get MVP. She hit the

winning shot. She's the reason we even made it to the championship. She led the team when I was out with my gallbladder surgery. I didn't even play the last few minutes of the game.

Jim places a gold statue of a girl shooting in my hands. *This isn't mine,* I think before I turn and start looking around for Jordan. But I can't find her and accidentally glimpse Shannon instead. *I can't. I just can't,* and I turn my eyes back up toward the empty stands.

REX

Look at you. Center stage. Holding your big, golden trophy. Just like you've never dreamed. Oh, but you like it, I see! Your nose way up in the air. I swear I hate you. You don't give a shit about my dreams. You don't care that I took a beating in the championship game because I was worried about you. You don't care that I probably lost my chance to go to a top school because of you. You haven't even looked in my direction. I mean, it's bad enough that you weren't there for me. But no words for me, either? Not even the silent, private kind? I swear you're worse than my father ever was. Maybe he never loved me all these years, but at least he had the decency to not pretend. Why pretend? Why tell me you loved me? So I could give myself away? So you could take and take and take? Well, I'm gone.

CARLI

"Your ass doesn't even like basketball!" Rex yells. I hear him before anyone else does. He's standing down below, to the left of the stage, staring at me with a hate so fierce it shoots straight through me.

I want to scream, *What are you doing? Shut up!* but shock has severed the connection between my brain and mouth.

Palming the small, gold basketball with his right hand, Rex sharply points the base of his trophy up at me. "You're such a fucking fraud!"

His words suck every sound out of the gym, and now all eyes are on him.

"Standing up there with that trophy when you know you hate basketball!"

Collective whispers and gasps from the crowd.

"Okay, I think that's enough," Jim says into the microphone, standing to my right.

But that doesn't stop Rex. "How you gon' be somebody's MVP when you're about to quit the team?"

Stop! Please stop! I plead with my eyes.

"Your ass ain't even playing next year. You don't deserve—" Rex's coach yanks him by the elbow and starts to march him toward the locker rooms.

A loud buzz from the crowd. Phones out recording.

My forehead feels clammy and I want to throw up.

"Well, folks . . ." Jim pauses, like he's trying to find the right words. "Emotions can run high at times like these. Why don't we give all the athletes another round of applause."

A few claps, but the buzzing drowns them out.

"I think we've all had a heck of a night," Jim says over the noise. "Let's be safe getting home."

I look back over my shoulder and see Rex and his coach disappearing into the tunnel leading to the locker rooms, the sting of his betrayal still piercing every inch of my skin. Those were my secrets to tell. Not his. Why would he do this? And in front of everyone?

I close my eyes, head reeling with confusion, and

imagine the last time I saw him, cheering wildly for me in the stands. *What the hell happ*— Damn, I missed his game. With everything going on, I wasn't even thinking about him. And he lost. In front of all the scouts.

Jordan grabs my shoulder and I turn around. "Is it true?" she asks, face screwed up with confusion.

"I was going to tell you—"

"Wait, are you serious? You're really quitting the team?"

"Yes, but—"

"I can't believe this shit! How could you keep this from me?"

"I wanted to tell you. I just—"

"Yeah, whatever," Jordan says, and walks off the stage. The rest of the team follows.

I forget to be careful and catch Shannon's daddy looking at me from the stands like I'm the biggest disappointment ever.

Even coming from him, I can't help feeling like I am.

REX

Nothing hurt. In the gym, in my haze of anger, I felt numb. Free. But heading back to Houston in the backseat of my father's Tesla, it feels like I just had a bad dream.

If only I had.

If only my mind—suspicious of itself, unwilling to believe I did what I did—was right.

Why did I have to do Carli so wrong?

Well, she did me wrong first. I didn't hurt her more any more than she hurt me.

I can't believe I'm sittin' up here defending myself. Another warm tear slides down my cheek, and I quickly wipe it with my funky warm-up sleeve.

Angie slides hand over hand over hand, like she's washing them. And I wish I could wash myself of myself—scrub my conscience clean.

Then she turns back to look at me over her left shoulder, her black wavy hair framing her face, and says, "People make mistakes, Rex. You were upset. You can't beat yourself up about it."

But that's exactly what you should do. My ass could use a good beatdown right about now.

My father looks at me in the rearview mirror. "Yeah," he says, "give it some time. Things will blow over."

Blow over? This shame I feel isn't blowing anywhere. It's clinging to every thought and feeling inside of me. I can't feel hurt without the shame. I can't feel sorry without the shame. I can't feel weak or stupid or sad or mad or disgusted or embarrassed without the shame.

I almost wish I hadn't run out of the locker room before the team came in and was riding back on the bus with them. Maybe they could curse and stare the shame out of me. Maybe Coach could continue yelling and finger-wagging the shame out of me. With the big bus engine rumbling beneath me and all the rage and disappointment piercing me, maybe the shame would seep out, little by little.

But there's no one sticking it to me in my father's car. No engine rumbling, either. The ride is smooth and silent. I try to hold on to the sound of the tires' revolutions, but it's too faint and I keep losing it to the shame.

I grab my headphones out of my backpack, blast J. Cole, and lean my head against the window, wishing I could run out into the darkness. Wishing I could run and run and run and never come back.

CARLI

No way I was riding home with the team. No way I was riding home with that man, either, even though it's his weekend to have Cole and me. After the award ceremony, I didn't even go near him. I rushed up to Mom, told her I knew about Shannon, and begged her to get me out of there.

Riding home in her Discovery, I have to ask, "All those years and you never knew?" I've never imagined Mom as the kind of woman who could pretend to be blind, but maybe I don't know her like I think I do. Wouldn't be the first time I got a parent all wrong.

"No," she says, briefly taking her eyes off the dark road to look at me.

I let out a breath I didn't even realize I was holding. "You never even suspected?"

"No. I mean, I always knew your dad was dealing with things he didn't want to share with me. But I always thought it was related to the pain around his parents' death, you know. And I thought I could help him, love him through it, you know."

I do know, because I thought I could do the same for Rex.

"I tried for years to get close to his pain, to try to help him heal it, but he always stayed guarded and we'd end up fighting. I even suggested he see a therapist, but he refused. So I left it alone, you know, left him to deal with it himself. But I had it all wrong. I never . . . ever ever ever would've guessed that he had a"—her voice breaks up—"a child he was seeing every week for the last fifteen years . . . a child born during *our* marriage."

Mom's pain envelops me like a thick fog. I can't imagine being married to a man for twenty years and finding out he had a secret child for most of them. I can't imagine getting that call from the other woman. And who is this other woman? How long was the affair? A night? Five years? I have questions, but there's no way I'm hitting Mom with them right now.

Mom takes one of her hands off the steering wheel to wipe her eyes.

"I can drive," I offer.

"No, I'm okay," she insists.

I grab her free hand and hold it.

"He still loves you, you know," she says.

As always, here she goes trying to turn the spotlight off her pain, around to mine. "But what about you? Do you think he still loves you?"

She puts both hands back on the steering wheel. "Love is not just some feeling, Carli."

Her voice isn't normal. It's not hard like she's pissed or high like she's annoyed, but it's not normal.

"There's a deep responsibility to it . . . a deep trust. And no matter how your dad *feels*, he's failed to love me."

It's defiant. That's what her voice is. She wipes her eyes again.

"And he can be mad about me divorcing him so quickly all he wants, but there's no way I will ever be able to trust him again. And I can't be married to someone I can't trust. Don't need time or marriage counseling to tell me that."

An image of my parents sitting in a room on opposite ends of a light-blue sofa pops into my head. And another one of them sitting closer on the sofa. And then together in the middle of the sofa with Cole and me on either end. "You don't even want to try?" I ask.

"Try?" she says, her voice going high.

"Yeah, try couples counseling," I say, pushing past her annoyance. You see, the scared part of me doesn't care about her annoyance. Or about betrayal or the responsibility and trust of love. The scared part of me doesn't care about how much that man has hurt Mom. Or me for that matter. All it cares about is me staying intact. Less ground shifting beneath my feet. Keeping my family together, my life together—myself together.

"Look, you may not understand it, Carli. But I've made my decision. Everybody has to live their life making choices for themselves, choices that will hopefully lead to happiness. We may get it wrong sometimes, but all we can do is our best. And this is me doing my best. I need to move forward, and this is the only way I know how."

"Well, I'm gonna move forward and divorce him, too."

"You say that like it's easy."

"Well, it looks easy enough for you."

"What do you want me to do, Carli? Cry forever? Stay in pain forever? That's no way to live. I love myself too much for that."

Love myself. I wish I knew what that felt like. I don't even know myself. How can I love what I don't even know?

"And there *is* no divorcing your dad."

"You sound like you've never heard of people divorcing their parents."

"Look, Carli. Clearly your dad has some work to do on himself—"

"You can say that again."

"But that doesn't change the fact that he's your dad. He loves you. You don't want to throw away that relationship."

"But she calls him Daddy."

"Shannon?"

"Yeah."

"Well, he's her dad, too."

"Well, she can have him. I don't want him anymore."

"Look, Carli," Mom says, and briefly reaches over to touch my thigh. "Your dad will always be your dad. Yes, he has another daughter. But that's a fact you're going to have to accept. You have every right to be shocked and angry and hurt. But at the end of the day, none of that will change what *is*. You need to talk to him. Tell him how you feel. Make him tell you what you want to know about the situation."

"But he's a liar," I say, feeling my heart swell up in my throat and warm tears run down my cheeks. I turn to look outside the window at the darkness on the side of the road, hoping for some kind of sign. But the darkness won't say anything.

"Yeah, but you can still talk to him. One of the reasons he probably lied all these years is because he was scared of losing our marriage. But that's already gone."

If only I could be gone.

IT
ALL
COMES
DOWN

REX

I have eight missed calls from *My Love* when I grab my phone off my nightstand the next morning. Ten a.m. and I'm still in bed. On weekends the sun usually wakes me up, but it's not out today. On the other side of my glass sliding door, dark clouds creep across the sky.

I tap *My Love* on my phone and change it back to *Carli*. Then I scroll down to the bottom of her contact page and press *Block This Caller*. I know I need to apologize, but I'm not ready to talk to her yet.

Outside, the pines are bending to the wind. I swing my legs over the edge of the bed and slide my boxer briefs on— ready to step outside and take in the smell of the coming storm, ready to feel its force against my bare skin—when

I notice an envelope in the middle of my floor.

My father must've slid it underneath my door this morning. Wait, that means my father must've come upstairs. I've never seen him upstairs. Maybe he even knocked on my door when I was asleep. Maybe it's a letter from him saying all the things that still need to be said.

I wipe the crust out of the corners of my eyes and go pick it up. It's light purple. Not exactly my father's style. Plus, it has a stamp in the upper right-hand corner. Typed underneath a strip of teal tissue paper in the upper left-hand corner, it reads *Carli Alexander*.

I think about tossing the envelope outside and letting the rain wash her words away, so I'll never be able to take them in. But I don't. Instead, I sit down with the envelope in the middle of my cold wooden floor and bring it to my nose—exactly the thing I shouldn't do. But it smells like her, and I can't help but to breathe it in deep.

Doesn't mean anything. After I apologize, I'm still done with Carli.

Each line of her return address, of my address, is typed underneath alternating strips of lime-green and teal tissue paper, which are all pasted on the envelope separately. She probably spent over an hour on the envelope alone. The least I can do is open it and see what's inside. It's not like it's going to change anything.

I poke my pinky finger in the corner of the backside of the envelope, slide it underneath the triangular flap, and lift it up. First thing I see is our faces in front of a big, swirly sun. I quickly close the flap and push the envelope away from me, back underneath the door. I've already seen too much.

 CARLI

The thunder outside my window sounds like it's ripping open the sky (not a good sign) as I call Rex for, like, the hundredth time. *Come on, Rex. Pick up the phone!*

I need to tell him about Shannon. I need him to understand why I missed his game. And he needs to know how much he hurt me by telling my secrets. Both of us need to apologize. And forgive. And afterward I need to slip in some of Mom's words about trust and responsibility, so our love can move forward toward something better.

I sit up in bed, hoping that a more upright position will somehow make him answer, and press 💜 Rex 💜 again.

Pick up! But there's only one ring before the computerized voice mail. More tears burning at the back of my throat find their way out.

Another knock at my door and I wipe the warm tears off my cheeks.

"Carli, I've got hot chocolate on the stove and it's getting cold." Mom's muffled voice comes through with N.E.R.D. playing in the background. First the doughnuts were getting cold with Missy Elliott. Then it was the blueberry scones with Mary J. She's been trying to get me out of my room with sugar and old-school hits all day.

I take a deep breath and manage to push out, "No thanks," without sounding like the hot mess I am.

"Okay, but you need to get something in your stomach."

"I will," I say in the most I'm-not-in-here-crying tone I can muster, hoping she'll be satisfied enough to go away. She is.

My phone pings and my heart leaps with hope. But it's only a text from Cole. **U okay?**

Yeah I answer, and it's not even a complete lie. Hearing from Cole is actually right on time. I miss him. I know we've only been separated for one night. But I need his overly loving presence around me right now.

Too bad he's stuck on the other side of town with that man. Shame he doesn't know the truth about him yet.

So u really done with 🏀 ?

Yeah

Why didn't u say something?

Thought you'd be disappointed

Come on . . . u know u can tell me anything

Yeah . . . but I know how much you love basketball

I hope u know I 💜 u more

Oh my gosh. I wish he was here to give me one of his hugs. I swear I would let him hold me forever. **I know**

💜💜💜

U need me to kick Rex's ass for u?

No but you can get him to pick up the phone

U still wanna talk to him after what he did 2 u??

I missed his game

Still! But that was pretty messed up. Where were u?

Locker room

R u serious???

There's stuff you don't know

Like what?

I think about telling him about Shannon. But I can't be the one to crush him. His dad needs to do that. **Can't tell you now but promise we'll talk soon**

What is it?

Can't say right now. Anyway Rex isn't picking up. Called 100 times

A little much don't u think?

But I need to talk to him

U need to stop calling

But I really need to talk to him

Trust . . . stop calling him & he'll call u

Fine, I text, swing my feet around to the floor, and stand up, thinking about how good those blueberry scones are about to be.

U saw the video?

I sit back down. **What video?**

Nothing. Don't worry about it

Tell me

It's nothing

Come on, Cole, I text, feeling myself getting mad.

Somebody filmed Rex's meltdown last night

What?

Yeah . . . already has over 200k views. A snippet even made ESPN.

Seriously??? Was it really that newsworthy?

U know ppl love the drama

**U made up your mind about where u wanna stay?
Gotta talk 2 the judge in a few days**

Staying with Mom

Dang . . . still staying with Dad

A light somewhere inside me goes out. **I thought we were going to stay together**

Come live with Dad

I can't

Well I can't live with Mom

Why?

Why can't u live with Dad?

If only he knew. I catch a picture of the man I formerly called *Daddy* on my wall beside this gold-foiled starfish I made. He's in Galveston sitting in a beach chair with sunglasses and a hat on. The back of my legs got stung by a jellyfish that day, and Mom had to rub meat tenderizer on me to soothe my stings. If only my wounds had such a simple remedy now. **Come on Cole** is all I can think to write back.

Come on Carli

Seriously??? So we're going to live in different houses and go to different schools? You know I'm only going to be here for one more year

Trust me . . . I know

I don't have a comeback for that. Only tears.

After a couple minutes, he texts again. **Sucks but everything will be okay**

Why do people always say that? It's, like, the biggest lie .

REX

When I go downstairs, the TV in the living room isn't on and there's a note on the kitchen counter from my father saying he got called in. On a Sunday, though? Couldn't he have said no? Blamed it on the storm? I mean, he saw what went down yesterday. He knows today has to be rough.

Clearly that doesn't matter to him, just like my game didn't matter to Carli. I don't know why I keep fooling myself into believing that anyone actually cares.

After eating three bowls of Honey Nut Cheerios while watching the rain come down on the trees in sheets, I head back upstairs. In the hall, outside my door, the purple envelope is waiting on me like it knew I would be back sooner or later. Like it knew I'm so pathetic that I would eventually need whatever love it has to give.

I pick it up and carry it into my closet, where I feel

safer. I lay it on my dresser, remembering Carli the night she sat here—her face, her lips, the new places I kissed and touched her.

I slip out the card. It's handmade and looks like a collage. On the front, Carli's handing me an orange-looking flower, and purple rays shoot from her chest to mine. I can't even lie—it's beautiful and it feels like magic. Like love is really flowing from her heart to mine.

I know I should put the card down, but I can't. I open it.

A whole page of her words that look like art. Handwritten letters that bend and loop and stay straight in curious places. *L*s that never want to be lowercase. *T*s that never want to be the same—short, straight, long, curvy, and crooked strokes crossing at wide-ranging spots along stems, which sometimes curve up at the ends. I remember seeing her handwriting all over her walls, but looking at it now makes me feel like I'm seeing a part of her for the first time.

Rex,

I don't think it's possible to tell you everything in my heart. I don't have the words for it. Like if I tried, they wouldn't be enough.

"I love you" isn't enough

I swear loving you is the only thing saving me right now. You just don't know, this past month has been the worst time in my life (other than when I'm with you or talking to you or thinking about you). My whole world is falling apart. It's too much to write here, but I will say I haven't been handling it well. It's like I don't know what to do or who I am and it's making me feel crazy.

Sorry I took the bad stuff in my life out on you. You don't deserve it. I'll never treat you like that again I promise. Please forgive me. I love you.

Yours forever (and the day after that, and the day after that),
Carli

I can't, I think, wiping tears from my face. *I just can't.* I leave the card in the closet and go get my phone.

CARLI

I finally see it. After single-handedly bringing the *Rex Carrington's Epic Tirade* video up to 300,000 views on YouTube, I finally understand. Rex never loved me. He couldn't have. He doesn't know love.

The anger on his face made one thing clear: all he knows is pain. Every square inch inside of him is drenched in it. He tries to hide from it, but there's no hiding. Tried to hide inside of me. He probably thought his hiding was love. I know I thought it was. And maybe I was hiding in him, too, I'll admit.

But no more. I'm out. Done with whatever this screwed-up thing is that he calls love. I can't do it anymore.

The booming thunder agrees. I'm still in bed, staring out my window, thoughts pouring down.

I deserve better than what he has to give.

Anyway, how could I ever trust him again after what he did to me?

I can't.

It's over.

My phone rings and I roll over in bed to grab it where I left it on my pillow, but it's not there. I quickly sit up and throw my Kantha quilt back, my sheet back. Still don't see it. Third ring. *This can't be happening.* I lift my pillow and my stomach growls in relief. Still haven't been out of my room to get those blueberry scones, but Cole was right. "Hello," I answer.

"Hi," Rex says, his voice as heavy as the rain coming down outside.

Hearing his tender voice puts me right back inside of him, and I send all the things I just told myself packing. I lie back down and reach to touch Rex's face on the wall right above my pillow. I have the picture of us on the sofa pinned up between a sketch of a sunflower forest and a line from Kahlil Gibran's *Prophet*.

All these things shall love do unto you that you may know the secrets of your heart,
and in that knowledge become a fragment of Life's heart.

I look at it every night before I go to sleep and every morning when I wake up, trying to figure out what it means.

"I'm sorry about the video. About what people are saying," I tell him.

"What video?"

"Never mind," I say, ready to play the tell-me game.

He doesn't press for more.

"And I'm really sorry for missing your game," I start to explain, "at the end of my game, Shannon—"

"Wait," he interrupts. "I just called to say I can't do this anymore. And I'm really sorry for what I did to you last night. It was wrong. I had no right. I was just so upset."

Clearly he can't mean what he's saying? I get it because I was just thinking the same thing, but I didn't mean it, either.

"You don't mean that," I say.

"Yes I do."

"No you don't."

"Yes I do."

"You're just upset. But if you let me explain—"

"Look, Carli. I mean what I said. I can't do this anymore. I was lonely before I met you, yeah. But I knew how to handle that. What I can't deal with is you loving me one minute and pretending you don't even know me the next. It's making me crazy," he says, and sniffs.

My heart disappears out of my chest as I try to decipher his words. "What do you mean loving you one minute? I've never stopped loving you. You don't understand—"

"Maybe you're right. Maybe I don't understand you. I thought I did, but really I don't have a clue what's going on inside you. But I can't keep trying to figure it out. It's messing up my life. I'm sorry, Carli, but it's over."

My heart is back, but it's a thousand-pound weight in my chest. I don't think my body can hold it. "What? No!" is all I can manage to say, tears strangling my words.

"I'm sorry, but I can't see you or talk to you anymore," he says, his voice cracking.

"Rex, please don't do this. I'm so sorry. I love you so much. I—"

"Nah, love isn't supposed to feel like this," he says, his voice firming up.

"I know. I'm sorry. Please let me explain—"

"Nah, man. Nah."

"But I thought you said you loved me."

"What? I poured it *all* out to you. Every little ounce of the love I had. You think you're the only one with problems?" His voice is hard. "Well, you're not. I'm dealing with some pretty fucked-up shit over here, too, Carli. Even still, I've always been there for you. From the very beginning. But you haven't done the same for me. And I've already heard all the apologies and *never agains* I'm going to hear. Look"—and he softens his tone—"I'm sorry. I just can't do this."

"Rex, give me a chance to explain," I beg.

"I'm sorry, Carli. I gotta go."

Dial tone.

I call him back.

One ring, voice mail.

Again.

One ring, voice mail.

Again.

One ring, voice mail.

Again and again and again with the rain pouring down outside my window.

Again and again and again until I'm coughing on my tears.

Again and again and again until I feel too stupid to keep calling.

He didn't even give me a chance to explain. I missed his game, yeah. But is that all it takes for him to throw me away? He's such a liar! He never loved me. He couldn't possibly have. If he loved me, he would've at least listened to me. He would at least pick up the phone. He wouldn't make me suffer like this. I swear I hate him.

I yank down the picture of us above my pillow. The forest of sunflowers. The Kahlil Gibran poem. Underneath it, there's a picture of our family in Kusama's *At the End of the Universe* exhibit. We're standing with our arms wrapped around one another in a small dark room at the center of tiny yellow lights that seem to stretch out infinitely. But ain't no more family! My walls are such a fucking lie!

I yank it down.

And the sketch of a silver flute I drew beside it.

And the handwritten Rihanna lyrics beside that.

I don't know who you think I am
I don't know who you think I am
I don't know who you think I am
I don't know who you think I am

And the trail of black stars drawn with various black marker tips underneath that.

And the picture of the Egyptian winged goddess, Isis.

All of the photos and quotes and ticket stubs and random written words and poems and facts and maps and magazine images and sketches and swatches of fabric and paper birds and birthday cards.

Every memory.

Oh, now the Mesopotamia fact wants to pop up. Written with purple crayon in perfect cursive. I hold it with two hands until sweat, pretending to be a tear, splashes on the curl of the capital *M* and reminds me of how all of this pain began. *Fuck the first kisses fact!* Off it goes to the floor with everything else.

Every love.

Every hope.

Every possible sign.

Until there's nothing left but scraps still holding on to tacks.

"Why are you still holding on? There's nothing left!" I scream, out of breath, and furiously start going after the last bits, ripping the tacks off the wall.

"Oh, Carli," Mom says behind me.

I didn't even realize she'd come in. She's looking around in disbelief. I've been putting things up on my walls since I was four, since first watching her tack up things on her design boards. And I haven't taken anything down since, just added layer over layer.

Until now.

And it's like I'm seeing my walls blank for the first time. Like they're closing in on me on all four sides, wanting answers about what I've just done. Whenever I used to look at my walls, it was like bits of my possible future staring back at me . . . but now there's nothing. What am I supposed to do with nothing? What is nothing supposed to tell me about everything?

● REX ●

Sitting in the middle of my hard, wooden floor, with the rain still pouring outside my windows, I search my name in YouTube. First new thing that pops up is a clip of the ESPN commentator Stephen A. Smith saying, "Since y'all wanna talk about Rex Carrington, when are you going to acknowledge that he just doesn't deserve the title you've given him. No. 1 high-school basketball player of the year? Puh-lease! And he's talking about what Carli Alexander doesn't deserve, who's a hell of a player, by the way. But can we get back to what he doesn't deserve?"

I swear I hate that dude. That smug look on his stupid, pointy face. He stays talking shit about somebody. Made a career out of it. Can somebody please tell me why people love to watch other people getting ripped to shreds?

I click on the clip below it: somebody's homemade video of me going off on Carli. It already has over 300,000 views. You can hear whoever's videoing in the background saying, "Oh shit! It's going down."

The video only plays for a few seconds before I press pause.

That's not me, I think. That dude whose eyes have no

tenderness. Whose mouth has no mercy. *Where did I go?*

I can't bring myself to watch anymore. Instead, I look through the comments.

mrmball

Rex is a fool. Definitely not top recruit material

Amara Queen

He just mad cuz he played terribly. Boy is so overrated

Lil Flacco

Has anyone else watched this 10+ times. Bruh, I swear I can't stop. Lol

Kasey C

That poor girl

Tarantula Girl

Her name is Carli Alexander. Put some RESPEK on her name

Wassup B

Dude is clearly off his pills

365BasketballTV

Check out my channel. BasicsofBallin

Trapgirl

Now this is good entertainment! Better than the Housewives of Atlanta

lifeonthecourt

Rex Carrington is still the truth. He does look like he needs therapy though

LisaLee529

It's obvious he's been hurt. You all need to leave him alone!

Blissfully Joi

Somebody needs to put a foot in his ass. Carli Alexander did not deserve that. If you don't know who she is, then look her up

Daquan

That was cold

That's not me! I throw my phone across the room, and it crashes into the glass box of beetles on my bookshelf. *Don't they get it? I'm not capable of that much cruelty!* It came out of nowhere, unfolding its brutal body inside of me. I couldn't stop it! And now *I'm* the one stuck with the mess. With people judging me, like they know me.

Nobody knows who I am!

Oh, but they've got their drama. They've got their views. And now coaches and scouts will have their reasons. And nobody will want me on their team! Is that what everybody wants? To see me lose everything? Well, they're in luck 'cuz it's gone. I can hang up going to the league after my first year of college. That dream is dead along with everything else.

Exhausted, I sit for long time, looking at the broken glass on my floor and the scattered beetles in between. When I was little, I used to stand on the ottoman to get them down from the top shelf in the living room. Then I'd hold them close to my chest while taking baby steps to the sofa, where I'd look at them for hours. I'd imagine Mom looking at them with me, telling me which ones were her favorites.

I look at a crack in the iridescent one's blue shell (her favorite). At the bright green beetle (her second favorite) and its thin, broken wing. At the purple-and-orange striped one who's now missing its antenna. At the black beetle on its back with only half of its jointed legs in the air.

Damn, after all these years, I can't believe I just messed up Mom's beetles, all because I got mad. Me. Not some kind of body snatcher who appeared out of thin air. Not the homie from way back when. I did this.

NEVER
WOULD'VE
IMAGINED

REX

After school I get back in bed. I'm rereading one of Mom's books about this dope landscape architect named Walter Hood and listening to her Otis Redding album (trying to keep Carli, basketball, and the beetles out of my head), when I hear a knock at my door.

"Rex?" My father's soft voice slips under the door into my room. Just like it slipped in Sunday after he got home from the hospital, yesterday after school, last night before I went to bed, and this morning before school.

But my father isn't the only one who can ignore somebody. Who can stay in his room and pretend the person they live with isn't actually there. Who could care less.

"Rex?"

I don't answer.

"Rex?" My door opens slightly. Widens. My father takes a step into my room in his green scrubs. And another one. And another one until he's standing in the middle of my room looking around at all of Mom's things.

As if on cue, the record finishes and the needle lifts.

He looks over at me.

I look back at my book like he's not even there.

"What are you reading?" he asks.

I hold up my book so he can see for himself.

"Oh yeah. Walter Hood is something special, isn't he? The *Street Trees* he's doing in Detroit and the *W.E.B. DuBois Double Garden* installation he did with Carrie Mae Weems are amazing," he says, and walks over toward my bookshelf.

Why is this man trying to act like he knows about Walter Hood?

"Your mom and I saw his installation at the Project Row House here in Houston when she was pregnant with you." He grabs the next record off the top of the stack— "What's Going On" by Marvin Gaye. Slides it out of its sleeve. "Do you mind?" he asks, his long fingers already lifting the needle to switch out the records.

Is he serious? This man is in my room, acting like he's been in here a thousand times. Over there casually mentioning Mom like we've had a million conversations about her. He never once talked about Mom! Never shared any stories about her. About what she was like. What they did. Where they went. Or what happened back when. Never! "Yes, I mind!" I shout.

"I'm sorry . . . I'm sorry," he says, gently places the needle back down, and slides "What's Going On" back into its sleeve.

"Sorry for what exactly?" I yell, standing to my feet with my fists balled up.

He turns to face me. "Sorry for—"

"For what?" I walk toward him, anger spewing out of me. It feels like a pipe—rusted, corroded, and under the pressure of being clogged for sixteen years—finally broke deep inside me. "Coming up in here acting all familiar? Or sorry for ignoring me all these years? For never being here?"

He looks up at me. He's tall, but I still have him by a couple inches. "Yes, for everything I—"

"Sixteen years! Sixteen years of leaving me on my own," I interrupt, screaming three inches from his face. "You know, I lost Mom, too. Actually, I never even had her. And I didn't have a father, either." Specks of spit fly out of my mouth, but I don't give a damn. "No, even worse.

I had a father who didn't want me. Who hated me. Didn't you know how much I already hated myself! I killed my own fucking mom! I've had to live with that!" Hot tears are streaming down my face and I don't try to hold them back.

"Oh no. Is that what you think?" he says, and reaches out to me.

I block his arms and step back. "Man, get off me."

"Rex," he says. "You have to know, it's not your fault," his voice soft and calm.

It's how he always talks, but right now it's on my goddamn nerves. "You can lose the bedside manner. I'm not one of your patients."

"You were only a baby. It's not your fault."

"Yeah, yeah, yeah. You can save all that."

"Rex, listen to me. I think your mom had some kind of undiagnosed heart condition. I don't know for sure because there were no further investigations done at the time. But we know a lot more about the dangers of undiagnosed heart problems in pregnancy these days."

The words *undiagnosed heart condition* stretches out inside me beside my guilt. And my guilt eyes it, sizing it up like I do when a new dude rolls up on the basketball court with the same build as me or the same height as me or the same shoes as me (basically with anything like me).

"Did I do this? Do you think it's your fault because of me? I'm so sorry. I've been such an awful father," he continues. "Your mother would've been so disappointed in me." He looks down briefly and then right back up, eyes full of tears. "Look, I've done a terrible job loving you, but you need to know it's not your fault. You were only a baby. It's a miracle you've turned out as amazing as you have. I just didn't know how," he says, his voice cracking. His tears start to fall.

"Nah, you don't get to cry. You were the adult! I was the child!" I scream, feeling *It's not your fault* trying to find its way deeper inside of me.

"I know, I know. I'm sorry. I checked out. And after being checked out for so long, I didn't know how to get back to you. How to talk to you. I was so depressed. Every time I saw you, I saw her. Even right now, looking at you, I see her. Her cheekbones. Her moles. The way she always slightly held her head to the side. The same pure look in her big eyes."

My father's words stun me. *Me look like Mom? Nah.* When I was a little boy, I used to be obsessed with looking at Mom's pictures. At her face, her outfits, her hair, her poses, her surroundings—anything that would clue me in about who she was. But after I realized her pictures ran out the day she gave birth to me, I stopped looking at them. And shortly thereafter, I stopped looking at myself. And now standing here, I can't really picture either one of us.

I back away from my father, walk over to my file cabinet, open my bottom drawer, and take out the white wooden box that houses Mom's old photos.

On top of the stack, there's a picture of her posing in front of a brick wall painted like pixels. She's sporting an afro with her arms on her hips and her head tilted to the side. She's a lot lighter than I am. And shorter. I can't see it.

"You got everything from your mom," my father continues. "The only thing you got from me was height and a little color. None of my personality, thankfully. Your mom was super passionate, like you. About life, about art . . . all kinds of art. And she loved trees. I mean, she really loved trees."

I always knew Mom loved trees. Well, I didn't know-know. It was the version of her I made up from this one picture I used to love. I start sliding photo off of photo, trying to find it. Here it is: Mom sitting crisscross in the grass in a grove of live oaks. Looking at her, looking up at the trees, I get the same feeling as when I'm lying in the woods behind the house, looking up at the crowns of the tall pines. It's the closest I ever get to peace.

"That's why I moved us out here to live among all these trees," my father says, walking closer to the sliding glass door. He interlaces his fingers behind his back and stares out at the hazy forest. "I thought waking up surrounded by trees every day would make you happy."

The subject of moving takes me right back to being pissed. "I was happy around Mom's old things. In the house she used to live in," I yell, stepping toward him. "I used to imagine her walking through the rooms. I used to imagine her sitting on our old sofa and cooking in our old pots and pans. That made me happy. This house is empty and sad. You didn't keep anything of hers. It's like you wanted to get rid of her," I say.

He turns around to face me. "No, no, no. I would never want to get rid of your mom. I love her. Always. My therapist thought it was critical that I move out."

"Your therapist?"

"Yes, he's been imploring me to move for years and years, and then something happened that made me listen."

"But you didn't even ask me first," I say, wondering what happened.

"I know. I'm sorry. I was in a really bad place. And I needed to get out quickly. Every second in that house brought back memories. Trust me, I would've stayed with those memories forever. But," he says, looking at me, "I had to keep living. I had to keep living for you."

Keep living? For a second my insides go black. Everything disappears, and I imagine being all alone in this world. Was he thinking about killing himself? Is that what happened? Even though he hasn't been there for me, the thought of losing another parent is unbearable.

"But I'm here. And I'm much, much better. And I promise to do better from here on out," he says, and reaches for me.

Part of me wants to fling my arms open and run to him, yelling *Daddy* like I'm five years old. But the anger, still seeping out beneath my skin, won't let me.

He walks toward me and wraps his arms around me. And now he's holding me for the first time I can remember. It's weird, I know he's trying to give me love. Love that I need. Shit, love that I've been wanting my whole life. But I can't feel anything.

CARLI

Judge Reed's chambers are creeping me out with all the dead animals. Beside her desk there's some kind of wild cat with a bird stuffed in its mouth. On the floor, in front of a wall of legal books, there's a ram's skull and horns surrounded by large bones. By the window there are two wolves on posts, heads up, like they're howling at the moon. And on the opposite wall—above the giant map of Texas—there's a duck with its wings spread, trying to fly away from it all.

Maybe a sign that I should try to get the hell out of here, too. But how?

The judge is leaning on her large mahogany desk, short legs stretched to the floor, holding a pen and legal pad. On almost every finger, she has some kind of expensive-looking ring. She's wearing dark jeans, cowboy boots, a light pink blouse, and a string of pearls underneath her black robe.

She's staring at me, wanting to know why I want to stay with Mom. I'm sitting in the leather armchair across from her trying to think of what to say. I'm not about to tell this judge about Shannon. Nuh-uh. I already know what she would write on her legal pad: *Black man had a baby by his sidepiece.* I mean, she probably wouldn't use *sidepiece*, but you know what I mean. Even though I hate him, I'm not about to let this little white lady reduce him to that.

"I'm just closer to my mom. She gets me," I finally answer.

"Can you elaborate, sweetie?" she asks, in her country (and when I say country, I mean *country*) voice.

I tell her about basketball and explain Mom is the only one I can talk to.

Judge Reed bites the inside of her left rouged cheek. "Are there other reasons? Besides basketball? It's really important you tell me all the reasons you want to live with your mom. It'll help me make a decision based on what I think is in your best interest."

"But I'm already telling you what's in my best interest," I say with more attitude than I want to.

She walks over and sits down beside me in the other leather armchair. "And I'll definitely take that into consideration," she says, and moves the vase of wildflowers from the round table between us to the floor. Judge Reed puts her pen and legal pad down on the table. The lined yellow pages are still blank. Then she props her elbow up on the table, rests her chin in the palm of her hand, and fixes her blue eyes on me. As if to say, *If you wanna stay with your mom, you'd better give up the goods.*

And I do. About everything that happened Saturday. About Sunday for as long as I can remember. About his lies. His double life. Let me tell you, the fear of the judge ordering me to live with that man has me spilling all the beans.

Judge Reed lifts her head. "Yeah, that's hard. I found out about my other siblings around your age, too." She leans back in her chair and puts her cowboy boots up on her desk. "That's when my mama died."

"I'm sorry," I say, surprised the judge has family drama like mine.

"Don't be, sweetie. We weren't close. You see, she left when I was a little baby . . . like four or five months old. Supposedly one of those big-time oil execs came into the IHOP where she worked, and she ran off with him. Left me and my daddy behind in Plainview and never came back. Never heard from her again," she says, and runs her fingers through her hair.

"Then one day," she continues, "I get this letter in the mail saying she died and left me and my siblings a whole bunch of money. My mama had three kids from her marriage with that rich man, you see. I didn't even know they existed. But now we've all been getting together for Christmas Eve dinner for some forty-plus years."

I picture myself having dinner with Shannon. Nope. Not happening. "But weren't you mad? I mean, your mom abandoned you and then went and raised all those other kids."

"I guess I could've been, but there's no use being mad at a dead woman. No use being mad at my siblings, either. They didn't do anything. Besides, all that money I got from my mama put me through college and law school. In a way, I probably wouldn't be where I am today if it wasn't for her running off."

The judge telling me all of her business has me feeling comfortable. So comfortable I think about putting my Blazers up on the desk to join her boots, but I don't. "True, true. But how can you still call her Mama?"

"Well, that's what she is, isn't she? What about your mama? You don't have grievances against her?"

The question throws me off. In all the sharing, I'd almost forgotten what we were here for. "I guess she works a lot," I answer, trying not to say too much. I need the judge to decide it's best for me to live with her.

"And that's okay with you?"

No one's ever asked me how I feel about Mom working so much, and now my words are trying to rush up and out, like someone just handed them a permission slip. "Well, I used to feel like her work was more important than me.

Like she loved it more than me or something. When I was younger, I used to hate staying in aftercare at school. And on top of that, I always saw other moms volunteering in the classrooms or organizing bake sales and stuff. My mom was never there. I mean, don't get me wrong, I was always proud of my mom. But I was also jealous of how much time her work took away from me."

"I understand. My kids felt the same way. When—"

"But now that I'm older I know she loves me more, no question about it," I interrupt, trying to turn my answer around before the judge goes on another talking spree. "But I also understand her work gives her something I can't give to her. And that's okay. I want something like that for my life, too. Basketball definitely isn't it. I'm still looking for it."

She takes her boots down off the desk, stands up, picks up her legal pad, and puts the flowers back on the table. "And you'll find it. I know you will."

Wait, is the interview over? I thought we were just getting started. I need to say more good things about Mom.

"Well, it was very nice talking to you. I have another appointment waiting, but I assure you I have everything I need to make a decision."

I look at the wild cat with the bird in its mouth and a strange pressure squeezes my throat. This lady wasn't being sweet and open. She was getting what she wanted—chewing me up. And now she's spitting me out.

Judge Reed walks toward the door and opens it. "Your parents should receive my ruling by the end of the week."

I want to beg her to let me live with Mom, tell her my whole life depends on it. But I stand up, say, "Okay, thanks," and walk out.

In the hallway Mom is sitting on a wooden bench on one side of the hall, Daddy (I guess I can call him that since that's what he is) is sitting on a bench on the other side of the hall, and Cole is standing in between. He met with the judge right before me.

And now Daddy is walking toward me. "You hungry?" he asks.

I shake my head and go try to sit beside Mom, like I've been doing all morning, but she stands up and walks closer to him.

I head toward my next safe place.

"How'd it go?" Cole asks, and gives me a hug.

"Okay, I guess," I say. "I don't really know."

"Yeah, same. Glad it's over, though."

"Me, too."

"You hungry? Because I'm starving."

"Yeah," I say.

Daddy appears over Cole's right shoulder. "Your mom and I thought it would be a good idea if you came to eat dinner with me and Cole went to eat with her."

Who thought what? I think, and shoot Mom an alarmed look.

Standing right beside him, she looks at me calmly and says, "It's for the best. Your dad can drop you back off at my house when y'all finish up."

She can't be serious. Why would she make me go with him?

"You ready, Angel-face?" he asks with a weak smile.

A bright flash of panic runs through me, and I think about taking off down the empty hall, about trying to get away from it all like that duck on Judge Reed's wall. But let's be real, the duck can't escape, and neither can I. I may not be stuffed with rags and cotton, but I'm stuck with Daddy for now.

REX

After my father leaves, I grab my phone off my desk, push the camera app, and flip it around to selfie mode. There's a bad crack traveling diagonally across the screen from when

I threw it across the room, but I can mostly see myself.

Still holding the picture of Mom, I bring our faces side by side. I can't believe I never saw it. Our strong cheekbones, our many moles, our hooded eyes—alike. Satisfaction quickly fills me up. But I keep staring, eyes floating back and forth between us until I'm in straight-up awe.

You see, I used to think of my moles as tiny sins, little reminders of what I did. But looking at Mom's moles is making them feel like tiny marks of sainthood or something. I know nobody's about to erect a statue of me in a sanctuary or anything, but looking at her face is making mine feel holy and bright. Like it's been washed clean.

But when I look up at the gray sky outside my window and back down at the big crack across the screen, I remember Mom's beetles belly up among broken glass. Man, I don't *even* want to think about that. But that doesn't stop my mind from going back to how heated I was when I hurled my phone. Or flashing to my tight fists dreaming of going upside my father's head.

Underneath the jagged line on the screen, the same angry face I saw on that video stares back at me. *Is this really me?* I swear to God that's why I don't even like looking at myself. All the stuff I try to keep buried is always trying to come up and make me feel something.

Why does everything have to keep coming up? Like what every coach and scout must think of me. *I know! I know!* And Carli. *But I've already apologized to her.* And the dream I lost—*hurts so bad it's sickening!* The anger that won't quit until everything I love is either broken or gone.

It has to stop.

I put Mom's picture down on my desk and lock eyes with myself. Man, I don't want to do this. I swear looking at myself makes my head and heart hurt. For a second I almost look away. Ready to get up and continue on with life like I always do, like everything is cool. But I can't even front like that's working anymore.

So I take a deep breath, blow it out slow, and force myself to keep staring at myself.

Until I can see past the crack in the screen into the face I always saw as my father's. Into the hate I always thought he had for me. The hate I always had for myself. I swear it's like a million wrecking balls swinging around, destroying everything inside of me. Feeling it is the absolute worst, but I'm not about to keep ignoring it and let it ruin me.

Tears rush down my face, and I wipe them and keep staring.

Until I see a little kid I haven't seen in years. Alone, playing with all his dead mom's things. A kid crushed by his father's absence and silence. A kid who spent all his time out of the house, either balling or under the tree out back talking to his mom and begging for her forgiveness.

I swear, the weight of it is enough to break me. But I square it up and make myself feel it. Tears dripping from my chin, I scoop up the little kid, squeeze him tight, and tell him what he's always wanted to hear, *It's not your fault.*

Over and over again.

It's not your fault.

It's not your fault.

It's not your fault.

Until I can feel the words sink into the innermost part of me.

Then I turn toward the pile of the injuries I've kept buried in me over the years. Every hurt I never wanted to feel. Still here.

But the closer I look at them, the more I see that most of them have nothing to do with me and everything to do with the people they came from. And after a while, most of them rise up, give me a few head nods (I think they like being seen), and start getting the hell up out of me.

I keep staring and staring until I'm in awe again. Of this dude with the two puffy eyes, snot-streaked lips, and flat, crooked nose. This dude who's been through some shit—I'm talking about some major shit—but who's still here, even after finally having the guts to take a good look at himself.

I swear I never thought looking at myself could feel like love. But it does.

CARLI

Tires crunching over gravel, I open my eyes to see what restaurant was worth the hour drive. But we're in a graveyard. First of all, I'm hungry. And second of all, really? He's never brought me here all these years I've been asking. All these years he's been lying about coming. But he wants to bring me now?

He turns the engine off, his million keys (I wonder if one of them opens the door to Shannon's house) hanging from the ignition. "I want to show you something," he says.

And? I think, but don't say a word. Hadn't said a word to him since we left the courthouse. I resume the position I had the whole way here: eyes closed behind dark shades, head against the window, thinking about Rex.

"Please, Carli," he says.

I keep my eyes closed, wishing he would shut up and take me to get something to eat.

"Come on, Carli," he says, a crow squawking in the background.

I wish they would both shut up. "Wake me up when we get to the restaurant."

"I'll take you right after we leave here, promise. It won't be long," he says, his voice perking up. I guess because I actually said something. *Oooo, I wish I would've kept my mouth shut.*

"Shannon told me what happened at the game. And I wanted to—"

Hearing her name leave his mouth is too real for me, and I quickly open the car door to get away from him, away from her. But as soon as I'm outside, this weird feeling hits me, like I've been here before.

It's that tree. Boy, would Rex love that tree. The one in the middle of the cemetery that looks like it's been here since the beginning of time. The live oak whose trunk looks ten feet wide. Whose long, winding, moss-covered branches extend way farther out than up, some dipping close to the ground. I know that tree.

I walk closer to it.

"You remember, don't you," Daddy says behind me.

I keep walking, and a picture flashes to the front of my mind of me swinging from a low branch. I was about two or three and Daddy yelled at me to get down.

"You're the only person I've ever brought here," he says, still walking behind me.

Then I see it. A tombstone right under the low branch engraved with *Camille Alexander.* His mother's name. But she's alone. She's supposed to be buried beside her husband.

Daddy kneels down in front of the tombstone. Below her name, it reads, *You will always be the girl of my heart, Love Randy.*

But that makes no sense. His parents both died in the same car accident.

I take off my shades so I can see better. The sky is as gray as these tombstones anyway.

When I look back down, Daddy's whole back is trembling, his shoulders shaking. I've never seen him cry. Sad, yes, all the time. But never crying. And all of a sudden it feels like my heart is opening on all sides, like I'm coming apart. Everything inside me wants to see what's hurting him. What's been hurting him my whole life.

I kneel down with him and put a hand on his back, and he lets more of it out, heaving and weeping. "My father lives twenty minutes outside of Austin in a town called Georgetown," he says, and briefly turns to me, his face redder than his freckles.

"What? I thought—"

"He wasn't in the car that night. He was with me," he says, still breathing like he just finished running a race.

I'm so confused that I don't know what to say. But I want to hear more. I need to hear more. So I sit down on the ground and grab his arm, encouraging him to do the same. It takes him a second to get his long legs crossed, but he does. And now we're sitting cross-legged in the grass facing each other.

"Him and Mommy were never married. He didn't even live with us," he says, his voice calming down. "They weren't even together that long. He couldn't deal with the disapproval of his family and friends. Couldn't deal with people staring at him walking down the street with a Black woman."

What? I knew his dad was white, but I had no idea that his mom being Black was a problem. I'd always imagined them living together in their own happy bubble.

"He used to drive down from Georgetown to see me every Sunday. Mommy would usually cook and do things around the house while he played with me. The night she died, she was making pancakes for dinner. But we were out of syrup. He offered to go get it, but she insisted he stay and have more time with me." He starts crying again, his face like that of a scared little boy.

The same little boy I've seen glimpses of my whole life. Only now, I know who he is. I touch Daddy's knee, gently encouraging him to continue.

"He stayed with me the whole week. When he dropped me off at my grandmother's house after the funeral, he said he'd be back to get me. Said I'd come live with him. Even left me with a set of keys to what was supposed to be my new house. But he never came back."

"Oh my gosh. I'm so sorry," I say, feeling way down deep in his sadness. The tears that have been gathering in my eyes fall down my cheeks.

"No, I'm sorry. I've ruined everything. But I wanted you to know the truth," he says, and hangs his head.

I wipe my face. Wait, does he think bringing me here and telling me all of this will somehow let him off the hook with telling me about Shannon? I know he hurts more than I ever knew, but I still need answers. "What about Shannon? Why did you keep her a secret? Who's her mother? Where did you meet her? How long was the affair? What do you do when you see Shannon every Sunday? Didn't you feel bad for lying to us? For keeping her from us? How could you?" All my questions come flying out all at once, scared that if they wait, they won't get answers.

He looks up but doesn't say anything.

"Sorry, that didn't come out the way I wanted it to. But I need to know."

"Oh, Angel-face," he says, a big tear falling down his right cheek. "Of course, I feel bad. I hate myself for what I've done," he says, and hangs his head for way too long.

"Come on, now," I say, trying not to get mad all over again.

"Okay. Amanda, Shannon's mom, was my neighbor and best friend throughout high school. She was the only one who knew the truth about Mommy and my father. I used to connect with her on Facebook. Then one day we met up for lunch. Then we met up again. I don't even know what happened, and then she got pregnant."

Oh, I know what happened, I think, but keep my mouth shut so he keeps talking.

"After I found out, I told myself I would tell your mom. Then days passed, months passed, and Shannon was born. And every day afterward, I kept begging myself to tell. Then years passed and the lie got so big . . . and you and Cole were getting so big. It killed me to think how much it would disappoint you. I felt so . . . so ashamed. What would people think? And I knew your mom would never forgive me. I didn't want to lose my family. I couldn't lose my family," he says, tears coming down fast and hard.

I feel sorry for him. Sorry for the part of him who's still that hurt little boy. Mostly sorry that the little boy is still there, hurting. Sorry that after all these years, Daddy still hasn't learned how to heal him.

But I'm still pissed. At all his lies, his betrayal of Mom . . . of our family. Even at how he treated Shannon. I can't imagine how knowing you're a secret child must feel. So much of what my dad did is messed up. So much of my dad is messed up.

How am I his daughter and know better than he does? It's not normal. I swear it's like we're in some kind of twisted world where our roles are reversed, where I must grab his hand and pull him along, even though it's not my job. "Well, you can't keep Shannon in hiding anymore. We have to get to know her," I say, not believing my own words. "And you need to tell Cole."

ALL
UP
IN
IT

● REX ●

In the car my father asks, "So, what's going on with Carli?"

I turn my head and eye him like, *Why you all up in mine?* but he's too focused on the road to notice. I'm really not used to him being in my business like this. All week he's been coming into my room, asking me about this or wanting to know that, I guess trying to have more of a relationship. I mean, in theory it's what I want, too, but dude, can we ease into it?

"Not much," I answer. I really don't want to talk about Carli. I already think about her enough. Every time I see a girl with big hair or a girl wearing jean shorts or leggings or Nikes or a thin gold chain. Don't even let me walk by a hedge of jasmine (nothing on Earth smells as good as Carli's hair). I can't even get a T-shirt out my drawer without thinking about her. Or go outside in the woods behind the house. Or blow my own nose. Basically, I can't do shit. It's like my mind isn't even mine anymore.

"You talked to her since last Saturday?" My father is exiting at Old Spanish Trail off Highway 288. To the right is the Houston Zoo and the Texas Medical Center and to the left is our old neighborhood. *Where is this man taking me?*

I asked him this morning when he came into my room talking about going somewhere, but all he said was "Just come on." Normally, I wouldn't let that fly. I mean, you gotta tell me *something*. But this morning I was happy to roll out. You see, I usually hoop Saturday mornings, but I haven't been able to bring myself to touch a basketball since the championship. I'm not ready to face the game without my dream of going to the league.

"Yeah, briefly. We broke up," I reply.

He puts on his left turn signal and looks in his left-wing mirror. My father is about as careful as careful gets when it comes to driving. Every move so precise, like he's performing surgery or something. He finally takes a left on OST. Now we're passing the corner store

I used to ride my bike to for chips and soda. "I thought you said you really loved her."

Where the hell did that come from? It's like he's speaking on her behalf. Like she's somehow managed to possess his mouth like she's possessed my mind. "I do . . . I did," I say, all worked up. "But I'm trying not to."

"Okay, okay. Sorry, wasn't trying to pry," he says.

If that's not a lie, I think, but stay quiet, satisfied with him dropping it.

He takes a right on Scott Street, past a big, new stucco house under construction. The streets are poppin'. So many people out and about. We ride by three old men sitting on the porch of a pale-green, wooden house on blocks. Two little girls with pigtails trying to share a scooter on the sidewalk. Four dudes in a grassy driveway—two crouched down looking at something on a motorcycle and the other two eyeballing us as we roll by.

I'd forgotten how much my old neighborhood feels like a real community. How neighbors actually come out of their houses and talk to each other . . . even rely on one another. Man, the woman next door used to drop her little girl off with Angie all the time when her babysitter was running late and she had to be at work. And I don't know how many times the old man on the other side of the house asked us to help jump-start his pickup. And this one time when my father forgot to pay the water bill, the dude who lived behind us let me hook up a hose to his house for a couple days. I always talk about missing my old house, but I've missed this neighborhood, too.

My father takes a left on Luca and parks.

I might be glad to be back in the old hood and all, but I don't know why he would he bring me back to our old house. Did he see me sign up for the TV show where you knock on some stranger's door, tell them you used to live there, and ask if you can take a look around? No, I don't think so.

"Come on," he says, and gets out of the car.

I stay put.

A few moments later, he's standing in the middle of these people's freshly cut yard, waving for me to follow.

Nah, dude. You can have that. I keep my seat belt on. The house still looks the same: dark blue-gray paint with white trim. White mailbox near the front door hanging crooked, like it always has. I tried to straighten it out once, but my dad stopped me. He didn't say why, but Angie told me later that my mom had put it up.

Now my father's standing at the front door, looking back at me.

I look back at him but still don't take off my seat belt.

He turns away from me and slides a key into the lock.

Huh?

Now he's inside. And he left the door open.

The house has all the old furniture that my father said he donated to the Salvation Army. Plus, there are side tables and pillows and chairs and paintings and photographs and masks and jars and bowls and platters and pretty pencils and matches and things . . . lots of things I've never seen before. The living room has a whole new wall of records and books. *A Love Supreme* is sitting in an old record player, same as the one in my room.

I walk over to the breakfast room, which looks like someone's been working in it. There's an unfinished painting of a blue bird hanging on an easel and a mug full of paintbrushes sitting on the table next to a palette.

"There was a whole storage unit full of stuff I couldn't bring myself to get rid of," my father says, standing in the kitchen. I can only see the middle section of his body. The rest of him is hidden behind upper and lower rows of pale teal-painted cabinets.

I walk around the breakfast room and into the kitchen. "Is this all of Mom's old stuff?"

"Yeah," he says, his hope for my approval tangled in his voice.

As much as I love the idea of being surrounded by Mom's old things, him saving and arranging it all as if she's still living here isn't right. I walk toward him. "Dad," I say, feeling the newness of the word on my tongue. "Dad," I repeat, mostly because I like the way it feels.

He must see that I don't approve because his eyes tear up and his face flattens into what I recognize as shame—familiar in the most terrible way.

"Dad," and I wrap my arms around him. It feels weird at first, but I force myself to hold him and keep holding him until it doesn't feel weird anymore. Hold him and keep holding him until I can feel my anger for the ways he's wronged me start to seep out. "I think we should sell the house."

CARLI

It's Saturday afternoon and I'm lying on the sofa in the living room, trying not to feel the ghost of Rex (his arms around me, my face sunk into his neck) or the nothingness of my walls (its weight like concrete on my chest) by slipping further down into the YouTube abyss.

I'm home alone. Better than being at work with Mom. She tried to get me to go with her this morning, to get me out of the house, but I'm tired of looking into her sympathetic eyes. And I swear to god I'll go apeshit if I hear *Are you okay?* one more time.

Better than playing basketball with Jordan, too. After I told her about Shannon, she forgave me. But now all she wants to do is ball. Says she needs to step up her game since I'm not playing next year.

And definitely better than being at Daddy's. He's supposed to have *the talk* with Cole. No need for me to go through all that again.

I've been watching random videos for over three hours. So long I swear I can hear my brain yelling, *Help! Get me out of here!* And I'm trying, but "The World's Funniest Family Feud Fails" is putting all ladders and ropes out of my reach.

Steve Harvey is standing between two women, both with one hand behind their backs and the other hand flat on their respective red buzzers. He says, "Name a number that all men exaggerate."

Not the number of extramarital kids they have, I think before the lady in the purple dress presses the button and answers, "One hundred!" A red *X* flashes on the screen and Steve Harvey confusedly points to the other lady, who says, "Sixty-nine?"

I mean, how stupid can they be. I swear these women are even more clueless than me. I seriously didn't think that was possible. No, I take that back. Daddy is definitely more lost than I am. He's like a five-year-old trying to read a road map.

I go off hunting for the boost, the boost I thought judging Daddy would give me, but there isn't one. There's only his history—of being an eight-year-old boy whose mom died and whose dad never came back, of being a man who had a family and lost it—and the path stretched out before him.

I try to imagine my path, but all I see is a large stretch of earth covered with green, untrampled grass.

That does it. Phone down. I'm up. Stretching my long arms out to both sides and arching my back. Rex's strong hands around my waist. His thumbs gently rubbing my ribs. And I pull my arms in, look for another distraction, something that might stop me from remembering the feeling of his long body lying next to mine under the tall pines.

Magazines. A stack of them in the brass tray on the ottoman in the middle of the room. *Don't even think about it*, I tell myself. I'd be trying to cut out stuff for my walls in no time.

Books. Rows and rows of them that stretch floor to high ceiling on the wall at the foot of the sofa. But reading truths about other people's lives always makes me wonder about the truths of my own. And I'd only end up with some kind of quote I'd want to tack up on my walls.

My bare walls.

Just thinking about them makes this oversized burnt-orange sofa feel like my forever home. When I used to step into my room, a ton of images and poems and quotes and facts would greet me. Little bits of everything I loved. Little things that gave me a way to look at my life . . . at all the possible meanings for my feelings . . . at all the possible signs for which way to go.

But when I'm in there now (which is only when I'm getting dressed in the morning . . . I've been sleeping on the sofa all week), there is nothing but me.

But who am I, really? Without basketball. Without all the little things that I thought made up who I was. And if I don't even know who I am, how am I supposed to know what to do with the rest of my life. Can somebody please tell me that?

I'm so tired of trying to figure it all out. But even more tired of being out here, hiding. Hiding doesn't do anything but make your problems worse. I guess Daddy's mess taught me that.

No more hiding, I decide, and take a step toward the hallway. And another one, my long bare feet marching off the thick, woven rug onto the wooden floor. One after the other after the other until I'm standing at my closed bedroom door, yellow light shining on the tips of my toes.

I go in.

Even though I know what to expect, seeing my bare walls still feels like death. I look back at the black box holding all of my old things, buried under magazines in the corner of my closet crammed full of clothes. Knowing that they're there, that I can still visit them, is at least some kind of comfort.

When I turn back around, I notice that the afternoon light flooding my room is creating shadows on my walls. The far wall has one of the whole window: sixteen slanted, golden squares. Something. Not nothing. I go sit across from it on the edge of my made-up bed.

Jagged shadows running through a few of the glowing squares make me look outside of my window at a small tree. Its branches are covered with tiny green buds on their way to being leaves. So many buds. I count the ones on a single twig. Twenty-one. On another one. Seventeen. And another one. Twenty-four.

Don't ask me why, but it feels nice counting. Moving from one bud to the next with no thoughts in between. It's making me feel more alive than I've felt all week. Until it brings me to thinking about Rex.

It's not horrible to think about Rex. Even after what he did, so many memories of him still feel good. But some literally make me sick. Like that look of hate on his face at the championship game, and how he never even listened to what I had to say. How could he— *Wait, why am I even thinking about this?*

I grab my notebook and pencil off my desk and turn my attention back to the twigs outside the window. Make a mark for every green bud I count. Draw a leaf for every ten buds. A hundred buds and counting.

But then I start to wonder why the buds are taking so long to become full-grown leaves (it's already mid-March).

And that leads me to thinking that maybe the buds are a sign. That maybe I'm like the buds, growing slowly. *But into what? I need to know.*

But I don't, so I go back to counting. Until all the buds begin to blur, and I feel like I should go outside and start tagging the twigs I've counted to keep track. But nobody's doing all that. So I turn back to the glowing squares and think about how there are sixteen of them and sixteen years in me. How it could mean— *No, not going down that road again.*

I start sketching the squares instead—eyeing the correct angle of their slant, erasing and smudging to create the glow effect. I sketch and sketch, until the weight of trying to figure out what everything means and what I'll do with my life falls away. Until there is only the pencil, the paper, and the image I'm bringing into being.

Maybe this is who I am, right here where this pencil meets the page, where my eyes meet these glowing squares. So basic, I know, but the lightness, the wholeness, I feel right now is telling me there's something to it. Not the sketching itself, but me totally doing it, this one small thing. Giving all of my attention to it is letting me be.

● REX ●

I'm in the living room, on the opposite end of the sofa from my dad, trading cool home design pictures via IG. I didn't even have to sign him up. He already had an account. One of those zero posts, no profile pic accounts, but still. Who knew?

"Look at this one," he says from the other end of the sofa, his big feet in white socks almost reaching mine.

"Okay, give me a sec," I say, eyeing the image of a black heart with a jagged line going down the middle that just popped up on my feed. Another post from Cole. I swear Cole has posted over twenty times today.

Not his usual portraits, which always seem to reveal the unseen parts of people. Nah, it's a whole bunch of I'm-going-through-some-shit-type posts like, *Don't trust anyone* or *I remember when life was good* or *How can one person tell so many lies* or *The saddest thing about betrayal is that it never comes from your enemies.*

That girl with the slick-back ponytail and the wide-open eyes must've done him real dirty. He's been posting about her like crazy the last few weeks. And now this. I thought about texting him earlier, but I was scared he wouldn't want to hear from me after what I did to Carli. But this public breakup stuff has been going on for way too long. I'm not only worried about him, I'm starting to feel embarrassed for him.

You alright? I DM him on IG.

He hits me right back. **My dad is a fraud**

I look at my dad on the other end of the sofa. He's nowhere near perfect, but he's trying his best. I message back, **He's probably doing his best**

"Did you see the last one I sent?" my dad asks.

I click on the chat with my dad and see a picture of an all-white living room with a long, gray sofa and sleek, dark wood furniture. "Nah, this is basically the same look we have now. Not comfortable enough. And not enough color," I say, and look around.

I pause on the wall of windows that extend all the way from the kitchen into the living room. Outside a darkening orange-pink sky hovers over the pines. I was trippin' before. Our house is sick. It's this cool modern house with these huge windows that bring all the trees it's surrounded by in. But we still need help making it feel like a home.

"The sofa looks way more cushiony than ours," he says.

"It's still gray."

He laughs, says, "Okay, okay," and returns to his phone.

I click back on the conversation with Cole. He hasn't written anything after my last message. I wonder what happened with his dad. Damn, I didn't even ask.

What's going on with your dad? I text.

U don't know?

No

U haven't talked to Carli?

Not about your dad, I type, wondering if he even knows we've broken up.

The three little bubbles telling me he's typing appear then disappear, appear, then disappear.

I hop over to *Barbara A*'s feed and shoot my dad a pic of a white, modern living room with colorful art and a sunken middle floor filled with bright blue velvet cushions. "Now this is what I'm talking about," I tell him.

"Let me see," he says. And then, "Now that's nice."

"Carli's mom did it."

"Carli's mom, huh?" he says, like he's trying to sniff something out.

I see what he's getting at, but it's not how it looks. "Carli's mom's design style is dope. Only showing you. This has nothing to do with me and Carli, okay," I say, setting him straight.

"Yeah, okay."

I check Cole's conversation again and see, **Shannon's our sister. My dad cheated on my mom and kept Shannon a secret all these years**

WHAT??!!! I message back, not processing what I just read. It's too much to take in. **Dude, I'm so sorry. Are you okay?** I want to ask who Shannon is but don't. The name sounds familiar, but I can't place it.

I HATE MY DAD

I know he doesn't mean that, but I respond, **Man I can't even imagine,** and look at my dad. Although I spent a good deal of my life thinking he hated me, I've never hated him. And trust me, I've tried. I don't even know if it's possible to really hate someone you came from.

How do you look your wife in the face? Your kids? Like EVERY DAY for 15 YEARS knowing u have another child? Who does that?

I don't know man. That's sooooo messed up. I'm so sorry

And the crazy thing is that if Shannon hadn't told Carli during the game we still wouldn't know. He was trying to take it to the grave

Shannon? Oh shit! Shannon! That's what happened to Carli at the game! That's why she was so upset. The night flashes back to me, and I can almost tell the exact moment she must've found out. When she went from draining everything, including threes, to letting Shannon take over.

What! Are you serious?! I message back.

Said he was afraid to tell us. Such a punk. Can't even look at him the same. Can't wait to get out of this house

Want me to come scoop you?

Actually my girl just pulled up outside. Gotta go

OK . Call me if you need anything

Thx. Will do

"Sent you another one from her site," my dad says.

"Huh?"

"*Barbara A.* She's really good."

"Yeah?"

"I was just saying I sent you another photo from her site."

I know he means *feed*, but I don't correct him. I'm too busy thinking about Carli. I can't even imagine what she's been going through. She tried to tell me, but I refused to listen. I could've been there for her, but all I did was break up with her on top of everything else she had to deal with. And all because she missed my game? My game is nothing compared to what she found out. Nothing!

I swear I hate myself. No, I take that back. Talking shit about myself has way too much power. But why didn't I listen to her? I close my eyes and shake my head, wishing I could press Rewind, go all the way back to the game, calm my ass down, and wait to hear from Carli. But there are no do-overs. Only what I can do now.

"What's wrong? You don't like it? Ignore the pink sofa. I was referring to the overall look."

"No, no. It's not that," I say, standing up, knowing I'm too late. But I take off running toward the stairs and up to my room to call Carli anyway. Too late is for damn sure better than never.

CARLI

After the sun goes low and the shadows disappear from my walls, I bust out my colored pencils and sketch some heavily cratered moons, a few blazing suns, and a ton of tiny stars around and throughout the pencil-sketched squares.

Then I allow myself to thumb through a magazine, where I find Sabina Karlsson and cut out her face and big, red hair. I place the bottom third of her face underneath a moon, her freckled chin disappearing off the page. The left side of her face to the right, between a sun and some bud-filled branches. And her right eye and big red hair at the top among the stars.

Make her a part of everything, one piece at a time.

I even have the nerve to allow myself to bust out some books of poetry and look for passages that speak to me. Not so I can try to figure out what they mean for my future (that was driving me crazy), but so I can experience what they make me feel right now. And because I love the act of doing it. Come to think of it, I've always loved hunting through pages and writing my favorite passages down in my prettiest handwriting.

From Tracy K. Smith's *Life on Mars*, I write:

> everything
> That ever was still is, somewhere

Something about the passage makes me feel like I'm okay. Like everything will be okay. I draw a speech bubble around the passage, across three squares in the middle of the page, and listen. I hear a faint ring. Dang, what does that mean? Wait, I'm trippin'. That's my phone.

I get up and run down the hall to the living room, but it stops ringing before I get there. I grab my phone off the sofa and see a missed call from Rex. I want to roll my eyes, but before I can, my heart starts spinning then leaping then going still like it doesn't know what to do with itself.

A text from him pops up: **Talked to Cole. Sorry about your dad. I can't even imagine what you've been going through. Sorry I didn't listen. I should've listened. I hope you can forgive me. And I hope you're okay. You don't have to call me back. I just wanted you to know how sorry I am**

With his words floating around inside me, tears flood my eyes. I read his text ten more times, and a million thoughts rush in.

Does his apology mean that he wants to get back with me? If so, what was that whole you-don't-have-to call-me-back business? Is he trying to play games? Maybe not, but he's still messed up. But what do I really know? I know he loved me. I know I didn't really give him a fair chance. I didn't even tell him anything going on with me and expected him to understand. That's still no excuse for what he did. But he said he's sorry. I wonder if he still loves me. Is love enough?

All this thinking about Rex is taking me far, far away from myself. And after finally being so close, I want to hold on tight for a little longer. I want to go back to my bare room, sit on my bed, and listen for the words to go in my speech bubble. And afterward, hunt for more images from magazines. Oooo, maybe some lava or a blazing blue fire or something fiery red or maybe even something beige. I'll know it when I see it.

But definitely more sketches around whatever images I find, and a fact or two or three or four. And I don't know what else. I just want to keep at it long enough to know that I'll always be here.

Sounds crazy, I know. Like, where else am I going? But this just-being thing I have going on with myself is new. And between dealing with thoughts and emotions and decisions and plans and parents and siblings and boyfriends, I need to be able to trust that I can always get away from the world and back to just being myself.

I look down at Rex's text. The only thing I know for sure about him, about us, right now is that I appreciate him apologizing. It makes the part of me that feels wronged by him want to close its case. **Thanks for texting . . . I'm okay**, I write back, and toss my phone on the sofa.

Above it, a waxing gibbous moon glows in the just-dark sky outside the window. I stand still for a while and take it in, resisting the urge to think about what the moon means for me and Rex, resisting the urge to think about anything.

NOTHING
AND
EVERYTHING

dom

● REX ●

Saturday morning and I'm crouching down in the mudroom, lacing up my LeBrons, when my phone pings. Man, I hope it's Carli. It's a stupid hope—when a girl thanks you for texting her, it's pretty much a nice way of saying she's done with your ass—but I allow myself to have it anyway.

I mean, maybe she misses me. I know I miss her. It's been a week since I've texted, but it feels like a lifetime. Nah, make that seven lifetimes because every day that passes without talking to her feels like a new death. But I'm trying not to bother her about us when she's dealing with so much else.

I stand up and dig my phone out of the pocket of my basketball shorts. **Still on?**—a text from Cole. He asked me to meet him up at the secret court today. He's spending the weekend at his dad's and wants to get out of the house. I definitely get that.

You know it, I text back. **Heading up there now.** I'd planned to go up there today anyway. Been going all week after school, too, since Coach is still too pissed to open the gym for me.

Yep, I'm back to ballin'. I figure to hell with what everybody is saying about me. What they think won't get me any closer to my dream. Yes, your boy's dream is still alive! Can't let it die. Shit, nobody's ever accomplished anything without trying. And I'm telling you, now, I'm about to put in work. Major work.

I thought we said 2, Cole replies.

Yeah, going early to get some shots in

Dang, I ●● u

Ha! I'm trying!

Below Cole's conversation is a conversation with Danny. He texted to invite me to a party he's having tonight. Said his parents were out of town for the weekend and he was getting kegs. Been to enough white-boy wasted parties (one) to know it's not my thing, but I plan to go anyway. Can't pass up the opportunity to try to smooth things over with the team.

Below the conversation with Danny, Carli's message of

thanks still sits, staring at me like a hand up in my face. I swear every time I see it, all the air rushes out my lungs.

This can't be the end of us.

I type, **Miss you**, and erase it. **Miss you** again and press Send before I can lose my nerve. Maybe she's done with me, maybe she's not. But how will I ever know if I don't start trying to fix what I've messed up.

CARLI

I'm driving back to Daddy's from my Photoshop class at HCC. Missed the first class of the session last Saturday, but I still killed it. And I was afraid I was going to be too far behind . . . afraid I wasn't going to be as good as those college kids. Chile, please! The teacher even said he was impressed by me.

Let me back up. After basically spending all last week filling up my notebook with sketches and quotes and facts and magazine clippings—each page with a totally different look, giving a completely different feel—I realized I was pretty good at collage.

Sounds crazy, I know. I've basically been doing it on my

walls since I was a kid. But I always thought putting ra——
things together in interesting ways would eventually tell me
what I really wanted to do with my life. I never considered
the possibility that it could actually be the thing I do. Duh!

And even when the possibility first popped in my
head, I was still like, *A collage artist? Me? Nooo.* But I am.
Not to say that it's all I'll ever be. Maybe it will be, and
I'll just keep getting better and better. Or maybe it will
lead to something else I love. Or maybe I'll end up doing
something completely different with my life.

All I know is that right now, I want to take my collage
skills to the next level. I want to learn how to do it digitally.
Where it takes me, who knows? But getting better at
something I love feels like a step in the right direction. And
that's all I can ask for.

Plus, it will keep me out of the house on the Saturdays
I have to spend at Daddy's. Oh, I forgot to tell you: the
judge decided that I'll live with Mom during the week
and Cole will live with Daddy. I still don't know how I'm
going to live without Cole, but at least we'll be together
on the weekends—first and third at Daddy's and second
and fourth at Mom's. If there's a fifth weekend, we get to
choose where to spend it.

Anyway, it's not like I'm still *that* mad at Daddy, but all he wants to do now is cry and apologize and explain the same things over and over again. It's like listening to the same sad song on repeat. A sad song that's not about to fix anything.

Pulling up to the house, I see Jordan's Jeep in the driveway beside Daddy's Tahoe. She beat me here. I had to beg her to skip ballin' today to come over here to be my backup. Figure things can't get too depressing with company around.

Walking up the driveway, I notice the magnolia tree is better. It has way less of that nasty white stuff on its limbs. Whatever the tree guy sprayed on it must be working. Makes me want to fish my phone out of my backpack and send Rex a pic, but I don't.

Got his text this morning—**Miss you**—and I swear I could feel him whispering it in my ear. But I'm in such a good place with myself. Don't know if I'm ready to risk that by starting things back up with Rex. Plus, I don't know if I can ever really trust him again.

Jordan thinks I should give him another chance. I think her exact words were, *Yo ass act like you've never messed up.* And I haven't even told her about his latest text yet. No doubt she's about to give me a hundred reasons to call him back. I grab the gold door handle—warm from the sun—push the latch down with my thumb, and press open the door, already hearing some of the reasons.

Now I can't hear anything. I can only see Shannon. Yes, old-enemy-new-sister Shannon. I know I told Daddy that we needed to get to know her, but I didn't expect to come back today and see her standing in the living room. Cole is giving her a hug.

Cole lets go of her and they both look over at me. Daddy, standing beside them, looks at me. Jordan, half-swallowed by the sofa, looks at me, too. Everyone's eyes are red and glossy like they've been crying, including Jordan's. And Jordan doesn't cry.

"Hey," I say, feeling like I'm not even here, like this isn't real.

"Hey," they say, voices dragging. No one even tries to fake a smile. Boy, was I wrong about things not getting too depressing with company around.

This has to end. It would be different if these were finally-united-and-it-feels-so-good tears. That would actually be nice. But tears from another stop on Daddy's apology tour? Nobody has time for that. I'm mad Jordan had to sit in on it. This heaviness is not hers. Really, it's not any of ours. It's Daddy's.

"It's super nice outside. Y'all wanna go up to the basketball court?" I ask, hardly believing the words coming out of my mouth. But dribbling and shooting under the sun would be way better than staying here in this funk.

Brighter faces all around. Except for Daddy's. He's looking down at the floor, his mind somewhere else.

Jordan climbs out of the sofa. "Hadn't planned on ballin' today, but you know I'm always down." She's wearing her Jordan 9 Retros. She doesn't usually ball in her Retros.

"I thought ballin' was always the plan," Shannon says, and bites the nail on her pointer finger. She's dressed in a baggy T-shirt, long shorts, and some Nike Dunks—clearly ready.

"Plan?" I look at Daddy, but he's still looking down at the floor. Then I look at Cole. His long, lightly freckled cheeks are going pink. Of course it was Cole. But you know what? I can't even be mad.

Shannon is our sister. Like, I have a sister. And she's real. She's standing in our living room with chewed-up nubs for nails (does she know how many hundreds of thousands of bacteria can live under just one dirty nail?) and her hair tied back in a bun. Wait, did she tie it back for me? I need to tell her she doesn't have to do that. I need to tell her so many things.

I mean, I'd be lying if I said Shannon being here doesn't feel strange. But it feels more normal than when I first walked in. And I'm sure it will feel even more normal when we get out of this house. Will it ever feel completely normal having a sister I only learned about at sixteen? I don't know. But life isn't about to sit around and wait on normal.

REX

Carli just walked through the opening in the hedges. No. Can't be. But the way the sun is glinting off the gold medallion on her chest, and the way her big hair is bouncing off her bare shoulders, tell me I'm not trippin'.

She's walking behind Cole—and wait, is that Shannon?—rockin' some high-top yellow Blazers with a tank top and some cut-off jean shorts. And now Jordan just walked in, too. Cole never said anybody else was coming.

Man, but Carli. I wasn't prepared to see her today. I swear to God I'm so happy I could cry. All I want to do is run to her and scoop her up in my arms. But I know I don't have the right. And the face she's making isn't giving me any type of permission.

You'd think that when every picture you've ever looked at of a person, and everything you've ever done with a person, constantly plays like reruns in your brain, that you would've seen every face they could possibly make. But this one is new.

She's looking straight at me . . . like what? Dude, I don't know. Definitely no smiling or sweetness going on. Probably too much to ask. But no anger or attitude, either. At least I could've worked with that. Normally when girls get mad, that means they still care. But Carli's face is straight-up blank, like she doesn't feel anything.

I drop the ball at the free-throw line and walk toward her, hoping to see something I'm missing.

CARLI

When I see Rex on the court, I swear the sun turns up a notch. It's like my world literally got brighter.

But should I be feeling this? I look back at the sidelines, at the shade along the chain-link fence with the tall, green bushes poking through. It looks so tempting. I could go sit down, lean back, and wait for some kind of sign to tell my confused heart what to do.

But I don't. I keep walking, putting one yellow Blazer (they're new) in front of the other on the green court. I wonder what it's made of. It's a lot softer than concrete, that's for sure.

Ahead of me, Cole gives Rex a hug. Then Shannon awkwardly hugs him, too, like she doesn't know what else to do. Jordan runs ahead of me, daps him up, and tries to beat Shannon to the ball.

My turn.

REX

How I've missed her little nose, her quiet brown eyes, and her fierce freckles. They snatch me up, pull me in, and I get lost inside.

CARLI

Being this close to Rex has my heart speaking in colors again. A kingdom of colors. Making all the arguments for our love that words and thoughts couldn't come up with. It's such an unbelievably good feeling. Like my heart just gave birth to it. Like I've never felt it before.

But I have.

And as much as I want to let the feeling carry me away, cocoon me in all the colors, I can't. Not yet. For now I feel safer with things being beige.

● REX ●

"Hi," I say, my eyes moving from the patch of freckles on her nose up to her eyes.

"Hi," she says, her eyes resting on mine, but somehow not giving me anything.

"I'm really sorry for what I did to you," I start. "I was just—"

"Wait, can we not do this?"

Damn, she doesn't even want to hear my apology? She's really done with me. But she doesn't even know that I've been working on myself. I need her to know. "Can I at least apologize?"

"You already did."

"But it's different in person."

"Yeah, but the sun is shining. And the sky is so blue. We're here. Back at the secret court. It's so soft," she says, and hops up and down a little bit. "I can't believe I didn't notice this the last time we were here."

I really don't know what's going on right now, but I hop up and down a little, too, try to see what sees talking about. I guess it's got a little spring to it. "Yeah, much better than concrete."

"Exactly," she says, staring at me.

I can't think of anything else to say, so I don't say anything.

And neither does she.

We stay like that for a while, and I finally see what her eyes are giving me. They're here . . . she's here . . . right now . . . with me. And I swear it feels like we're out of our skin. Like there's nothing covering us. Nothing in the way.

It's the best feeling in the world, but I can't even lie, it's making me feel kind of shy. "So, Shannon is here," I say, and turn to look back at everybody else. Shannon grabs the rebound from Cole's missed shot before Jordan does.

"Yeah, Cole set it up."

"Gotta love Cole."

"Yeah, I'm pretty sure he set this up, too," she says, and twists her lips. But her eyes have the happiness of a thousand smiles. Okay, maybe not a thousand but at least one.

"Looks like it," I say, a monument of hope springing up inside of me.

"So how are we about to do this?" Cole yells over to us. "We got five. Quick game of horse to see who sits out first?"

"No, y'all go ahead. I'm not playing," Carli yells back.

Takes everybody a second to process, but then Jordan finally shouts, "Damn, that's right!"

CARLI

Didn't feel like sitting on the sidelines. Wanted to be in the mix with everybody else, so I'm the ref. Just called Cole for his third foul on Rex.

"You've gotta be kidding me!" Cole complains, throwing his hands up in the air from the baseline. "You're clearly giving Rex preferential treatment. I can't even look his direction without you calling a foul."

"Yeah, you can't be out here playing favorites if you're the ref," Shannon backs him up from the middle of the key. Didn't take her any time to get comfortable with sibling bickering.

"Nobody's playing favorites," I snap back, and grab the ball from underneath the basket. "It's not my fault y'all haven't found a way to guard him yet. Stay in front of him. Keep a hand in his face. Block him out so he doesn't keep getting all the rebounds."

"Oh, so now you're the ref and the coach?" Cole replies.

"Tell me about it!" Shannon echoes.

I dribble the ball a few times, noticing how it pops up quicker than it would on a normal court. "Whatever. Don't be mad at me. I'm just callin' it like I see it."

"Y'all are funny," Jordan says, and walks to the low block.

Rex walks to the free-throw line, looking uncomfortable with being in the middle of all the arguing.

"Oh, I almost forgot," Jordan says, turning toward me. She reaches into her sneakers and pulls out a piece of paper rolled up into a flattened scroll. "Here," she says, and holds it out.

"Ew, I'm not touching that," I reply.

"Girl, would you look," she says, eyes wide, and unrolls it. The hospital menu.

I quickly slide the ball between my left elbow and hip and take it. The paper is damp from Jordan's sweaty feet, but I don't care. I flip it over, and there it is in blurred blue ink:

The very first kisses were blown in Mesopotamia as a way to get in good with the gods.

Tangible evidence of where it all began for me and Rex. A sign of where we're going? Maybe, but who has time to try to figure that out?

Don't get me wrong. I'm not totally giving up on my signs. I still believe that if I pay attention, signs will pop up and let me know I'm on the right path. But all that business of thinking everything was a potential sign had to stop. Some things just are what they are, and trying to give them extra meaning all the time was overcomplicating my life.

Take me and Rex. Regardless of the first-kisses fact, our fate will depend on how we treat each other—how much of the good in ourselves we're willing and able to give each other—simple as that.

But should I at least give him the menu? So he can always have it as a reminder of how I've felt from the very beginning, no matter what happens to us?

"Any day now," Cole says, walking up to the block opposite Jordan.

Shannon sets up beside him, already looking ready to rebound even though Rex hasn't even shot his first free throw.

I bounce pass the ball to Rex with my right hand, still trying to decide what to do with the menu in my left.

Rex catches the ball and dribbles—one, twice, three times, and swish. No kisses.

I grab the ball and pass it back to him.

Again—once, twice, three times, and swish. No kisses.

The first time he went to the line and didn't blow a kiss, I thought he might've forgotten.

The second time I allowed myself to hope. That he'd stopped asking forgiveness from his mom. That he'd realized her death wasn't his fault. That he'd somehow let go of his pain and rearranged himself into a boy who would never hurt me again.

Now three times, and the hope in my chest slides on its wings and starts flapping all over the place. I can't help but think that there will be more between us. Much, much more.

But only the future knows.

I slide the menu into my back pocket, where I keep it for myself. And the game goes on. With us and only what belongs to us. Nothing else.

ACKNOWLEDGMENTS

Book two. *Say what?* I feel so incredibly grateful to be putting more words into the world. For me, writing has always been an exercise of going deep within, extracting bits of my human experience, and shaping them into a universal story. The fact that people are reading my stories and connecting to them feels so rewarding. So, to all my readers: thank you, thank you, thank you! You don't know how much you mean to me.

To my little family, Amina and Larry: you give my heart a home. A home filled with light and beauty and joy and kindness and peace. I'm so grateful to have you both. I love you.

Seneca Shahara Brand, aka Sha Love: I'm so lucky to have such a loving, artistic friend. Thank you for being so generous with your creative gifts. This book wouldn't be the same without you.

Rochelle and Stan, aka Mom and Dad: None of this would be possible without your continued love and support. Thank you. I love you.

Loveis Wise: I love your name. I love the energy you put into the world through your work. Thank you for putting that energy into this book's cover. It's gorgeous, and Carli and Rex are perfect.

To my agent, Jennifer Carlson: Thank you for being my advocate. I am happy I have you.

To my editor, Virginia Duncan, and everyone at Greenwillow Books/ HarperCollins: thank you for turning my words into a book and getting that book out into the world.

The Complete Book of Mothers-in-law

The Complete Book of Mothers-in-law
A Celebration

LUISA DILLNER

ILLUSTRATED BY STEPHANIE VON REISWITZ

ff

faber and faber

First published in 2008
by Faber and Faber Limited
3 Queen Square London WC1N 3AU

Typeset by Faber and Faber Limited
Printed in the UK by CPI Mackays, Chatham

A CIP record for this book
is available from the British Library

ISBN 978-0-571-23819-4

2 4 6 8 10 9 7 5 3 1

To John, my children Sam, Madeleine, Mathilda and Lydia,
my mother Theresa and mother-in-law Maggie
THANKS TO YOU ALL

Contents

My Mother-in-law Maggie

I can't remember when I first met my mother-in-law and she's vague on when she first met me. This suggests that we are not sentimental about our relationship and it doesn't consume either of our lives. I have heard friends talk about this first meeting with a future mother-in-law as something significant, setting the tone (sometimes acrimoniously) for their future relationship. Not so Maggie and me. 'I seem to remember you were very pleasant and we had tea,' is how she recalls our first meeting. We have existed ever since on a similar plane, without drama, intensity or, until recently, particular intimacy, for ten years. I'm not married to her son, but I might as well be. We have a reconstituted family of two older children (mine) and two younger children (ours), a house and a people carrier. Only the addition of a pet could make us more entwined.

As an unmarried mother when I met her only son John, I may not have been every mother's dream, but Maggie is too matter-of-fact to harbour matrimonial aspirations for her children. 'If you are good enough for him,' she says, 'that's good enough for me.' I doubt I will be so laissez-faire about whoever my son embraces as a partner. Since she already has three daughters she didn't need me to be the daughter she'd never had. I didn't have any negative preconceptions about mothers-in-law. I have a good, close relationship with my own mother and expected to like the mother of the man I was going to live with. I assumed that if I was reasonably pleasant, she would like me. And so it has turned out.

Maggie was never going to be a hands-on mother-in-law because she would hate to be intrusive. Anyway she has her own life and it is, for a woman in her seventies, remarkably busy and while not outrageous, mildly unconventional. You might not think her unconventional on first meeting her – she lives in a neat white house in Finchley with a blue Volkswagen parked outside, with a well-tended garden (except for the sprawling weeping willow which recently fell over into the neighbours' garden) and school pictures of her grandchildren and children (looking very 1970s) throughout the living room. It is like a granny's house, quiet and neat with flowers in vases, although Maggie doesn't keep Rich Tea biscuits in a stripy tin. She has books, mostly biographies, in various states of being read, many of which seemed rather highbrow when I first met her. In the early days I felt I was a disappointment to her, invariably looking blank when she asked me if I'd read any Trollope (no) or was familiar with some school of architecture (even less likely). I should have taken it as a compliment that she presumed I was so well read.

She is unconventional, if you would apply that term to someone who was a French teacher but took early retirement to become an escapologist's assistant and later a Pearly Queen. I think that is unusual and I don't know anyone else's mother-in-law who has such exotic credentials. She was not only a justice of the peace for thirty years but did voluntary work for the Family Planning Association at a time when it wasn't widely accepted in British society that anyone was having sex (certainly not enjoying it). She dispensed, she remembers, mostly jelly. So this, in essence, is the potted list of some of my mother-in-law's accomplishments. Physically she is comfortably round in a Restoration comedy way. If you asked her what she liked least about her appearance she would say 'My hair,' because it is thin and wispy, too insubstantial for such a generous personality, but despite it she is handsome. She has a lovely rich voice that would sound great on radio. Sometimes mid-conversation for no obvious reason she will look baffled in a professorial way, furrowing her forehead and raising her eyebrows, as if readjusting her face. She looks young for her age (the genetics of good skin) and she guffaws a lot – Maggie likes a good laugh. She doesn't have catchphrases but her conversation is littered with thespian asides and dramatic flourishes and she will lapse into local dialects and characterisations mid-sentence. She is never, thank goodness, dull and is good-natured enough that should she repeat a story about a play she has been in or an actor she's met, you can tell her and she'll say 'Oh well,' but not take offence.

Maggie was born in London in 1932 but her parents moved to Hertfordshire before she was two because the air was better there. She was an only child (her mother intimated once that she couldn't have more children) and was brought up in an adult, politicised world. Her father was a committed Labour man and her mother was unusually political for a woman at that time, becoming an agent for the East Islington Labour Party after the war. They had spent the war eating rabbit in St Anne's-on-Sea as Pop's work at the Ministry of Fuel and Power moved there for five years. Pop, beloved of his grandchildren, was known for being 'straight, fair and honest', a man of high principles who, when after the war he was offered the chance to buy a home in Canonbury, refused because he didn't approve of the Marquis of Northampton owning the leasehold. Maggie is her father's child, straight and scrupulously honest, an advocate of fair play. Her mother, Agnes, was colder and more practical than Pop, and quite likely to breeze into a room and tell Maggie sharply that the skirt she was wearing looked all wrong. Agnes embraced political life probably more intuitively than motherhood, sufficiently to became Mayor of Islington. There is an old Pathé newsreel of Agnes showing the Queen around an Islington labour exchange in the 1950s with the voice-over saying dramatically, 'And then the Queen was introduced to a black man.' When we transferred it from film reel to DVD we kept replaying that part, laughing at the political incorrectness of it all. I've never asked Maggie where she stands politically, as a daughter of Old Labour, but I would guess she is a liberal. She's a regular churchgoer, the epitome of a good Christian woman, although she moved churches when the new vicar started preaching against gay people. She's not into fire and brimstone and many of her friends are gay men. She can't stand discrimination.

Her first acting was at school, precociously taking part in a production of *She Stoops to Conquer* at the age of thirteen and thereby launching her career as a character actress. She studied French at university and did the occasional revue, meeting her future husband Eric (a Northern grammar-school boy with considerable charm) on the same course on the first day, although it wasn't love at first sight. He had a girlfriend, a domestic science student, but he dumped her for Maggie and they married six years after they met. Four children followed fairly quickly – due to her inherent fertility and how easy she found the whole process, rather than a conscious desire to compensate for her being an only child – John and Lilly, the twins, being the last. Maggie was one of the founders of the Hornsey Housebound Wives, a group of mothers who got together after one of them wrote to the *Hornsey Journal*, saying that she had a six-month-old baby and, because she'd been working, didn't know anyone in the area. If anyone wanted to have coffee would they get in touch? The first batch of women who did so started up three playgroups (there hadn't been any), occasional lectures and monthly newsletters. There was a rota of houses where a mother with pre-school children could go for coffee each day – the only rule was that no one could show off with homemade cakes, only biscuits were allowed. By the time Maggie went back to work as a French teacher there were 240 members of the Hornsey Housebound Wives.

Her career took a more unconventional turn when she met up with Larry Barnes, an old friend from home whom she'd lost touch with. Maggie was doing some amateur dramatics, and he was performing a professional Harry Houdini cabaret act. He asked her to be his assistant, largely to protect him from over-enthusiastic members of the audience who on one occasion made him pass out by swinging him around on his crotch strap. Maggie was anxious about what it would involve. 'I'm too old to wear a leotard and tights,' she told him. 'So wear an evening dress,' said Larrry. "I've got rotten hair,' said Maggie. 'So wear a wig,' said Larry. Initially their work was at weekends and evenings, squeezed around school hours. Maggie's job was to pluck two burly men out of the audience to put Larry in a straitjacket and then to count him out of it with a stopwatch. Larry always got out.

As a sideline Larry was the Pearly King of Thornton Heath (it is an inherited honour) and although his wife and daughter should have been his Pearly family, they refused to wear the outfits. Larry needed a Pearly Queen to accompany him to charity events and Maggie was sufficiently unselfconscious to agree to help him. They had to ask permission from the Pearly Kings and Queens Association (because Kings and Queens should be married) but soon Maggie was accompanying Larry to fetes and galas, shaking hands and doing a few variety turns to raise money for charity. One can only imagine how her teenage children felt about their mother singing 'My old man said "Follow the van"' in full Pearly regalia. 'Children don't like their parents making a fool of themselves,' says Maggie, 'and they probably thought I was making a fool of myself.' Maggie's other variety turn couldn't have afforded the children any more comfort: dressed as a male impersonator, with a boater over one eye, she would do a selection of the French songster Maurice Chevalier's most famous tunes for the British Music Hall Society. Ever one to work an audience, she would encourage them to sing in French, which they couldn't speak, but I expect Maggie made them feel they were doing it splendidly.

By the time I met Maggie she was living on her own, having divorced Eric ('I'd rather gloss over that – we probably married too young'), within a five-mile radius of her children, working in repertory companies most summers (usually doing period thrillers) and occasionally as the voice of Dr Evelyn Smythe in a series of audio plays based on Doctor Who. The part of Evelyn is loosely modelled on Maggie. She is a fifty-five-year-old history professor who is the sixth Doctor's companion and doesn't take any nonsense from him – she will question his decisions but also guide him wisely through his darker moments.

Smythe has a fondness for chocolate (Maggie prefers red wine and the occasional cigarette) and has a heart condition that was made worse when she was injected with blood from Killoran prisoners. Occasionally Evelyn fans will ask Maggie for photographs of herself, which she dutifully signs, or take her out to lunch. Who they think they are having lunch with is unclear. She does less Pearly Queen work but tradition decrees she will have the title until she dies. Her children are grateful she can't pass it on.

Her relationship with her own mother-in-law was difficult and has moulded her approach to the role. 'I don't think she ever thought I was good enough for her darling son, who was the apple of her eye. She had ruled his childhood. Things got on her nerves and she was terribly neurotic.' Maggie would never want to be that sort of mother-in-law and I wonder if this has made her overly sensitive to being one at all. She is so unintrusive that I used to wonder why she never popped in, because where I was brought up people often arrived unannounced. I thought that maybe she was too busy seeing her daughters to engage with our family. It was only when I asked her why we didn't see more of her that I understood. In her view, her children and their partners have their own lives and social arrangements and she wouldn't just arrive unannounced on any of their doorsteps. So she is a good granny but will wait to be asked before offering to look after the children.

I am touched by how she treats my children in the same way as her grandchildren, with interest and generosity. She is careful not to have favourites either amongst her children or grandchildren, which helps to keep the family close. She is uncritical of all of us, because, she says, it's unfair to be critical, which is true of course but for many people criticising is irresistible. Rather than make me feel her son could have done better ('he was never at my beck and call, so it felt natural for him to meet someone') she has said she couldn't be more proud of me than if I was one of her own children. She mentions to friends that I write but doesn't herself, I notice, buy the newspaper that my articles appear in.

Such is Maggie's disinclination to impose on us that when she called and asked if we would be in one evening because she wanted to come round, I asked if anything was wrong. 'No,' she said. But I suspected she wasn't telling the truth. She sat us down and said that a doctor, on examining her for an insurance policy, had found a lump in her breast. She had had a mammogram and been told she had breast cancer.

She didn't falter and told us in a matter-of-fact way, but she must have been alarmed, although she played the part of calm and collected mother quite perfectly. She told me later that she didn't want to upset the children. What she, and others who lived through the war, are good at is being pragmatic and getting on with things. She has refused to feel sorry for herself, although having surgery and expecting to have chemotherapy meant she had to cancel a cruise to New York. 'You've just got to get on with it' is her philosophy. Having trained as a doctor (but for reasons too dull to go into, stopped practising some years ago) I was probably too bossy about what questions she should ask (I stopped short of getting her to ask questions about her likelihood of survival when she gave no indication of wanting to know) and sought out my own experts to verify what she was being told by her doctors. She is happy to go along with what the doctors tell her, believing that they know best. She looks fantastically well but the family, who valued her pretty highly before, are keener than ever to spend time with her.

Like many daughters-in-law I encourage my partner to phone and see his mother because men forget they have any relatives at all. But I see more of her myself now and will phone her up to chat, instead of going through John. I talk to her more openly, as if she were a real person whom I could have met and liked myself, rather than treating her more remotely as my partner's mother. Last summer we went to see her at Nottingham's Royal Theatre in *The Ghost Train*, a 1920s thriller. I don't know what I imagined but it was a beautiful, real theatre, with an elaborate domed roof, gold-leaf cherubs on the front of ornate boxes and people who had paid money to come and see my mother-in-law.

She played, as she often does, the character part of an elderly spinster who gets squiffy when she's plied with brandy for her nerves. There's a lot of 'What would the vicar say?' and a wonderful line where she pats the face of the young hero, draws herself up tall and says, 'I may have been a spinster – but, young man . . . I was not neglected.' We were not really surprised to find that she can hold her own and is a real actor, but there was some relief mixed in with our pride.

My mother-in-law is a strong believer in marriage although in ten years she must have asked us only once when we were going to get married. It seems churlish not to make her a real mother-in-law while she is well enough to enjoy it. When we told her we were getting married, her response was theatrical but, I believe, genuine. She threw up her arms and shouted, 'That is the best news.' This enthusiastic response, after ten years of my being a potential daughter-in-law, bodes well for the future of our relationship. I'm just as pleased to have her as my mother-in-law.

Mothers-in-law worldwide

Afrikaans: *skoonmoeder*

Albanian: *vjehërr*

Czech: *tchyně*

Danish: *svigermor*

Dutch: *schoonmoeder*

Esperanto: *bopatrino*

Estonian: *ämm*

Finnish: *anoppi*

French: *belle-mère*

German: *Schwiegermutter*

Greek: πεθερά *(petherá)*

Gooniyandi: *marriyali*

Hebrew: חמות (khamót)

Indonesian: *mertua perempuan*

Interlingua: *matre affin*

Irish: *máthair chéile*

Italian: *suocera*

Krisa: *sami* (husband's mother)

Latin: *socra*

Norwegian: *svigermor*

Polish: *teściowa*

Portuguese: *sogra*

Romanian: *soacră*

Russian: *свекровь* (wife's mother-in-law);
тёща (husband's mother-in-law)

Scottish Gaelic: *màthair-chèile*

Seri: *aaquéect cmaam* (husband's mother-in-law)

Slovak: *svokra*

Slovene: *tašča*

Spanish: *suegra*

Swedish: *svärmor*

Tupinambá: *mendy* (wife's mother-in-law); *aîxó*
(husband's mother-in-law)

Turkish: *kaynana*

Mothers-in-law: an Essential History

There have always been mothers-in-law and most of us will end up either having or being one. The role of mother-in-law has existed throughout the ages; a part that no one actively chooses and anyone would be forgiven, considering the negative stereotypes, for thinking it has little to recommend it. Mothers-in-law have been variously feared, loathed, ridiculed, appreciated and adored but rarely ignored. Historically you can find mothers-in-law of all varieties: admirable, loving, scheming, bad, divine (literally) and quite ordinary. The mother-in-law phenomenon is global. Native Americans have mystical stories about mothers-in-law, Lithuanian women sing poetic, tragic songs of suffering at the hands of their mothers-in-law and Aboriginal men avoid them entirely, tradition forbidding them to look directly at them or talk to them. Jokes about mothers-in-law exist in all languages, covering the same themes of mothers-in-law as interfering battle-axes who visit too often, create conflict in the family and would be better off living as far away as possible – if at all. Anthropologists and social scientists have thoroughly studied mothers-in–law; the Scottish anthropologist Sir James George Frazer once remarked that 'The awe and dread with which the untutored savage contemplates his mother-in-law are amongst the most familiar facts of anthropology.'

All languages have a name for mothers-in-law although in some societies the rules of kinship are more complex and there are separate names for the husband's mother-in-law and the wife's mother-in-law. *The Oxford English Dictionary* defines a mother-in-law as 'the mother of one's husband or wife' and dates its first written appearance to 1440 as 'moodur-in-lawe' in the 'Promp. Parv.' (shorthand for the title of one of the first Latin–English lexicons). The term 'in-law' was initially also used to describe those relationships which are now prefixed by 'step', such as stepmother. Despite the faltering of marriage, the term mother-in-law is still used by non-married, particularly cohabiting couples. The title is unlikely to become extinct and there is no shortage of mothers-in-law or of stories about them.

History is full of quotations from mothers-in-law who have underestimated their sons-in-law. The Norwegian composer Grieg's mother-in-law said of him, 'He is nothing and has nothing, and he writes music which no one wants to hear.' The first meeting between the mother-in-law and daughter-in-law is also the stuff of legend because it can decide the course of the relationship. It was with these concerns in mind that the film star Marilyn Monroe was introduced to the mother of the playwright Arthur Miller, to whom she was already engaged. The couple went for dinner at Mrs Miller's small apartment in the Bronx and Marilyn was getting on well with her prospective mother-in-law, but just before they left she had to go to the toilet. There was only a flimsy door between the living room and the toilet, and to avoid the embarrassment of them hearing her in the other room she turned the taps fully on. She came out, they said goodbye warmly and the next day Arthur phoned his mother and asked, 'How did you like her?' To which his mother replied, 'She's sweet. A wonderful, wonderful girl but she pisses like a horse!'

Like the role of women generally, that of the mother-in-law has changed throughout history, its influence affected by prevailing political and social conditions. We can start our history with the Bible which includes one of the most idealised stories about a mother-in-law and daughter-in-law. For those who may not know the story, here is a short reprise. Naomi was an Ephrathite and her daughter-in-law Ruth a Moabite (the two races were long-standing enemies). When Ruth's husband died, Naomi, also a widow, set off home to Bethlehem and Ruth was bound by custom to follow her. Ruth would have been expected to marry one of Naomi's other sons and remain within the family, but her mother-in-law had no other sons. When Naomi and Ruth reached the road to Moab, Naomi, realising her daughter-in-law would be condemned to a loveless and childless life, begged her to leave her and return home. To which Ruth gave her legendary reply: 'Don't ask me to leave you. Let me go with you. Wherever you go, I will go; wherever you live, I will live. Your people will be my people and your God will be my God. Wherever you die, I will die and that is where I will be buried.' Why Naomi deserved such unconditional love is assumed rather than explained, although releasing Ruth from her obligation to accompany her to Bethlehem would have been a considerable sacrifice. Ruth went on to marry Boaz, a relative of Naomi, providing her mother-in-law with a child who was effectively her grandson (and through whose line King David was born). As the women of the family said to

Naomi, 'Your daughter-in-law loves you and has done more for you than seven sons.'

A more unsavoury mother-in-law makes an appearance between 405 and 359 BC in Persia, when Plutarch describes how Queen Parysatis poisoned her daughter-in-law, Statira, who had offended her. Poison was put on one side of a knife and used to cut a small bird served up at the supper table. The Queen took the non-poisoned side and had a taste to reassure her daughter-in-law, who promptly took one bite, convulsed and died.

In ancient Rome, the satirist Juvenal in the first century AD took a harsh view of mothers-in-law. 'Give up all hope of peace as long as your mother-in-law is alive,' he wrote, arguing that they taught their daughters 'evil habits'. Do not assume, however, that mothers-in-law were singled out for vitriol: Juvenal had little good to say about any women, who were considered inferior to men in Roman society. This prevailing misogyny makes Terence's comedy *The Mother-in-law*, written in the second century BC, even more remarkable for its sympathetic portrayal of mothers-in-law. The story is of a newly married couple, Pamphilus and his young bride Philumena. While Pamphilus is at war, his wife finds out she is pregnant, which causes a problem because her husband believes they have never consummated their marriage. In fact he was the mysterious man who raped Philumena before the betrothal. Philumena rushes home to her mother, leaving her poor mother-in-law Sostrata accused of cruelty – for why else would the new bride have run away? Terence captures an early stereotype of the mother-in-law as Sostrata's husband rails at her: 'Mothers-in-law and daughters-in-law, they're all of one mind –

hating each other.' Sostrata answers, 'It's no easy matter to clear myself when they've got it into their heads that all mothers-in-law are unkind. I know I'm not: I've treated the girl as my own daughter and I just can't think how this could happen to me.' In the event it is the couple's two mothers-in-law who sort out the comedy of misunderstandings and reunite them.

Rome had its own formidable cast of flesh-and-blood mothers-in-law who were caught up in political intrigues, limited by only being as influential as the men in power allowed them to be. Servilia Caepionis, a strong-willed and wealthy patrician, was the mistress of Julius Caesar in 63 BC. Caesar was said to have loved her passionately, giving her a priceless black pearl as a sign of his devotion, but Servilia had other allegiances, notably an association with a murderous son-in-law. She may have been fond of Caesar but it was her son Brutus and son-in-law Cassius who assassinated him and met afterwards at her home. Servilia's involvement could not be proved and she managed not only to escape punishment but to keep her wealth during the following reign of Augustus.

Mothers-in-law in Rome could never be complacent. At any moment, political expediency could mean they could lose a daughter-in-law or be forced themselves to marry a man who had once been their son-in-law. Marriages in Rome were for the advancement of the patriarch's political ambition and could become absurd. The Emperor Augustus, for example, made Tiberius Claudius Nero divorce Vipsania, whom he deeply loved, and marry his own mother-in-law Julia – the two were never happy together.

Antipathy as a motif for the mother-in-law and daughter-in-law relationship was already prevalent in the stories of the day.

The most famous Roman mythological example is that of Psyche and Venus (Psyche and Aphrodite in Greek). The tale reflects well-recognised themes of this relationship: a mother-in-law envious of her daughter-in-law's beauty and so devastated at the transference of her son's love that as soon as she gets the opportunity she makes her daughter-in-law's life a misery. Psyche was a beautiful mortal whose loveliness made Venus, the goddess of beauty, so jealous (mortals were getting confused and beginning to worship Psyche) that she asked her son Cupid to make Psyche fall in love with the most hideous creature in the world. Cupid, however, falls in love with Psyche himself and they marry, the idyll only being broken when his wife steals a look at him. Cupid rushes home to his mother and Psyche follows him, begging her mother-in-law to let her see him. Venus sets her an increasingly impossible set of tasks which she manages to complete only with the help of the gods. Eventually Jupiter intervenes and under pressure Venus embraces Psyche as a daughter. Unfortunately, in real life, divine intervention is not available.

It wasn't until the Middle Ages that mothers-in-law became more visible. Previously they had been discussed historically as bundled with other older women who had household and childcare duties. Viking mothers-in-law stayed at home while their sons-in-law went off on expeditions and for this period of history they, like all women in that society, had a relatively high status. Upon marriage a bride-price was paid by the bride's mother, who would have been involved in arranging the marriage, but it was kept by the bride. Mothers-in-law are not pilloried in Viking stories of the time (it is gossips and servants who are the butt of jokes about family life), nor are they in Anglo-Saxon or Norman times. This may be because marriages did not last long, frequently being ended by early deaths, and also because kinship was of increasing importance. The term 'in-law' comes from French and was imported after the Norman Conquest of 1066. Prior to that mothers-in-law may have been referred to by the Latin term *socra*.

By the late Middle Ages mothers-in-law emerge in the writings of the time as women who have a recognisable position in the family. But they are the villains of choice in these sources. Chaucer is not known for his sympathetic female protagonists but he surpasses himself in 'The Man of Law's Tale' by creating two of the most pernicious mothers-in-law in literature. The story is an allegory of unshakeable Christian belief; Constance is the Christian heroine who is beautiful, good and chaste, while her first mother-in-law is a Muslim and that of her second marriage a pagan. Both try to kill her (the pagan one also tries to kill Constance's newborn son) using the same technique, casting her adrift in a boat, but Christianity prevails and Constance, her son and her second husband are reunited. Both the mothers-in-law come to a sticky end, the pagan one being killed by her own son. Chaucer's characterisations show the unnaturalness of the mother-in-law and daughter-in-law relationship; the pagan mother-in-law has no natural maternal feelings for either her daughter-in-law or her baby grandson.

Chaucer did not reflect the contemporary realities of this relationship in British society, where the lives of mothers-in-law and their daughters-in-law were becoming more closely intertwined from economic necessity. Mothers-in-law had some superiority because of their age and perceived wisdom, but the two women typically worked together. If the men in the household had to travel for work, their role was to look after their husbands' and sons' properties. The fifteenth-century Paston Letters are a collection of over four hundred letters from a prominent Norfolk family, over a hundred of them written by three generations of Paston women. Agnes is the mother-in-law, Margaret her daughter-in-law and Margery the wife of one of Margaret's sons. The letters depict the patriarchal society they lived in (each of the women brought lands with her when they married into the Paston family). They show their responsibilities for running the household and arranging marriages but also their role in running the properties and the retainers (an occasionally violent occupation as aristocrats tried to appropriate their lands) while their husbands were working away from home. It was Agnes who arranged for Margaret to meet her son John. She wrote to her husband about the first meeting: '. . . as for the first acquaintance between John Paston and the said gentlewoman, she welcomed him kindly and courteously and said he was truly your son. And so I hope no great negotiation shall be needed between them.' There was no protracted negotiation; Margaret brought even more land into the Paston family than her mother-in-law had done. After the marriage Margaret referred to Agnes as 'Mother'. Writing to her husband as he lay sick in London, and concerned that he was not being adequately cared for, she wrote: '... on my word of honour, my mother and I have not been easy in our hearts from the time that we knew of your illness until we knew for certain of your improvement.'

Mother-in-law and daughter-in-law often had to stand shoulder to shoulder against attacks on their properties, both enduring and shouting insults. Margaret told John of one such attack on her chaplain James Gloys by John Wymondham, a follower of an aristocratic family with designs on the Paston lands, who set upon Margaret and her mother-in-law as they were coming out of Mass: 'Wymondham called my mother and me flagrant whores ... We said he lied, knave and churl that he was.' In the face of such an onslaught, mothers-in-law and daughters-in-law would have felt solidarity. Margery, Margaret's daughter-in-law, writes a letter to her mother-in-law in 1477 arranging for her to meet her own mother in Norwich and affirming her affection for her mother-in-law. 'I trow ther is not a kinder woman leueing then I shall haue to my modyr in lawe ...'

It is, as usual, left to Shakespeare to first describe a relationship between mother-in-law and daughter-in-law that has any emotional depth. *All's Well that Ends Well* is perhaps an early example of a modern phenomenon, that of a mother-in-law approving more of her daughter-in-law than of her son.

Bertram, the love of Helena's life, is unaware of Helena's devotion, but when she courageously saves the King of France's life, the King grants her the choice of a husband. She chooses Bertram who cruelly rejects her, refuses to live as her husband and leaves the court.

The Countess, who is Helena's mother-in-law, has loved her for many years, having protected her since her father died. She supports Helena in her campaign to win her son's heart and, while she loves her son, is furious with him, declaring, 'She deserved a lord, / That twenty such rude boys might tend upon / And call her hourly mistress.' The Countess even has to suffer the possibility that Helena's plot to win her son's affections has gone wrong and that her son has murdered her beloved daughter-in-law. When Helena returns, having won her husband's love, to claim her place as his wife, the emotional climax of the play shifts to the maternal relationship she has with her mother-in-law, who has collapsed under the strain: 'O dear mother, do I see you living?'

In the bloody and bawdy Tudor times some mothers realised that good marriages for their children could provide influence for themselves (see Chapter Seven). As mothers-in-law they schemed for power with variable success. In France Catherine de' Medici was a tour de force as a mother-in-law, grabbing back the crown jewels and brushing aside her disrespectful daughter-in-law Mary (who would go on to be Mary Queen of Scots) within hours of her son Francis II of France dying of an infection. Catherine, as the mother of France's next king, tried to secure the best marriages she could for her children, essentially to safeguard France's future. When she tried to get her own daughter Mary to marry King Philip of Spain's brain-damaged son (and thus obtain more protection for France), Philip, who was himself already a son-in-law of Catherine through marriage to her oldest daughter Elizabeth, made a series of excuses to avoid any further connection with his mother-in-law. He had had enough of her dynastic ambitions already.

Mothers-in-law generally became more prominent over the next few hundred years. Britain and much of the world were patrilocal societies in which brides and their properties joined their husband's families. But does this mean they invariably lived with their mothers-in-law? The historical evidence does not support this, although the influence of the mother-in-law may have been exerted outside of the couple's dwelling. Data collected from thirteen English parishes between 1600 and 1799 shows surprising demographic characteristics: for most of this period the average age of marriage was twenty-seven to twenty-eight for a man and twenty-five to twenty-six for a woman (these ages fell later in the eighteenth century). Wealthy families may have been large but most working-class families were small, their children being sent away to work as soon as they were able.

It was actually unusual to have three generations living together. In one study of parish data between 1574 and 1821 only five per cent of families lived in this arrangement. Kinship responsibilities clearly extended beyond the locality. The diaries of the Reverend Ralph Josselin (1617–83) show how the wider kinship system worked. His uncle helped him to get his first living, and Ralph helped his sister school her children when her husband died. His relationships with his wife Jane's immediate family were close. His father-in-law came for a visit and stayed for two years; her mother came to help after Jane had their first baby.

Mothers-in-law were meanwhile gaining a reputation for being able to humiliate their sons-in-law. An early example played out in France in the late 1700s, where Louis XVI had a formidable mother-in-law in the Empress Maria Theresa. He and his wife, Marie Antoinette, were known to have problems consummating their marriage and Maria Theresa was quick to write to her ambassador at Versailles saying, 'I refuse to believe it is my daughter's fault.' She insisted her son-in-law had a narrowing of his penis which meant it didn't work properly (in fact he didn't know how to have sex with his wife and was removing his penis without ejaculating). This widely disseminated letter didn't do Louis's standing much good, although the ridicule brought upon the King by his mother-in-law was not the only reason he was executed.

Around this time evidence was accumulating which would later point to the evolutionary significance of the mother-in-law and daughter-in-law relationship. Try as they might to be civilised to each other, mothers-in-law and daughters-in-law have considerable evolutionary baggage to negotiate. This evidence was discovered in an area of north-west Germany called Krummhorn by two twentieth-century evolutionary psychologists, Eckart Völand and Jan Beise, who trawled through the local parish records between 1750 and 1874. There were around six thousand legitimate births during this period. Völand and Beise found that if a woman lived in the same parish as her mother-in-law she had an increased risk of having a stillborn child. The risk rose if her own mother was dead, to two and half times higher than the average rate, and this effect was still there when other factors known to increase the likelihood of a stillbirth were taken into account. Having a mother-in-law nearby also increased the risk of having a baby die in the first month of its life. How could mothers-in-law have such a deadly impact? If they had conflicts with their pregnant daughters-in-law, this could have caused sufficient stress to inhibit the growth of the developing fetus, and smaller babies would have had an increased risk of dying in the first month of life. There was a telling proverb at the time, '*Mann's Moo'r is de Düvel over de Floo'er*,' which translates as 'The husband's mother is the devil in the kitchen.'

Assuming mothers-in-law were not really devils, what would be the evolutionary rationale for their presence having such an adverse effect on their daughters-in-law? The answer lies in their conflicting interests. Mothers-in-law were committed to progressing their sons' lineage, acting as 'mate guarders' to ensure that their sons were not cuckolded (a terrible humiliation). In the absence of modern technology their oversight might have involved some degree of harassment of their daughters-in-law and the occasional false accusation to keep them on their toes. The families of that time, in that area, were strict Calvinists and the mothers-in-law may have put their daughters-in-law under considerable stress with harsh discipline and close monitoring of daily activities. Mothers-in-law were also in conflict with their daughters-in-law because their power was dependent on their bonds with their sons and this was the primary relationship they sought to maintain.

Even in economic terms, the interests of mothers-in-law and daughters-in-law were not aligned. Mothers-in-law might have preferred their daughters-in-law to toil in the fields rather than see any of their own family working hard. It was an exploitative relationship, where newborn babies were largely replaceable, as were young wives, as long as there were enough women of childbearing age around (which was not always the case).

These farming communities were not sentimental. So out of these often cruel conditions, daughters-in-law told stories and sang songs about their wicked mothers-in-law. Young women would also have been told these stories before marriage, as cautionary tales. If they didn't work hard or were disobedient, their mothers-in-law could force them to do impossible, backbreaking tasks and deprive them of food, clothes and their husbands' love. This evolutionary conflict of interests is so widespread among populations, being noted in such diverse regions as the Sudan, the Bolivian highlands, Israel and rural Taiwan, that it may persist at a modern, albeit subliminal level. There is no need, in survival terms, for women not to get on with their mothers-in-law but perhaps there is a residual unease. Underlying this conflict, after all, is a factor that has not changed over thousands of years – the belief that a mother will put her son's interests above that of her daughter-in-law.

In Britain, the late eighteenth century was the age of the domineering mother-in-law. Novelists and playwrights created some masterpieces of mothers-in-law, characterisations of loud, dominating women who would put any suitors off marrying their daughters. Mrs Bennet in Jane Austen's *Pride and Prejudice*, written between 1797 and 1813, is a comic depiction of a woman so totally wanting in 'propriety' that she is a liability and risks making her daughters unmarriageable. When Darcy, the proud and solemn hero, proposes to Elizabeth Bennet he blurts out that he has struggled to overcome his attachment to her because her mother is so vulgar. Elizabeth initially doesn't take this too well, but true love prevails and is preserved by the silly Mrs Bennet being too scared of her son-in-law ever to visit the couple. However, revisionists have been more sympathetic to Mrs Bennet, arguing that to have five girls to marry off would make anyone slightly crazy.

In comparison mothers-in-law in French literature were being given a more tragic treatment. *Thérèse Raquin* by Emile Zola, written in 1867, is a grim tale of a mother's nightmare, the murder of her son by her daughter-in-law and her daughter-in-law's lover. Madame Raquin, a poor widow, is not a good judge of character. She says of her daughter-in-law, 'Her face looks unfriendly, I know, but her heart is warm with every kind of affection and devotion.' So what does her daughter-in-law say about Madame Raquin? 'I don't give a damn about her.' Madame Raquin has no idea of her daughter-in-law's guilt. It is only when she is old and paralysed, in the care of Thérèse and her lover in her cramped little haberdashery shop, that the couple admit their guilt in her presence. Madame Raquin can say or do nothing to denounce them and her suffering is painfully described. For her at least there is a happy ending; her torment ends when the evil couple self-destruct in front of her.

Was it the cramped conditions that encouraged such perfidious daughter-in-law behaviour? If so there would have been an epidemic. From the later 1700s up until the 1900s living standards in Europe were gradually rising, life expectancy was increasing and people were marrying at a young age. Rather than being responsible for the creation of the isolated nuclear family (which did already exist) the industrial revolution may have actually promoted more extended families. Factory workers often lived with their parents after marriage, as did other members of the family. Housing was too expensive and sometimes too scarce for young married couples to do anything other than move in with one set of in-laws. Married daughters would often move in with or close to their mothers, relying on them for childcare if they needed to work and for advice and reassurance in their new role. Mothers-in-law began to impinge more on the lives of their sons-in-law, eliciting reactions that would play out in the music halls and later in the repertoire of stand-up comics.

Husbands often felt excluded and threatened, afraid that their wives were moaning to their mothers about them and being influenced by their old family ties. Their children often had close relationships with their 'Nanas' and when re-housing schemes threatened to split up these generational supports, families would resort to visiting their in-laws with their children at weekends. But the age of the 'evil' mother-in-law was over. It was daughters-in-law who now held the power in most westernised countries; mothers-in-law might meddle, but they had no direct authority over their daughters-in-law. The Victorians, buoyed by a strong sense of morality and kinship, valued the extended family and would have been openly respectful to their mothers-in-law. But now mothers-in-law, because of demographic changes and the increased proximity they had to their daughters' families, became the butt of humorous songs, stories and jokes, told exclusively by men. Mothers-in-law were lampooned with impunity in music halls from the 1850s onwards and portrayed on saucy seaside postcards as lascivious and sexually repulsive. The jokes were overwhelmingly hostile and abusive. Feminists have argued that such humour is a form of social control; mothers-in-law can't take offence because they will be accused of not being able to take a joke, which is a serious indictment (see Chapter Nine).

Through the two world wars, mothers-in-law became almost an endangered species; nearly one million young men were killed in the First World War alone, leaving a generation of unmarried women and a consequent shortage of mothers-in-law. One mother-in-law whose heroism we should note in passing was Alice, Princess Andrew of Greece, mother-in-law of Queen Elizabeth II. During the Second World War Alice hid the Cohens, a Jewish family, from the Nazis in occupied Athens (their father had helped the Greek royal family during a flood in 1913), pretending that the widowed mother was her former governess, and ensuring that she and her sons escaped the death camps. For this, Alice (who never spoke about her role in saving the Cohens) was posthumously awarded by the Holocaust Memorial in Jerusalem the title 'Righteous among the Nations'.

After the wars, despite a programme of house-building in the first half of the twentieth century, there were still shortages and even where there was housing it was sometimes so expensive that married couples chose to stay with their in-laws. In the United States at the end of the 1940s a third of newly married couples lived with relatives in the first two years of marriage. In Britain and the US television sitcoms made humour out of the tensions between young couples and their mothers-in-law: in particular, the inability to have sex for fear of being heard was a recurring joke.

Mothers-in-law now became subject to the scrutiny of psychotherapists and social psychologists and were judged to have a pernicious influence on those around them. Freud had already declared in *Totem and Taboo* that sons-in-law in 'savage societies' avoided their mothers-in-law in order to reduce the risk of incest between the two. More populist research brought up the

now familiar areas of conflict, daughters-in-law who felt they
would never be good enough, mothers-in-law who felt excluded
from the lives of their married sons. No less a mother-in-law
than Margaret Thatcher, Britain's first woman prime minister
and notable 'Iron Lady', was accused by her daughter-in-law
Diane of creating a 'mummy's boy' capable of regressing to a
helpless child who depended on his mother to do his washing

and ironing. Their marriage collapsed after eighteen years, but
this may have had more to do with Mark's alleged involvement
in a coup plot in Equatorial Guinea than the few shirts ironed by
his mother.

So what will become of mothers-in-law during this millen-
nium? More women are working, the population is ageing,
marriage is on the decline and even in societies where mothers-
in-law have traditionally been powerful figures, such as India
and China, their influence is waning. It is already a more temporary role, as in western societies two out of five marriages
end in divorce and cohabiting relationships are even shorter.
Mothers-in-law who want to keep seeing their grandchildren
often have to go through their ex-daughter-in-law, an access
that can depend on the quality of the two women's relationship
and has led to pressure groups of grandparents arguing for
legal rights. As mothers-in-law themselves work and have busy
lives they may be both less judgemental of their daughters-in-
law and less available to do the meddling they have traditionally been accused of. Now the charge is more likely to be that
they aren't around enough to help.

In the West, marriages and cohabiting relationships between
couples of the same sex have made the role of mother-in-law
accessible to more women. But there has been opposition to
this extension. When the US secretary of state Condoleezza
Rice swore in Mark Dybul, an openly gay man, as Global AIDS
Co-ordinator in 2007, it caused some stirrings in conservative
quarters, but this was nothing in comparison to the outrage she
provoked when she referred to Mark's partner's mother as his
mother-in-law. 'To treat his partner like a spouse and treat the
partner's mother as a mother-in-law, which implies a marriage

between the two partners, is a violation of the spirit if not the letter of the Defence of Marriage Act,' complained the Family Research Council, a US conservative think-tank.

Twenty-first-century mothers-in-law still arouse strong feelings, perhaps more from their daughters-in-law than sons-in-law. These feelings have found a vent on the internet where websites have sprung up with stories of the rudeness of mothers-in-law, their emotional cruelty and, worst of all, their terrible choice of presents, from crotchless pants to prenatal vitamins (see Chapter Eleven).

As this generation of mothers-in-law ages it is unlikely that their sons and daughters-in-law will look after them. The difficulties of doing so are captured touchingly in David Haynes's novel *Somebody Else's Mama*, which tells the story of Paula, who insists on taking her sick, elderly mother-in-law, 'Miss Kezee', to live with her husband and two children in St Paul in the mid-West of America. Cantankerous and ungrateful Miss Kezee has a commentary about her daughter-in-law running in her head: 'Cheap little gal. Stingy and ornery. Wouldn't give a drowning man a glass of piss water . . .' Yet her view of her daughter-in-law changes over time: 'She may be simple and have soddity ways but her heart is as big as the moon. She tries to cover it, but I can see through her. She bruises easily as a peach.' By the end of the novel the two embark on a road trip together that will take Miss Kezee back to her own home. But outside fiction, close relationships between ageing mothers-in-law and their daughters-in-law, with wisdom passed on from years of experience, are likely to become rarer.

A more contemporary and funny real-life portrayal is that of Suad Amiry's ninety-two-year-old mother-in-law in *Sharon and my Mother-in-Law*, which describes how Amiry had to rescue and house her during the Israeli occupation of Ramallah in 2002. As Amiry reaches her mother-in-law's house during a break in the curfew, Um Salim starts crying with relief at seeing her. Amiry tries to get her to hurry:

'OK mother, let's get out of here as soon as possible. The army is surrounding the building and we have to move quickly.'

'Shall I bring my purple dress?' she enquired.

'Fine, yes, purple is nice.'

'But where is it?'

Once they find it Um Salim has another question.

'Do you think yellow goes with purple?'

'Yes, yellow is very nice with purple; all colours are nice with purple.'

'But I cannot find my yellow blouse.'

The first thing Um Salim says when she wakes up the next day, in the safety of her daughter-in-law's house, is, 'What a pity we did not carry the begonia pot with us that you gave me on Easter Monday.' Amiry blames the Israelis not only for occupying Ramallah but for forcing her to live with her mother-in-law. (Um Salim's honorific title itself underlines her role as mother-in-law – it means 'mother of Salim'.)

This generation of mothers-in-law may be more sensitive about their role, more introspective, more aware of why they might have conflicting feelings when their children develop long-term relationships or marry. They may desire to do better than their own mothers-in-law. In the novel *Mother-in-law Diaries*, Lulu Penfield, a former 'free spirit', finds that when her son announces he has been living with someone for six months, she cannot help but be venomous to both him and his girlfriend.

She feels she has had the role of mother ripped from her, to be replaced with the unwanted one of mother-in-law. But she rapidly retreats from her position, realising how her rejection has crushed them. 'There's one thing I've learned for sure. Mothers-in-law possess a power, whether we want it or not. Every phrase we speak carries pressure ... When I see you during our visits, I can bring in the shadow of my presence either good or evil; without even realising it I might sweeten your morning or lace it with alkali. So now daily I learn a new kind of diplomacy: thoughtfulness, restraint.' As we shall see in Chapter Twelve, these qualities are the ones most likely to make the mother-in-law–daughter-in-law relationship successful.

So as this history closes, what do we think of mothers-in-law today? Canadians are apparently very fond of them, with over ninety per cent saying they 'love' their mothers-in-law and nearly one in ten saying they are closer to their mothers-in-law than their own mothers (admittedly these figures are from a survey by Hallmark, which sells cards for people who love their mothers-in-law). From Florida comes a moving and remarkable story of Staff Sergeant Roberto Carrizales, a Communications Squadron ground radio journeyman who donated a kidney to his mother-in-law after her own kidneys were damaged by diabetes. None of her blood relatives had been a suitable donor but Roberto volunteered to be tested and found he was a match. His mother-in-law is now in good health. 'Saving a life is a good feeling in itself and the feeling is even greater when it's someone you love,' he said.

Meanwhile, in Warrington in the north of England, loving your mother-in-law took on a different meaning when in 2007 Clive Blunden married his former mother-in-law. The two fell in love four years after he had divorced her daughter. In marrying his mother-in-law he made a successful legal challenge to an ancient law forbidding this practice. This is, however, unlikely to precipitate a rush of similar events. The accounts of relationships with mothers-in-law throughout the rest of this book are of the more usual kind.

Melanie on her mother-in-law

I think one of the most interesting aspects of my relationship with my mother-in-law is that we come from very different worlds. We come from opposite ones in some ways and there was a bit of a clash at the beginning due to mutual ignorance. But we have grown to respect each other. I am from a Greek-American background, with the usual associations of hospitality, generosity, family-orientation and big emotions. My mother-in-law, on the other hand, is Dutch. What defines her is frugality; a certain Calvinist dourness or lack of affection or emotion; an intense practicality; and a certain kind of black-and-white stubbornness. I didn't understand these qualities for many years and I thought they showed cynicism and selfishness. Now I've come to understand them better. I realise that I've come from a country (and generation) of plenty, whereas she lived through the Second World War in Holland when it was occupied by the Germans. There was so little food she had to eat cat meat.

My mother-in-law continues to be frugal and she thinks that the generosity my family instilled in me (a cultural tradition) is wasteful. She doesn't find it touching. I found her intimidating at our first meeting. She had and continued to have long conversations with my husband in Dutch and by doing this she seemed aloof and exclusive. She seemed to judge me for everything. I am a poet and I work at home. I could tell that she thought my having a nanny, so that I could work, was wasteful and that it was ridiculous that I didn't cook every night. In her mind I didn't need a nanny because I didn't have a proper career. Her idea of a career is something that is regular and makes proper money, like working in a large corporation. I had had other prospective mothers-in-law and they had all been warm to me and interested in me. My mother-in-law didn't seem to have anything in common with me. We did have a big fat Greek wedding because my family is from the generation that needs to show off. It was nothing like the simple Dutch weddings my mother-in-law was used to. Some of the Dutch relatives said it was like a Mafia wedding. But my mother-in-law never criticised us about any aspect of our wedding.

As I grow older I don't see things in such black-and-white terms any more. My husband and I went through a bad patch in our marriage and I felt as though I had one foot out of the marriage for a time. What my mother-in-law thought of me, therefore, mattered less. And part of my acceptance of my mother-in-law was that I became able to see things from her point of view. I could see why, because she grew up with so little, she thought I was wasteful. I know there are some things I do that will never please her but I know that we both wish each other well.

She recently asked my husband and me to help her fill out some forms to do with 'dying with dignity'. She does not want to ever be put on life support unnecessarily and so she has taken the practical step of filling out forms detailing her wishes. I imagine that's quite rare. And although she is frustrated with her health, she accepts it. She looks after her husband, whose health is similarly erratic. They do not complain, or ask us for help, whereas my own parents, after a lifetime of giving and giving to their children, would have very high expectations of being looked after by us, even at the expense of our own families, work and happiness.

My mother-in-law is clear that she does not want to be a burden to us; she is very stoic. So I can see that her ability to be practical above emotional works very well in certain circumstances and that it can be admirable. I can see the upside of a personal trait that was initially unappealing to me.

We all grow up thinking that the way we are is the only desirable way to be but as we mature we realise this isn't so. I'm not a perfect daughter-in-law. I know for example that I forget to send birthday cards when in Dutch culture it is important to send birthday cards. My parents are full of love and grand gestures for their grandchildren but can't really help me out because they live three thousand miles away, whereas my mother-in-law who lives nearby is very much an absentee grandmother. She was never interested in babysitting or helping out. I used to resent this, because it was so different to what I know. But now I realise this is part and parcel of her culture, and not a reason to judge her.

Mothers-in-law in Different Cultures

It was the anthropologist Margaret Mead who said, 'Of all the people I have studied, from city dwellers to cliff dwellers, I always find that at least fifty per cent would prefer to have at least one jungle between themselves and their mothers-in-law.'

This leaves a sizeable proportion of sons- and daughters-in-law, however, who can manage without an impenetrable natural barrier between them and their mothers-in-law. This is remarkable given that the patriarchal societies of many cultures have been conducive to fostering the worst possible relationships between mothers-in-law and their daughters-in-law. The mother-in-law in Asian, Middle Eastern and some Mediterranean cultures has traditionally been the queen bee of the household, a revered older woman whose job it is to socialise her daughters-in-law into her family's customs and ways of life. Whether she does this with kindness or cruelty is not mandated. In many Asian countries daughters-in-law call their mothers-in-law 'mother'; to do otherwise would be rude. A daughter-in-law joins a family not for romantic reasons (marriages are traditionally arranged by go-betweens and mothers) but for production purposes. Her role is to serve her new family and to provide the heir. The servitude, in her mother-in-law's mind, ideally lasts long enough for her to look after her elderly in-laws as they become infirm. When the daughter-in-law has a son and becomes a mother-in-law herself, it becomes her turn to rule the household and have governance of her own daughter-in-law. Sons-in-law are largely absent from this account, either because their mothers-in-law live some distance away and they never see them, or because they are forbidden, for reasons to be discussed shortly, to look at or touch their mothers-in-law.

Many of these practices are gradually being eroded, but historically daughters-in-law often felt desperately lonely and confined in their new homes. They poured their sorrow into songs and stories. Their plight is summarised in the Japanese proverb: 'The daughter-in-law who was bullied by her mother-in-law bullies her daughter-in-law in revenge.' Whatever the reality, this sentiment has international resonance. It is repeated in similar sayings in many different languages. How systemic this sort of relationship was is difficult to know. Mothers-in-law could also be kindly to their young daughters-in-law and guide them gently into their new homes, helping them with domestic affairs. Such behaviour was unlikely to inspire songs and poems, so it is the legacy of unkindness that endures.

Increasingly, however, the status of older people in many societies is being diminished, leaving mothers-in-law vulnerable in their old age. Urbanisation and the desire of women to live apart from their mothers-in-law and to work outside the home have left poorer mothers-in-law in particular more likely to try to placate than berate their daughters-in-law. There is now a saying in southern India: 'Here it is the daughter-in-law who lies on the bed ordering her mother-in-law around.'

Before we look at the changes in the status of mothers-in-law, we should have some sense of their traditional standing.

Some of the oldest cultures have elaborate customs around mothers-in-law due to their particular marriage rituals. The Australian anthropologist Adolphus Peter Elkin remarked in the 1930s that 'The tendency amongst the Australian Aborigines is to select the mother-in-law rather than the wife.' The senior men in the village would agree to a young girl being allocated to a young man, but this did not mean that those two would get married when they were older. Under this arrangement the girl would grow up and marry someone else and it would be her daughter who would marry the specified man. The young man was actually being allocated a mother-in-law and would have to wait a generation before this arrangement produced a wife for him. Husbands were thus much older than their wives. The term given to the young girl at the time of her allocation was *tualcha mura*, meaning 'the mother of the woman who is allotted to me'.

This is tricky enough, but the closeness in age between the son-in-law and his mother-in-law meant they were also much more likely to find each other sexually attractive, necessitating strict social avoidance rituals to avoid any sexual contact developing between them. The results of such a union could be disastrous. If a man had sex with his mother-in-law she could give birth to a daughter who would then be expected to marry her own father. Professor Elkin wrote, 'The severest taboo is that which is observed all over Australia between a man and his wife's mother . . . son-in-law and mother-in-law must neither see nor speak to each other.' Mothers-in-law and their sons-in-law where this practice occurs must therefore not look at each other; they must sit facing different directions if in the same vehicle and only sleep in the same house if a physical barrier is placed between them. Mothers-in-law and sons-in-law can talk to each other only through someone else, such as their daughter, and they use avoidance language, a variation of everyday language with similar grammar but a more restricted vocabulary – for example, in one Aboriginal tribe the word *ginga* (a porcupine-like animal) in 'mother-in-law language' makes do for two words in usual vocabulary, *gumbyan* (porcupine) and *ginga* (pig). The use of avoidance language and behaviour is extended to cover the wife's grandmother and brothers, indeed anyone who is related by blood through the same line of women. Avoidance is still used in Aboriginal societies although marriage choice has been relaxed and it is now not uncommon for couples to choose each other and live together before marriage.

This mother-in-law avoidance is also practised among the Korowai in Papua New Guinea, who live in tropical rainforests in the west of the country. Marriages tend to be between younger women and older men, arranged by senior relatives, usually men, when a man has shown interest in the young woman. Usually it is the woman who moves to her husband's home when married, but she is likely to have her own mother to stay fairly often. Her own mother and her husband must not come into each other's line of vision and to make sure they do not bump into each other in the same house, they shout out warnings to each other. Mothers-in-law do not use the son-in-law's name but refer to him in terms of his relationship with their grandson or wife, for example 'the father of Adoni'. They will talk to each other but only with a barrier between them (houses are built with panels for this purpose) and using avoidance language. Their food is cooked separately; they will not use each other's towels or sheets or drink from the same cup.

The reasons for this are based more on superstitions than on concerns that mothers-in-law and sons-in-law will have carnal relations. If a mother-in-law and son-in-law accidentally see each other, both will worry that the wife or the children will become sick and die. It is against the natural order of the family for the two to overlap in any area that should belong to a son-in-law and his wife. This avoidance continues even if the wife dies, but may be broken if the son-in-law is not approved of or hasn't provided sufficient presents at the wedding.

American Indians had different customs for mothers-in-law, depending on their tribe. Navajo men, for example, observed avoidance rules but in the Cheyenne tribe, where a man would move into his mother-in-law's lodge, the reason for not speaking was that he had to prove himself worthy before doing so. When a son-in-law had proved himself in battle and brought trohpies back to his mother-in-law, she would fully acknowledge him by presenting him with a buffalo robe that would have taken her months of work to make.

China has historically given mothers-in-law considerable power in the family but in the context of a strong patriarchal society where women were largely invisible even within the home (where they would sit apart from the men behind panels). The reverence due to mothers and fathers (and hence to in-laws) was based on a small book called the *Classic of Filial Piety*, a lesson from Confucius to a disciple on how everyone in the family has his or her place and how if sons did not show loyalty and care to their parents, chaos would ensue. The feelings of women are under-represented in Chinese history, where the literature was overwhelmingly written by men.

In the Sung period between 960 and 1279, when life generally got worse for all women (for example footbinding became widespread), sons stayed home to continue their bloodline and a young bride would be moved from being submissive within her own family to being further subjugated in her new one. Marriages were arranged as unions of families and ideally one's children married 'upwards', regardless of how far away a husband's family lived or whether he still had teeth. Writers of the time describe daughters-in-law sewing, cooking and serving their mothers-in-law devotedly, as to allow servants to perform these tasks would be disrespectful to the mother-in-law.

Daughters-in-law became parodies of subservience in their relationships with their mothers-in-law. Sometimes this was out of fear. There were tales of mothers-in-law so strict that they would not allow their daughters-in-law to sit in their presence, and husbands who beat their wives to death for standing up to their mothers-in-law. A biography of a judge in the Sung period records the case of a man who killed his wife. His excuse? 'My mother was yelling at my wife and my wife was talking back. I couldn't take it and in my anger I beat her. By accident I killed her.' The judge was sympathetic and did not sentence him to death: 'Beating an unfilial daughter-in-law is not the same as killing a wife.' A young woman by the name of Sun Ju-Ching, on the other hand, was glorified in the writings of the day as the ideal daughter-in-law who refused to allow her mother-in-law to perform any physical tasks. When she became ill she nursed her, praying that her own life would be shortened if her mother-in-law could only live longer.

It was not until the Chinese Revolution and the onset of Communist Party rule in 1949 that things changed. The family, being so central to Chinese life, was bound to face reform and as early as 1950 the Marriage Act (or Divorce Act as it came to be known) dramatically reduced its power. A woman was still expected to move to her husband's house and look after his parents but she had the right to choose whom to marry and she could be paid for work outside the home. The old tradition of a bride-price and the marriage of child brides were made illegal, and women had the right to divorce. The Communists proudly announced they had ended the 'feudal marriage system arrangement'. Meanwhile in the villages older women resisted and there was a rise in murders and suicides of married women who presumably tried to take advantage of the new law but were obstructed by their families. Communist propaganda magazines of the time told stories of abusive mothers-in-law who were slow to change but were capable of redemption, which consisted of looking after the grandchildren while their daughters-in-law went out to work. In one fictional account, a mother-in-law admits to having the wrong kind of thinking. 'The law is right. Men and women should be equal. Mothers-in-law and daughters-in-law should live in harmony, we are all human beings. It was my old-fashioned mind that messed up everything and I'll have to change.'

Land reforms in the countryside reduced the amount of land available to families and many were split up, with some family members moving to the cities. Even so today's sons are still expected to uphold Confucian ideals and look after their parents, especially financially. Traditionally the oldest son still lives with his parents and gifts are still exchanged at the marriage. The man is expected to provide the house, the wife's family to furnish it and provide presents of clothing, jewellery and fabric, largely for the mother-in-law. If the daughter-in-law does not live with her mother-in-law she will still be expected, at family occasions, to make and serve the food and clean up afterwards while the mother-in-law and her daughters enjoy themselves. The best relationships between mothers-in-law and daughters-in-law are based on respect but this respect precludes them kissing or affectionately touching each other.

In Taiwan, the relationship between mothers-in-law and daughters-in-law has also changed in the past fifty years, with over half of all married women in paid employment outside the family even in rural areas. Financial independence and the growing acceptance of marrying for love, thus having a more equal relationship with their husbands, has put daughters-in-law in a more powerful position. In her study of mothers-in-law and daughters-in-law in Taiwan the anthropologist Rita S. Gallin interviewed sixty-five-year-old Mrs Shen, the wife of a farmer, who lived with her son and daughter-in-law and helped them look after their five children. She bemoaned her daughter-in-law's higher status. 'When we were married we cried because we belonged to another family. We had to cook and to serve others. We used to worry would they like our cooking. If they didn't your mother-in-law beat you. Now we are worthless. Women today are afraid of their daughters-in-law. They dare not criticise them. If you criticise a daughter-in-law she will run away. Daughters-in-law look at you with ugly faces.'

Japan, like China, has a history of servile daughters-in-law and dominant mothers-in-law which has also changed in recent years, in particular since the Second World War. In feudal Japan young women had arranged marriages and put up with husbands who were absent or unkind and with mothers-in-law who demanded absolute loyalty. Daughters-in-law could be sent home in disgrace if they did not pass muster and were meant to stay in the background, uncomplaining, even if their husband had concubines. This was the way of life for young brides up until the middle of the twentieth century.

The diary of a young bride called Makiko, started in 1910, enabled her descendants to see how family life was lived in the past. It details largely routine matters such as how her mother-in-law taught her to cook. Her husband was a merchant in Kyoto and her mother-in-law, Mine, whom she calls 'mother', is kind and supportive, encouraging her to learn western cooking and treating her like a daughter. Mine does her share of work in the house (Makiko's husband accuses his wife of depending too heavily on his mother's willingness to do housework) and allows Makiko time for herself – encouraging her to pursue outside and even rather racy interests such as seeing comedy troupes with a friend. The accounts of their relationship are given a businesslike airing with occasional exceptions, such as when Mine comes home after a trip away. 'Mother came back home around four o'clock this afternoon. While she was gone the house seemed empty and cold. I missed her very much, feeling cold and lonely, just like the weather has been the past few days. I am glad the house has come alive once again!' Mine died shortly after Makiko's first child was born and she undoubtedly missed her very much.

While the eldest son in Japan may still live with his mother, most marriages are no longer arranged although couples still seek approval from their parents. Daughters-in-law are twice as likely to work now as they were in the 1960s but the population is ageing sufficiently fast for the government to predict that by 2025 one in every two women will be involved in looking after a bedridden senior – usually a mother-in-law. Daughters-in-law may not choose to live with their mothers-in-law but families are still expected to look after their own when they are old and frail. Mothers-in-law must hope that this tradition endures.

The relationship between mother-in-law and daughter-in-law in India is largely known through stories of the avaricious demands of mothers-in-law for dowries. It has been illegal to demand a dowry for a bride for nearly half a century, but the tradition is so entrenched that it has continued relentlessly. Long after the wedding is over, it is not unusual for a husband to continue to ask his bride's family for financial help whenever he needs it, to buy a car or to set up a new business. Shamefully it is the mothers-in-law who put the most pressure on their daughters-in-law to finance their sons' schemes; brides who fail to provide enough money can be beaten, starved and even set alight. In a society that values men so much more highly than women, sons are said to have an 'umbilical attachment' to their mothers that isn't severed at birth. The combination of arranged marriages, oppressive demands for dowries and the tendency for some Indian mothers-in-law to treat their sons as deities has largely maintained the status of mothers-in-law at the expense of their daughters-in-law.

Daughters-in-law in India were brought into their husbands' families, and to prevent them feeling secure and becoming close to their husbands (which could tilt the balance of power in the family away from the mother-in-law) they could be subjected to a bitter regime of beatings, ridicule and rough work and denied contact with their husbands, at the mothers-in-law's behest. But economic changes such as the growth of job markets in urban areas have again shifted the power in this relationship. In her study of mothers-in-law and daughters-in-law in South India, the anthropologist Penny Vera-Sanso found that mothers-in-law in poorer urban areas lived in dread of being abandoned by their sons and daughters-in-law. Young couples here are more likely to set up nuclear families after a few years of marriage and it is left to the son who is in the least hurry to escape his parents to provide for them in later life, a more unstable arrangement than in previous generations. There is still a great deal of respect for elderly parents but enough stories about neglect to make mothers-in-law anxious.

To ensure that they will be looked after by their sons and daughters-in-law, elderly widows who are taken into their son's nuclear families have to adopt strategies that can include doing some of the menial work once reserved for their daughters-in-law. They will be found doing some of the demeaning jobs such as doing the laundry and cleaning toilets and are expected to contribute money if they are working outside the home. In situations in which mothers-in-law live in houses on subdivided land, with a son in the property next door, Vera-Sanso noticed that the mother-in-law's home tended to be more of a 'tumbled-down shack' while their son's property would be not only well maintained but usually improved. Mothers-in-law who doubt that any of their sons will look after them can 'buy' security in their old age by giving some of their property to a daughter who will then be obliged to support her.

Daughters-in-law are certainly less compliant than they used to be, but these women are still unusual and not supported by Indian customs or law. The Delhi High Court ruled recently that a husband can divorce his wife if she refuses to get on with her mother-in-law. A wife who left the family home because she hated her mother-in-law and refused to return until her mother-in-law had been sent away was judged to have deserted the marriage. A spokesman from the voluntary organisation HelpAge India commented, 'If people respect the senior members in a family it will create a peaceable atmosphere.'

If they are unable to do so it can have tragic consequences. The *Hindi Times* reports how in the village of Brahamansahi, in Ganjam, a married couple tried to kill themselves by drinking pesticide after arguing incessantly over who should look after the son's mother who was bedridden. His wife, Sumitra, who could no longer cope with the full-time nursing of her mother-in-law, died. Her husband survived in hospital. The mother-in-law, hearing of her son and daughter-in-law's suicide attempts, managed to crawl out of bed, find some pesticide herself and drink it. She too died.

In European countries disputes between mothers-in-law and their daughters-in-law may not lead to murder or suicide but they do lead to acrimony and divorce. In Italy mothers-in-law are being blamed for the rise in the divorce rate. A report from the research institute Eures found that the divorce rate had increased by nearly half between 2000 and 2002 and that three out of ten marriages were reported to have failed because of the unusually close attachment of Italian men to their mothers. There is even a word to describe sons who cling to their mother's apron strings: *mammoni*. Such is the love that Italian mothers stereotypically have for their sons that they will come round to their homes and take over the traditional role of the wife: cooking and ironing, and giving the impression that they know best. Dr Annamaria Cassanese, a Milanese psychologist who frequently sees daughters-in-law in her practice who feel marginalised by their mothers-in-law, believes that such mothers have an excessive form of maternal love that makes them feel jealous of their daughters-in-law. When a mother is crying at the wedding of her son, she warns, it is from the sorrow of losing him rather than the joy of seeing him happy with another woman.

Of course some of this stereotyping occurs in many cultures. At the risk of this book alienating mothers-in-law of every nationality, Greek and Turkish mothers-in-law, as well as Jewish mothers-in-law (about whom jokes abound), also stand accused of blind devotion to their sons, finding it inconceivable that any woman could be good enough for them. The Jewish Torah advises mothers-in-law and daughters-in-law to get along by respecting each other's contribution to the man they both love. Mothers-in-law must not live vicariously through their children. The Torah advises, 'A man shall leave his father and mother and cleave unto his wife.' If only it was that easy.

Eleanor on her Chinese mother-in-law

When the Communists came in they were keen to stamp out arranged marriages in China- it was one of the first things to go. Before then the first time you would have met your mother-in-law would have been when she (and your father-in-law) picked you out for their son. Parents wanted their children to marry up – it was like a Jane Austen novel.

Traditionally women married out of their family into the husband's family, but these days this is less likely to happen because young educated city women want their own home. The traditional way didn't necessarily mean that the mother-in-law treated the daughter-in-law like a slave. The husband's family may have chosen a young girl who would be brought up in the family, with the expectation that she would become a good wife and cook and clean well. One of the tests of a good wife, which she would have wanted to pass, is that she should be pleasant and obedient to her mother-in-law. Women weren't necessarily brutalised into being obedient, they often aspired to be so. There are many fictional stories of daughters-in-law and mothers-in-law but these sources are biased towards the miserable because it sells.

My mother-in-law is not typical. She is very intelligent although she is quite superstitious and was keen that we got married on a day that wasn't unlucky. When she heard we wanted to get married she put out feelers to my husband to find out if a bride-price needed to be paid. I realised that she saw this as a marriage between two families, so it was much more real to her when my relatives turned up. I knew she didn't approve of me at first; I was four years older than her son and she had never met a western woman before she met me. Western women have a reputation for being sexually fickle, so she wasn't pleased, but she was too polite to take me by the scruff of the neck and throw me out. For a Chinese mother-in-law the ideal wife for her son is a young girl who is sweet and biddable. It is good if she is educated but not good if she is better educated than her husband. My mother-in-law had to get over the fact that my husband wasn't going to marry someone like a nurse or a kindergarten teacher: domesticated, and educated – but not too educated. But bless her, she managed to adjust, she is as tough as nails herself and not at all biddable.

The family would have been within their rights to have expected us to get married faster than we did. I was teaching English in China when I met my husband and once you have declared yourselves (which we did) you are considered to have made up your mind, and to date other people would make you seem fickle. I knew my husband for ten years before we married because we lived apart for some of the time as I was working in different countries. The Chinese are used to the idea of long-distance relationships, as couples who lived a long way away from each other were fairly common up until the nineties: they might see each other only once a year.

When my husband first met my parents, I was gobsmacked by the level of devotion he showed to them, the effort that he put into pleasing my parents. Was he trying to pass the Chinese test of 'Am I a proper son-in-law?'

Expectations vary now in China, especially between the countryside and the city. Most of the students that I taught moved into new flats when they got married, that were partly paid for by the husband's family. There is still the expectation that you would take in your parents when they are old. The Chinese think that westerners are not good to their family members; that we kick out our children when they are sixteen and don't look after our old people when they are ill. Daughters-in-law in particular would be expected to be kind to their mothers-in-law and look after them if they were ill.

My mother-in-law is a lot more vocal in her opinions and particularly in how she wants to be a grandmother than western mothers-in-law would be. She will think nothing of being quite personal in what she says: 'Come on, you're in your mid-thirties, come along or you'll be too old.' It wouldn't be easy if we lived under one roof but we live in England and she lives in China so we manage.

My mother-in-law has accepted that I try to be a pleasant daughter-in-law and that pushing me around will not help. I will have a better idea of how she is when my husband's younger brother moves on and gets a wife. He gave my in-laws an exact description of the house he wanted, with a garage to keep his car in. So they bought the house for him and all three of them moved in. They are thinking ahead – he will be the one to look after them in their old age. And he will have a garage to put his car in.

To my mother-in-law
LEE SOOK-JUNG

Finding in the attic the bundle of hemp cloth you used to raise nine children and that you left behind, I thought of your sigh as you lamented the synthetic fabric they would spin out now like your hemp cloth, and I felt the tears start. You made the cosy baby blanket for my first baby, with the cotton you asked from a villager who grew it on the small side of a mountain. That baby is now grown taller than I and his thick black hair, seen from the back, is exactly as yours used to be.

When I was filled with anxiety watching my children sleep, you told me that I know your heart and that you know mine, but you left my side before I was old enough, wise enough to really understand your heart. Even though the teeth you lost every time you gained a child made chewing difficult, you loved zucchini pancakes; now, every time I prepare zucchini pancakes, the lump in my throat keeps me from swallowing. When the afternoon drowsiness flooded in, you put two pillows side by side and told the long-ago stories of your son, my husband, as if there would be, could be, no end, but when will you hear the stories that have piled up since you left our side?

Putting your hand, rough as arrowroot brambles, on the inner flesh still white and soft, you looked at your hand. I saw in your eyes our lack of devotion, but it was too late to revoke your sorrow. On the day when the family heir was born, you held him in your arms and asked him where he had been. And where are you now?

In the snow and in the rain, in the alternate rise and fall of the sun and the moon, your expression was always hardened, but stepping out from the front door with the first child on your back, bent with years of hardship, where did you get such light feet, such bursts of joyous energy?

Your smile as you told me that the new baby of our house has a heel softer than an egg has inspired my patience. The day you left, my white mourning dress wound around the coffin and would not let go.

In the midst of time that allows neither going nor coming, you and I have separated, but in the taste of the bean paste of our house, your heart is still deeply buried.

The sad lot of daughters-in-law in Ukrainian and Yiddish folksongs

UNTITLED POEM FROM BESSARABIA

Oh, mama
What should I do?
I have a cruel mother-in-law,
She's dissatisfied with me.

If I walk fast,
She yells that I'm tearing my shoes.
If I walk slowly
She yells that I'm crawling.

If I cook fish,
She says that it has no taste;
If I don't cook
She makes a to-do at home.

If I make chicken soup,
She says it has ashes in it;
If I don't make any
She makes a fuss at home.

Matinko moia kokhana ('*Beloved mother of mine*'),
UKRAINIAN SONG COLLECTED IN PODOLIA IN 1922

Beloved mother of mine
Why did you love me?
Why did you love me?
And give me away to a cruel mother-in-law?
If I was washing my clothes in the river,
My mother-in-law says – in alcohol.
My daughter-in-law is lazy, lazy,
She doesn't want to work at all.
If I put the clothing on the fence
My mother-in-law says – they're in the dirt.
My daughter-in-law is lazy, lazy,
She doesn't want to work at all.

UNTITLED YIDDISH SONG FROM THE VILNA AREA

I lay my head down
On my mother's bed;
My mother passes by.
All she does is beam:
'Sleep, my beautiful daughter;
You have little eyes.
Sleep in good health!
Sleep in good health!'
I lay my head down
On my mother-in-law's bed;
My mother-in-law passes by.
All she does is curse:
'My daughter-in-law is no bargain.
She doesn't do any work!
She just sleeps,
She just sleeps.'

Na krakivs'kim mosti iarar ruta skhodyt
('ON THE CRACOW BRIDGE BRIGHT RUE IS COMING UP')

This song recorded in the Teopil region has a daughter-in-law answering back to her mother-in-law.

A daughter-in-law never satisfies her mother-in-law.
Even if the daughter-in-law got up at midnight,
Her mother-in-law would say: she slept until noon . . .
Even if the daughter-in-law sewed a rose flower,
Her mother-in-law would say that she hadn't done any
    thing.

You shouldn't have sent your son to me;
You should have sent him to the village head's daughter.
She would have brought you some four cows,
Some four cows and a heifer as the fifth.
You would have had a rich daughter-in-law.

Janice on her mother-in-law Agi

My mother-in-law Agi is young for her age and is fun and
easy to talk to. She treats me like the daughter she never
had because her two children are both boys. I have a
lovely relationship with her and I don't have anything
negative to say about her. I respect her views on most
things. My mother-in-law has had an unusual life. She's
Hungarian, in her seventies and she defected in 1956 and
escaped into Austria and then to Britain. She and my
father-in-law, Sisi, had to leave Hungary suddenly to get
away from the Soviet Communists. My mother-in-law
was only twenty-two when she left, she was a sports
photographer, which was then an unusual job for a
woman, and my father-in-law, Sisi, was the first freelance
journalist in Hungary.

They couldn't speak English when they came and they
were initially put into a refugee camp in Lincolnshire, arriv-
ing on Christmas Eve. My mother-in-law learnt English as
quickly as she could and set up a photographic studio, trying to earn a living taking family portraits. Her mother-in-
law came over from Hungary to join them afterwards and
she lived with them for the rest of her life. I think that must
have been difficult for Agi.

I first met my mother-in-law after I had been going out with Rob for nine months. Every Sunday he and his brother went home for lunch or for the afternoon, to see his parents. The day I met her was the day that Rob and I came back from a two-week holiday. When we got back to Rob's house his parents were knocking on Rob's door within two hours.

I wasn't worried about meeting my mother-in-law because it never occurred to me that we wouldn't get on; I intended to be as nice as possible. I didn't feel threatened by that first meeting. Rob and I had had a great holiday, and we were very much in love. And from the moment we met she has always been really, really nice to me. From then on Rob and I went to see his parents together at weekends. I have never felt that his mother didn't want me to be with him and however strongly I know she loves him, I have never had the feeling she was jealous of me. When we said we were getting married, Agi and Sisi were really pleased. We organised the wedding, and arranged everything exactly how we wanted it. Neither of our families interfered at all. I didn't know if that was unusual but people have told me since that families can have terrible rows over a wedding. When we came back from our honeymoon, Agi and Sisi had left flowers and put milk in our fridge and they wrote a letter saying thank you and how lucky they felt to have me as the daughter they had never had. I was touched by that.

I really like Agi and I'll stand up for her if I think Rob is not treating her fairly. I always talk a lot to my mother-in-law. I give her information; tell her what has been going on in the family, female banter that she has never had from her boys. I have as much contact with her as Rob does because I make all the arrangements for us to meet up. Now and again I pop in to see her on my own and sometimes take the girls in to see her if we are near by. I will always call her first. A few years ago Agi and Sisi moved to be closer to us and I was glad about that and it means we can make more unplanned visits.

They have always been so fantastic with our children, they not only babysit but they have them at weekends and do interesting things with them, such as taking them to museums. The girls have always adored them. They are their only grandchildren so they are very close. My in-laws are never critical of us. I cannot imagine my mother-in-law saying to me, 'I wouldn't do things like that.' They had two boys and now with my children they have two little girls. Girls are so different and my mother-in-law appreciates having girls in her family.

My mother-in-law always lets us get on with things; she's not an interfering mother-in-law although she will offer to help out. She always tells her friends how much she likes me but she also makes that clear to me and to Rob. She has always been a very strong, together woman but now that my father-in-law has had a stroke she is struggling because she has to look after him all the time and the stroke has changed him. He doesn't like it when she's not around. They don't have the children quite so much and I know she misses that and we've discussed what we can do about it because they are so much a part of her life. The other day Rob watched the rugby with his father and Agi and I took the girls to the park and it was lovely.

I must get on their nerves because I am always busy but to be honest we have spent far more time with Rob's parents than with my mum. His parents are very involved in our lives. If we haven't spoken to them for a couple of days, they're on the phone, saying, 'We haven't seen you for ages.' If we went a week they would phone and say, 'Can we just pop in?' When we get home from holiday there is always a message.

They are very well read and intelligent. I met an ex-girl-friend of Rob's who said to me, 'Aren't his parents daunting, they are so intellectual?' But they have never made me feel like that. I suspect I will be a much more controlling mother-in-law. I can see me trying to be a friend to my children when they're grown up. I only hope I have a relationship with them similar to the one I have with Agi and Sisi.

Motherly Mothers-in-law

John Keats, one of England's best-loved poets, died of tuber-culosis at the age of twenty-four before he could acquire a bona fide mother-in-law. But Mrs Samuel Brawne, the mother of Fanny, Keats's fiancée, was, throughout the three years they knew each other, the genuine article. In the tradition of the best mothers-in-law she loved Keats as a son. Literary friends of Keats, while doubting Fanny's suitability, invariably referred to Mrs Brawne as 'that kind woman'. For Keats, she took the place of his own mother (also called Fanny) whom he had nursed when she had tuberculosis but who had died when he was just fourteen years old.

As his passionate poetry suggests, Keats was not a conven-tional catch for Mrs Brawne's eldest and accomplished daughter Fanny. He was a dishevelled poet, suffering from con-sumption, who couldn't tie his cravat, was penniless and con-stantly wrote her daughter letters that combined a lover's yearning and insecurity with a disturbing desire for death. 'I have two luxuries to brood over in my walks, your loveliness and the hour of my death,' he wrote to Fanny. Mrs Brawne could never rejoice in their attachment. The attachment, how-ever, was immediate and intense and would be severed only by death. Even then, Fanny mourned him for three years, cutting off her hair, wearing black and wandering distraught round Hampstead Heath.

Mrs Brawne was a thirty-seven-year-old widow when Keats met Fanny. Her husband had recently died of tuberculosis, leaving her to bring up three children. In 1818 Mrs Brawne moved into rented accommodation in Wentworth Place. The white stucco-fronted property in Hampstead was made up of two adjoining houses that shared an entrance and large lawned garden. The Dilke family, friends of Keats, lived in one; the other side was rented to the Brawnes by another of Keats's friends, Charles Brown. The Dilkes and the Brawnes rapidly became friends, sharing a love of chatting (Mrs Dilke was more of an indiscreet gossip than Mrs Brawne) and a fondness for Hampstead society. Keats was lodging round the corner with his brother Tom, who was in the last throes of tuberculosis (he died shortly afterwards), and was forever visiting the Dilkes. This was where he met Fanny.

Fanny was elegant, intelligent and strikingly attractive, although she disliked her aquiline nose and sallow complexion. She had inherited her mother's love of books and was brought up to speak French and play the piano. Keats was immediately smitten but gave nothing away, writing to his brother George rather casually that he met Fanny occasionally for a 'tiff and a chat' and thought her a 'minx' and 'ignorant', when in reality they talked about Tom's illness and about literature, sparred a bit and became deeply attached to one another.

Mrs Brawne, too, was enamoured of Keats, enjoying his conversation and ability to make puns. When the Brawnes left Brown's house to move round the corner to Elm Cottage, Mrs Brawne, while wary of the romance growing in front of her, invited him round and he spent Christmas there in 1818.

Keats wrote of Mrs Brawne as a 'very nice woman'. Fanny said afterwards that this was the happiest time of her life. Keats, however, had developed a recurrent sore throat: the first sign of his tuberculosis.

Biographers do not agree on when Fanny and Keats developed an understanding to marry. Keats was never good at putting dates on anything he wrote, but it was some time between that Christmas and the winter of the following year that he gave Fanny a garnet ring. Mrs Brawne was troubled but philosophical. She felt that Fanny, at eighteen, was too young to wed an impoverished poet and hoped they would both grow out of the relationship. She insisted that they wait for a while before being properly engaged.

Being both sociable and fond of Keats, Mrs Brawne continued to invite him round for suppers. To her good friend Mrs Dilke she confided her concern that Keats was a 'mad boy' and that despite being proud of his poetry, she wished he had become a doctor (he had abandoned his training early on). Keats's affection for her shows up in much of his correspondence. When Charles Brown wrote some sneering verses, provoked by jealousy, about Keats's relationship with the Brawnes, Keats immediately wrote his own stanzas poking fun at Brown and sent them to him.

Mrs Brawne's decision to move back into Wentworth Place when the opportunity arose was rather surprising. By doing so she brought her potential son-in-law and daughter as physically close as was socially acceptable. Sitting under the plum tree, with Fanny near by, Keats wrote some of his most famous poetry – 'Ode to a Nightingale' was scribbled down one afternoon before tea.

But the idyllic days were about to end. Brown rented out his half of Wentworth Place, as he did every summer, to go travelling and took Keats with him, away from London and Fanny. This released Keats's insecurities and jealousy and in July 1819 he wrote to her from Shanklin, 'Ask yourself my love whether you are not very cruel to have so entrammelled me, so destroyed my freedom.' The letter, which desperately asked Fanny to reassure him about her feelings and fidelity, still ended with a civil 'present my compliments to your mother'.

When Fanny, who hadn't heard from Keats for weeks, was handed the letter, she rushed upstairs to read it. For the next few months Mrs Brawne watched a rapid exchange of letters and the disquieting effect they had on Fanny. Keats increasingly felt unwell and morbidly dispirited. When he wrote, 'I hate the world: it batters too much the wings of my self-will and would I could take sweet poison from your lips to send me out of it,' Fanny, perhaps on her mother's advice, promptly told him to stop writing 'any more such letters'.

He didn't return to London for nearly four months but as soon as he did, he moved back into Wentworth Place. One night in February 1820, returning from town he coughed up the bright red arterial blood of tuberculosis. It was, said Keats, his 'death warrant', and with remarkable fortitude, he prepared to die.

In doing so, he didn't hide what was happening from Fanny, 'On the night when I was taken ill – when so violent a rush of blood came to my lungs that I felt nearly suffocated – I assure you I felt it possible I might not survive and at that moment thought only of you.' Fanny broken-heartedly told her mother, but Mrs Brawne had suspected it anyway. Not only had she nursed her husband with the disease, she lived in fear that her delicate son Samuel was also in the early stages of tuberculosis. She began to watch over Keats with as much motherly attention as she did Fanny.

From then on either Fanny or her mother saw Keats every day. Mrs Brawne made him preserves (the raspberry, he told Fanny, was too sweet) and scolded Fanny when she thought her good-night letters to Keats were exciting him too much. He noticed the more sisterly lilt in her writing immediately: 'Do not let your mother suppose that you hurt me by writing at night. For some reason or other your last night's was not so treasurable as former ones.' Fanny tried to stay away to avoid exciting him and relied on Mrs Brawne to relay his progress to her.

When Mrs Brawne visited him she was upset by his pallor and listlessness but always brought back optimistic reports for Fanny. When Keats found himself writing a particularly bleak note to Fanny he interrupted himself to say, 'I am writing in too depress'd a state of mind – ask your mother to come and see me – she will bring you a better account than mine.'

So Mrs Brawne became the intermediary between her daughter and her potential son-in-law. 'Remember me to your mother and tell her to drag you to me if you show the least reluctance,' wrote Keats. Only to Mrs Dilke did Mrs Brawne confide her anguish about the relationship which Mrs Dilke reported as 'quite a settled thing between John Keats and Miss Brawne. God help them. It's a bad thing for them. The mother says she cannot prevent it, and that her only hope is that it will go off. He don't like anyone to look at her or speak to her.' Mrs Brawne understood and was sympathetic to how Keats's illness made him jealous and resentful of Fanny. To Fanny she tried to downplay the extent of Keats's illness, although her daughter guessed it from the anxiety on her face.

Keats was forced to move to Kentish Town to stay with friends, despite his poor health, as Brown once again let his house out for the summer. For the sake of propriety it was Mrs Brawne who went to visit him. She found him emaciated and exhausted. He was preparing, on his doctor's advice, to spend the winter in Rome, the only treatments for tuberculosis at that time being warm weather and intermittent bleeding.

He was never happy in Kentish Town and when one of Fanny's letters was delivered to him with the seal open, he could no longer bear to stay in his friend's house. He left immediately, stumbling in a feverish state to Wentworth Place. Mrs Brawne opened the door and took him in. This time, realising that the end could be imminent, she dispensed with propriety and, with Fanny, nursed him for the last six weeks he was in England.

It was an unconventional arrangement. Engaged couples did not live together in nineteenth-century England and the house at Wentworth Place was small. By nursing him the Brawnes not only put their reputation but their lives at risk. The mode of spread of tuberculosis was not known but many felt it no coincidence that it spread through families. If the Christmas of 1818 was Fanny's happiest time, this, poignantly, was one of Keats's more contented periods. In the care of Fanny and his would-be mother-in-law he felt both loved and hopeful.

By spending the winter in Rome Keats hoped to be buying future time with Fanny. Mrs Brawne encouraged them to put their engagement on a more established footing. The Brawnes discussed how Keats would return, marry Fanny and live in his mother-in-law's house. Joseph Severn, a painter, agreed to accompany him to Rome, but Mrs Brawne was worried that he did not have the maturity to look after Keats. As the Brawnes said goodbye to Keats they doubted that they would ever see him again.

Keats never wrote to Fanny again and refused to read the letters that she wrote to him in Italy, asking that they be buried with him when he died. When his boat landed in Naples he wrote his only letter from Italy and it was to the woman who would have been his mother-in-law. To her, he said that he was 'about how he was', the sea air improving him but the accommodation and food harming him so any beneficial effect was cancelled out. 'I would always wish you to think me a little worse than I really am; not being of a sanguine disposition I am likely to succeed. If I do not recover your regret will be softened, if I do your pleasure will be doubled.' He shared with her his torment over Fanny. 'I dare not fix my mind upon Fanny; I have dared not think of her.'

Unbearable as this must have been to Mrs Brawne, it is the brief postscript that is so moving. Keats cannot bear to write to Fanny directly, so ends his letter by saying, 'Goodbye Fanny. God bless you.' It was heart-rending for Mrs Brawne to give Fanny this message – so hard did she try to shelter her from the reality of Keats's illness. She forever regretted not accompanying Keats to Italy.

So central was Mrs Brawne in the last period of Keats's life that when Joseph Severn had some good news, he wrote a long and detailed letter to her immediately.

My dear madam,

I said that the first good news I had should be for the kind Mrs Brawn [sic] . . . I most certainly think I shall bring him back to England. Nature again revives in him, I mean where art was used before. Yesterday he permitted me to carry him from his bedroom to our sitting room, to put him clean things on, and to talk about my painting to him.

Present my respectful compliments to Miss B who I hope and trust is quite well. Now that I think of her my mind is

carried to your happy Wentworth Place. O I would my
unfortunate friend had never left it for the hopeless disad-
vantage of this comfortless Italy. He has many many times
talked over the happy days at your house, the only time when
his mind was at ease. I hope still to see him with you again.

Mrs Brawne promptly wrote back to Severn. It is the only sur-
viving letter of hers and is kind and solicitious: 'Severn, I beg
you to take care of your health do not omit taking nourish-
ment as it is absolutely essential to support you during fatigue
of the body and mind under which you may be labouring.'
She wishes, she writes, that Keats was still in England so that
she could nurse him, and asks Severn to tell Keats that she
and Fanny will look after his sister (also called Fanny) and
that the two Fannys are already writing to each other. She
ends by saying, 'When you talk of bringing him to England it
cheers us for believe me I have considered it among the happiest moments of my life to see him here in better health.'

When Keats did die, Fanny and Mrs Brawne grieved
together. Fanny barely went out for the first year and tried, with
her mother, to get to see Keats's sister Fanny who was still living with her guardian, Mr Abbey. Fanny Brawne wrote to her,
'You must consider my mother as more than a stranger for your
brother loved her very much, and used often to wish she could
have gone with him and had he returned I should have been his
wife and he would have lived with us.' Mr Abbey blocked visits
from the Brawnes and it was not until 1825 that Fanny Keats
was allowed (at the age of twenty-one) to leave her guardian
and come to Wentworth Place.

Just as Keats had enjoyed the warmth and care of Mrs

Brawne, so did Fanny Keats, who had been similarly deprived of affection. Mrs Brawne, who retained a foothold in Hampstead society, entertained for Keats's sister and it was through such social events that she met her future husband Valentine Llanos. So close were the families that the Llanoses moved next door to the Brawnes.

Meanwhile Samuel Brawne was seriously ill with tuberculosis. In March 1828 he died at the age of twenty-three. Mrs Brawne never recovered. She made her will and one night in November, while guiding a guest by candlelight across the wide front lawn of Wentworth Place, her dress caught fire. She died the next day from her severe burns, at the age of fifty-seven. Four days later a letter from Brown arrived for Fanny, asking, as ever, after Mrs Brawne's health.

Edgar Allan Poe was another literary genius who had an intense relationship with his mother-in-law. So close was he to his beloved 'Muddy' that he is buried between her and his wife Virginia. Muddy's real name was Mrs Marie Clemm and she was also Poe's aunt. Poe, who had been orphaned aged two, went to live with her in 1831 at the age of twenty-two. He had already written three volumes of poetry, his first a slim book called *Tamerlane and Other Poems*.

Mrs Clemm's household was supportive but financially precarious; she was a widow and had little money apart from a pension from an elderly relative. Virginia, his cousin and future wife, was only eight years old when Poe first moved in. Poe started writing prose to sell to journals but while his horror stories showed remarkable maturity for a man in his early twenties, much of his work went over the heads of those reading it.

Eventually he won $50 for a short story, 'Manuscript Found in a Bottle', and found work on the staff of various magazines, even though he had to move away from his adoptive family.

In 1835 he began editing the *Southern Literary Messenger* and wrote frequently to Mrs Clemm sending her as much money as he could afford. Modern sensibilities may find it uncomfortable that Poe fell in love with Virginia when she was only thirteen and he twenty-six, but sympathetic biographers suggest that Virginia had a beauty and maturity that belied her years. Whatever the basis of her attraction for Poe, he was devastated to get a letter from Mrs Clemm asking whether she should allow a relative, Neilson Poe, to take over the care of Virginia.

Poe wrote back in tears, declaring his passionate and devoted love for his cousin and his fears that his surrogate mother and his future wife would go with Neilson Poe, never to be seen by him again. He ends with a postscript to his cousin: 'My love, my own sweetest Sissy, my darling little wifey, think well before you break the heart of your cousin Eddy.'

Poe's state of mind at this time was one of profound depression. He was always a troubled, sensitive man, who was prone to drinking excessively and fearful that he would slip into madness. His brand of genius was generally beyond the understanding of readers and critics of his day. Mrs Clemm, who must have seen his emotional instability, did not pursue Neilson Poe's offer of protection and she and Virginia joined Edgar in October 1836 in Richmond, where they lived together in modest lodgings. It is not clear why she tolerated Poe's love for her barely adolescent daughter but her motherly attentions and the presence of Virginia improved Poe's spirits.

His status as a literary critic grew, although he had trouble finding a publisher for his short stories. The following year he married Virginia, not only with Mrs Clemm's blessing but with her connivance; she claimed her daughter was twenty-one while in fact she was only fourteen years of age. Mrs Clemm was forever part of this union. She watched over Poe's interests, and loved and tried to protect him for the rest of his life.

The following year Poe took his wife and mother-in-law to New York where he published *The Narrative of Arthur Gordon Pym*, a horror story of a murderous mutiny, which did not sell well. His plan was always to do some editing and writing to earn money, but when New York did not provide the riches that Poe hoped for, he decided to move his family to Philadelphia. There he found work on a couple of magazines and produced some of his finest writing, such as 'The Haunted Palace', *The Conchologist's First Book* and 'The Murders in the Rue Morgue'.

In 1842 Poe met Charles Dickens, who had come to Philadelphia on a lecture tour. Dickens was sufficiently taken with Poe to try to get his book *Tales of the Grotesque and Arabesque* published in England (although he failed to do so). The meeting, while not the beginning of a friendship, revealed enough of Poe's responsibilities and poverty to touch Dickens. When he returned to America on a second tour, Poe had died, but Dickens, on hearing that Mrs Clemm was living in poverty, gave her one thousand dollars.

That the Clemms provided Poe with the constant love and security that he needed is without doubt. By all accounts his home life, however financially insecure, was always happy. Virginia was widely regarded by friends and even foes of Poe as an accomplished, beautiful and devoted wife. His mother-in-law was equally devoted to him. When Virginia was suddenly taken ill following what biographers describe loosely as a 'broken blood vessel' Poe thought she would die and responded by drinking so heavily he was frequently unconscious. Virginia did rally and enough normality was restored for Poe to take her to New York where he hoped again to find more lucrative employment. He had never before, apart from when he went on his honeymoon, taken his wife anywhere without his mother-in-law.

The first person he wrote to on their arrival was his beloved Muddy, saying how much he missed her and how 'we hope to send for you very soon'. Mrs Clemm, meanwhile, was trying to sell her son-in-law's books but by accident sold a volume of the *Southern Literary Messenger* that did not belong to Poe. The incident tarnished Poe's reputation but such was his love for his mother-in-law that he defended her reputation blindly. She was later to do the same for him.

In 1845 he wrote 'The Raven', one of his most famous poems, which resonates with the pain of lost love. James Russell Lowell, the author, poet and editor, recalls meeting Poe and Mrs Clemm around this time, describing Mrs Clemm as rather ordinary. He was even less impressed with Poe, who he noted was drunk and pompous. Mrs Clemm must have read Lowell's opinion of her son-in-law some time after Poe's death as she wrote furiously to him defending her 'darling Eddie'. Her defence is even more laudable as she needed Lowell to help sell Poe's works and thereby provide her with some income. In her letter to Lowell she declares that Poe was not himself when he met him, that such had been her concern that she never left the room during their meeting, and that it broke her heart to hear her poor Eddie spoken about so unkindly and untruthfully.

Virginia never fully recovered from her earlier illness and developed tuberculosis. The couple moved to a cottage outside of New York, in the hope that the air would be better. George Colton, the publisher of 'The Raven', went to visit them with Mrs Mary Gove, a writer, homeopath and health reformer. There they met Mrs Clemm, who had come to act, as Gove described it, as 'a sort of universal Providence for her strange children'. She was, by Gove's account, a 'tall, dignified lady, with a most ladylike manner'. During the visit Poe split his shoes, and Mrs Clemm, ever the practical member of the household, begged Gove to ask Colton to publish another of Poe's poems so that he could afford another pair of shoes. Such was the force of Mrs Clemm's entreaties, Gove agreed.

Although Poe was writing more stories and poems and his fame was spreading, the family remained in poverty. As Virginia lay dying, Poe and Mrs Clemm nursed her as best they could until she passed away in January 1847. It was then Poe's turn to need nursing and his mother-in-law, herself distraught, did her best to tend to him. As soon as his 'brain fever' had abated, he resumed his writing. 'Ulalume', a poem about spiritual love, was promptly sold, as was *Eureka*, a prose poem about the universe.

Poe had a few erratic and passionate relationships after Virginia's death and was engaged first to a poet, Sarah Helen Whitman, and then to his childhood sweetheart, Sarah Elmira Royster. His plans after marriage to Elmira included having Mrs Clemm live with them, and Elmira wrote affectionately to Mrs Clemm, introducing herself and reassuring her that Poe was sober. She had good reason to reassure Mrs Clemm, as throughout much of this time Poe drank heavily and on occasions became paranoid. He wrote to Mrs Clemm from Philadelphia telling her he was sick and begging her to come to him so they could die together.

Mrs Clemm felt intensely responsible for Poe, particularly on her daughter's behalf. She wrote to a friend explaining why: 'Can I ever forget those dear eyes looking at me so sadly, while she said, "Darling, darling Muddy, you will console and take care of my dear Eddy – you will never never leave him? Promise me my dear Muddy and then I can die in peace." And I did promise. And when I meet her in heaven I can say, "I have kept my promise my darling ..."'

Poe's next letters to Mrs Clemm pleaded for her to come to him – they had only been apart for a matter of weeks, but he was desperately homesick for her and, not realising she had not replied because she had not got his letters, worried about her health. 'If you are but alive and if I but see you again, all the rest is nothing, I love you better than ten thousand lives – so much so that it is cruel in you to let me leave you; nothing but sorrow ever comes of it.' In this the last year of his life he wrote the poem 'To My Mother', which was for Mrs Clemm.

His last letter to Mrs Clemm is written from Philadelphia in September 1849, telling her how well his lectures had been going but that he was unable to send any money. Mrs Clemm, still not having seen him, tried to get the money to visit him from friends, but was unable to do so. Poe left Elmira in Richmond, after which she wrote to Mrs Clemm saying that he had a fever and was both sick and unhappy. A few days later Poe was found in Baltimore, in mysterious circumstances that have never been explained, half-conscious and half-dressed. He was taken to hospital where he died on 7 October 1849 from an inflammation of the brain, although rumours persist that he was murdered or suffering from a brain tumour. He was buried two days later, without Mrs Clemm, who only heard of his death by reading a newspaper notice.

The women who had loved Poe were quick to comfort Mrs Clemm, asking her to stay with them and writing to her as 'mother'. Elmira wrote to say she was sure that Poe had been on his way home to his 'dear Muddy' when he died. Some, such as Sarah, referred to Poe as Mrs Clemm's son. She herself always felt she was Poe's mother and her uncritical love of him reflects that.

Mrs Clemm had no claims on Poe's estate compared to those of his sister and she struggled financially for the rest of her life. One critic, Rufus Wilmot Griswold, even arranged with her to publish a posthumous collection of Poe's works supposedly for her benefit, when in reality all she received was six copies of the two-volume set to sell privately. Griswold disliked Poe, describing him as irascible, envious and arrogant, and his opinions were widely influential. Nathaniel Willis, a fellow writer, came to Poe's defence, citing Mrs Clemm's devotion to him as proof of his good character. Mrs Clemm had once asked Willis for a job for her son-in-law, explaining that he was ill at the time and that her daughter was an invalid. Willis writes of Mrs Clemm's refinement, describing her as an angel. 'What does not a devotion like this – pure, disinterested and holy as the watch of an invisible spirit – say for him who inspired it?' Mrs Clemm would have been grateful indeed.

To My Mother

Because I feel that, in the Heavens above,
The angels, whispering to one another,
None more so devotional as that of 'Mother,'
Therefore by that dear name I long have called you –
You who are more than mother unto me,
And fill my heart of hearts, where Death installed you,
In setting my Virginia's spirit free,
My mother – my own mother, who died early,
Was but the mother of myself; but you
Are mother to the one I loved so dearly,
And thus are dearer than the mother I knew

By that infinity with which my wife
Was dearer to my soul than its soul-life.

Eliza Calvert Hall was the pen name of Lida Calvert
Obenchain, an author and supporter of women's suffrage, who
due to family circumstances became a full-time mother-in-law.
She was born in 1856, and while a mother of four and housewife found time to write stories set in her home state of
Kentucky that highlighted the injustices of women's lives. She
wrote in her short story 'Sally Ann's Experience', 'I'd like to
know how it is that a woman that had eight hundred dollars
when she married, has to go to her husband and git down on
her knees and beg for what's her own.' President Theodore
Roosevelt recommended the first chapter of her collection of
short stories, *Aunt Jane of Kentucky*, 'for use as a tract in all
families where the men folks tend to selfish or thoughtless or
overbearing disregard of the rights of their womenkind'.

By 1916, Lida, as she was known, had four adult children
and her husband had died. She was excited about becoming
a full-time writer. Instead she had to assume the role of
mother-in-law, helping out her son-in-law. Lynn Niedermeier,
her biographer, says that she took to the role with a mixture of
motherliness and martyrdom.

Lida's elder daughter, Margery, had married Val Graham
Winston, an arms manager for the Winchester Repeating Arms
Company, and after the birth of their son Val, Lida took it upon
herself to have a house built for them in Texas, largely to her
own specifications. Lida stayed at home in Bowling Green in
Kentucky, writing her fifth book and finishing off some essays,
but wrote to a friend predicting she would be needed in Texas.

'My poor little girl is almost broken down with the care of a nervous sleepless baby and I must go to her help. No wonder women's work does not measure up to the standard of men's work. No novelist or poet ever had to suspend his work to nurse his grandchildren.'

Margery's tiredness developed into a chronic illness. It is not known if Val asked his mother-in-law to help out, but Lida arrived promptly, even as she complained to a friend, 'God knows when I will be able to do any writing.' Margery, despite being ill, gave birth to a daughter, also called Margery, in 1917. Lida wrote to a relative, 'There were three days that Val and I will never forget, when we wrestled with the children, all the work of the house and waited on Margery . . . For the last two years I have done little except nurse sick people and babies and

I think I'll get a trained nurse's outfit and wear it for the rest of my life.'

Margery was diagnosed with tuberculosis and went into a sanatorium. Lida reverted to housewife and mother while Val travelled for work but she couldn't resist being self-important about her assumption of Margery's role. Lida wrote to her mother, Margaret Younglove Calvert, 'The children have never cried for her and Little Margery calls me "Mamma" half the time.'

When Margery came home, Lida continued to run the house for Val while her daughter was slowly dying. Lida and her son-in-law did not always agree on what was best for the children. Lida felt they were sickly and needed their tonsils removed. Val disagreed. 'Val is scared to death at the thought of his children being operated on but it ought to be done,' Lida wrote to her mother. Lida may have got her way – the children had their adenoids out a year later. Whether their tonsils came out too is unrecorded but it was common for them to be removed at the same time.

After Margery died in 1923 Lida remained at Val's house, looking after the children. However motherly Lida was to her grandchildren, such was her character that Val must have found his mother-in-law opinionated, forceful and difficult to live with. He remarried barely a year after his wife's death, perhaps anxious to dislodge Lida. As soon as he married he moved out of the Dallas home and left Lida behind. Val seems to have cut his mother-in-law out of his family's life and Lida barely saw her grandchildren. She was furious with him. She wrote bitterly to her sister Josephine, 'These family quarrels are disgraceful, but it's all Val's fault. I did not want Margery to marry him and her marriage has given me more trouble than anything that ever happened to me. Send the children candy if you want but remember that their father does not want them to have anything to do with their mother's family. When the children are older they may be different and I feel that some day they will come back to me. I hope it is not necessary for me to tell you to have no communication with Val.'

Lida died in 1935, still estranged from her son-in-law. Her biographer says that Lida always felt responsible for everyone around her, including her son-in-law and his children, but that she also resented not being able to pursue all her literary ambitions. She did, however, through her support of the suffragettes, contribute to a legacy for her little Margery. By the time Lida died, the Nineteenth Amendment had been passed extending voting rights to women.

Janice's mother-in-law Agi on her own mother-in-law

When we escaped from Hungary and the Communists in 1956 my husband Stephen and I left everything behind – including his mother. Stephen was her only son and it was always her ambition to come and join us but it took three years for her to get a visa and passport. When she arrived in Britain she didn't know anybody except us and she was utterly lost. It never occurred to us that she would live alone in a little flat somewhere. She couldn't have an independent life, she couldn't speak English – she didn't know how to use the tube, or make a doctor's appointment.

I knew the only way for her living with us to work was for me to be even-tempered and patient. Also that if anything needed to be said, or any laws needed to be laid down, then it had to come from her son. So Stephen told her that when we had friends round, she would not be joining us. If she had done the evening would have been very different, everyone would have sat round politely, smiling at her. So she never appeared when friends came round, which she didn't like but she put up with. Once a very old friend bumped into her in the corridor and said, 'Do you know there's an old lady walking towards your loo?' I said,

'She's living with us, she's Stephen's mother.' It may sound cruel but it was the only way one could cope with it. We also always had separate holidays.

I lived with my mother-in-law for twenty-five years which was a hell of a long time. She was a very sweet woman but she had no sense of humour and my and Stephen's sense of humour was to tease each other and our children. Our children would tease us in return. She could not understand it. 'Do you think it is wise for you to let the children talk to you like that?' she asked me. I said it is awfully wise; that it gets me the respect a friend would have from them. But I could see that she was hurt.

The guilt complex may not exist so much in British households but it is a big continental Jewish thing. We decided when we had children that they would not be made to feel guilty. My mother-in-law was a classic example of someone who would try to make you feel guilty. The advantage of living with your mother-in-law is that you never need a babysitter. I used to work, come home and spend time with the children and then Stephen and I would go out. My mother-in-law would stand in the kitchen looking at us in the hall and would say with a big sigh, 'Well I hope you have a good time.'

She was good with the children in an old-fashioned way. She would say, 'You must brush your teeth before you go to bed,' but then she would produce chocolates and crisps and I would say, 'I don't want you giving them that stuff,' and she would say, 'But how will they know I love them?'

She was agreeable, she loved the children, and her son was at the top of her world. An example of how she treated him: one evening we were having supper and the salt was very near to Stephen but he asked for someone to pass it to him. Mama jumped up and ran round the table to give it to him. Any household activity was always out of the question for him. Women are here to serve men. In Hungary my father had never done anything either. If my mother-in-law hadn't lived with us Stephen might have done something in the house. He is amazed that our sons can cook. My mother-in-law would say to my son, 'No Robin, don't boil an egg, I'll do it.'

There were lots of irritations and I got used to a very different way of living. When our sons left to go to university we couldn't be free because she was there. We couldn't be spontaneous and make love on the staircase in case she came out of her room. It became more difficult to leave her to go out because she grew scared of being alone.

She was eighty-five when she died. She died very elegantly. She felt unwell so I took her to the hospital, she had a heart attack and died the next day.

I don't feel like a mother-in-law. The word has connotations. When you hear it you think, 'Here comes an old bitch who will screw up the household.'

Living with my mother-in-law hasn't stopped me having opinions as a mother-in-law. I will say what I think but I never interfere. I think, 'It's your life.'

I liked Jan, my daughter-in-law, as soon as I met her. I had an instinct that something very good was happening to my son. She arrived at our house in an open-top red sports car with her blonde hair flowing. My husband immediately thought, 'Wow, this is good.'

The third time we met we were having supper with my other son Nick who can be argumentative in a humorous way and I was worried they wouldn't get on well. Within the first five minutes he said something and Jan came right back at him and gave as good as she got and we all burst out laughing. And I thought. 'This will be all right.' And it's important because a young wife can ruin a relationship between her husband and his sisters and brothers.

I know the pitfalls of being a mother-in-law and I must have them but I can't think of what they are. If I saw Jan was in the right about something and Robin was not then I wouldn't hesitate to say that I thought Jan was right.

The day Stephen had his stroke I was leaving to pick up the grandchildren to take them home from ballet. I heard a crash and Stephen was lying there and he said politely, 'I'm having a stroke, can you call the ambulance?' I called the ambulance and phoned the school to say there had been an emergency and could they get hold of the children's mother to pick up the children. I don't know how she did it but Jan was here before the ambulance.

Years ago I made a decision that if I am a widow I will never live with either of my sons. It's very hard for a couple to live with their mother-in-law.

Royal and Presidential Mothers-in-law

Queen Victoria, with her nine children and forty-one grand-children, was known as the Grandmother of Europe. She could equally have been Europe's mother-in-law, allegedly planning her oldest daughter's marriage before her christening had taken place. The role of Europe's mother-in-law was not without its challenges. She not only had to find spouses for her children but was responsible for keeping the family peace when the countries they had come from went to war with each other.

Her matchmaking was driven by the need to make political alliances. Her eldest and most intelligent daughter, Princess Victoria, was married (at the age of seventeen) to the Crown Prince (and future Emperor) Frederick William of Prussia, with the mission of influencing Prussian politics by introducing British liberalism.

Despite needing to make marriages to further Britain's interests, Queen Victoria was unusual in insisting on finding husbands and wives who would make her children happy. Her own love match with Prince Albert, which lasted for twenty years until he died (after which she mourned him in virtual seclusion for three years), made her want nothing less than this 'miracle' for her children. She even allowed one of her daughters, Princess Louisa, to marry a commoner. In her journals, diaries and letters she writes about her sons- and daughters-in-law in the most glowing and affectionate terms – it would be hard to find another mother-in-law so generous about her children's spouses. In her family life she usually managed to put her queen's role to one side and tried to be even-handed in her treatment of her sons- and daughters-in-law, never openly taking sides in disputes but listening sympathetically to grievances from her in-laws and her children.

For a woman busy building an empire she still retained a mother-in-law's capacity to offer advice on domestic details. She insisted Princess Victoria should not get pregnant for a year (this was ignored) and warned her that men 'are selfish in marriage', which did not please 'Fritz'. It may explain why he wrote to Albert rather than his mother-in-law to tell him Princess Victoria was expecting. When the Queen heard she called it 'horrid news' and when the confinement came despatched English doctors to attend on the grounds (which again didn't please Fritz) that German ones would kill her daughter. The future Kaiser Wilhelm was delivered by a British obstetrician but had a difficult birth; he was a breech baby and in being pulled out, the nerves in one arm were damaged, leaving it useless (historians have suggested this as a contributory factor in his desire to take over Europe, as a means of compensating for his infirmity – such is the power of a mother-in-law's decision). Her intervention did not stop there; Victoria wasted no time in expressing her view of breast-feeding as 'disgusting' and insisted her daughters and daughters-in-law should not make 'cows of themselves'. Later she took an active interest in improving her grandchildren (privately thinking they had indulgent upbringings and were over-excitable) with Bible studies and plain nursery teas.

Victoria's influence as mother-in-law extended to deciding what employment her in-laws should take. Princess Helena, her third daughter, was married to Christian, Prince of Schleswig-Holstein, and they lived (at the Queen's request) within walking distance of Windsor. When the Queen saw Prince Christian (who had been given the untaxing job of Ranger of Windsor Park) lying against a tree, she promptly sent him a stiff note advising him to find something better to do with his time. Since the sons-in-law who settled in England were mostly given posts for the convenience of the Queen, so that she could keep a continuing eye on her daughters, there was little chance of any of them having fulfilling positions.

Her favourite daughter-in-law was the Danish Princess Alexandra, who was married to her most problematic son, Albert Edward, the Prince of Wales. Bertie, as he was called, was a disappointment to his parents, lazy in the schoolroom and with what his mother called 'a total want of chin'. He was incapable of either fidelity or good judgement, leading the Queen to seek not merely a daughter-in-law but 'his salvation'. In 1885 she gave Princess Victoria a list of her requirements: someone who was 'beautiful, resolute, virtuous and dutiful'. Given such a list, it took five years for her to come up with Princess Alexandra, whom the Queen initially opposed because of her Danish and thus insufficiently grand connections. Thorough investigations of Alexandra by her future in-laws took the form of testimonials from people who had known her from birth. Princess Victoria reported that she had plenty of sense although she 'was nothing of a genius', and that she was beautiful, tactful, 'charming, sweet and amiable'. It was enough for the matchmakers to engineer a 'chance' meeting between Bertie and Alexandra in Speyer Cathedral, with the result that Bertie said he had never met a woman who pleased him so much.

But being Bertie he nearly destroyed his chances of a future with Alexandra. Anxious for their oldest son to make something of himself, Albert and Victoria sent him off to the Curragh Camp near Dublin on attachment to the Grenadier Guards. Not only was Albert unable to achieve any rank of significance, he created a scandal when a young actress was found in his bed. His father was devastated, believing the royal family should be the bastion of morality and fearing this would ruin his chances of marrying Alexandra. Prince Albert was already unwell; within the month he was diagnosed with typhoid and died in December 1861. Victoria was heartbroken and held Bertie partly responsible because of his behaviour. She could barely look at him for two years and when she reconsidered his marriage prospects it was with the opinion that her future daughter-in-law was likely to be too good for him. She finally allowed Bertie to propose. 'I assured her', he told his mother, 'you would love her as your own daughter.'

Alexandra still had to endure 'trial by Osborne House', the Queen's residence on the Isle of Wight. There, without Bertie (he was off sailing), the seventeen-year-old girl spent ten days being observed by her future mother-in-law, managing to win the most effusive praise. For Victoria she was 'one of those sweet creatures who seem to come from the skies to help and bless poor mortals and brighten for a time their path. She lives in complete intimacy with us and she is so dear, so gentle, good, simple, unspoilt . . .' She gave her future daughter-in-law a sprig of white heather that her own Albert had given her and 'told her I hoped it would bring her luck'. For marriage with such a philanderer she would need more than a sprig.

Such were her feelings for Alexandra that the Queen didn't want her to marry Bertie without her knowing that he was not an ideal catch. She asked Princess Victoria to tell Alexandra's mother that he had been in a 'scrape' that had deeply hurt his parents but that she was very confident that he 'would make a steady husband'. It didn't put Alexandra off and the couple were married. Despite the Queen's wish that her new daughter-in-law should not be known by any nicknames, she was soon referred to as Alix, even by the Queen herself.

The first political fallout from the marriage was rapid. Prussia and Austria invaded the Danish dependencies of Schleswig and Holstein and Queen Victoria found her family divided. Alix and Bertie supported Denmark, while Princess Victoria was on the side of her Prussian husband. Since Alix and Bertie had considerable popularity among the British people, public opinion was tilted Denmark's way. On this occasion political imperative overcame mother-in-law's affection. Queen Victoria was strongly in the Prussian camp. At a family party she said that good as her daughter-in-law was, she was not worth the price of her family connections. Her 'darling' Alix was in the 'enemy camp' and she'd always wished she'd been German. Throughout her reign Victoria suspected her daughter-in-law was trying to push Danish interests up the British political agenda.

Alix's first child was born prematurely and the Queen rushed to their home in Frogmore to offer her assistance, suggesting unhelpfully that her daughter-in-law's 'general weakness' and 'not lying down enough' might have been the cause.

She appointed a Mrs Innocent to help with the baby, repenting as soon as she realised the nurse was 'very troublesome, cross, grand and a great nuisance' and that Alix didn't like her. The Queen had strong opinions on everything she saw at Frogmore. 'Alix does not sleep well as she sleeps too much in the day,' she wrote to Princess Victoria, claiming that her daughter-in-law disliked the 'whole business extremely and is utterly disgusted with it all'. Queen Victoria was as ever, keen to be an involved grandmother. 'This dear baby will indeed be an object of great interest to me if I can be of real use to it, but [Bertie] is so odd that he often listens to the greatest nonsense of stupid, inferior people and is inclined to follow their advice rather than that of wise and sensible people.' The Queen clearly saw herself in the latter camp.

The royal mother-in-law did not approve when Alix had a further premature son, followed quickly by two daughters, who Victoria thought were 'frail' and 'puny', and she fretted that her advice was not appreciated. She wrote long letters telling the couple the names she thought would be suitable for the boys and forbade Alix from taking the children to see her parents in Copenhagen until she had seen her own physicians, and even then only for the shortest time. Her daughter-in-law was understandably put out and may have shown it, because Victoria wrote, 'Alix and I never will or can be intimate, she shows me no confidence whatever especially about the children.' The children, she feared, were running wild, and the princess was not rising until 11 a.m., leaving her husband to breakfast alone. Yet a month later she proclaimed after a walk with her daughter-in-law that no one could be nicer or dearer.

After a visit from her grandchildren, the Queen wrote to Bertie, 'You must let me see them often . . . The great thing which I have observed from watching them is to keep to as much regularity of hours as possible; letting them get out early and go to bed in good time . . . Then not to have them too long at a time downstairs when you cannot watch them and above all not all together.' In her opinion her grandson Eddy was lethargic and the girls fussed over too much by Alix. But she could be as sensitive as she could be dictatorial. Eddy may have had some hereditary problem and Alix thanked her for her support in the face of Bertie's impatience. 'I am so glad you seem to have understood his disposition.'

The Queen never underestimated how difficult it was for the woman who had married her weak-willed son. She tried to protect her son's reputation by dictating which homes they could visit and asked for a daily report of life from their home to reach her at Windsor. She was not amused to hear of house parties full of 'horse dealers' (this from Tsar Nicholas II) nor of practical jokes where live lobsters were put into guests' beds.

But the Queen couldn't protect her son from himself and he was involved in a number of sexual scandals.

Alix knew of his infidelities but believed he loved her, whereas the Queen found it much harder to forgive her son. Alix, she said, with understatement, had a lot to put up with.

Her affection for Alix grew over the years. When the Queen insisted on wearing a bonnet for her diamond jubilee it was Alix who was sent in to beg her to wear a tiara. On this occasion she was 'snubbed', but such was their closeness that only Alix had rushed to Windsor to be with her mother-in-law when her dear friend and servant John Brown died. 'Nothing', said the Queen, 'could exceed her tender sympathy and complete understanding of all I could feel and suffer.' Alix, in turn, was effusive about her mother-in-law. After being sent a birthday present and affectionate wishes she wrote to Victoria saying, 'Many many thanks for your affectionate letter with all the kind things you say of me; but I really feel quite ashamed of so much praise as I don't deserve a quarter of it, though at least one thing is true – how entirely I return your affection, which I value above all things.' As Princess Victoria had promised her mother many years previously, Alix would indeed be like a daughter to her. Alix signs her letter, 'Ever, dearest Mama, your loving child, Alix'.

If Alix was her favourite daughter-in-law, Henry, who was married to her youngest daughter Beatrice, was Queen Victoria's most loved son-in-law. This was quite an achievement as the Queen had been bitterly opposed to Beatrice ever marrying. She had determined Beatrice's role in life as looking after her ageing mother, and so firmly was the Queen committed to this plan that she forbade anyone even to mention the word 'wedding' in her daughter's hearing and only allowed her to dance with her brothers. But the Queen must have momentarily lost concentration because Beatrice met Henry, Prince of Battenberg and an officer in the Prussian household cavalry, at a royal wedding and was instantly smitten. When Beatrice told her mother, she was so angry she wouldn't speak to her for weeks, only relenting when Liko (as he was known) promised to live in England so as not to deprive the Queen of her daughter. This arrangement, coupled with his sunny, lively temperament, won Victoria's approval.

Within two days of their honeymoon the couple had to go back to Osborne House to attend to the Queen. This was the pattern for much of their married life and it nearly ruined it. Beatrice complained that her mother's demands meant that she only had time alone with Henry from eleven o'clock at night. Henry, however, was not only an attractive son-in-law; he was also attentive and full of life, at a time when the Queen was feeling old and tired. He was her 'bright sunbeam', the only son-in-law to secure a smoking-room – the Queen was strongly opposed to smoking. But Henry wanted more than his mother-in-law's approval and the honours she bestowed on him. His training in the Prussian army made him desperate for more challenging work than opening fetes. When a situation arose over the slave trade in West Africa, Prince Henry volunteered to go and the Queen eventually buckled under Henry and Beatrice's protests.

It was to be the end of him. In January 1896 he died of malaria off the coast of Sierra Leone. It was hard to know who was the most distressed, the wife or mother-in-law. The Queen wrote of her great grief and how the shock had unnerved her.

In the last few years of her life she continued to visit and suggest improvements in the lives of her children, her sons- and daughters-in-law and her grandchildren and great-grandchildren. For someone who was once quoted as saying there was too much marrying going on, she'd made her own significant contribution to matrimony in Europe.

The next British queen found herself facing widespread hostility because her behaviour as a grieving mother-in-law fell short of what the country expected. For a few days in September 1997, after the death of her former daughter-in-law Diana, Princess of Wales, in a car crash, Queen Elizabeth II came close to being the most hated mother-in-law in England, if not the world. It was her refusal to show any distress, or to modify any royal protocols at a time when her people were participating in unprecedented displays of emotion, that had commentators asking if the monarchy was so out of touch with its people that it was a worthless institution. In Diana's death, as in her life, it was impossible to separate the roles of mother-in-law and queen. That the Queen is like no other mother-in-law is indisputable.

The Queen had championed Diana as a potential daughter-in-law; having known her since childhood (Diana's father was an earl and tenant of the Queen and many of her relatives had held posts in the royal household) and believed her to be 'one of us'. Diana may not have been as rigorously investigated as Princess Alix was by Queen Victoria, but Queen Elizabeth, before advancing her prospects to Prince Charles, knew she was a virgin and put her through a similar trial to that undergone by Princess Alix: by house party at Sandringham. Diana passed this with flying colours, stomping through mud, revelling in the shooting of pheasants and appearing to be an open, giggly young woman who understood etiquette. Charles, who had had two recent short-lived relationships and was, as he would continue to be, emotionally attached to the then married Camilla Parker Bowles, sought her out and enjoyed her company. Both he and Diana always insisted their marriage had not been arranged, but the Queen was getting frustrated by her thirty-two-year-old son's indecision in relationships and pushed him into settling down – she was the first person he rang after Diana accepted his proposal.

The Prince and Diana were not, as history has shown, well suited – she being much younger, less serious and more informal than him. The Queen had been optimistic in her appraisal of Diana's inherent ability to fit into her new position; her prospective daughter-in-law was in reality too young and insecure to go from nursery-school teacher to the consort of the heir to the throne. Unlike the Queen, Diana had had little guidance in what would be expected of her. She had a poor relationship with her mother, hated her stepmother and had experienced a wafer-thin slice of what was known as the Sloane Ranger life-style. In Sloane Ranger land nice girls went to finishing schools and took trivial jobs because their real career was in marriage. Diana was from a broken home (which had fractured with tears and recriminations that hurt all the Spencer children) and of a generation that made her believe she was entitled to personal happiness. She married both to be happy and to wed a prince – not primarily to serve her country.

The Queen's role has always been to serve her country as head of state – this is why she exists. She was bred for her role, her childhood rigidly controlled and largely devoid of contact with the outside world. Duty has been embedded from an early age. The Queen's marriage to Prince Philip was a love match but while she has had to put up with repeated and lurid stories about his infidelity, she would never have questioned her marriage. She left Prince Charles as a baby to tour Australia and New Zealand (just as her parents left her) but would never have thought to put motherhood above the priority of state visits. Courtiers have been quoted as saying she is not a tactile mother and has a presence that can be chilling.

The Queen did not intend, however, to be negligent or cold to her prospective daughter-in-law. Prior to the wedding, Diana stayed at Buckingham Palace, where the Queen met her for meals and expressed the hope that palace life with its luxury but also its demanding protocols wasn't too much of a strain for her. She encouraged Diana to call her 'Mama' but was still intimidating to her future daughter-in-law. Diana was always terrified of upsetting her. But royal life was already too much for her. She was suffering from the eating disorder bulimia and was devastated to discover that Prince Charles was having a relationship with Camilla Parker Bowles. By the time of her wedding she was painfully thin.

If the Queen wasn't naturally patient or familiar with eating disorders, she tried to support Diana (who was already being accused of shouting at Prince Charles and having hysterical outbursts) and defend her against other members of the royal family. The wedding was a success as far as the Queen was concerned and she was visibly moved to see them return to Balmoral for the second half of their honeymoon, where they looked genuinely in love. This honeymoon was shorter than the first half – living in her mother-in-law's house, with its rules that put the Queen and Queen Mother's needs before hers, upset Diana deeply – she mourned the loss of Charles's undivided attention.

Diana's continuing distress must have tried her mother-in-law's patience. When she made her well-known cry for help by throwing herself down the stairs at Sandringham House while pregnant with Prince William, her mother-in-law, who had been so pleased that Diana was expecting a baby, was mystified as to why she should be quite so unhappy and encouraged her to get help from a series of psychiatrists and counsellors.

The upper classes do child-rearing differently from other people – usually through nannies and diffidence. Queen Elizabeth had not been a loving mother and found Prince Charles to be her most difficult son, perhaps making it inevitable that she would struggle to get on with his wife. As with Queen Victoria, it wasn't until the Queen had grandchildren that she became indulgent, although she still watched their behaviour with the eye of a queen. After Prince Andrew's wedding, in which William was a page boy, she summoned Diana and Charles to tell them that their son had not behaved well enough, as he had fidgeted and had messed up his outfit. Mother-in-law and daughter-in-law could not have disagreed more about parenting – Diana believed in affection and talking to her children, getting them to understand social injustice and be able to speak to ordinary people; the Queen had delegated her parenting to nannies and although her children went to school (a break from royal tradition), they never mixed with 'ordinary' people.

Diana may not have been well equipped to join the royal family but her common touch was unparalleled. She often chose unfashionable charities – her work with people with HIV and her campaign against landmines helped make her an international icon. The public loved her accessibility, comparing her favourably with the fusty royal family. She also appealed on a more trivial level; her glamour ensured that a change of hairstyle made her front-page news.

As the marriage disintegrated the Queen continued to hope it would improve – it was unthinkable that the heir to the throne and his wife would divorce. As the marriage unravelled Diana sought out her mother-in-law, frequently crying during their meetings and saying afterwards that she had 'the best mother-in-law in the world'. The Queen, however, resisted taking sides and did not directly confront either Charles or Diana, even when there was a crescendo of rumours about their separate lives and infidelities. The Queen's response was inversely proportional to her status: she became a spectator as events unfolded with almost pantomime effect.

It was only when a series of scandals about her son and daughter-in-law became widely public that the Queen acted, and again more in her capacity of head of state than as a mother-in-law, because she became convinced the behaviour of her son and her daughter-in-law, played out in public, was damaging the monarchy. First there was the book by Jonathan Dimbleby that Charles had endorsed and that revealed his infidelity; then Andrew Morton's book, sanctioned by Diana, detailing Charles's cruelty; then the interview with Charles admitting adultery with Camilla Parker Bowles, followed by Diana confessing on the BBC to her affair with James Hewitt. The Queen acted swiftly: in December 1995 Diana was sent a letter expressing the Queen's frustration with her behaviour and her desire for a swift divorce. Charles was eager for a divorce but Diana was less so. When she met the Queen in February 1996 she needed some persuading, although the Queen was so adamant it was in her grandsons', the family's and the country's interests that Diana quite quickly agreed to a divorce. What other mother-in-law could have such persuasive arguments?

That Diana never saw the Queen as adversarial, admired her enormously and desperately sought her admiration is agreed on by biographers. She also wanted her mother-in-law to acknowledge the work she had done for the family. The Queen, in turn, maintained that she had written many letters to her daughter-in-law expressing support and offering to help but had never felt her interventions to be wanted, although her letters were signed affectionately 'with love from Mama'. She also, in more unguarded moments, expressed the opinion that Diana's behaviour bordered on the subversive.

There was little time to find out how the future, after the divorce, would play out – Diana was killed in a car crash in Paris on 31 August 1997. If she had been a troublesome daughter-in-law in life, it was nothing to the damaging effect she had on her mother-in-law after death. Her early death did many things, but one of the most profound was to show the inability of her ex-mother-in-law to understand the mood of the very country for which she had given a life of service. For an institution that lived by protocol and precedent, the salient points regarding Diana's death were that she was no longer in the royal family and so was not entitled to the royal plane to bring her body home, or to a state funeral, and her death did not necessitate any change in the routine of the royal family. The public wanted Diana's in-laws to join in their grief, but the monarchy behaved as if nothing had happened. In particular the public wanted to see the royal family in mourning and to have some ritual around Diana's death; a flag at half mast out-

side Buckingham Palace was deemed essential. The royal standard, the only flag to ever be raised at Buckingham Palace and
then only when the Queen is in residence, is never lowered to
half mast for anyone's death because the monarch lives on, but
the public didn't know that.

While outpourings of public grief filled the grounds of the
Princess's home at Kensington Palace, the Queen remained
silent and invisible. When the new prime minister, Tony Blair,
spoke of Diana as 'the people's princess', it widened the divide
between 'the people' who mourned her and her former
mother-in-law who didn't seem to be doing so. Many people,
after the revelations in Andrew Morton's book, felt that Diana's
troubles had been partly caused by the insensitivity of her
mother-in-law and husband. Newspapers asked, 'Have you got
a heart, ma'am?' and said, 'The British monarchy has been
given a warning that it is overdue for renewal. Let it take heed
and act.' By agreeing to a state funeral, to address the public on
television (after which she reputedly asked, 'Was that contrite

enough?') and to have the Union Jack at half mast outside Buckingham Palace, the Queen was forced to break with tradition and protocol. Her ex-daughter-in-law, in death, continued to dominate her mother-in-law's life.

Is the Queen fond of any of her children's spouses? She has not been the most fortunate mother-in-law. Three of her children have been divorced, causing her to question, as any mother would, how she might have contributed to their inability to remain married. She has not always been the best judge of the suitability of her daughters-in-law. The media was quick to claim that it was bouncy Sarah Ferguson who was the Queen's favourite daughter-in-law. She had seemed to be exactly what the family needed – lively, unpretentious but well balanced, an 'asset'. It was Diana who introduced her to Prince Andrew (they had met as children) at a house party at Windsor Castle during the week of Royal Ascot in 1985. The Queen liked her immediately, sufficiently to overlook her past (she had had boyfriends) and to believe that her worldliness would make her more able to settle into royal life. The Queen was grateful that she would want to marry Andrew, who for some time had been a 'handful'. The couple married the next year (becoming Duke and Duchess of York) and had two children within the next four years. Sarah, like Diana, was terrified of her mother-in-law.

Sarah's life experiences made her no more fit for royal office than Diana had been. She was barely on nudging terms with the monarchy – her father, Major Ronald Ferguson, was Prince Charles's polo manager – but it mattered less because Andrew was not going to become king. The Queen liked the fact that Sarah was a good horsewoman and cracked jokes, and hoped she would be company for Diana.

The Queen indulged Sarah's expensive tastes, her daughter-in-law being initially overawed and then eager to invite friends round to sample the 'goodies' as she called them. The media rapidly latched on to this love of the freebie, accusing her of never living in newly built Sunninghill Park, a vulgar ranch-style mansion costing £5 million, because she was too busy taking free trips abroad. Royal officials' attempts to limit her travel led her to petition the Queen, who allowed her daughter-in-law to have her way. Prince Andrew spent little time with his new wife; his life in the navy meant he was away from home for most of the year and Sarah blamed her in-laws for not supporting her, although the only option would have been for her to follow him, which was not thought safe.

To the Queen the break-up of this marriage also was a public relations disaster, but not the constitutional nightmare that loomed between her eldest son and Diana. Her daughter-in-law's behaviour became embarrassing with a series of tabloid revelations about affairs. Once Sarah had separated from Andrew, she continued within the family until she was caught by a tabloid in August 1992 having her toes sucked by an American business 'adviser' while sunbathing topless. Prince Philip was outraged, the Queen sufficiently appalled to agree to her immediate expulsion.

Sarah Ferguson now had to support herself. Through a combination of media work and book writing she paid off her £4 million personal debt and did, to some extent, gain the respect of her now ex-mother-in-law. The Queen was appreciative of the way in which Sarah's commercial behaviour was largely focused in the US, with her ex-daughter-in-law seeming to be careful not to hurt the image of the monarchy. Sarah's public remarks about her mother-in-law illustrate the impossibility of separating out the mother-in-law from the monarch. She is 'one of the greatest icons of all time but she is terrifying'; on the other hand she is 'one of the finest ladies I've ever met in my whole life. I'm so honoured to be able to say we are friends. I love her. She's given up her whole life to her country.' When Sarah was invited, for the first time in five years, to a royal family event, the memorial service for Princess Diana in 2007, she refused on the grounds that she felt like an outcast, despite having a good relationship with the Queen. Yet, according to Richard Kay, the *Daily Mail*'s royal correspondent for seventeen years, the Queen's relationship with Sarah is maintained for the sake of her grandchildren.

According to Kay, it is the unassuming Sophie Wessex who is the Queen's favourite daughter-in-law. Sophie, a former public relations executive who married Prince Edward in 1999, is the lowest-born of all the Queen's in-laws (her father sold car parts) and is ostensibly the least suited to royal life. Yet it is she who has had the closest relationship with the Queen. The Queen, by preferring the wife of her most favourite son, is in this respect no different from other mothers-in-law.

America may not have royalty but in the Roosevelts and Kennedys it had families who were similarly revered. The relationship between Sara Roosevelt and her daughter-in-law Eleanor has been subject to much speculation by historians. Was Sara domineering and controlling, or was she the victim of misrepresentation, largely by her daughter-in-law?

Sara and Eleanor knew each other from a distance before Eleanor met her future husband (and distant cousin) Franklin.

Eleanor had had an unhappy childhood; her mother died of diphtheria when Eleanor was eight and her father was an alcoholic and drug user who died a few years afterwards. Eleanor was brought up by her grandmother and assorted aunts and uncles who all drank a lot and largely neglected her. When she met Franklin she was desperate for affection and security. The two became engaged rather too quickly for Sara, who felt they were too young to get married and urged them to wait before making the engagement public. Franklin was Sara's only child and she undoubtedly adored him and devoted her life to him, her husband having died when Franklin was seventeen. Sara was an heiress and for all his life bankrolled Franklin and his family.

Before the marriage Sara would spend afternoons with Eleanor, trying to be a mother to her, offering advice and support. After the wedding she bought them a house adjoining hers. The houses had a common entrance and interconnecting rooms on certain floors. Eleanor was unhappy there, complaining that she was not adequately consulted and the house did not feel like her own, but overall she was grateful to her mother-in-law for assuming control. She wrote later: 'For the first year of my married life I was completely taken care of. My mother-in-law did everything for me.'

When the Roosevelts had children, Sara again assumed control, employing a nursery nurse at Eleanor's request. Eleanor was never good with babies and even as her children grew up she preferred to pursue political causes of her own rather than spend time with them. When the children were ill Franklin would call Sara for help rather than get Eleanor to look after them. The relationship Sara had with her grandchildren grated on Eleanor later on. Eleanor argued with her mother-in-law over the expensive gifts she bought them for Christmas. One grandson was given a car having crashed his previous one, although Eleanor had clearly said he needed to buy his own.

Mother-in-law and daughter-in-law also clashed over Franklin's political aspirations. He was president from 1933 to 1945 but although Eleanor was herself politically active in the Women's Trade Union League, African-American rights and the plight of families in the Depression, she was rather luke-warm about her husband's political achievements. Sara would stand in for Eleanor as First Lady for some of the more tradi-tional activities, which Eleanor did not like. Franklin sent his mother to Europe on a two-month tour as his goodwill ambassador. Such ceremonial activities made Sara a much-loved national figure. The nation initially took longer to warm to Eleanor, who was less con-ventional in her choice of political interests.

In fact Eleanor refused the title of First Lady, insisting on being called Mrs Roosevelt. Newspapers of the day asked who had the most influence over the president – his wife or mother? Since Franklin had had a paralysing illness in 1921, Eleanor became used to making public appearances on his behalf. As she grew more confident (she held her own weekly press conferences and had a daily newspaper column about her work) she became more disparaging about her mother-in-law.

Sara however only spoke admiringly about her daughter-in-law. She remarked that while her generation did not do the sort of work in supporting causes that Eleanor and the women of her generation did, she thought they were 'splendid'.

Undoubtedly Sara could be strident in her opinions. When she heard Eleanor was planning to drive around Europe with her children on holiday, she let Eleanor know she thought it undignified. Eleanor snapped at her and complained that her mother-in-law was a snob. When Eleanor and Franklin's children had a series of divorces and remarriages, Sara was adamant that Eleanor should take them to task. She feared they had never been taught right from wrong. As Eleanor was later to remark, she was not entirely sure what was right and wrong herself.

Eleanor oscillated between being critical of her mother-in-law and grateful for her help. When she organised Sara's eightieth birthday party she lamented to staff that she had not been a good daughter-in-law. Yet she fuelled the rumours that Sara was a dominating mother-in-law and after her mother-in-law's death co-operated with the play and film *Sunrise at Campobello* which depicted Sara as a harridan. Sara's grandchildren were horrified at this characterisation, as were household staff.

Part of the blame for the chasm that opened up between Sara and Eleanor lies with Franklin's affair with Lucy Mercer. Sara was furious and mortified for Eleanor who she knew would be severely damaged by this betrayal. Sara told Franklin that if he divorced Eleanor he would no longer have his mother's financial support. The marriage was saved but Eleanor never felt the same about her husband and Sara's unconditional love for him was irritating to her. When Sara died her reputation was gradually eroded by stories of her controlling behaviour, particularly as a mother-in-law, but her grandchildren were staunch in their defence of her. Elliot Roosevelt wrote of his mother's austerity and distance. He claimed that the warmth and all the good things in life when they were little came from their grandmother.

The Kennedy family also had a strong matriarch in Rose Kennedy, the mother of President John Kennedy and mother-in-law of Jacqueline Lee Bouvier (who after the assassination of her husband John went on to marry Aristotle Onassis). Rose was born into a strongly Catholic family with political aspirations. Her father became a charismatic mayor of Boston and imbued a love of politics into his eldest daughter that persisted throughout her life. She married Joseph Patrick Kennedy in October 1914, after a long courtship. Her father had been opposed to the match but when he was involved in a scandal over his relationship with a girl of Rose's own age, Rose asserted her will. This brush with infidelity was a recurrent theme in Rose's life, a weakness that ran through the male line. Her husband amassed a huge fortune as a businessman and his political aspirations were realised when Roosevelt made him his British ambassador in 1938. His lack of support for the

Allies in the war (he infamously predicted the end of democracy) led to his resignation and the end of hopes for high political office. Rose devoted herself to raising children, nine within seventeen years. She was devastated by her husband's infidelities but perversely this made her intolerant of the distress of her own daughters-in-law over their husbands' infidelities. Wives, she believed, should hold marriage sacrosanct and turn a blind eye to their husbands' affairs.

Rose's first chance of being a mother-in-law occurred when her daughter Kathleen announced she was getting married to Billy, a Protestant. Although Billy wrote to her asking her forgiveness for falling in love with Kathleen, Rose was 'heartbroken and horrified' and instead of attending the wedding was admitted to hospital to avoid reporters who understood too well how Rose felt about the union.

Rose soon had a real tragedy to contend with. Her oldest son, Joseph, brought up to realise the Kennedy political ambitions, was killed in a flying mission during the Second World War. The focus now fell on John Fitzgerald Kennedy, or Jack as he was known. To be a credible political contender he needed a wife who would enhance his prospects. Jacqueline Bouvier was the 'Inquiring Photographer' for the *Washington Times-Herald* when she met Jack at a dinner party. She was intelligent and from a privileged background but Rose was not enamoured of her. Jackie's independent spirit ran counter to Rose's philosophy of putting the Kennedys' interests above all others. Before their wedding Jackie and Jack spent time at the family's summer home in Hyannis Port, where Jackie refused to engage in the competitive tennis matches and touch football games that characterised Kennedy get-togethers. Rose was particularly incensed by Jackie's habit of sleeping late. After their marriage Rose continued to be cool to Jackie and unsympathetic to Jackie's distress over Jack's playboy behaviour. Jack's rapid political progress from senator to president in 1960 made infidelity an insignificant flaw in Rose's opinion. Rose herself had campaigned with vigour for her son, showing remarkable energy for a woman of seventy. She was his warm-up act, touring ahead of him across the country and extolling his virtues in a series of speeches.

Her tolerance of infidelity was convenient because her other daughters-in-law, Ethel Skakel, who married Robert, and Joan Bennett, who married Edward, all had to put up with it. Rose applied the high standards she had adhered to in being a wife and mother to her daughters-in-law. As a mother she had compiled a list of improving books for her children to read, such as *Kidnapped* and *Treasure Island* by Robert Louis Stevenson. Her children had also taken part in family quizzes and Bible readings. She expected her daughters-in-law to be as careful in intellectually stimulating their children as she had been. She was critical of profligacy and looked for evidence of this failing in the homes and habits of her daughters-in-law. As a mother-in-law she was forceful and opinionated.

Ethel was the daughter-in-law most willing to look to Rose for inspiration in bringing up children. She encouraged her children to be physical, as Rose had done with her children, even though the fighting between them was sometimes violent, and she discussed newspaper articles with them over supper. She had few disagreements with Rose although her mother-in-law was shocked by Ethel's love of fine wines and irritated by her extravagant housekeeping, noting her displeasure at hearing Ethel was having crab for supper.

In Rose's autobiography *Times to Remember* she includes a note that she sent Ethel rebuking her gently for putting an expensive clock in a maid's room. Her motivation for pointing out the clock's value (around $90) was to stress the importance of respect for personal possessions which, she felt, for many people were hard-won. Her autobiography also includes another letter to poor Ethel, telling her that her children were ignorant about the history of Thanksgiving and suggesting that Ethel might review history and current affairs more thoroughly with them. Rose's level of interest in the well-being of her grandchildren verged on the intrusive. She went so far as to write to Ethel to tell her to make her children take their bikes in at night. If they didn't, they should be banned from riding them the next day.

Rose was known to be rather vain in her old age and disinclined to pose for photographs that put her close to her daughters-in-law. Jackie rapidly became the most glamorous member of the Kennedy family and as First Lady developed a style that became admired throughout the world. Rose gave no indication that she felt any jealousy. She was delighted when Jackie chose to call her 'Belle-mère', the French term for 'mother-in-law', which she saw as rather glamorous. Rose did grow to appreciate Jackie's differences, crediting her with encouraging Jack's interests in art, poetry and music. Her view of their marriage, however, was either disingenuous or genuinely optimistic. She wrote of their 'loving, understanding and devoted relationship'. At times, such as after Jackie suffered a stillbirth, they were undoubtedly close, but Jack's campaigning and infidelities made their marriage more problematic than perfect.

Rose and Jackie spent most holidays together but it was Jack's assassination in 1963 that brought a genuine intimacy to their relationship. Both women were devastated. Rose was to speak of her admiration for Jackie's bravery and dignity. Jackie was always loyal to Rose and only criticised her once, in an interview after Jack's death in which she referred to Rose's lack of affection towards Jack. In Rose's autobiography she, like the other daughters-in-law, supplied a eulogy. Jackie extended her regard to all mothers-in-law by writing, 'And I think it's so sick when you hear these mother-in-law jokes on the radio or any of the media. They used to make me sad even before I had a mother-in-law. They really used to make me almost angry when I hear them, because I'd think, are people really like that? And then this woman, my mother-in-law, she just bent over backwards not to interfere. If she gave a suggestion, it was in the sweetest way.'

Jackie's view by this time was no doubt softened by compassion for the tragedies that had hit Rose. After Joe's death, Kathleen had been killed in a plane crash, and Jack's assassination was followed by Robert's. Rose had been remarkably brave, breaking down only once in front of Jackie, when she grasped her hand and forbade anyone to feel sorry for her.

For a woman who had been so passionately devoted to her sons and so involved in the upbringing of her grandchildren, Rose was remarkably generous in her response to Jackie's subsequent marriage to Aristotle Onassis. Jackie, she wrote, was so warm-hearted and such a lovely woman that she needed to marry again. Jackie was thrilled by her support. 'When I married Ari she of all people was the one who encouraged me, who said, "He's a good man," and, "Don't worry dear." She's been extraordinarily generous. Here I was, married to her son and I have his children, but she was the one who was saying, "If this is what you think is best, go ahead."' Rose was a frequent visitor after their marriage. She outlived Jackie, who died in 1994, although she had a stroke that confined her to a wheelchair. She died in 1995 at the age of 104. Jack once remarked that she was the glue that held the family together. But it was her daughter-in-law Jackie who provided the compliment that must have pleased her the most. Jackie said of her, 'What a thoroughbred.'

Katharine Whitehorn on mothers-in-law and daughters-in-law

The relationship between mother-in-law and daughter-in-law has no obvious rules so with the best will in the world it will go wrong. In my work as an agony aunt for *Saga* magazine, I get letters from mothers-in-law who have been treated terribly by their daughters-in-law. One daughter-in-law wrote out a contract for her mother-in-law that she had to agree to before she could come over. She had to agree never to bring food and never to pop round without ringing first. I think the daughter-in-law was terrified of the mother-in-law taking over.

There was a couple who were living in the same house as their son and daughter-in-law and they tried to be helpful. The daughter-in-law would often dump the grandchildren on them on the pretext of feeling ill. The mother-in-law would sometimes cook for both the families to save her daughter-in-law the trouble and, so as not to intrude, would leave the dish on the stairs where they could collect it. One day after she'd done this, her son came back with the dish and she asked if they had liked the meal. 'I don't know,' he replied, 'Joanna shoved it in the bin as soon as she saw it.' Now why did the son tell her and why did the daughter-in-law do this?

What is really heartbreaking is when mothers-in-law who have been pivotal in looking after their grandchildren lose access to them when their son and daughter-in-law split up. The daughter-in-law thinks it is bad enough to have to give access to her hated husband but wants to draw the line when it comes to her mother-in-law.

Mothers-in-law can be difficult. There was a daughter-in-law I have heard of who, when she looked at the wedding pictures, saw her husband's mother was standing there very close to him, holding his hand. When he died suddenly she was terribly upset that he hadn't left her any money, but what son, when he's making out his will, would think he was going to die before his mother?

A lot of the trouble is caused by the lack of a real relationship between mother-in-law and daughter-in-law and when they get to know each other as real women and share experiences it works out fine. One of the *Saga* letters I remember vividly because I was so appalled by it said, 'My daughter-in-law never has anything to say unless we are talking about her family. We meet regularly for tea and family occasions but unless we talk about her family she doesn't speak.'

I thought: there is no social interaction here at all. I told them to unfreeze these formal situations; they had to meet at other times. These nice family occasions can be terribly formal and for a mother-in-law to get to know her daughter-in-law they have to have time alone together. If it stays formal it is hopeless. Mothers-in-law don't think of the girl in her own right, instead they think of 'my son's wife' or 'the grandchildren's mother'. It can be a tricky thing when the mother-in-law thinks they are terribly helpful offering financial or actual help because sometimes if you asked the young girl they would rather be left to get on with things themselves. The less sure you are of what you're doing, the less help you may want.

My daughter-in-law Nancy is splendid. She may have another take on our relationship but I think we get on well and she is very nice to me. Bernard, my oldest son, turned up with her one day, unannounced, and I am sure he did it on purpose so as not to make a big deal of it. When they had their daughter Ruby I offered to help when Nancy went back to work in the mornings, but it was always fudged, so I wrote to her and said, 'Look, this is ridiculous, I'm an under-used resource, use me. I can do one morning a week.' So then I would come to the house at 9 a.m. and get Ruby to the nursery by fair or foul means. When Nancy came home we would go for lunch and that was when I got to know her. Nancy's mother was dead, so I guess there was a spot for me. I see them about once every two weeks now and we'll go for a walk on Hampstead Heath with their children and then we have a meal together and talk about all sorts of things.

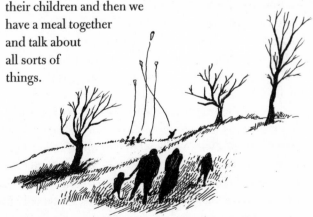

It's wonderful – they are both very agreeable. Nancy and I are very different people, so it's important that we did get to know each other. She's very Green, for example.

She's also a much better mother than I am and I think I let her know that. The way they bring up children is excellent but exhausting. They limit the television and computer which is good. What's tiring is that the house is run as one big democracy, so no one ever says, 'That's it, I decided, chop chop, let's go.' Instead it's 'Here are six reasons why you need to do something.' When my husband Gavin died, they were very supportive to me. Nancy's the best thing that's ever happened to Bernard. She gives him a reason for everything he does. Their wedding was touching and hilarious. I paid for a third of it but I didn't interfere, the young arrange things themselves. They got married in a Unitarian church because they don't go on about God too much. Bernard was wearing his first ever suit and Nancy had on a Laura Ashley dress with sparkly high shoes. There were sixty to seventy people of whom twenty were children who had never heard the word no. A friend of theirs gave a lovely reading wearing a lilac satin suit and bovver boots and her son was peering through the bars of the pulpit like a gorilla. It was hilarious and moving. I was weeping and laughing at the same time.

Initially I was very lucky with my own in-laws. My mother-in-law was super. She used to have this phrase that made me laugh. She'd open her mouth to rebuke my husband Gavin about his table manners and then she would stop and say, 'Well you're Kath's problem now.'

My mother-in-law did two lovely things. Gavin and I got engaged in Greece and when we came back I finally went to

Birmingham to meet her. She had done this beautiful album of Gavin from his birth up that she gave me. Then they wrote to me afterwards and said how pleased they were he was marrying me and used the phrase 'not only his choice but ours'.

Initially my mother-in-law and I got on like a house on fire. But later on I think they identified me too much with all the things they didn't like about modern life. Ann was a Quaker; she never drank, except for having a drop of champagne at our wedding. She had never had a proper job after she married but when her children were grown up she did a few days a week in the Friends' office in Bournville. She was working on updating the lists of people who were registered as Quakers. Gavin was twenty-eight at the time and she asked him if he still thought he was a Quaker. She said to him, 'You're a grown-up, now make up your mind. Do I put you on the new list or not?' Although Gavin had been in the air force during the war he told his mother that he was still a Quaker. Later my mother-in-law told me that she could have transferred him to the list perfectly well. She said the Friends wouldn't have minded that he had been in the air force or that he drank but what they wouldn't have understood was a man of twenty-eight who couldn't make up his mind.

Gavin and I were lucky because we could leave our children with my parents and Gavin's parents so we could spend weekends together. Ann was very good with small children but then everyone was better with small children than me. Gavin always said his mother was not so good with adolescents. He remembers confiding in her when he was in love for the first time and she said, 'Oh don't be so silly.' She lived for her family. She was a very good, conventional wife, married to a man who was an accountant, who joined a firm at sixteen and retired from it at sixty-seven. The atmosphere in her house was always bubbly, lovely and easy-going. It didn't matter if you were late coming down for dinner. By the time my parents had died in the early 1980s it was nice to have an older generation around who were familiar and warm.

The relationship got more difficult as they got older and Gavin started drinking too much. They never said anything but when something goes wrong with your lovely little offspring you probably do blame their wife or husband. Maybe they thought that I was having this marvellous twentieth-century life and that I wasn't being a caring wife. But although they identified me as a disruptive influence at the end they were marvellous for most of the time I knew them. It is probably true that no mother wants to think her son can be at fault. One has a great deal of tribal loyalty and it is a great mistake to underestimate it.

Mixed Feelings about Mothers-in-law

Mothers-in-law are more likely than most people to arouse mixed feelings. Not quite family but close enough to matter, their position makes them vulnerable to falling in and out of favour.

Maria Cecile Weber, the mother-in-law of Mozart, has been depicted as the 'evil spirit' in Mozart's destiny by the music historian and critic Alfred Einstein and is portrayed in some biographies as a woman on the look out for a meal ticket for her family. Worst of all, however, is Einstein's accusation that the mother-in-law of Mozart, one of the greatest composers the world has ever known, was unmusical. In fact there is no evidence that Frau Weber was unmusical, and while Mozart's attitude lurched from love to detestation and back to adoration, she was always fond of him.

Leopold, Mozart's father, was such a dominating man that he made the friendly Weber family seem particularly welcoming to his son. By the time Mozart met the Webers, his father had hawked him round the world's courts as a child prodigy and was putting considerable pressure on him to make his fortune in music. As a young man, lodging in Vienna and employed in a series of court appointments, he was delighted to accept Frau Weber's offer to lodge in her house. Mozart had met the family a year previously when he had fallen in love with the eldest daughter, Aloysia, a talented opera singer who married Joseph Lange, a German actor. At the time Mozart was devastated but he recovered quickly. By the time of this second meeting Mozart's mother (whom he had adored) had died, making him susceptible to kindnesses from motherly women. On accepting her offer, Mozart wrote to his father, 'Old Madame Weber was so kind to take me into her house, where I have a pretty room, and am with obliging people, ready to supply me at once with all that I require . . .' When his father was lukewarm about the arrangements, reminding him of his previous infatuation with Aloysia, Mozart defended his adopted family. 'I was a fool about Madame Lange, I own, but what man is not when he is in love? . . . Believe me when I say old Madame Weber is a very obliging person, and I cannot serve her in return in proportion to her kindness to me, for indeed I have not had time to do so.'

In Einstein's analysis Frau Weber plotted for her family to 'sponge' off Mozart. Her husband had died leaving nothing but a small box of linen, according to the probate court reports of the time, and funding the upbringing of her children through the acquisition of sons-in-law may have been a reasonable plan. Einstein is unsympathetic. She was, he insists with venom, 'an evil genius that shadows many men's lives, which they can no more escape from than a fly can keep out of a spider's web'.

Mozart was soon writing to his father, mentioning another daughter, Constanze Weber: 'I banter and jest with her when time permits.' Rumours soon spread. In July 1781 he informed his father that for the sake of Constanze's reputation he was changing his lodgings.

*I repeat that I have long had it in my head to remove to
another lodging, solely from people's gossip and very much
do I regret being obliged to go on account of such nonsense, in
which there is not a word of truth. I should really be glad to
know why certain people take pleasure in spreading ground-
less reports. Because I live with them, I am to marry the
daughter. Nothing was said as to my being in love with her;
that was entirely passed over – merely that I lodge in their
house and am to be married . . . Frau Weber says it would
grieve her to be the innocent cause of annoyance to me. This
is the sole reason why I have for some time (since people
began to gossip) thought of changing my residence.*

Mozart's change of residence did not interrupt his composi-
tions, or his contact with the Webers whom he continued to see
daily. Despite his assurances to his father that there was nothing in his relationship with Constanze, he asked for permission
to marry her in December 1781. In his letter to his father he says
he is a religious man who would neither want to seduce an
innocent girl outside of marriage or to 'fool about with
whores'. He told Leopold that he wanted domesticity, similar
to that which he had seen in the Weber household, and swore
that he loved Constanze 'with my whole soul, as she does me'.

Leopold did not leap for his pen to send congratulations,
instead voicing concerns about both the suitability and timing
of this engagement. But pressure was being put on Mozart to
marry Constanze. Frau Weber may have been innocent of forcing Mozart's hand but her daughter's guardian Johann
Thorwart intervened. Mozart detailed Thorwart's accusations
in a letter to Leopold. They were, he wrote, that: 'I had no

fixed income, that I frequented her society too much, that I would perhaps leave her in the lurch and thus make the girl miserable. The guardian became very uneasy at these insinuations. The mother, however, who knows me and my integrity was perfectly satisfied and never said a word to him . . . The guardian besieged the mother with his remonstrances till she told me of them and begged me to speak to him myself, as he was to be there shortly.'

Thorwart was apparently not convinced of the sincerity of Mozart's intentions and insisted that Frau Weber end the association. Mozart told his father, 'The mother said, "I cannot forbid him my house; he is too good a friend of ours, and one to whom I am under great obligations. I am satisfied; I trust him. Settle it with him yourself." So he forbade my seeing her at all, unless I gave him a written engagement.' Was Frau Weber's assurance sincere? The contract demanded that Mozart promise to marry Constanze within three years and that if he failed to do so he would pay her three hundred florins a year. Mozart told his father that such was Constanze's indignation that she took the contract and tore it up.

If Frau Weber had been trying to push the couple even closer together, this ploy worked. 'This trait endeared Constanze still more to me . . .' wrote Mozart. Leopold was outraged by Frau Weber and Thorwart, telling Mozart they should both 'be put in chains, made to sweep streets and have boards hung round their necks with the words "seducers of youth"'.

He refused to give his consent to the marriage. He had concerns about the suitability of the entire family. In one letter he said that Frau Weber was rumoured to drink excessively.

Mozart quickly responded, 'Your postscript about her mother is justified only in so much as she likes wine, and more so I admit than a woman ought to. Still I have never seen her drunk and it would be a lie if I were to say so. The children only drink water – and although their mother almost forces wine upon them, she cannot induce them to touch it. This often leads to a lot of wrangling – can you imagine a mother quarrelling with her children about such a matter?'

In August Constanze went to stay with Baroness von Waldstadten, who was known to both the Webers and Mozart as a music patron. This allowed Constanze to see Mozart more easily but Frau Weber became almost hysterical about the risk to her daughter's reputation. She threatened, via her daughter Sophie who was visiting her sister, to send the police in to bring Constanze home. It was with real desperation that Mozart wrote to the baroness to ask, 'Have the police really the power to enter any house they please? Perhaps this may only be a snare to lure her home. But if it could be so, our only resource is that Constanze should marry me early tomorrow or this very day if possible; for I will not expose my darling to such an insult, from which as my wife she is secure.'

They were married, in the presence of Frau Weber, on 4 August 1782. Mozart continued to be furious with his mother-in-law for having threatened to call the police and the couple got on badly with her for some time after the wedding. Constanze would often be found sobbing after meeting her mother and Mozart banned all visits apart from special occasions. It was only the birth of their first child that reconciled Mozart to his mother-in-law. In telling his father of the birth of his 'fine, sturdy boy' he says, 'My mother-in-law by her great kindness to her daughter had made full amends for all the harm she did her before her marriage. She spends the whole day with her.' The reconciliation allowed his mother-in-law to insist on feeding the baby milk, rather than giving him water, as Mozart had been given as a newborn.

Mozart's relationship with his mother-in-law became closer from this time. Frau Weber was overtly proud of her son-in-law and often attended his concerts and operas. She increasingly devoted herself to his comfort and happiness. When Leopold finally agreed to visit the married couple and meet his grandson, Frau Weber made an enormous effort to serve him a supper that he would approve of. Leopold, who was not easily pleased, was completely won over, writing to his daughter Nannerl, 'I must tell you the meal, which was neither too lavish nor too stingy [sic] was cooked to perfection. The roast was a fine plump pheasant; and everything was excellently well prepared.' In such a manner the rift between Leopold and his son's mother-in-law was healed. The relationship was also eased by Leopold's pride in his son's piano concertos and string quartets – even the emperor was heard to shout 'Bravo Mozart!'

Life outside of Mozart's brilliant composing was difficult for the young couple. Constanze's repeated pregnancies and miscarriages made her ill and Mozart paid for her to go to various spas in Baden to recover. Alone in Vienna, he would meet his mother-in-law for supper and take her to his operas where he would give her the libretto to read beforehand. 'We may well say of mamma that she sees the opera, but not that she hears it,' he wrote to Constanze. Einstein takes this to mean Frau Weber had no ear for music – it is just as likely that by now she was partially deaf.

Sophie, her youngest daughter, later wrote of her mother's relationship with Mozart during the last few weeks of his life, 'Well, Mozart became fonder and fonder of our dear departed mother and she of him. Indeed, he often came running along in great haste to the Wieden (where she and I were lodging at the Goldner Pflug) carrying under his arm a little bag containing coffee and sugar, which he would hand to our good mother, saying "Here mother dear, now you can have a little 'jause' [afternoon tea]." She used to be as delighted as a child.'

Mozart was under considerable stress at this time, having been engaged by a wealthy and mysterious patron to write a requiem mass. A combination of poverty, missing his wife and ill-health made him convinced that the masterpiece he was composing would be his own requiem. When Constanze came back from Baden she was horrified to find him exhausted and seriously ill.

Sophie wrote of how, during this illness, she and her mother made him a padded dressing gown to protect him from the cold. 'We visited him constantly . . . one Saturday when I was there Mozart said to me, "Now dear Sophia, tell your mama that I am going on very well and that I shall be able to pay her a visit during the octave of her name day to congratulate her." Who could be happier than I was at bringing such joyful news to my mother – news which indeed she could scarcely have expected.' It was clear how much Mozart meant to his mother-in-law. The relationship that had started so warmly had become so again.

Sophie's memoir of the last day of Mozart's life shows the Weber family's love for Mozart, as well as, touchingly, her own self-interest. She is mulling over whether she should go into town to see him (he had looked better anyway the previous day and she didn't like to wear nice clothes when she walked into town) while she makes some coffee, and as she does so the candle goes out, despite the room being 'airless'. Sophie shudders involuntarily and takes the candle as an omen, confiding her feelings to her mother who says she must rush into town to see Mozart 'but bring me back word immediately how he is . . .'

Mozart is clearly dying and asks Sophie to stay and comfort Constanze, but understands Sophie's promise to his mother-in-law to tell her how he is. 'How shocked my poor mother was,' writes Sophie. Mozart died that night, aged thirty-five. He was buried in a pauper's grave and his remains have never been recovered. His mother-in-law, already old and frail, was devastated by his death and died two years later.

Geniuses may not be easy for anyone to get on with, let alone for mothers-in-law. While her mother-in-law was alive Virginia Woolf belittled and despised her. Yet after her death she wrote about her in affectionate terms. Such was her ability to capture the foibles of a person, and so vulnerable was her mother-in-law to ridicule, that one hopes Marie Woolf (known as Lady) never rifled through her daughter-in-law's diaries. Virginia was never going to be the dutiful daughter-in-law. She did have room in her life for a mother figure; her own mother Julia had died when she was a teenager and Virginia later immortalised her in the knowing, ethereal character of Mrs Ramsay in *To the Lighthouse*. Lady, however, was not the type of woman that Virginia would seek as a maternal replacement.

Virginia met Leonard Woolf, her husband, within the Bloomsbury group of writers, painters and critics whose society was intellectually terrifying and exclusive. Leonard could not facilitate any warm relationship between his wife and mother as he himself did not have a close relationship with his mother. Lady had had nine children altogether (she had been widowed at the age of twenty-two and married Sidney Woolf, the executor of her late husband's will, who also died young) and expected to be adored in the same extravagant way that she adored her children. Leonard wrote of her: 'She lived in a dream world which centred on herself and her nine children. It was the best of all possible worlds, a fairyland of nine perfect children worshipping a mother to whom they owed everything . . .' His impatience was communicated to Virginia who realised she would have no competition for his affections from her mother-in-law. Leonard felt he was his mother's least favourite child.

Leonard took Virginia to meet his mother for dinner, an event that Virginia predictably ridiculed afterwards. The Woolfs were Jewish, although liberally so, all of Marie's children marrying outside the religion. Virginia congratulated herself on being liberal enough to marry a Jewish man, but was not sufficiently so to excuse 'their nasal voices' or to prevent her writing cruelly about his mother and sisters. The first meeting did not go well; Virginia took against her future mother-in-law's voice and manners, rather shamefully writing in her diary, 'I think Jewesses are somehow discontented.' She was irritated by Marie's 'prattling on'. 'She has, I think, the qualities of a person who has never altogether grown up, in spite of nine children and all her cares. She gossips and enjoys herself and bursts into tears because she feels she ought to burst into tears; but she tells her stories with spirit and somehow deals with life very freely and easily and with the liveliest childlike interest in it all, mixed with the most absurd conventions.' What Marie thought of Virginia is not documented, but Marie was no fool and would have quickly got the measure of her clever but sarcastic daughter-in-law.

Throughout their relationship they had a running joke that whenever the couple went round to Marie's house for tea, as soon as Virginia walked into the room after Leonard, Marie would say, 'And Virginia?' and Virginia would smile and say, 'Conceal your disappointment at the sight of me.' Following which Marie would laugh and give Virginia a kiss and a pat on the arm. 'We were on friendly laughing terms, always at the same stock joke which carried us through those two-hour teas. "And tell me what you have been doing?" And I would have some story ready.' Virginia, on reflection, said it had taken them years to reach this level of intimacy.

Marie was not invited to their wedding, but was dignified when Leonard wrote to tell her that they were having a quiet wedding. 'My dear Len,' she wrote, 'To be quite frank, yes, it has hurt me extremely that you did not make it a point to have me at your marriage.' But she ended her letter with loving sentiments. She always treated Virginia kindly and having been depressed herself, had some sympathy for her daughter-in-law's bouts of paralysing depression.

For a woman whose family was her life, she struggled to understand Leonard and Virginia's bohemian lifestyle and the absence of children (Virginia was not keen on sex and there were fears she was too fragile physically and emotionally to have children). Marie was unlikely to have been spared rumours of Virginia's affair with Vita Sackville-West but kept her own counsel. Leonard and Virginia visited dutifully and, as Marie grew older and infirm, took their turn in taking tea in the claustrophobic hotel room she had moved into in Earl's Court.

After Leonard had his mother to stay for a weekend, Virginia was sufficiently exasperated to write to her sister an account of the visit, in the style in which Marie talked. In the letter she mimics Marie talking effusively about Len (his clear brain and splendid qualititles and how he could have been a successful barrister) before randomly launching into, 'Have you read Radclyffe Hall's book I have got it from Harrods . . .' Her words, Virginia sneered, were a stream of consciousness, a description often applied albeit more flatteringly to Virginia's own writing. Marie was now in her late seventies and such chatting would have been understandable in an elderly lady. She remained mentally active and was desperately concerned about the plight of the Jews in Germany in the 1930s, with which Virginia, rather harshly, accused her of being obsessed. Lampooning easy targets was one of Virginia's less attractive qualities.

Marie was a sentimental, generous woman, presenting them with a huge cake and electric coffee maker on their silver wedding anniversary. At the age of eighty-seven she had a fall and died in hospital shortly afterwards. Leonard wrote honestly after her death about his lack of patience with her sentimentality and optimism. Virginia wrote more poignantly in her diary that she went to the service at the synagogue but felt it had nothing to do with 'Lady'. Her observations in her diary reflect the complexity of feelings but also her predominant affection for her mother-in-law.

> *What was she like then? Let me see – she was small, narrow shouldered – things slipped off – she wore a low blouse with a pearl necklace – & rather heavy. Her head nodded. She had stiff grey black hair . . . Yet there was something spontaneous about her. A great joy in family, in society . . . she could make friends out of anyone; was very popular with elderly gentlemen . . . She would tell the whole story of Gone with the Wind for example, talking as if they were real; a trait odd to me in so shrewd a woman, for she had as she was often boasting, brought up 9 children. Never went to bed, she said, without a basket of socks by her side . . . Sometimes tho' she made me feel the daughter emotion – when I kissed her when Clara [one of her daughters] died. She attaches to nothing in my own life; except the comment she made that she was the elder generation: & I (now the elder, to most people) was the younger. I never saw her save in her own surroundings. These were fussy, yes, but full of stir; always presents of flowers: children's letters . . . I know nothing of interest about her, now that I come to write, only little anecdotes, about Holland, nothing that makes her a real person – save is Virginia coming? Which touches me.*

The poet Dylan Thomas only wrote about his mother-in-law fleetingly in letters, but his relationship with her was close at times, although he found it frustrating to be cooped up with her. He was a man of huge charm but could be intolerable to live with. Yvonne Macnamara is unusual among mothers-in-law of famous men in that some of her letters have been preserved. Her letters to Bill Read, an American biographer of her son-in-law, are mostly functional but show glimpses of her fondness for Dylan, her pride in his work and her desire to ensure that after his death he is fairly represented. She spends considerable time writing notes, hunting for iconic photographs of Dylan for Read and offering corrections for his manuscript. 'You give such a picture of Dylan, not too sweet, not too unpleasant,' she writes approvingly. 'I hope you will get good reviews when it comes here.'

Yvonne Macnamara was, for her day, an unusual woman. Caitlin, her beautiful blonde daughter, who married Dylan, recalls in her autobiography that her mother neglected her three daughters 'deploringly'. Yvonne, who was half French and half Irish, left Caitlin's father, himself a poet and drinker, and in the mid 1920s bought a house near the New Forest, called the New Inn. There the girls had an eccentric upbringing; Yvonne had an affair with a neighbour called Nora Summers. Her preoccupation with Nora allowed the girls considerable freedom to roam the New Forest. Caitlin had a few exotic love affairs before meeting Dylan, whom she married in the absence of her mother or any other relatives or friends in Penzance registry office.

Dylan's brother-in-law had phoned Yvonne Macnamara before the wedding to warn her not to let her daughter marry

Thomas (for reasons that may have been genuinely to do with the family's concerns that he shouldn't marry anyone), but Yvonne seems not to have acted. After their honeymoon in Wales, she allowed them to live with her at the New Inn, where they stayed for six months, although Dylan found the country-side dull. He would write every day in a room that was a converted woodshed, with a writing table in front of a large window. The couple sometimes cycled or walked through the New Forest but often ended up in the local pub.

It was fortunate that Yvonne was as casual a mother-in-law as she was a mother. The young couple would spend after-noons in bed together, eating sweets and reading to each other, before returning to the pub. Caitlin was drinking as much if not more than her husband but her mother seemed to have no con-cerns about her daughter living as a sodden poet's muse.

Dylan wrote and revised a good volume of poetry, being largely undisturbed. From the woodshed appeared 'I make this in a warring absence' and 'After the Funeral (In memory of Ann Jones)'.

Yvonne was perhaps more maternal to Dylan than she was to her own children. When he felt down, as he often did, she would feed him bread and milk to comfort him. At the end of one of his stays he noticed that he had put on a couple of stone in weight.

Dylan and Caitlin left his mother-in-law's house only to return to it when Caitlin was heavily pregnant. Thomas wrote to a friend, 'This flat English countryside levels the intelligence, planes down the imagination, narrows the a's, my ears belch up old wax and misremembered passages of misunderstood music, I sit and hate my mother-in-law, glowering at her from corners and grumbling about her in the sad, sticky, quiet of the lavatory.' Did he really hate his mother-in-law during those weeks before his son was born? Yvonne may have been a scapegoat for his frustration at being stuck in Hampshire. He was unlikely to have been easy to live with and his mother-in-law may well have disapproved of him in the two weeks after his son was born because he was permanently drunk.

Yvonne, suspecting that neither her daughter nor son-in-law would be capable of looking after a baby, engaged a former nanny to look after little Llewelyn and continued to shore up the couple's fragile relationship. By the time they had their next child, a daughter, Dylan was rarely sober and such was their insolvency that Caitlin would go home to her mother's house with the children while he roamed between Wales and London. The family came together in Wales for a while but

Llewelyn spent most of his time at Yvonne's house. When Dylan began to earn more money, and his mother-in-law asked for some financial assistance, he refused.

Caitlin and Dylan's marriage was violent and beset by infidelities and jealousy. When he died of pneumonia Caitlin was unaware of it, having been committed to a private psychiatric hospital after a drunken episode at his bedside. Yvonne, rather remarkably, did not bear grudges, even on her daughter's behalf. Although by the time Bill Read contacted Yvonne many years had passed since Dylan's death (Yvonne was seventy-eight) and Caitlin had remarried and been sober for some years, she is remarkably generous in her memories of her son-in-law and amnesic about his failings. It is unlikely that Dylan, a romantic but troubled and drunken genius, ever appreciated these qualities in his mother-in-law.

For the Australian singer Peter Allen, there were many qualities in his mother-in-law that he admired, but even more that were insufferable. Judy Garland not only chose him to be her daughter's husband but expected him to be a knight in shining armour for both of them. When Judy Garland saw his act in a Hong Kong hotel in the spring of 1965, she was smitten not only with his singing but with his easy-going personality. She was at this time a deeply troubled woman, addicted to drugs and alcohol. She had been fired by her film studio and was trying to salvage a singing career. She had recently taken an overdose (her attempts had long since run into double figures). Meeting Peter seemed to rejuvenate her. At their first meeting she talked about becoming his manager but was already imagining herself in the role of his mother-in-law.

He would, she thought, be the perfect husband for her oldest daughter Liza. Peter reminded Judy of Liza's father, who, like Peter, later revealed he was bisexual.

Peter, who had grown up in a violent household in small-town Australia (his father beat him and his mother and later shot himself), thought Judy was warm and charismatic and believed that she was offering him the possibility of stardom. Judy brought him to England to meet Liza, introducing him with: 'This is the boy I've been telling you about. Peter, this is my daughter I've been telling you about. You'd be perfect for each other.' They had at least one thing in common; both were the unhappy and disturbed children of alcoholic parents. It was enough for them to announce an engagement within three weeks. In interviews Liza spoke of how Peter was exactly like her, and how they had been good friends before they fell in love. In already knowing Judy, and being himself a performer, Peter, she said, understood his future mother-in-law and the stress she was being put under. 'So he could say to Mamma, "Relax", and she would listen to him. She adores him.'

It sounded like Liza was marrying him for her mother. He was always more brotherly to Liza than a passionate lover, frequenting the gay bars of Manhattan with his singing partner throughout their relationship. But even before they married Peter was a devoted son-in-law; he helped Judy to pay her bills, calmed her down and looked after Judy's younger children Lorna and Joey whenever she had a mad alcoholic rage and smashed mirrors and furniture in front of them. There were times when his affection for her was tried. Judy, barely knowing what she was doing, would angrily throw her children out of the house, leaving them to run round to Liza and Peter's apartment. Peter would soothe them before ringing Judy and brokering a peace. Judy, oblivious to what had happened, would often blame Peter, accusing him of kidnapping her children.

On the day of Liza and Peter's wedding, there is a picture of Judy dressed in satin with a smile broader than the horizontal stripes on her dress. She was reported as saying she loved being a mother-in-law because it was such a 'normal' thing to be.

When Judy died in 1969 (she was forty-seven and Liza was twenty-three), it was Peter who took the call and broke the news to Liza. Both were devastated. The next year they separated and Peter's music career took off. He died of an AIDS-related illness in 1992. One of the songs in his repertoire was written for his mother-in-law and always got a standing ovation.

'Quiet Please, There's a Lady on Stage'

Quiet please, there's a lady on stage.
She may not be the latest rage,

But she's singing, and she means it.
And she deserves a little silence.

Quiet please, there's a woman up there,
And she's been honest through her songs
Long before your consciousness was raised.
Now doesn't that deserve a little praise?

So put your hands together, help her along,
All that's left of the singers, all that's left of the song.
Stand for the ovation,
And give her one last celebration.

Quiet please, there's a person up there,
Who's singing of the sins that none of us could bear
To hear for ourselves,
Now give her your respect if nothing else.

So put your hands together, help her along,
All that's left of the singers, all that's left of the song.
Rise to the occasion,
And give her one last celebration.

Quiet please, there's a lady on stage.
Conductor, turn the final page.
When it's over, we can all go home.
She lives on on the stage alone.

So put your hands together, help her along,
All that's left of the singers, all that's left of the song.
Stand for the ovation,
And give her one last celebration.

Put your hands together, help her along,
Let's just stay here all night; let's sing every song.
Won't you rise, rise to the occasion,
Yes, give her one last, just one last celebration.

Mothers-in-law who Took a Stand

A mother-in-law can be a formidable force when she thinks her son-in-law is treating her daughter badly. The men in this chapter are formidable themselves, which makes these mothers-in-law the more notable for taking a stand against them. They also stood up to their sons-in-law at times in history when it wasn't generally done for women to oppose the will of men.

No one would suggest that David Livingstone, Scottish missionary and African explorer, was not a great man, but he wasn't as careful of his family as he might have been. This rather infuriated his mother-in-law, Mary Moffat, who was a prominent missionary's wife in Africa but is now almost unheard-of outside of missionary circles. The conversion of 'heathens' may not be seen so romantically these days, but in the nineteenth century a missionary life was not only a self-sacrifice but a dangerous one – the risk of malaria and tick-borne fevers being far greater than that from the 'heathen' population.

Mary Moffat was born Mary Smith into a comfortable and happy family in a town near Manchester. She went to the Moravian school at Fairfield where she was so inspired by reading reports from missionaries in Africa that she declared, while still a young girl, that she would lead a missionary life. Part of her attraction to Robert Moffat, who would become her husband, was his readiness to join the London Missionary

Society. Not long afterwards Robert left her in England to spend three years building up a mission in Africa before she sailed out to meet him in Cape Town in 1819, where they were married.

They settled at the mission in Kuruman, north of Cape Town, an arid, inhospitable area, where they tried to introduce the locals to Christianity and an English way of life that included encouraging them to wear clothes. For an English woman, the transition from comfortable home to partial shelter, where crops were hard to grow and there was no obedience to English etiquette (locals would come uninvited to stay the night), was challenging. Tribes often fought each other and when Mr Moffat left to do missionary duties away from Kuruman, his wife, with their children, waited anxiously at the station. Mrs Moffat, however, did not complain. She was a strong-minded woman who learnt to cook, do the laundry, garden, nurse anyone who needed it and create a home for her family where standards of cleanliness were legendary. She taught local children to read and count and encouraged them to sew and make some clothes for 'the sake of decency'. When her husband was away she continued to run the mission, visiting sick people and teaching and saying prayers with whomever she could get to listen. Hard as this life was, Mrs Moffat was happy and devoted to her husband and the role of a missionary's wife. As she told a friend in England, 'I always studied my husband's comfort, never hindered him in his work, but always did what I could to keep him up to it.' She worried, however, that her children (she gave birth to nine altogether, although they did not all survive) would not be educated well enough to serve God, and sent her eldest girls, Mary and Ann, to a school in Cape Town. The girls spent two years away from their mother, staying with friends in the holidays because the trip home was too arduous. Mrs Moffat wrote to a friend in England telling her of the success of their work. 'I am happy to inform you that the converts are going on well ... The standard of morality is considerably raised, so that those who are no way particularly serious abstain from those sins which were formerly committed with impunity. They are becoming generally more civilised.'

At one stage the family returned to England and Robert Moffat undertook a speaking tour of England, telling audiences of his work and trying to raise money. Both Mrs Moffat and her oldest daughter Mary missed Africa. Mrs Moffat found life as a Victorian housewife constricting and unsatisfying. It was while the Moffats were in England that they met David Livingstone, a serious young man who was a great admirer of Robert. Livingstone was born in Scotland of working-class parents and trained as a doctor, deciding to combine this with his strong faith to become a medical missionary. Later his missionary zeal would be diverted into exploring the interior of Africa and to expounding strong anti-slavery views.

Livingstone was twenty-seven years old when he first arrived in Africa, working at the Kuruman station for two years before the Moffats returned. He then moved north to set up a new mission in Mabotsa. While he was there he was mauled by a lion and taken back to Kuruman to be nursed by the Moffats. It was this that led to his marrying the Moffats' daughter Mary. She was plain but selfless and full of common sense. Having been nursed by her, Livingstone decided she would support rather than detract from his work and the two were married in

1845. Mrs Moffat had some concerns. She was delighted her daughter would remain in Africa, but suspected that her son-in-law had a reckless streak. She was aware of his plans to reach communities deep in the continent's interior and feared for her daughter's safety. She also suspected that his drive and vision would dominate their lives and Mary's happiness would be sacrificed for the greater good of Livingstone's vision.

Mrs Moffat's fears were soon realised when early on he took Mary back to Mabotsa, where she quickly became pregnant. He then left her to find somewhere to launch a new mission. Soon after the baby (a son called Robert) was born they moved to Chonwane, an undeveloped, arid region where Mary was soon pregnant again and rapidly became ill and exhausted. Mrs Moffat bravely came to visit her, with local attendants but without her husband. She was shocked by her daughter's appearance and they both quickly realised that however much Livingstone loved his family, he would sacrifice anything for his missionary work. His mother-in-law was relieved when the couple returned to Kuruman for Mary to deliver her second child. It was difficult for her to take issue with her son-in-law because his justification was that what happened to them was God's will and he had to pursue God's purpose.

In pursuing God's purpose Livingstone decided to take the family by ox-cart to Lake Ngami, with Mary once again pregnant. It was a calamitous trip. The region was full of mosquitoes carrying malaria, which the children caught, the baby was born prematurely and died, and Mary had a stroke. Livingstone said it was God's will, but Mrs Moffat, who had intrepidly and fortuitously decided to visit them once again, blamed her son-in-law. Livingstone, she felt, was not only risking his wife and

children's lives by taking them into malaria-infested areas but was also leaving their home in a terrible state of disrepair. Convinced that he was too high-minded and impractical to care for his family, she took them back with her to Kuruman once again to feed them and restore their health, only for her son-in-law to undermine her work when they returned to him.

Mrs Moffat begged her daughter to promise never to accompany her husband on trips again, but Mary, once again pregnant, wrote to her mother telling her of his plans for another family exploration trip. Her letter was intended to make her mother ask Livingstone to change his mind. Mrs Moffat took the hint and wrote to her son-in-law reminding him of how dangerous their last journey had been. Mrs Moffat's anguish is palpable in her letter:

> *Was it not enough that you lost one lovely babe, and scarcely saved the others, while the mother came home with paralysis? And will you again expose her and them in those sickly regions on an exploring expedition? All the world will condemn the cruelty of the thing to say nothing of the indecorousness of it. A pregnant woman with three little children, trailing around in the company of the other sex, through the wilds of Africa, among savage men and beasts! Had you found the place to which you wished to go and commence missionary operations, the case would be altered. Not one word would I say, were it to the mountains of the moon. But to go with an exploring party, the thing is preposterous. I remain yours in great perturbation, M. Moffat.*

The arguments were incontrovertible but her son-in-law ignored them. During the expedition Mary gave birth and once again became paralysed down one side. It was this, not his mother-in-law's entreaties, that made Livingstone decide to send his family to England so that he could explore more freely. Here Mary was to encounter her own mother-in-law, but the plan for them to live with Livingstone's family in Scotland was quickly revised. Mary and her mother-in-law did not get on, although no correspondence as to why has survived. Mary's children probably did not conform to her mother-in-law's rigid standards of behaviour and Mary herself was miserable and drank brandy, which was shocking to Livingstone's parents but had been recommended by her own mother as a cure for various ills. Whether or not Mary drank too much has been a matter of speculation, but during the two years that her husband left her to bring up their four children she was certainly unhappy. He returned to a hero's welcome and the lecture circuit but by the time he left for Africa again with Mary, she was pregnant again and Livingstone swiftly arranged for her to go to Kuruman to give birth, while he continued his expedition.

When she finally met up with him again three years later it was to embark on another expedition to Lake Nyasa. Within a few months she became feverish and her body swelled alarmingly. Livingstone, realising suddenly that she was seriously ill, did what he could, but she died. His love for his dumpy, loyal wife was reflected in his inconsolable grief. To his mother-in-law who had often been critical of his treatment of her daughter, he revealed the extent of his sorrow: 'My dear mother, With a sore heart I give you the news that my dear Mary died here on the 27th. This unlooked for bereavement quite crushes and takes the heart out of me. Everything else that happened in my career only made the mind rise to overcome it. But this takes away all my strength. If you know how I loved and trusted her you may realise my loss . . . There are regrets which will follow me to my dying day.'

His mother-in-law was already mourning the loss of her son Robert when she heard of her daughter's death. She wrote to her grandson Robert, Livingstone and Mary's son, in October 1863, 'The mournful tidings of the death of your dear mother only came to our ears just when our hearts were yet bleeding over that of her brother, our own dear Robert. For some time after these mournful bereavements I did not feel able to use my pen, and when strength of mind was yet restored, it was only to address those dear ones who were partakers of our sorrow. For your dear father too, we feel much, and dread any increase of his trials.'

Mrs Moffat died only two years before her son-in-law (Livingstone died in 1873, probably of malaria) and did not see him again, although to her grandchildren at least, she remained supportive of his work. She died after returning to England, the inclement winter weather giving her a fatal chest infection.

Mme de Montreuil, mother-in-law of the Marquis de Sade (best known for lending his name to sadism and for his sexually explicit writings), had a monumentally different sort of son-in-law to contend with and was eventually his nemesis. She contrived to put her son-in-law in prison to protect her daughters, money and family name. There may be many mothers-in-law who disapprove of how their sons-in-law treat their daughters, but few can have had more claim to do so than Mme de Montreuil.

The Marquis has his supporters, who cite the sexual honesty in his literary writings and the hypocrisy of the French aristocratic classes as mitigating factors for his scandalous and debauched sexual practices. These practices, which usually involved torture, coprophilia, blasphemy and orgies, would have recommended him to few people, whatever the other aristocrats were doing.

Donatien Alphonse François was born in Paris in 1740, the son of a rather serious and physically fragile mother and promiscuous, opportunistic father, Jean Baptiste de Sade, a former captain in the army who then worked in ambassadorial positions. The Comte de Sade was a member of the French nobility who fell out of favour with the King, leaving his family in a financially perilous state. This combined with the Comte's dissolute lifestyle made him intolerable as a husband. Donatien's mother took herself off to a convent and remained there until she died. Donatien, who went on to look for replacement mothers for the rest of his life, was brought up largely in a Jesuit school under the eye of his uncle. As he reached adulthood he rapidly became known for his uncontrollable rages and depraved sexual practices and, on a more mundane note, as a haughty loner who felt his insights into life were the only ones of consequence.

Donatien saw active service in the army but never rose through the ranks. He was disliked by some colleagues and pursued gambling and whoring with such singlemindedness that it gained him a bad reputation, no mean feat in the French army of that time. He came out of the army in 1759 with venereal disease, a penchant for dancers and actresses, an obsession with sodomy (then a capital offence in France), and little else.

His father, who had until now revelled in his son's activities, began to see him as a liability and decided to marry him off.

The French nobility did not rush to offer up its daughters, having heard of Donatien's reputation. However, a wealthy and respectable family, the Montreuils, who had some recent noble connections but wanted a link with older nobility, expressed an interest. It was ironic they thought the name de Sade would boost their social standing. Mme de Montreuil was forty-three years old and was regarded as an intelligent and strong-minded woman. Her husband had bought a high office in the judiciary and Mme de Montreuil, known as 'la présidente', was admired for her charm and steely determination. When rumours reached her of her prospective son-in-law's deviant behaviour, she coolly remarked that all young men had committed 'follies' every now and then. The Comte de Sade couldn't believe his luck. Far from taking a stand against Donatien, it looked as though Mme de Montreuil had succumbed to his considerable charm.

Donatien was less enthusiastic about marriage but his father insisted, tying up a marriage agreement that was of financial benefit only to him. The bride, Renée-Pélagie, was plain but Donatien had no choice. He behaved impeccably well, prompting his mother-in-law to write to his uncle congratulating him on his nephew's good breeding and fine manners. He was, she said, a 'most amiable and desirable son-in-law'. The Comte was amazed at how his son had captivated Mme de Montreuil. She now called him 'that amusing child' and while she quickly realised how thoughtless he was, she was confident that he had a good heart and that marriage would settle him down. The two bickered occasionally but there was a mutual fondness, Donatien telling people that he was delighted with his mother-in-law and father-in-law, who were looking after his interests with 'an incredible eagerness'.

In Mme de Montreuil, Donatien had found a second mother, who unlike his first was eager to support him. He wrote of his joy in addressing her as 'mother'. Their relationship was more confiding than most relationships between mothers and sons. He claimed to have discussed with his mother-in-law both the merits of anal sex and his ambivalence about her daughter. Mme de Montreuil, he felt, understood his need to seek sexual adventures elsewhere. Five months after the wedding in June 1763 he did exactly that. He had managed to survive some months with his in-laws in Normandy but on his return to Paris he picked up a prostitute called Jeanne Testard, took her to a house he had rented for such purposes and subjected her to an ordeal which included threatening her with torture and subjecting her to profanity and blasphemy, swearing he would kill her if she did not take an enema and defecate on a crucifix. The next morning Testard told the police and they quickly found the house and the identity of the man behind her ordeal. Louis XV was only too pleased to sign a *lettre de cachet* – an order that the King himself would sign that circumvented the law and could not be appealed against through legal channels – ordering his imprisonment. When Donatien was given permission to contact someone outside he chose his mother-in-law.

How he managed to convince his mother-in-law that the affair had been exaggerated is unknown, but the redoubtable Mme de Montreuil bought permission for him to be remanded into her custody in their Normandy chateau and hushed up the affair. She was still optimistic about her son-in-law, hopeful that her little boy would mature into a more respectable young man. Donatien was thrilled with how capably his mother-in-law had cleaned up after him. It wasn't long before she needed to do so again.

The death of Donatien's father deeply upset him and for a while his mother-in-law thought his grief might be having a stabilising effect on him. It did not, however, stop him from increasing the size of the dossier on his sexual activities with prostitutes that was now held by the police. His mother-in-law began to lose patience, particularly when he slighted her daughter by publicly passing off a dancer as his wife. He continued to behave in a scandalous manner, and was wanted by the police after one particularly unpleasant episode when he was alleged to have abducted and tortured (by pouring hot wax into wounds he cut into her back) a working woman called Rose Keller. De Sade had fled immediately after the incident to his mother-in-law's house where he gave his sanitised version of events and begged for help in evading the police. This diluted the effects of any other versions that reached his mother-in-law and she stepped in and bribed Keller not to give evidence, reassuring herself that her son-in-law's offence was an 'act of folly'. In reality it was a sadistic attack on a woman who had been terrified for her life. Between such acts of folly her son-in-law had been busy producing two children with her daughter and helping himself to considerable amounts of Montreuil money.

It took a few more scandals, including de Sade's seduction of his wife's younger virginal sister, sodomy with servants and a sadomasochistic incident with a group of Marseilles prostitutes which included some accidental poisonings, for his mother-in-law to realise her son-in-law was not only unmanageable but now notorious among Paris's eighteenth-century equivalent of the vice squad. She moved swiftly. This was Mme de Montreuil's finest hour. Renée-Pélagie was enthralled with her husband and would never have turned against him, but Mme de Montreuil knew she had to act quickly to protect her grandchildren from their father's reputation and to stop her son-in-law squandering the family fortune.

Understanding how French justice worked she bought a *lettre de cachet* authorising her son-in-law's imprisonment. She then used the illness of his mother to entice him to Paris – Sade so rarely communicated with his mother that he had not known she was sick. By the time he arrived (simultaneously planning sexual exploits while visiting the sickbed) his mother had died, a fact his mother-in-law was already aware of. Meanwhile Mme de Montreuil, anxious that de Sade should not realise she was plotting to imprison him, responded warmly when he wrote to her of his mother's death and asked her to be a mother to him. He later claimed he wasn't fooled by her reply and knew she had turned against him, but in fact he was shocked by what he felt was a terrible betrayal. He saw himself as the loving son who had rushed to his mother's side, only to be captured by agents of his mother-in-law and marched off to a dungeon at Vincennes. He wrote to her from his prison cell, 'Of all the possible ways that vengeance and cruelty might have chosen, you will agree, madame, that you have selected the most horrible. I came to Paris to be with my mother during her last moments, my sole purpose was to see her to embrace her once more if she was still alive or to mourn her if she was no more. And it was that moment you chose to make me your victim once again.'

The love he felt for his mother-in-law was transformed into hatred. He threatened to kill himself, but these were threats he had made before. He pleaded with his in-laws, saying that he had hoped they would adopt him now his parents were dead, not incarcerate him. He wrote to his wife: 'Your abominable mother is most annoyed that I have not yet taken my life, it is as if this infernal monster set loose against me by all the demons of hell has declared, "Yes I want to see you grow to hate everything that is dear to you; I want to wrench apart all the bonds that might link you with others . . . Your children were dear to you; I shall scatter my serpents even over them, it is my wish they too will revile you."' His wife wrote a furious letter to her mother, but Mme de Montreuil was steadfast in her determination not to help him.

His novels went on to contain the most disgusting descriptions of mothers and quasi mothers-in-law being raped and tortured. His letters to his wife were full of obscenities directed at Mme de Montreuil. It is unlikely, however, that his mother-in-law ever read anything he wrote after this time. When his pleas for freedom were ignored, he begged his mother-in-law to take care of his children, to love them and to educate them so they could avoid the 'misfortunes' of his 'misplaced upbringing'. His mother-in-law managed to get a court hearing to clear her son-in-law's name but it was a cleansing operation only – de Sade had been sentenced to death in his absence by a French court for the poisoning incident and she did not want her grandchildren to be stigmatised by their father's crimes. She ensured that he stayed behind bars and promptly ordered the destruction of the torture chamber in his ancestral home. De Sade railed at her, mostly through her daughter. Hell, he said, never spewed out anything as horrible as his mother-in-law.

Mme de Montreuil stood firm, declaring that she would be neither his 'dupe' nor his 'confidante'. Through his mother-in-law's efforts and the disinclination of the French ruling class to free him, he was kept in jail for over a decade, being released only during the revolution, when the *lettre de cachet* was declared illegal. He had reinvented himself as Citizen Sade to blend in with the new regime and on his becoming a free man his long-suffering wife promptly divorced him. His freedom lasted some years but the pornographic literature he had published was considered obscene and he was thrust back into jail, as was his publisher. His mother-in-law died at the age of eighty-one, in the same year that her son-in-law was imprisoned again.

Lord Byron was no Marquis de Sade, but his sexual permissiveness would have tried the patience of most mothers-in-law (see Chapter Ten for an account of his relationship with Lady Melbourne, the mother-in-law of Caroline Lamb, with whom he had an affair). The influence that his mother-in-law, Judith Milbanke, had over his life was quite profound. It prompted him to say, 'I should, many a good day, have blown my brains out, but for the recollection that it would have given pleasure to my mother-in-law; and even then, if I could have been certain to haunt her.' It should be presumed that Judith Milbanke would indeed have danced on her son-in-law's grave.

Byron was twenty-four years old when he decided to marry Annabella (Anne Isabella) Milbanke. She wasn't really his type, being rather serious and modest, but she came from a wealthy family and Byron's confidante, Lady Melbourne, who happened to be Annabella's aunt, heavily promoted the match to both parties. Lady Melbourne's promotion was motivated by self-interest: she wanted to extract Byron from an affair he was having with Lady Caroline Lamb, the wife of her son William. Annabella had developed an interest in Byron after reading his acclaimed poem *Childe Harold's Pilgrimage* and their social circles overlapped, although Byron did not take much notice of her until he was sent a copy of some poetry she had written, which he thought was rather good. In October 1812 he proposed to her, on the basis that she was pretty, rich and calm enough (after Caroline's violent outbursts) to suit him. Annabella, however, refused, fully aware of his public and dramatic affair with Caroline, although she did so in a way that made Byron say he was more proud of her rejection than he would ever be of another's acceptance.

Annabella rapidly became convinced that actually she was in love with Byron and had made the wrong decision. She set about courting him, writing a stream of letters and sympathising with him over widespread rumours that he was having an incestuous affair with his half-sister Augusta. It may have been a temporary yearning for domestic normality and an interest in the Milbanke money that made him propose once again to Annabella. Perhaps he hoped, somehow, that Annabella would save him from himself. Whatever his motivation he had to overcome his dislike of her mother. At the time of his first proposal he wrote to Lady Melbourne, 'My only objection (supposing of course that ye Lady's was got over) would be to my Mamma from whom I have already by instinct imbibed a mortal aversion.' The feeling was mutual. Judith Milbanke was not enamoured of Byron but she was so indulgent of her only daughter, whom she had had at the relatively advanced age of forty, that she would never have denied Annabella her choice of husband. During the couple's four-month engagement she convinced herself of the desirability of the match. Annabella, she told Lady Melbourne, had never been interested in any man other than Byron; he, meanwhile, had 'proved that his attachment is steady and sincere'.

Judith Milbanke was over sixty when she met Byron. She was clever and from a top-drawer family but had none of the social charm or remnants of beauty that attracted Byron to

Lady Melbourne. She had been devoted to her husband, and the scale of infidelity that her son-in-law had pursued was anathema to her. During the engagement Byron stayed with the Milbankes and could not fathom Lady Milbanke at all, finding her silent and suspecting her of trying to find out his weaknesses. He was sure, and correct in his assumption, that she did not like him, although he could have won her approval had he treated her daughter better.

The wedding went ahead but no sooner were they driving away in their carriage than Byron apparently began behaving badly, warning Annabella that she would pay for initially refusing him and telling her how much he hated his mother-in-law. In fairness, these accounts came from Annabella after she was estranged from her husband, but Byron himself made derogatory comments about their marriage shortly after the wedding. Annabella began to suspect that Byron did harbour a passion for his half-sister although she was unsure if it had been consummated. What was just as intolerable were his rages, drinking, gaming and general neglect of her. She had romantically imagined that she could reform him but quickly realised this was impossible. While she was pregnant he regaled her with stories of the mistresses he was seeing and when Lady Milbanke came to see her in London, Annabella informed her of the true state of her marriage. Byron's mother-in-law was horrified and promptly succumbed to an asthma attack. Both women took to their beds, Annabella to give birth, her mother to recover from the shock of hearing about Byron's behaviour. Annabella gave birth to a daughter and while reports of Byron's response vary they agree that he was not delighted. His wife, however, who was plotting her escape from her marriage already, was tormented by the fear that he would try to gain custody of their child.

Lady Milbanke, anxious to look after her daughter and granddaughter, invited the whole family to their home in Kirkby. Byron took advantage of the offer to tell Annabella rather flippantly that she was welcome to leave and he was inclined to be a single man again. Annabella left with her daughter and Lady Milbanke was swift to engage a legal opinion – the lawyer advised a separation. Annabella may not have been ready for this but her mother had taken control. Friends had advised her that Byron was so unstable that her daughter was no longer safe with him, and she was ready to fight to extract Annabella and the baby from a life that she considered to offer violence and misery. Byron suspected his mother-in-law was behind Annabella's now entrenched position and had Augusta write to his wife, asking if the separation was really at her request. If it was, he said, he would not oppose it. He conveyed a dramatic change of heart towards Annabella, declaring in a series of increasingly passionate letters that he had loved her and didn't want a separation.

Lady Milbanke wasn't having any of it. She was convinced that he was playing a game with Annabella and feared that his brutality towards her for refusing his first marriage proposal would be nothing compared to how he would treat her after this separation. 'Is that mad man to have care of the child?' she asked a friend. She became convinced that he would give the baby to Augusta to bring up. Even after the separation was agreed, mostly due to her efficient work, she was wary of her son-in-law. She bought a pair of pistols that she swore she would use to protect her granddaughter from any kidnap attempt by Byron. Her son-in-law continued, through Lady Melbourne and Augusta, to try to influence his wife but eventually signed the separation papers and shortly afterwards left for Italy. He continued to write to her during the last eight years of his life, fervently believing that his mother-in-law had been the instigator of their separation. While he never sought custody of his daughter, after death he was reunited with her. His daughter, who had been called Augusta after his half-sister, had left instructions in her will to be buried next to him.

Andy on his mother-in-law Von

Within the family lexicon, the word 'mother-in-law' comes second only to 'stepfather' for negative connotations. As it happens, when I gained a mother-in-law, I also became a step-father. So it's perhaps no surprise that I have little sympathy for the popular myths that surround these particular familial designations. Better still, nor does Von, my mother-in-law.

When I first met Von fifteen years ago, her only daughter was not long separated from her first husband, with whom she had two children. Our future was uncertain, to say the least. It could so easily have been an uncomfortable situation. That it was instead a memorable pleasure was due in large part to the tact, charm and warmth that are Von's signature qualities. Nor have we had a disagreeable moment since.

My wife is originally from New Zealand, and that's where Von continues to live. I don't doubt that there are some men who must dream of their mothers-in-law being located twelve thousand miles away, but I have no reason to be one of them. On the contrary, as much as I enjoy Christmas visits to Auckland every couple of years, I often regret that Von doesn't live round the corner.

For one thing, she's a fabulous grandmother, thoughtful and loving with that conspiratorial informality that kids instinctively know to respect. But I'd really like to see more of her for selfish reasons. Not only has she been immensely supportive but she is also unusually good fun.

How many mothers-in-law, I wonder, would suggest a visit to the cinema with their sons-in-law to see a French film with the title *A Pornographic Affair*? And trust me, it wasn't a romantic comedy. If that makes her sound a little too racy, then I'm conveying the wrong impression. There's nothing 'improper' or 'eccentric' about Von. It's just that she is a stranger to social awkwardness in all forms.

At seventy-nine she retains a lively intellectual curiosity that men and women half her age can no longer match. Yet – how can I put this? – I would be dishonest if I claimed that her attractions lay entirely in her bright and approachable character. A head-turner who must have caused more than her fair share of neck strains in her youth, she remains a strikingly elegant woman.

When reminiscing about her early romances, my wife likes to complain that her boyfriends seemed more interested in her mother. And while I may seem guilty in this appreciation of continuing that unchivalrous tradition, I have to confess that my admiration is only further enhanced by the lightness with which Von has always worn her looks.

Perhaps this all sounds rather too good to be true? Surely there must be some lurking tensions or unspoken differences, the kind of dark material that lies beneath most family relationships if you dig deep enough. Well, the answer is yes, in a way. But not between Von and myself. Such difficulties that have arisen have been between mother and daughter. Nothing dramatic or frequent, just the minor frictions that all parents and children generate, regardless of age.

I haven't had a chance to nurture any of my own resentments (and that would require a neurotic effort beyond my imaginative powers), because, when push comes to shove, or misunderstanding to mild grievance, I tend to take Von's side. So much for the cliché of the mother-in-law undermining her daughter's husband.

Just recently Von came to stay with us for a couple of weeks. Her husband, Jerry, is too infirm to travel, and he was taking a recuperative break in hospital. When I make the long trip to New Zealand, I tend to behave as if I were the first person in the history of international travel ever to suffer jet lag. It takes me about ten days to recover, during which I'm to be seen in a washed-out state reminiscent of advanced heroin addiction.

Von arrived at Heathrow, after her twenty-four-hour flight, looking as if she had just stepped out from a fifteen-minute taxi ride. Completely uninterested in the abundant opportunities for moaning, she sang the praises of the flight and its attendants, and then volunteered to make dinner when we got home.

We went on a family holiday to Cornwall for a week. I have friends who couldn't share house space with their mothers-in-law for twenty-four hours without fleeing to the pub. But each day was a joy. A veteran of Himalayan hill-walking, Von used to display the kind of unstinting energy that left me exhausted just watching. Happily, she has slowed down to the point that we now operate on the same holiday regime: a brief walk, a long lunch and an afternoon nap. That's my kind of woman.

I have an image of Von from that holiday that is stored for good in my memory. She is on the beach of Watergate Bay with her granddaughter, our seven-year-old. It's a brilliant blue-sky day, the Atlantic waves are rolling in, and the two of them are playing hide-and-seek, lost in a moment of their own making, while my wife and I watch from the comfort of a nearby restaurant. There's something about this scene – aside from the fact that I get to sit and drink wine – that makes a kind of holistic sense of life.

When my own mother died six years ago, I mourned that she wouldn't watch my daughter grow up. And I also mourned the fact that she would no longer watch over me. It was as if, without her witnessing them, the good things or achievements in life had been robbed of meaning. It's a testament to Von that in her presence, and even in her letters and phone calls, that meaning seems to make a miraculous return.

Mad, Bad and Scheming Mothers-in-law

It is the misfortune of mothers-in-law to have their stories told by people (sons- and daughters-in-law) who may dislike them. As such they risk being portrayed as shadowy, spiteful figures who are to blame for their family's troubles. It's hard to know how true these depictions are because there is usually no one to speak up for the mothers-in-law. They are unlikely to be as famous as the people writing about them, so nobody will have collected their diaries and letters to provide any evidence to the contrary. Such is the case for William Makepeace Thackeray's mother-in-law, who is vilified in his letters and through vicious characterisations in his novels. Then there are other mothers-in-law, such as the Countess of Lennox in Tudor times, who are guilty of no more than ineffectual scheming. Finally there are the truly wicked mothers-in-law, guilty of torturing and even murdering their daughters- in-law.

Thackeray's best-selling novel *Vanity Fair*, published in 1847–8, put him, as he told his mother, 'all but at the top of the tree'. (The very top was occupied by Dickens.) The story of Thackeray's life is as melodramatic as any Victorian novel, with a depressed wife, attempted drowning, mad mother-in-law and a doomed young love. He began working as a hack with ambitions to write, but when he met his future wife he was relatively unsuccessful and had little to offer a woman. Isabella Shawe was a surprising choice for Thackeray, a worldly man in his mid twenties, while she was a scrawny seventeen-year-old, living in a boarding house in Paris with her formidable mother. Isabella was a delicate girl with fine features and red hair who was prone to worrying about her health, particularly constipation, and spent many hours lying on her bed. She had nothing obvious to recommend her but her letters show her to be affectionate with a good sense of humour. Mrs Shawe, an Anglo-Indian widow with four other children, had mood swings that seemed merely eccentric for the time but nowadays would probably fit the diagnostic criteria for several psychiatric disorders. Thackeray, who drew fantastic caricatures, later produced a cruel one of his mother-in-law, showing a sour woman, dressed bizarrely, with a mad glint in her eye. He was so caught up in his obsession with Isabella that he did not consider the significance of her mother's emotional instability.

Mrs Shawe was not happy about a penniless would-be writer marrying her fragile daughter, but despite her opposition the two became engaged. As Thackeray wandered backwards and forwards between Paris and London trying to find employment, he wrote to Isabella frequently, pressing his suit but painting a rather unappealing picture of domesticity and bullying her to write to him. He implied that marriage would separate her from her mother, which didn't go down well with Mrs Shawe. To reassure them both Thackeray said that when they married they would have a 'snug apartment in Paris with a spare bedroom where please God your mother will occupy long and often'. The separation, he explained to Isabella, related solely to what would happen in their bedroom. Nevertheless it prompted Mrs Shawe, on some pretext about her daughter's health, to restrict Thackeray's visits with the aim of breaking their engagement.

Thackeray was devastated, writing to Isabella, 'I can't live without you that's flat,' and promising to ask her mother's permission to call once or twice a week. On the positive side he hoped the rift 'will put the intimacy which ought to exist between your Mother & me upon its proper footing for I think that when we are not too intimate or familiar we shall be much better friends'.

The estrangement, if anything, mysteriously precipitated their marriage on 20 August 1836; Mrs Shawe must have approved in order for it to proceed. The ink had scarcely dried on the marriage certificate before Thackeray declared his true feelings for his mother-in-law: returning from a social gathering he wrote to his mother, 'My Mother in-law who was present talked as big as Saint Paul's; she is a singular old devil, and has become quite civil of late. I don't know why I dislike her so much.'

But as so often happens, the birth of their first child (Mrs Shawe's first grandchild) in 1837 brought reconciliation. She was the first person Thackeray wrote to, with proud excitement. 'We had intended to keep profoundly secret an event which had just occurred. Mrs Thackeray after walking to Piccadilly on Monday . . . requested me to find a medical gentleman which I did and on my return had the pleasure to find another Miss Thackeray arrived in my family . . .' Thackeray was pursuing writing work wherever he could but Annie was born into debt and by the time Isabella was pregnant again, later that year, the situation was even more desperate.

This is really a story of two mothers-in-law, because Isabella quickly established a correspondence with Thackeray's mother,

Mrs Carmichael-Smyth (she had remarried after Thackeray's father died), who in her own way was as disastrous a mother-in-law as Mrs Shawe. Isabella had hoped for a warmer relationship than she had with her own mother, but Thackeray's mother suffered from the unhelpful syndrome of believing no one was good enough for her son. While Isabella's letters to her are informative and affectionate, she was sufficiently critical of Isabella's 'laziness' and inability to nurture her son that poor Isabella ended at least one letter to her pleading with her mother-in-law not to be angry with her. Thackeray himself had to ask his mother not to be so openly critical, as a mutual friend had passed her comments on to Isabella. 'Mrs P repeated to Isabella just before her confinement every word you said, about her faults not doing her duty and so on and in the course of her depression the poor thing had worked up these charges as to fancy herself a perfect demon of wickedness.'

Isabella's second child, Jane, was born in July 1838 and died in March the following year. Isabella bore this bravely at the time, although her letter touching on Jane's death to her mother-in-law shows her despair, but Thackeray underestimated the toll this tragedy had taken on his young wife. He was not an emotionally supportive husband but to some extent his behaviour was driven by the desperate need to earn money. He continued in his bachelor ways, getting commissions as a journalist that required him to travel and network in gentlemen's clubs, while Isabella slipped slowly into depression. When Harriet was born in 1840, Isabella's mental health was miserably stretched. Her letters to her mother-in-law give the first indication of this overwhelming depression. 'My body has been unhealthy and consequently my spirits low . . . I confess to you I feel myself excited my strength is not great and my head flies away with me as if it were a balloon.'

Thackeray, despite her pleas for him to stay home, had gone to Belgium for work and when he returned was shocked to see her 'excessive lowness of spirits'. Sea air was the ticket, he decided, and took her to Margate where she improved temporarily although her daughter Anne later described an incident unseen by her father in which Isabella had tried to drag her, resisting, into the sea. When they returned home he concluded, conveniently, 'there can be nothing the matter with her (but indigestion . . .).' Isabella however remained 'low' and Thackeray complained to his mother that it was hard to work with 'the pitiful looks always fixed on me'. His remarks seem callous today, as Isabella clearly (in the modern light of day) had severe postnatal depression.

In desperation Thackeray thought that a spell with his mother-in-law could revive Isabella, and they set off for Cork, where Mrs Shawe now lived. Thackeray clearly hoped with his mother-in-law's help to minimise the disruption to his life caused by his sick wife. Mrs Shawe had other ideas. She was deeply unimpressed by his self-centred excuses for not wanting to care for his wife. She was incensed by his letter, saying, 'Do what he will a man is but a bad nurse and you and Jane [her sister] must look to the little woman and get her back to spirits again.'

Instead of an unconditional welcome, Mrs Shawe had written to say she would be happy to see them but her house was not big enough to accommodate them. Thackeray had been outraged. However, once they arrived in Cork and Mrs Shawe took over his wife's care, he was relieved enough to admit that his mother-in-law had done Isabella 'a great deal of good'. Mrs Shawe confided in her son-in-law that she herself had been 'affected with melancholy when she nursed'. Isabella's emotional state was more than just melancholic. Thackeray's initial relief at handing over the care of his wife to his mother-in-law was all the more intense because of the drama that had occurred on their journey from London. On the crossing to Cork, Isabella had tried to commit suicide by throwing herself into the water and been found, floating on her back, paddling feebly with her hands. Thackeray eventually told his mother about the incident (out of fear that Mrs Shawe would gossip sufficiently for it to reach her ears). 'I see now she had been ill for weeks before and yet I was obstinately blind to her state,' he wrote. Isabella, he said, had been insane.

Within a couple of days of being in Cork Thackeray became exasperated with his mother-in-law, who incessantly bragged about her self-sacrifice in nursing her daughter, but he was prepared to excuse her on the grounds of madness; she was, he wrote, 'really and truly demented'. Isabella continued to improve and as she did so, Thackeray accused Mrs Shawe of being 'unmotherly' and putting concerns about her own nerves above her daughter's needs. 'The woman is mad, more desperately self-deceived than any I ever knew ... Every time I see the woman I pray God (for poor Isabella's sake) to keep me out of a quarrel.' His anger reflected his own guilt over Isabella. Mrs Shawe did not spare him her opinion that he had neglected her daughter and, while he had never brought her to visit in happier times, was pretty quick to dump her on her doorstep when she was sick. She asked him directly if he had ill-treated Isabella and was openly rude to him. For Thackeray, who was devastated over the change in his wife and felt responsible for at least failing to notice her declining mental health, the atmosphere became unbearable.

When his own mother wrote offering to look after the Thackeray family, he replied, 'I have been half tempted to fling it in Mrs Shawe's face and say there Madam you who prate about self-sacrifices, you bragging old humbug see the way in which my mother welcomes your daughter and think how you have received her yourself. But the woman is mad that is the fact . . . it is in vain to talk reason to her.'

Things didn't improve and Mrs Shawe became 'so odious' to Thackeray that he packed up Isabella and the children and, without telling his mother-in-law, took the steamer back to England. He was beside himself with rage at what he thought was Mrs Shawe's appalling treatment of his family. On the steamer he wrote a vitriolic nine-page letter to his mother-in-law but didn't send it immediately. Instead, on disembarking he sent her a short note alluding to this longer letter and saying that he would consider whether she had been as much at fault as he thought or whether he had been in a 'passion'.

Thackeray never forgave or had a civil relationship with his mother-in-law again, but he did not send the letter, suggesting that on reflection, he did feel he had been in a 'passion'. Mrs Shawe never forgave Thackeray either, believing he had driven her beloved daughter into madness by pursuing his own interests while his young bride was left isolated and penniless. She wrote to other members of her family, condemning Thackeray for his cruel treatment of Isabella. Poor Isabella never recovered from her severe depression and needed nursing care for the rest of her life. Mrs Shawe refused to help Thackeray financially, and it was the other mother-in-law, the complex and demanding Mrs Carmichael-Smyth who had never been the uncritical supporter that Isabella needed, who stepped in to look after the children. Later Thackeray wanted to end the war with his mother-in-law, writing to his brother-in-law Arthur to ask if he could get her to recognise her responsibilities to Isabella, and thereby end the 'enmity' as it was 'hard to be at war with any mortal'.

Mrs Shawe never did put an end to the feud and Thackeray responded by channelling his enmity into some of his writing. He took to inserting a collection of self-important, bellicose mothers-in-law in his novels and stories. 'A Little Dinner at

Timmins's' is a fine example; the ghastly Mrs Gashleigh, with her incessant chattering, interfering and pungent opinions, is heavily based on Mrs Shawe and includes almost every negative stereotype there is of mothers-in-law. Mrs Gashleigh, who is Fitzroy Timmins's mother-in-law, sticks her nose into every aspect of her son-in-law's household. She asks servants how the baby is being brought up, rifles through papers in her son-in-law's study and confiscates his cigars. The loathing is mutual. 'Mrs Gashleigh has never liked him since he left off calling her mamma and kissing her.' Their relationship never recovered from an incident where Mrs Gashleigh caught him flirting with a shop assistant. When the Timminses decide to have a dinner party, the plans for which quickly exceed their budget, Mrs Gashleigh has her say about everything, particularly the extravagant use of a leg of beef to make stock. 'Never whilst I am in this house, never in a Christian English household; never shall such sinful waste be permitted by me.' And so she goes on, 'bawling over the house', upsetting everyone and all the arrangements until the household contrives to exclude her from the dinner party. In Thackeray's world, no one can so easily escape a bad mother-in-law. The expensive dinner party has so nearly ruined the Timminses that Mrs Gashleigh suggests she comes and lives with them, bringing her 'little sum' from the bank. Poor, good-natured Fitzroy is, as Thackeray believes is true of many men, powerless to resist his mother-in-law. 'The poor wretch is so utterly bewildered and crestfallen that it is very likely he will become her victim.'

Thackeray's biographers, failing to find any evidence to exonerate his mother-in-law's behaviour, have largely colluded with his version of Mrs Shawe.

There isn't anyone, either, to stick up for the Countess of Lennox, whose behaviour as a mother-in-law was entirely self-serving. To gain social advancement or wealth through the marriage of one's children is an age-old practice. Margaret Douglas, Countess of Lennox and a close relative of Elizabeth I, was a career mother-in-law who tried through her children to regain family lands in Scotland and become a powerful political force both north and south of the border. If you're a mother who has daydreamed about the advantages of an upwardly mobile match, here is how not to do it.

Margaret already had a prime lineage: her mother was Margaret Tudor, sister of Henry VIII, her father the rather less illustrious Earl of Angus, whose lands had been plundered by Scottish lairds. It was the loss of these lands that years later largely determined Margaret's first choice of daughter-in-law. Margaret grew up in the court of Anne Boleyn and when Anne was beheaded she herself was accused of having married a nobleman called Thomas Howard, and thereby displeasing the King, although the twelve-year-old Margaret and fourteen-year-old Thomas had done little more than say they loved each other. Margaret was given her first taste of the Tower of London and Henry used the episode as an excuse to pass a law making it a criminal offence for anyone to marry a relative of the king or to deflower them without his permission – the latter a request that seemed unlikely to be granted. It was this legislation, passed because of Margaret's behaviour, that was used against her when she became a mother-in-law.

As Margaret grew up she became more obviously a Tudor, with pale skin, reddish hair and a forceful, argumentative personality. At the relatively advanced age of twenty-six, she married Matthew Stewart, the fourth Earl of Lennox, who had claims to the Scottish throne. Henry Darnley, their son, who was doomed to marry Mary Queen of Scots, was born in 1545. He was only a toddler when Margaret started casting around for future daughters-in-law but by the time Darnley was old enough to marry she had decided that Mary would be the most suitable wife. She should have investigated more thoroughly. Mary was already a widow, having been married to the French Dauphin Francis, and her relationship with her then mother-in-law, Catherine de' Medici, had not been cordial. Mary had referred to her mother-in-law as a 'Florentine shopkeeper's daughter'. When Francis died shortly after becoming king, Catherine's dislike of her daughter-in-law was sufficiently robust to ensure she swiftly took back the running of the royal household, relieving Mary of the crown jewels and leaving her to grieve alone. She also ensured that Mary's attempts to marry into any major European royal families were thwarted.

Mary's suitability had nothing to do with a mother's desire for the matrimonial happiness of her son and everything to do with the acres of land in Scotland that Margaret wanted to reclaim. Darnley was not quite the elevated match that Mary was looking for but Margaret bided her time, asked for the support of the French and Spanish ambassadors and sent a miniature of Henry to her intended daughter-in-law, which showed how handsome he was. In reality Henry was attractive, but had, under his mother's influence, become a spoilt, immoral and disagreeable young man. When he did finally marry Mary, in 1565 in Scotland, Queen Elizabeth was incredulous that anyone could have chosen him as a husband. He was, she said, 'more like a woman than a man', being 'beardless and ladylike'.

She clearly had different tastes in men from Mary, who declared he was 'the lustiest and best proportioned long man'.

It is hard to know how angry Elizabeth really felt about the marriage. If Elizabeth died without children, Mary, a hated Catholic, would be queen, but as a threat to her monarchy it would have been worse for Mary to have married a French or Spanish prince. This did not stop Elizabeth protesting loudly at the marriage, saying it was perilous to the 'sincere amity between the queens and their realms', and immediately putting Margaret (who had stayed in England while the couple got married – she had not met her daughter-in-law) under arrest in the Tower. Secretly Elizabeth must have been pleased; intelligence reached her that the marriage had plunged some powerful Scottish earls into open rebellion and, most gratifying of all, that within months Mary reportedly 'repenteth her marriage and hateth Darnley and all his kin'.

While the mother-in-law Mary had never met was languishing in the Tower of London, Mary was openly showing her disenchantment with her husband. As she toured round southern Scotland, visibly pregnant, she made it clear that she was happy her husband had stayed at home. Darnley continued drinking heavily, visiting brothels and becoming increasingly incapacitated and psychologically confused by syphilis, a disease he had caught before meeting Mary. His wife sought support from her Italian secretary, David Rizzio, support that was platonic but played into the hands of Rizzio's enemies. The Earl of Moray convinced Darnley that he was being cuckolded, and in a haze of drunkenness and syphilitic madness Darnley and a stellar cast of Scottish co-conspirators stabbed Rizzio to death in front of the now heavily pregnant Mary. Mary, a con-

summate conspirator herself, initially chose to forgive them but
then began to plot her husband's downfall.

Margaret had paid a high personal price for this marriage, as
she was still in the Tower. Mary, despite declaring that she
hated her husband and his family, had some compassion for
her mother-in-law. She continually asked Elizabeth to release
her, which may have entrenched the English Queen's position.
She wrote to Elizabeth in 1566 pleading that it was harsh to
imprison a mother for only wanting the best for her son. When
this entreaty failed Mary sent an emissary to work on improving Margaret's prison conditions and to continue to press for
her release. Margaret did manage to get letters smuggled out to
Mary, some of which were critical and deeply upset her.

When Mary's son was born, Margaret could only hear about
her grandson from the Scottish emissary. She would also have
heard that her son had not attended her grandson's christening
on the grounds that he believed that he was not the baby's
father. What she would not have heard about were the plans
being made to murder her son. While Mary pretended to nurse
her husband, who was now seriously ill with syphilis, her lover,
the Earl of Bothwell, with the help of other Scottish earls,
planted gunpowder around the house in Kirk O'Field in which
they were staying. Mary, on some pretext, left the house, which
promptly exploded into flames. Any hope of pretending this
was an accident, however, was lost when Darnley was found not
as a charred body in the house, but lying strangled in the garden.

Elizabeth, on hearing the news, was compassionate enough
to release Margaret immediately. She had been a prisoner for
nineteen months, imprisoned, as she wrote in an inscription on
the fireplace of her quarters in the Tower, for the 'marefe of her

MARGRET·DOUGLAS
HERE·IMRISONED
FOR·THE·MAREfE
OF·HER·SONNE·
MY·LORD·HNERY·
DARNLE·AND·THE
QUENE·OF·SCOTLANDE

sonne my Lord Hnery Darnle and the Quene of Scotlande'.
Margaret had been told of her son's murder while in the Tower
and a doctor had had to be fetched to stop her harming herself.
Sir William Cecil, Elizabeth's counsellor, told her that
Margaret 'could not by any means be kept from such a passion
of mind as the horribleness of the fact did require'. Margaret
knew that Mary was responsible for the murder. For a while
motherly love overcame the imperative of ambition. Putting
her lost Scottish lands to one side, Margaret denounced Mary
to the Spanish ambassador.

Elizabeth not only forgave Margaret but promised to avenge
Darnley's death – for once the women were united against a
common enemy. This unanimity, however, did not last.
Elizabeth had concerns that Margaret's ambition would make
her try to re-establish ties with Mary, a concern that had greater
resonance because Mary's son James had both English and
Scottish ancestry.

Margaret, however, was distracted by the need for financial security (she was now a widow) and rather foolishly decided to try the marriage route once more, this time through her son Charles. Why she thought being a mother-in-law for a second time would be any more lucrative than the first is unclear. She decided upon Elizabeth, the daughter of her friend Bess, Countess of Shrewsbury. Why the two mothers did not ask the Queen for permission is a mystery, but whatever the reason, they hatched a risible plot that involved Margaret falling ill on the way to Yorkshire with Charles, being taken in and nursed by Bess, and Elizabeth falling in love with Charles. Margaret and Bess's excuse that propriety insisted the young couple be married immediately did not convince the Queen.

Elizabeth reminded both mothers-in-law that the law said that only the Queen could arrange marriages for members of the royal family, but while she put the bride and her mother under house arrest, she put Margaret back in the Tower. This was not because the marriage threatened her in any way, but it was a good excuse to put the scheming Margaret in a safe place, away from any renewed plotting with Mary Queen of Scots. For however much Margaret protested that she loathed the daughter-in-law who had murdered her son, if it became politically expedient to realign herself with Mary, she was prepared to do so. Even as she wrote to Cecil that she could never make peace with her daughter-in-law, she began to write to Mary again, sending her a square of embroidered tapestry, which Mary apparently treasured.

Although the two never met and even in correspondence never warmed to each other, in Mary's death (she was imprisoned and then beheaded by Elizabeth) Margaret achieved her ambitions. Her daughter-in-law had changed her will to leave Margaret the lands she was entitled to through her father, the Earl of Angus. Mary had also put Charles second in line, after her son James, to the Scottish throne.

Having achieved and even exceeded her aims, Margaret effectively retired from scheming, although uncharitable court gossips put her devotion to her grandchildren down to her desire to continue plotting through the next generation. When Margaret died at the age of sixty-three, it was James, the son of her daughter-in-law Mary Stuart, who paid for her magnificent tomb.

Mad and scheming mothers-in-law are one thing, but torturing and murderous mothers-in-law are a breed apart. In Delhi's Tihar jail a third of the total number of prisoners, fifty out of a total of 150, are mothers-in-law convicted of crimes against their daughters-in-law, mostly relating to dowries. These crimes generally involve threatening or bullying their daughters-in-law in order to extort more money from their families, but the most serious crimes include murder. There have been cases reported where a bride has been doused with paraffin and set alight under the pretext of an accident while cooking. The National Crime Records Bureau in India recorded one dowry death every seventy-seven minutes in 2005: the staggering number of 6,787 altogether. Usually these mothers-in-law are in cahoots with their sons and many crimes are hidden and unpunished.

Britain was shocked more recently by the 'honour' killing of Surjit Athwal, carried out by her mother-in-law and husband. Surjit, a Sikh, wanted a divorce from her arranged marriage because she had fallen in love with someone else. Her mother-in-law Bachan Athwal, a seventy-year-old grandmother, was bitterly opposed to the divorce, although the family knew that for the ten years of her marriage Surjit had been deeply unhappy. Bachan announced that a divorce would disgrace the family and would only occur over 'her dead body'. The 'her' in this tragic story was Surjit herself, for her mother-in-law lured her to India and arranged for her murder, telling the relatives and police who made enquiries on behalf of Surjit's friends and family that she was a 'slag' who had run away with another man. Surjit's body is believed to be in the river Ravi. Her mother-in-law, who was given a sentence of twenty-seven years, will die in prison.

The ultimate fate of a less successfully murderous mother-in-law is unknown. In 1888 the *New York Times* reported an account via a Paris correspondent of a Russian mother-in-law, Madame d'Elson, who was insanely cross with her French son-in-law, a M. Favart, who had met and wooed her daughter while they had been travelling in Italy. The marriage, however, was unhappy and M. Favart divorced his wife in a court in Nice, which gave a judgement in his favour. His mother-in-law and wife appealed to a higher court in Nîmes, but the husband won again. This time the enraged Mme d'Elson appointed herself as judge and went round to her son-in-law's hotel, armed with what the *New York Times* described as a 'big revolver'. On entering his room she said, 'I have a letter here from your wife,' and as he read it, she shot him four times, one bullet entering his jaw. 'Although weakened by the loss of blood,' recounts the *New York Times*, 'M. Favart was able to seize and disarm the infuriated woman and to shut her up in a room before she could effect any more mischief.'

*Von on her son-in-law Andy and being
a mother-in-law*

The first meeting I had with Andy was memorable but I
can't remember the occasion. I was immediately attracted
to him, probably because he is a handsome man and
because I knew how much Louise was in love with him.
It was also the way that he responded to her that made me
feel so secure about him. Louise is my only daughter.
Perhaps it is because they met when they were older but
their relationship seems very precious. When we met,
Andy asked me lots of questions about myself, as if he was
interested in getting to know me, which I found moving.
I'd never been involved with her boyfriends before but
with Andy it was really quite different. The times that we
saw each other were so brief because I live in New Zealand
and he and Louise are in London.

When the book *Atonement* came out he sent me a copy
with a personal dedication inside it, saying, 'I thought you
might like this – knowing what it was like to live in digs.' I
hadn't thought he'd recollect that I had lived in digs when I
was nursing soldiers in the Second World War. He remembers all sorts of little things that Louise and I have talked
about.

Louise had been married before (they had two children) and when it broke up I was desperately unhappy for her. Her ex-husband used to talk to me; I remember one terribly sad lunch we had together in a hotel in Piccadilly. I tend not to interfere and keep my thoughts to myself.

It was quite a while afterwards that Louise met Andy and when I met him all the sadness that I'd felt about the divorce, and the worry about the children not having their father living with them, went away. He was so marvellous with the children – I was so relieved as it could have gone horribly wrong. He was quite mature and that helped.

When their daughter Issie was born, I came to England and saw what an enormously emotional experience it was for Andy. Perhaps he had wondered if he'd ever have a child. We spent a few days alone together while Louise was still in hospital, which is unusual for a mother-in-law and son-in-law but it made us close. I've met his mother and father; his mother was a lovely, gentle woman and I have on my computer the eulogy he wrote for her at her funeral. It's my way of knowing so much more about Andy. The eulogy is beautiful. It's wonderful writing.

We've just come back from a holiday in Cornwall together, motoring around, visiting places. It was a lot of fun. In some ways distance does provide enchantment. We see each other every two years. We've never had disagreements. There has never been a time when I have thought, 'Oh, why did he say that – what a pity.'

I barely knew my own mother-in-law. She had a sad and unhappy marriage.

I like being a mother-in-law and I get on with my daughters-in-law. I always feel I gain a daughter rather than lose a son. As a mother you hope your children will have children if they want them. But what you want more than anything is for them to be happy in their relationships.

My daughter-in-law who is married to my second son asked me to go for lunch with her a while ago and showed me a letter she had been sent. It was from a young man living in Australia, he was thirty-five and he had found her through Jigsaw, an organisation through which you can trace your parentage. She had become pregnant when she was young and had had the baby adopted. None of us had had any idea. Her son came to see her and we all met him. It was so wonderful. She must have had him in her mind all of her life.

I have always been close to her. She had only been married to my son Geoffrey for a year when her mother died. Her mother said to me, as she was dying, 'I want to give Trish to you.' I told her that Trish had always been my daughter. Trish and I have never discussed this but I often think about it. I felt her mother gave me the most precious thing she had.

Mother-in-law Cocktail

2.5 ounces Bourbon
1 teaspoon Cointreau
1 teaspoon Maraschino
1 teaspoon simple syrup
2 dashes Paychaud's bitters
2 dashes Angostura bitters
2 dashes Amer Picon

Stir the ingredients with ice. Strain into a cocktail glass.
Garnish with a cherry.

Fairy-tale Mothers-in-law

Once upon a time there was a mother-in-law who was always the villain in fairy tales, except when the story had a wicked stepmother instead. Originally, however, it was the mothers in fairy tales who did evil things, usually to their children, but the Brothers Grimm re-edited their collection of tales to reflect, some scholars believe, a more romantic view of motherhood in late eighteenth- and early nineteenth-century Europe. It was no longer Hansel and Gretel's mother but their stepmother who tried to lose them in the wood.

Mothers were therefore free to be pure and idealised and mostly left out of fairy tales, having usually died before the story started (as in *Cinderella* and *Snow White*). The evil, unnatural mother-in-law is the perfect counterpoint to the 'good' and pure mother and the antithesis of the heroine who is usually the daughter-in-law.

At the time when the Grimms were collecting fairy stories in Germany, there were others doing the same thing in France, Scandinavia, Sicily and Scotland as well as in Asia. Scholars of folklore have found enormous similarities between these stories as well as regional variations, and these differences in the core content of the stories reflect the living conditions of the day. This is not to say all fairy tales are true, but they may contain aspects of everyday life.

Linda J. Lee, a folklore scholar at the Center for Folklore and

Ethnography at the University of Pennsylvania, has studied the role of mothers-in-law in fairy tales and written many of the academic papers upon which this chapter is based. She finds that the mother-in-law is a common hostile figure who shares many similarities with the more ubiquitous stepmother in being domineering and frankly villainous. The terms themselves overlap, with the English term 'stepmother' being interchangeable with 'mother-in-law' (the law, through the marriage, conferring motherhood) until the middle of the nineteenth century. In France both stepmother and mother-in-law are called *belle-mère* (beautiful mother).

In the patriarchal society that gave birth to these oral tales, you can see why stories of wicked mothers-in-law and downtrodden daughters-in-law were told, either as cautionary tales to girls before they married, or as happy-ever-after stories in which good (usually the married couple) triumphed over evil (the mother-in-law). In these societies young women would leave their villages to marry and live in their husband's family home. There they would be under the control of their husband's mother and be expected to wait on the family. The benevolence or brutality of the regime varied but the promise underlying it remained the same. Once the daughter-in-law gave birth to a son, her status in the household would rise and once that son married and brought a wife home, the daughter-in-law would become the mother-in-law and rule the household and the next generation of daughters-in-law.

For a mother-in-law to protect her position, she had to get between her son and daughter-in-law to maintain her influence. If her son no longer had a primary emotional attachment and responsibility to her, the mother-in-law's security was threatened. So while a mother wanted her son to marry, society programmed her to try to insinuate herself into that marriage. While she may have wanted grandchildren, the patriarchal rules of engagement meant that these children threatened her position by strengthening that of her daughter-in-law.

There are also fairy stories that reflect the risks mothers-in-law faced in not being able to maintain a position of power once their daughter-in-law became part of their household. There are tales of wicked daughters-in-law who scheme to make their mothers-in-law go hungry and deny them access to their sons and grandchildren.

Scholars have found a systematic structure to most fairy tales. Bengt Holbek defined the five moves in every fairy tale: in the first two the hero or heroine overcomes a crisis of some sort and becomes an adult. In move three the hero and heroine usually marry and in moves four and five there are threats to their children and usually questions about the paternity of these children. In stories where there is a mother-in-law, the son does not usually see the enmity between his mother and wife and leaves the home to go to war, leaving his young bride in his mother's care. The mother-in-law makes her presence felt in moves four and five. As in real life, the tensions between the daughter-in-law and mother-in-law are heightened during pregnancy.

In the typical fairy tale *The Maiden without Hands*, a father mutilates his daughter (by cutting off her hands) on the grounds of her refusal to marry, and she is rescued by a prince who marries her. The prince's mother is furious because her daughter-in-law has no relatives or status. The prince leaves his pregnant wife in his mother's care and while he is away, his mother writes to him telling him that his wife has given birth to puppies (the implication being that she is unfaithful – the variation is that she gives birth to monstrous babies). The prince replies that he will settle everything on his return but trusts his mother to safeguard his children. His mother pretends his letter has asked for the children and his wife to be killed but her attempts to murder them are thwarted, her daughter-in-law's hands grow back and she is embraced by her husband. The mother-in-law is banished (but variations include her being beaten and killed). In most such fairy tales the daughter-in-law is innocent of the wrong-doing of which her mother-in-law accuses her, and love invariably triumphs. The level of violence is extreme and disturbing – women (usually the mother-in-law at the 'happy ending') are boiled alive in oil, mutilated by having their tongues cut out and in turn accuse their daughters-in-law of eating their own children.

There are subtle variations. In one Sicilian fairy tale the mother-in-law appears to be kind to her daughter-in-law but in reality she is plotting against her. One evening the mother-in-law suggests that her daughter-in-law should get some air on the balcony. In doing so the daughter-in-law is seen by the male villain, who then tries to seduce her by pretending he knows her body intimately (such as where she has a birthmark). The husband orders her to be killed, but she survives to prove her innocence through a series of adventures and is reunited with her husband.

Adultery is an important theme in these fairy tales, reflecting that mothers-in-law had a role as 'mate-protectors' – when their sons were away they were expected to ensure their daughters-in-law remained faithful and did not introduce illegitimate children into the family line. The ultimate insult for a man was to be cuckolded. Lee points out that fertile young women were an important resource and needed to be protected from predatory men – who could do this better than their mothers-in-law?

Sometimes it is not the mother-in-law who directly harms her daughter-in-law or grandchildren, but her agent. In Scandinavian fairy tales the Red Knight is a common villain, sent out by the mother-in-law to harm her daughter-in-law, thereby keeping her one step removed.

There are some regional differences around the role of the daughter-in-law. In many fairy tales she is fairly bland (surely the Machiavellian mother-in-law has the better part) but some Indian stories have a theme where the daughter-in-law outwits her mother-in-law and from then on holds the power in the household. In *The Clever Daughter-in-Law*, a southern Indian tale, the daughter-in-law is subjected to daily beatings and verbal abuse from her mother-in-law: 'You slut, you hussy, you want to wash away our house in your tears and bring bad luck, you daughter of a whore.' During the story the clever daughter-in-law not only outwits the goddess Kali but turns the tables on her mother-in-law and husband when they try to burn her alive. She scares them both sufficiently to make her mother-in-law say, 'From now on I will do as you say. Just forgive everything I have done to you. Will you, my darling daughter-in-law?'

Conversely there are also some Indian tales in which the daughter-in-law is cruel and emotionally and physically tortures her mother-in-law, usually by denying her food or shelter. The mother-in-law is humiliated and only rescued when her son realises what is happening.

Fairy tales about sons- and mothers-in-law are notably missing, probably because men rarely saw their mothers-in-law. In patriarchal societies the wife left her family behind when she married. The jokes that men tell against their mothers-in-law have the same intent, to relieve tension, but in them mothers-in-law are not the sinister presences they are in fairy tales. Instead they are laughable, crazy women, without the power to harm anyone seriously.

We may no longer tell fairy tales to each other as adults, but these stories have been replaced by accounts of personal experience and modern cautionary tales (many of them also on the internet) which do not favour the mother-in-law either. But as the power of the daughter-in-law now largely exceeds that of her mother-in-law in western society and she controls access to the son and grandchildren, these oral stories may change and the daughter-in-law may not forever be the heroine.

The following are two very different fairy tales, the first from southern India about a wicked daughter-in-law, the second a Grimms' story about an evil mother-in-law.

Ninga on my Palm

A mother-in-law and a daughter-in-law were always at loggerheads with each other. They quarrelled all day, and the son was sick of listening to their complaints. So he built a separate house for his mother and settled her in it.

Every day, he would give his mother some old blackened rice that his wife sent with him. The mother lost weight and grew thin. One day the son noticed it and asked, 'What's happened to you? Don't you eat properly? Are you unhappy or what?' He also said, 'Maybe you need some buttermilk for your rice. Come to our house and take some.'

One day the mother thought she would try and get some buttermilk from her son's house. She went there when he wasn't in. She was ashamed of begging from her son, but she was desperate for some buttermilk. When she asked for some, her daughter-in-law said, 'You didn't want anything from us when you left. Now you want some buttermilk, do you? If you want it, you'll have to do as I say.'

'Tell me what it is you want me to do. Let me at least hear it,' said the mother-in-law.

The daughter-in-law told her, 'You must take off your sari and everything you're wearing, and dance naked, chanting, "Ninga on my palm, look look at my shame!" Do you think you can do that?'

The mother-in-law cursed under her breath, 'You wretch, why did you have to marry my son?' That day, the daughter-in-law relented and didn't insist on her condition. She gave her some buttermilk, greatly diluted with water.

The next day, the mother-in-law couldn't eat the plain rice. 'Let's see if the wretch will give me some buttermilk,' she muttered to herself, and went to her son's house. The daughter-in-law reminded her of what she had to do. 'Isn't it enough to tell you once? Do I have to tell you every time you come here?' she asked.

The mother-in-law took off her sari, put it on her head, and danced naked, chanting, 'Ninga on my palm, look look at my shame!' The daughter-in-law watched her with satisfaction and gave her some buttermilk.

When she went home, the mother-in-law was disgusted and couldn't touch the buttermilk. 'She humiliates me and then she gives it to me. Who needs it?' she thought, and stayed home. In her misery, she grew even thinner.

Her son asked her the next time he saw her, 'Why, what's the matter? Doesn't my wife give you any buttermilk?' She told him how she had to dance naked for it. He heard it all and simply said, 'Come tomorrow. I'll be there.'

When he went home, he asked his wife, 'Don't you give my mother any buttermilk? She's getting thinner by the day.'

'Why, of course, I give it to her whenever she comes here. Should I be delivering it to her house when she refuses to come here? What's she saying?' she asked.

'Just give it to her. She'll come here today,' he said. But his mother didn't come all day. He had to go somewhere. He instructed his wife, 'Even if I'm not here, give her the buttermilk.'

Then he left through the front door and sneaked back through the side door, and hid himself. His mother arrived soon after, saying, 'I couldn't come all day. Give me a drop of buttermilk.'

'It's good you came now,' said the daughter-in-law. 'But you know what you must do.'

The mother-in-law took off her clothes, made them into a bundle, put it on her head and danced naked, chanting, 'Ninga on my palm, look, look at my shame!'

When she was gone, the son silently got down from the atta. He now knew why his mother looked so miserable and thin. Pretending to come in from the outside, he called his wife and said, 'We must arrange a ceremony for our household gods.' Then he went out and invited everyone he met. He sent a town crier around to nearby villages and letters to villages that were farther away. Then he went to his wife's parents' place to invite them personally for the occasion.

He told his parents-in-law, 'Father-in-law, mother-in-law, your daughter is deathly sick. If you want to see her before something happens to her, come soon. We've consulted priests and astrologers about her disease. No one could give us a remedy. Today we went to a guru, who asked us to undertake a vow. He said that you, her parents, must agree to come, naked as you were born, without a thread on your bodies. If you can do that and take part in a ceremony at our place tomorrow, we can have some hope for your daughter. Tomorrow, at two o'clock. Please.'

Then he went home and decorated the doors of his house with festoons of mango leaves. He removed all the clothing in his house from his wife's reach and locked it up in his room.

The next day he gave all the guests a grand dinner and distributed betel leaves and nuts. He requested them all to sit down, saying, 'Sit down for a while, if you please. I've a small speech to make.'

His wife was unhappy throughout the dinner that her parents had not been invited to the ceremony. He consoled her by assuring her that they had been invited. 'They will be here in a few minutes. Just be patient till two o'clock,' he said.

Meanwhile, he had arranged for his mother to bathe, eat and be comfortable. At two, his wife's mother came in stark naked, running anxiously into the house, crying out, 'O my daughter, my daughter, what's happened to you?' Her father cried, 'Tell us, what's happened to you?' He too was naked.

His daughter nearly died of shame. She beat her forehead, looked around for some cloth, any cloth, crying, 'O god, if only I could lay my hands on a piece of cloth to cover them!'

As the assembled guests were wondering if her parents had gone mad, her husband began his speech.

'Listen. In our house, we were three once. My mother and my wife didn't get along. So I arranged for my mother to live in a separate house. She has been growing thinner by the day. All her life, she has been used to milk and buttermilk. So I had said to her, "Come to our house and get some buttermilk. Don't eat the dry rice." Whenever my mother came here to ask for a little buttermilk, my wife made her do shameful things. My mother had to strip herself naked, put her clothes on her head and dance,

chanting, "Ninga on my palm, look, look at my shame!"
Only then would she get a little buttermilk to take home.
Today, I wanted to teach my wife a lesson. So I tricked her
parents and asked them to come before you as they did.'

Then he gave his wife the key to his room and said, 'Go,
open the door and bring your parents some clothes.' She
silently took the key and brought them clothes to cover
their shame.

From that day on, the mother, the son and his wife lived
in peace in the same house.

The Six Swans

Once upon a time, a certain king was hunting in a great
forest, and he chased a wild beast so eagerly that none of
his attendants could follow him. When evening drew near
he stopped and looked around him, and then he saw that
he had lost his way. He sought a way out, but could find
none. Then he perceived an aged woman with a head
which nodded perpetually, who came towards him, but she
was a witch. 'Good woman,' said he to her, 'can you not
show me the way through the forest?' 'Oh, yes, Lord King,'
she answered, 'that I certainly can, but on one condition,
and if you do not fulfil that, you will never get out of the
forest, and will die of hunger in it.'

'What kind of condition is it?' asked the King.

'I have a daughter,' said the old woman, 'who is as beautiful as anyone in the world, and well deserves to be your
consort, and if you will make her your queen, I will show
you the way out of the forest.' In the anguish of his heart

the King consented, and the old woman led him to her little
hut, where her daughter was sitting by the fire. She
received the King as if she had been expecting him, and he
saw that she was very beautiful, but still she did not please
him, and he could not look at her without secret horror.
After he had taken the maiden up on his horse, the old
woman showed him the way, and the King reached his
royal palace again, where the wedding was celebrated.

The King had already been married once, and had by his
first wife seven children, six boys and a girl, whom he loved
better than anything else in the world. As he now feared that
the stepmother might not treat them well, and even do them
some injury, he took them to a lonely castle which stood in
the midst of a forest. It lay so concealed, and the way was so
difficult to find, that he himself would not have found it if a
wise woman had not given him a ball of yarn with wonderful
properties. When he threw it down before him, it unrolled
itself and showed him his path. The King, however, went so
frequently away to his dear children that the Queen
observed his absence; she was curious and wanted to know
what he did when he was quite alone in the forest.

She gave a great deal of money to his servants, and they
betrayed the secret to her, and told her likewise of the ball
which alone could point out the way. And now she knew
no rest until she had learnt where the King kept the ball of
yarn, and then she made little shirts of white silk, and as
she had learnt the art of witchcraft from her mother, she
sewed a charm inside them. And once when the King had
ridden forth to hunt, she took the little shirts and went into
the forest, and the ball showed her the way. The children,

who saw from a distance that someone was approaching, thought that their dear father was coming to them, and full of joy, ran to meet him. Then she threw one of the little shirts over each of them, and no sooner had the shirts touched their bodies than they were changed into swans, and flew away over the forest.

The Queen went home quite delighted, and thought she had got rid of her stepchildren, but the girl had not run out with her brothers, and the Queen knew nothing about her. Next day the King went to visit his children, but he found no one but the little girl. 'Where are thy brothers?' asked the King. 'Alas, dear father,' she answered, 'they have gone away and left me alone!' and she told him that she had seen from her little window how her brothers had flown away over the forest in the shape of swans, and she showed him the feathers which they had let fall in the courtyard, and which she had picked up. The King mourned, but he did not think that the Queen had done this wicked deed, and as he feared that the girl would also be stolen away from him, he wanted to take her away with him. But she was afraid of her stepmother, and entreated the King to let her stay just this one night more in the forest castle.

The poor girl thought, 'I can no longer stay here. I will go and seek my brothers.' And when night came, she ran away, and went straight into the forest. She walked the whole night long and next day also without stopping, until she could go no farther for weariness. Then she saw a forest-hut, and went into it, and found a room with six little beds, but she did not venture to get into one of them, but crept under one, and lay down on the hard ground, intending to pass the night there. Just before sunset, however, she heard a rustling, and saw six swans come flying in at the window. They alighted on the ground and blew at each other, and blew all the feathers off, and their swan's skins stripped off like a shirt. Then the maiden looked at them and recognised her brothers, was glad and crept forth from beneath the bed. The brothers were not less delighted to see their little sister, but their joy was of short duration. 'Here canst thou not abide,' they said to her. 'This is a shelter for robbers. If they come home and find thee, they will kill thee.' 'But can you not protect me?' asked the little sister. 'No,' they replied, 'only for one quarter of an hour each evening can we lay aside our swan's skins and have during that time our human form; after that, we are once more turned into swans.'

The little sister wept and said, 'Can you not be set free?' 'Alas, no,' they answered, 'the conditions are too hard! For six years thou mayst neither speak nor laugh, and in that time thou must sew together six little shirts of starwort for us. And if one single word falls from thy lips, all thy work will be lost.' And when the brothers had said this, the quarter of an hour was over, and they flew out of the window again as swans.

The maiden, however, firmly resolved to deliver her brothers, even if it should cost her her life. She left the hut, went into the midst of the forest, seated herself on a tree, and there passed the night. Next morning she went out and gathered starwort and began to sew. She could not speak to any one, and she had no inclination to laugh; she sat there and looked at nothing but her work. When she had already

spent a long time there it came to pass that the King of the country was hunting in the forest, and his huntsmen came to the tree on which the maiden was sitting. They called to her and said, 'Who art thou?' But she made no answer. 'Come down to us,' said they. 'We will not do thee any harm.' She only shook her head. As they pressed her further with questions she threw her golden necklace down to them, and thought to content them thus. They, however, did not cease, and then she threw her girdle down to them, and as this also was to no purpose, her garters, and by degrees everything that she had on that she could do without until she had nothing left but her shift. The huntsmen, however, did not let themselves be turned aside by that, but climbed the tree and fetched the maiden down and led her before the King. The King asked, 'Who art thou? What art thou doing on the tree?' But she did not answer. He put the question in every language that he knew, but she remained as mute as a fish.

As she was so beautiful, the King's heart was touched, and he was smitten with a great love for her. He put his mantle on her, took her before him on his horse and carried her to his castle. Then he caused her to be dressed in rich garments, and she shone in her beauty like bright daylight, but no word could be drawn from her. He placed her by his side at table, and her modest bearing and courtesy pleased him so much that he said, 'She is the one whom I wish to marry, and no other woman in the world.' And after some days he united himself to her.

The King, however, had a wicked mother who was dissatisfied with this marriage and spoke ill of the young Queen.

'Who knows', said she, 'from whence the creature who can't speak comes? She is not worthy of a king!' After a year had passed, when the Queen brought her first child into the world, the old woman took it away from her, and smeared her mouth with blood as she slept. Then she went to the King and accused the Queen of being a man-eater. The King would not believe it, and would not suffer any-one to do her any injury. She, however, sat continually sewing at the shirts, and cared for nothing else. The next time, when she again bore a beautiful boy, the false step-mother used the same treachery, but the King could not bring himself to give credit to her words. He said, 'She is too pious and good to do anything of that kind; if she were not dumb, and could defend herself, her innocence would come to light.' But when the old woman stole away the newly-born child for the third time, and accused the Queen, who did not utter one word of defence, the King could do no oth-erwise than deliver her over to jus-tice, and she was sentenced to suffer death by fire.

When the day came for the sentence to be executed, it was the last day of the six years during which she was not to speak or laugh, and she had delivered her dear brothers from the power of the enchantment. The six shirts were ready, only the left sleeve of the sixth was wanting. When, therefore, she was led to the stake, she laid the shirts on her arm, and when she stood on high and the fire was just going to be lighted, she looked around and six swans came flying through the air towards her. Then she saw that her deliverance was near, and her heart leapt with joy. The swans swept towards her and sank down so that she could throw the shirts over them, and as they were touched by them, their swan's skins fell off, and her brothers stood in their own bodily form before her, and were vigorous and handsome. The youngest only lacked his left arm, and had in the place of it a swan's wing on his shoulder. They embraced and kissed each other, and the Queen went to the King, who was greatly moved, and she began to speak and said, 'Dearest husband, now I may speak and declare to thee that I am innocent, and falsely accused.' And she told him of the treachery of the old woman who had taken away her three children and hidden them.

Then to the great joy of the King they were brought thither, and as a punishment, the wicked stepmother was bound to the stake, and burnt to ashes. But the King and the Queen with her six brothers lived many years in happiness and peace.

'I'm Getting Ready for my Mother-in-law'

My wife met me at the door,
Letter in her hand,
Said: mother soon will visit us,
Now isn't that just grand;
She says she'll stay about six months
Or longer if she can.
If she don't come I'll know I'll be
A disappointed man.

I'm getting ready for my mother-in-law,
Getting ready for the fun,
When she puts her face
Inside the place
She'd better take it on the run.
If she should stay for just one day,
I can hear the church bells chime;
Oh! Mother, mother, mother, mother, mother,
You'll have a dandy time.

I taught my bulldog how to bite,
Parrot how to swear,
I sawed the springs and legs and things,
From our best rocking chair;
I sprinkled soap on the kitchen floor,

And polished it with fat,
If she falls down and breaks her neck
Can I be blamed for that?

Chorus
I'm getting ready . . .

I fixed a little room for her,
Without one window pane,
Turned on the steam
And fixed it so it won't turn off again.
No pictures on the wall at all,
It looks just like a cell.
When she gets in bed,
She'll think that she is in a Turkish bath.

Chorus
I'm getting ready . . .

Somebody wrote a song one time,
Which made me awful mad.
The song said, everybody worked
Excepting poor old dad.
If he could see me nowadays,
I know he'd change his tune,
I'm working like a truck horse now,
From morning night till noon.

Chorus
I'm getting ready ...

I'll take her to the Hippodrome,
Get seats right near the stage,
I want to be real sure that she
Is near the lion's cage.
I've heard of lions breaking loose,
Don't think that I'm a dunce,
But things like that are almost sure,
To happen more than once.

Chorus
I'm getting ready ...

I'll hire an automobile,
This fact I told my wife,
She said, ain't you afraid something
Might happen to mother's life?
Am I afraid things might happen?
Such questions make me sick,
I know that something must happen,
And happen mighty quick.

Chorus
I'm getting ready ...

She'll want to visit Brooklyn Bridge,
But she'll get a shock,

I'll fix it so we reach the bridge
Some night near six o'clock;
They have a jubilee down there,
Each night from six to five.
And she can thank her lucky stars,
If she comes out alive.

Chorus
I'm getting ready . . .

9

Mother-in-law-baiting

Tell people you're writing a book about mothers-in-law and they'll either ask if it's got jokes in it or volunteer a gag themselves. 'What do you do if you miss your mother-in-law? Reload and fire again.' Or, 'What's the definition of ambivalence? Seeing your mother-in-law reversing off a cliff in your new Mercedes.' There are jokes about mothers-in-law in many languages and they translate rather too easily. They follow familiar themes: that mothers-in-law talk too much, interfere, are domineering, overbearing, think no one is good enough for their son or daughter, are mean, ugly and wholly disagreeable.

Whether the mothers-in-law are Jewish, Italian or British, the formula they follow is the same.

In a small rural community a farmer's mule kicks his mother-in-law to death. Such a huge crowd turns out for her funeral that the minister is amazed. He says to the farmer, 'She must have been a very popular woman for so many people to take the afternoon off to come to her funeral.' To which the farmer replies,

'They're not here for her funeral. They've come to buy the mule.'

George goes on holiday to Israel with his family, including his mother-in-law. They are visiting Jerusalem when his mother-in-law drops down dead. George, who comes from New York, goes to the American embassy with his mother-in law's death certificate to make arrangements to send the body back to the States for burial. A member of the embassy staff, hearing the story, advises George on what to do. 'My friend, it is very, very expensive to send a body back to the States. It can cost over $6,000. In most cases like this, the person responsible for the remains decides to bury the body here because this only costs around $1,000.' George thinks for a while and then replies, 'I don't care how much it costs to send the body back. It's what I want to do.'

The member of staff feels himself going misty-eyed. 'You must have loved your mother-in-law very much, considering the difference between $1,000 and $6,000.'

'No, it's not that,' says George. 'It's just that I know of a case many many years ago of a person who was buried here in Jerusalem and was resurrected on the third day. It's a chance I don't want to take.'

The mother-in-law joke is synonymous with music hall, where comedians sang or told jokes about the terrible things they wanted to do to their mothers-in-law whenever they came to stay. These songs and jokes came from personal experience; men often lived near or even with their mothers-in-law due to housing shortages and the tradition continued until the advent of the frilly-shirted comedians of the 1970s such as Les Dawson. These jokes were phased out when alternative comedians arrived. Mark Rough, who has been a stand-up comedian in Britain for over forty years, remembers how the end of mother-in-law jokes became synonymous with the death of old-style humour. 'In the 1970s comedians would tell a string of gags, whereas alternative comedians told stories about their lives and these stories were not racist or sexist,' he says. 'Mother-in-law jokes became frowned on and thought of as misogynistic, which some of them were. But some of these comedians had lived with their mothers-in-law and they did make jokes about how frightened they were that the women in the house would gang up on them. Mothers-in-law were never skinny in the comedy context; they were always strong, big figures. As a son-in-law, living with your mother-in-law you would have felt outnumbered by women. Comedy after all is about truth. If a comedian is writing about something that happened to them, you can tell because their intonation and tone is different. The comedian Les Dawson was the greatest proponent of mother-in-law jokes but they were told with kindness. It was like he was talking publicly about a private battle with his wife about his mother-in-law.'

Les Dawson's widow, Tracy Dawson, maintains her husband told his mother-in-law jokes with a twinkle in his eye. 'He was lovely to my mother,' she says. 'His mother-in-law jokes were told with affection and my mother always thought they were very funny. But the jokes had nothing to do with her. He thought they were a bit old hat but when he tried to drop them people wrote in and said, "Please, will you tell your mother-in-law jokes." There was no offence in the jokes, but people related to them because they were the sorts of things people said; "Oh no my mother-in-law is coming for the weekend."'

In 1998 Butlin's holiday camps announced that not only were they modernising and replacing the term 'camps' with 'centres', they were also outlawing mother-in-law jokes in their entertainment programmes. But the baiting of mothers-in-law as a blood sport continued. Stand-up comedians may have dropped mother-in-law jokes from their repertoire but laughing at mothers-in-law persists in situation comedies and films all over the world.

In the 1950s in Britain the film *Sailor Beware* presented a slice of postwar working-class life. It was a comedy where a mother-in-law, played by the well-known character actress Peggy Mount, presided over a household where she henpecked her hopeless husband, bullied her spinster sister and was horrified to discover her precious daughter had chosen an orphaned sailor for her husband. Somewhere deep down she had a good heart but she was an overbearing stereotypical mother-in-law.

The series *Bewitched* had a mother-in-law in a more peripheral role but one that was more gently amusing. *Bewitched* was an American sitcom which ran from 1964 to 1972 and covered the family life of Samantha, a witch who did magic by twitching her nose, and Darrin who was her mortal advertising-executive husband. Some of the best scenes involved Darrin's mother-in-law Endora, who was, of course, also a witch and used her magic to interfere with their marriage. In one episode, for example, she gets another witch to try to seduce Darrin to prove he, like all mortal men, is unfaithful. Whatever spells Endora casts, however, she can never destroy their relationship and each episode ends with the couple cuddling up, having confounded her attempts.

Endora never develops any affection for Darrin – she wilfully refuses to remember his name, calling him anything from 'Darwin' to 'Dumb Dumb' – but she loves her daughter enough to realise that Samantha wants her mortal marriage to work. In one episode she makes her estranged husband, Darrin's father-in-law, bring Darrin back to life after he has made him disappear in a puff of smoke.

The situation comedy *The Mothers-in-Law* ran for two years in America in the late 1960s and featured two couples, the Buells and the Hubbards, who lived next door to each other. One has a daughter, the other a son, and the two marry and live above the Hubbards' garage. The series started with arguments over the wedding and the in-laws joining the newly-weds on their honeymoon.

Perhaps the longest-running American sitcom (its repeats are still shown in many countries) with a prominent mother-in-law was *Everybody Loves Raymond*, in which long-suffering Ray, a sportswriter, lives with his wife Debra and their children across the street from his parents and brother. Debra and her mother-in-law Marie do not get on. Marie is the archetypal intrusive and overbearing mother-in-law who, although she appears to be sweet and helpful, cannot resist bustling into her daughter-in-law's kitchen and criticising her cooking as well as her parenting skills. If she smells anything strange Marie will immediately ask, 'Is Debra cooking anything?' Continuing the well-rehearsed theme of mothers-in-law who believe no one can look after their son properly, Marie sneaks into Debra's house not only to redo her cleaning and laundry but to make personal remarks: 'Ah Debra, I see you've bought some new underwear – rather more revealing than usual.'

Generally the mothers-in-law in these comedies were loud-mouthed but lovable. The British series of *Carry On* films had less lovable and more unpleasantly stereotypical mothers-in-law, usually played by an English character actress such as Joan Sims. These mothers-in-law were sexually repressed, domineering and judgemental. In *Carry On Behind*, the mother-in-law turns up with two large cacti to accompany her daughter and her son-in-law Arthur on holiday and is forever barking at Arthur, 'I won't have swearing.' In her mind Arthur is a poor excuse for a husband. 'He may be your husband but he never has been and never will be a gentleman. He's just like your father – he's coarse.'

More recently, but still unsubtly, the 2005 romantic comedy *Monster-in-law* gave a starring role to the mother-in-law. Jane Fonda is Viola, a pantomime-like mother-in-law who is so desperate not to let professional dog-walker Charlotte, played by Jennifer Lopez, marry her only son that she nearly resorts to poisoning her at the wedding rehearsal dinner. Viola has recently lost her job as a television interviewer and plans to resume her close relationship with her son. He is, she admits, all that she has in her life, which may account for why she phones him ten times a day. Her barbed comments to and about her potential daughter-in-law – 'I was a virgin when I wed, we'll just have to pretend with you,' and 'I could kill that dog-walking slut' – are accompanied by behaviour that is mentally unbalanced. Viola, as part of a ploy to drive Charlotte away from her son, insists on organising the wedding, pretending to collapse, seriously ill, when her offer is refused. Rather than being a genuinely threatening character, Viola is the extreme stereotype of the mother-in-law, a parody of self-interest, who is suffocating her son. On the wedding day she turns up wearing a white dress to upstage the bride, but is upstaged herself when her own mother-in-law Gertrude appears and is as unpleasant to Viola as Viola has been to Charlotte. Only then does Viola realise she has behaved abominably and apologises. Charlotte welcomes her into their family, promising to include her in all their holidays and special occasions.

Far from the saccharine of Hollywood mothers-in-law is a British sitcom called *The Royle Family*, which follows the fortunes of a northern working-class family who spend most of their time on the sofa watching television. In 2006 the show's Christmas special, 'The Queen of Sheba', focused on the mother-in-law, Nana, who has steadily grown older through the series and now lies in bed taking up a large part of the front room and looking at everyone through an enormous magnifying glass. She is at the heart of the family despite being bedridden, and holds court from her pillows. The humour is more subtle and realistic, although there are still the familiar gags. When someone announces, 'Oh look, Nana's awake,' Jim Royle, the son-in-law, remarks wryly, 'Better luck next time.' Jim is furious when he can't find the batteries for the television's remote control and realises they have been put in Nana's fan to keep her cool. He refuses to come out of the kitchen, shouting, 'She thinks she's the Queen of Sheba.' Yet when Nana dies he is inconsolable: 'I would give anything to have her back to have a row with her,' he says. In *The Royle Family*, mothers-in-law may be laughed at but they are also deeply loved and respected. Jim's emotion at the loss of his mother-in-law is moving because it is so believable – she was irritating but he loved her. There is only one place where his mother-in-law's ashes can go: they take pride of place on top of the much-loved television.

Yet some of the humour in recent films is more unpleasant; mothers-in-law are here shown as one-dimensional, sexually rapacious but repulsive middle-aged women. The dreadful British comedy *Sex Lives of the Potato Men*, which was rightly panned by critics, has a deeply unattractive mother-in-law who insists on her son-in-law giving her own mother a cheap thrill by letting her feel his genitals.

It is this more uncomfortable type of humour that Pamela Cotterill, a lecturer in sociology and women's studies, examines in her book *Friendly Relations? Mothers and their Daughters-in-law*. Humour, she argues, can be used as social control. Mothers-in-law are put into the unenviable position of having jokes told at their expense, being expected to chuckle along or be accused of not having a sense of humour. There is noticeably no history of jokes being told about mothers in the same way, nor about fathers-in-law or sons-in-law. Cotterill interviewed thirty-five mothers-in-law and daughters-in-law in Stoke-on-Trent and found that real-life mothers-in-law often did not take offence because the jokes seemed so far-fetched they couldn't possibly apply to them. Women generally in her study did not find mother-in-law jokes amusing, the daughters-in-law realising that such humour could be used against them. The mothers-in-law were sensitive to the negative stereotyping their position attracted, particularly in the media.

This media interest in mothers-in-law is not just a western phenomenon. Mothers-in-law appear in telenovelas in South America and in dramas in Japan. In India, a popular soap opera, *Kyunki Saas Bhi Kabhi Bahu Thi*, follows a dysfunctional extended family among whom there is traditional infighting and jealousy. Tulsi, the heroine, is one of three daughters-in-law, married to the eldest son (the two eloped). She is a tough young woman and has to work hard to overcome the prejudices of her mother-in-law, born out of the fact that her own family (her father is a priest) are relatively poor. The series is built on Tulsi taking stands against her mother-in-law's behaviour. The title tellingly translates as 'Because the mother-in-law was once a daughter-in-law'.

Mothers-in-law are likely to continue to be used for blood sports. Some of that humour may be affectionate and derived from living so closely to mothers-in-law that telling jokes about them is a release of tension. Other humour feels more uneasy and controlling. But mothers-in-law do have their defenders. One such was Will Rogers, the American cowboy humorist, who said, 'After looking at mothers-in-law and seeing sons-in-law – I always felt that the jokes were on the wrong ones.'

Mother-in-law's Chicken Soup

INGREDIENTS

4lb whole chicken
2 pints of chicken broth (made with bouillon cubes)
1 onion cut into quarters
1 stick of celery
6 carrots chopped – 3 into large chunks and the rest
    finely to be added later.
½ lb medium egg noodles

DIRECTIONS

1 Rinse the chicken and remove the skin with a
knife. Put the chicken into a large saucepan on
the top of the stove and pour the stock over it.
Bring it to the boil and add the large chunks of
carrots, celery and onion.

2 Once the liquid is boiling turn it down
and simmer for about 45 minutes to an
hour, until the chicken literally falls off
the bone.

3 Take the chicken out of the broth and leave
it to cool down. Take the onion, carrots
and celery out.

4 Shred the chicken from the bones and leave covered.
5 Add the remaining carrots to the broth and shortly afterwards the noodles, and simmer for about five minutes until the noodles and carrots are tender.
6 Add the shredded chicken and serve.

Racy Mothers-in-law

Mothers-in-law are not obvious sex objects, although there is a pornographic magazine, founded by media baron Richard Desmond, called *Mothers-in-law*. A search on the internet also reveals some racy stories from men who claim carnal knowledge of their wives' mothers.

There has been more academic interest in the sexuality of mothers-in-law. Sigmund Freud examined the phenomenon in 1913 in *Totem and Taboo: Resemblances between the Mental Lives of Savages and Neurotics*, which discussed the horror of incest in 'uncivilised people'. He reflected on the Australian Aborigines' avoidance customs which ensured there was no sexual activity between a mother-in-law and son-in-law. The mother-in-law taboo, Freud noted, involved incestuous wishes which 'civilised' people had completely repressed, but which the 'less civilised' struggled with at a conscious level. Freud's view of mothers-in-law may have been influenced by his poor relationship with his own mother-in-law, Emmeline Bernays, whom he found bossy and self-obsessed. Emmeline had hoped her daughter Martha

would find a better suitor than Freud, who at that time was a penniless atheist. The Bernays were an orthodox Jewish family who later moved from Vienna to Hamburg to escape their father's humiliating bankruptcy and in doing so separated Martha from Sigmund, who desperately wanted to marry her. Martha and Sigmund wrote to each other and survived a four-year engagement before finally being allowed to marry and live pretty much happily ever after.

Who knows what Freud would have made of Mrs Robinson in the novel and screenplay *The Graduate*? She is the Taboo itself in fishnet stockings, a sexual predator of a certain age who contrives to seduce her friend's son Benjamin, who has just graduated from college, not realising that she is destined to become his mother-in-law. Mrs Robinson is, as Benjamin calls her later, a 'lascivious alcoholic' who makes her intentions clear at Benjamin's graduation party by asking him to unzip her dress and to lie down with her on his bed. She then contrives to remove all her clothes and corners him, naked, in his bedroom. 'I want you to know that you can call me up any time you want and we'll make some sort of arrangement.'

The arrangement they make is based on regular sex in a nearby hotel room, which Benjamin, after a while, finds unsatisfying. 'Mrs Robinson,' he asks, 'do you think we could have a conversation?' The fact that the affair is fizzling out is the least of Benjamin's problems, as he is under pressure from his parents and Mr Robinson to date Elaine, the Robinsons' daughter. Against the odds, Benjamin and Elaine fall in love. Mrs Robinson, who is furious that Benjamin could become her son-in-law, tells Elaine of her affair with him but the young couple ultimately go off together. Mrs

Robinson's parting shot to Elaine about her future son-in-law is, 'Marry this conniving son of a bitch and you're on your own.'

Historically there is a dearth of mothers-in-law with notable sexual reputations. Lady Elizabeth Melbourne in the eighteenth century perhaps comes the closest, a woman whose own son said of her, 'A remarkable woman, a devoted mother, an excellent wife – but not chaste, not chaste.' The son, William Lamb, became Queen Victoria's first prime minister and was thought not to be his father's son but the result of an affair between his mother and Lord Egremont. According to the rumours of the day Lady Melbourne's affair with Lord Egremont had been arranged by her previous lover and she had received a cut of the money that had changed hands. At Cambridge William's younger brother George had been taunted with, 'Your mother is a whore,' by fellow students. Out of her six children, no one was quite sure which were related to her husband, Sir Peniston Lamb.

Lady Melbourne was a famous beauty and consummate hostess in Whig society and became the confidante of Lord Byron. Her social gatherings attracted the elite, including the Prince of Wales who became her lover in the 1780s (George Lamb was his son). Lady Melbourne was clever enough to ensure they remained life-long friends.

Lady Melbourne was a highly involved mother-in-law, not necessarily in the best of ways. It was said of her that she never saw a happy marriage without trying to destroy it, and the unions that she arranged were disastrous. As a mother-in-law she was closest for a while to Lady Caroline Lamb who married William, her favourite son. Lady Melbourne quickly became her confidante, as she did with other individuals whom she sought to control.

William had adored Caroline as a teenager but she was known to be reckless and unconventional. William may however have inherited some of his mother's sexual promiscuity – ironically Caroline wrote to her mother-in-law to complain. 'He called me prudish – said I was straight-laced, amused himself with instructing me in things I need never have heard or known and the disgust that I at first felt for the world's wickedness I till then had never even heard of.'

Their marriage began to break down within a few years: Caroline had two stillborn babies and then a child who would today probably be identified as being on the autistic spectrum, while William became heavily involved in politics. Lady Melbourne had to suffer her daughter-in-law's confidences about an affair with Sir Geoffrey Webster and the rumour that Caroline had had herself carried to the dinner table at Devonshire House under an enormous silver dish, from beneath which she had emerged naked. These were minor indiscretions compared to her notorious affair with Byron. Caroline had wanted to meet him as soon as she had read his work, saying, 'If he bites his nails and is as ugly as Aesop, I must know him.'

They launched into a consuming affair. Lady Melbourne's only objection was that it was so indiscreet and public. She and Caroline's mother suggested that Caroline retire to Ireland for a while, which cooled the affair, although Caroline spent her time writing to her mother-in-law, ruminating on the details of her relationship with Byron and how she longed for him, which was strange given she was married to Lady Melbourne's

son. Lady Melbourne, in turn, was writing to Byron, ostensibly
to try to gain intelligence of his view of the affair but soon out
of pure enjoyment. Lady Melbourne and Byron continued
their correspondence for many years, exchanging confidences
and trying to promote each other's usually selfish and devious
interests. Byron said of Lady Melbourne, 'When I do see a
women superior not only to all her own sex but to most of ours
I worship her.' Lady Melbourne not only encouraged
Caroline's confidences but was known to forward them to
Lord Byron. Caroline later complained of Lady Melbourne's
infatuation with him.

When the affair dissolved, driving Caroline into obsessive
madness, her mother-in-law simply moved on to corresponding with Byron about his latest affair, this time with Lady
Oxford. The two flirted shamelessly in their letters, Lady

Melbourne asking Byron why he didn't run off with her and teasing him if he was slow to visit her. What is striking in their letters is the level of sexual intrigue – Lady Melbourne passing on confidences from just about anyone. After one house party she wrote to him, 'Your former favourite Lady Susan Ryder has been there displaying all her Graces to the Master of the Mansion who does not seem inclined to Grace her in return.' Yet even she was shocked to hear that Byron had had a child with his half-sister Augusta, which she called 'atrocious' although his behaviour did not stop her promoting Byron's marriage to her own niece Annabella, largely as a ploy to stop Caroline's overt infatuation with him.

Lady Melbourne was quick to become her niece's confidante, although she thought her rather priggish and would not otherwise have chosen to befriend her. Once again she enjoyed the intrigue of obtaining confidences from both Annabella and Byron and passing on information to both parties. She found a home for the newly-wed couple in London and when Byron again quickly fell into having affairs, confronted him with his wife. It made no difference and Lady Melbourne was probably an unconvincing censor. As we have seen in Chapter Six, Annabella left Byron shortly after their only child was born and her family were quick to blame Lady Melbourne for the disastrous marriage. Judith Milbanke, Byron's mother-in-law, knew, through her daughter, of the letters that had passed between Byron and Lady Melbourne and considered the latter a terrible influence.

Lady Caroline Lamb was also gunning for Lady Melbourne. Caroline's novel *Glenarvon*, a barely disguised autobiography, portrayed her as vulgar and bigoted, a nasty Gothic villainness.

Lady Melbourne was anxious to get rid of her troublesome daughter-in-law but William was too fond of his wife to agree. Lady Melbourne died in 1818 without completing this final piece of intrigue. Four years before her death Byron wrote of Lady Melbourne to his wife, 'I do love that woman better than any being on earth.' Caroline maintained that Lady Melbourne was 'infatuated' with the poet. The love that Byron had for Lady Melbourne may not have been consummated but with such a highly sexual woman it was never just platonic.

Rebecca on her mother-in-law

I first met my mother-in-law three weeks before my first child was born. I had been with James for five years before we met (we had been married for two and a half years and my in-laws didn't come to the wedding). His dad phoned up one day and asked us if we would have a meal with them. We met them in an Italian restaurant and we made small talk. I had met James's dad a couple of times on the quiet before, which made me feel embarrassed as my mother-in-law didn't know.

I hadn't met my mother-in-law before because she had refused to see both James and me. James had left a previous relationship with a woman called Olivia and their three children because he was having an affair (this was before he met me). His mother had cut him out of her life, so this Italian meal was the first time for years that she had seen James either. She used to write hate mail to him: 'How could you leave her to look after those children on her own? You're no son of mine.'

I do believe my mother-in-law had a point. When James left Olivia, their youngest was only nine months old. His mother sided with the daughter-in-law and grandchildren. She only had sons and Olivia was the daughter she had always wanted. So she battled to keep this daughter and was willing to denounce her son because she was terrified she would lose contact with her grandchildren.

By the time I met James he had left his wife two years previously but his mother still felt so strongly that he would come to his senses and go back to her that she didn't want to accept me. It was hard for her to accept that James was going to marry me because he had never married Olivia and his mother is religious and hates the fact that her grandchildren were born out of wedlock. My mother-in-law often talks about church but I have always felt that if they were as Christian as they say they are they would have embraced us, not cast the first stone.

My mother-in-law had always said she would never meet me because it would be disloyal to Olivia and James's children. However, I knew that if I got pregnant she would have a dilemma because I had a sense of how important her existing grandchildren were to her.

When I fell pregnant I said to James, 'I know what will happen now, she will want to know me – if she phones me she can just fuck off.' But by the time she did phone I had begun to think that I had no right to deny my children access to their grandparents. I went into the restaurant with pregnancy hormones forging round my body and I felt very benevolent towards her. I was ready to be whatever she wanted me to be. We gave each other gushingly friendly smiles and it was very formal but I do remember thinking she had a much kinder face than I had imagined.

I heard last year through one of James's children that my mother-in-law has said she was grateful to me because I had been so good about things. But have we ever discussed it?

No. Have we discussed anything more meaningful than the price of milk? No. I forgive her for how she treated me.

I have never felt I could compete with Olivia. She was already the daughter-in-law; I am not needed. She already phones my mother-in-law twice a week. I have been at family occasions at the same time as Olivia and I can see that my mother-in-law feels awkward at showing any affection to me in front of Olivia. She seems closer to Olivia than to her own son. Even now I would never phone or drop in on my mother-in-law. We see them three times a year, including once around Christmas.

My mother-in-law is very kind to the grandchildren and puts them before anything. I can't help but warm to her when I see her with our two boys. I watch her with them and she never gets irritated by them, she answers their questions, she is attentive, never short with them. She really enjoys them and she loves hearing about them.

They came to see us at our house shortly after Dan was born and I had one of those baby books where you fill in all the information about your family and she happily filled in her bits about where she went to school and where she met her husband. I felt embarrassed asking her to fill in the book because she felt like a stranger to me.

When I first had my boys I was upset I didn't have a girl. I found myself immediately projecting forward to when they would have their own children and I thought, sadly, that paternal grandparents never get the look-in that the maternal grandparents get.

I have been left alone with my mother-in-law while James goes to the pub with his dad and we talk about safe, neutral things, like places I have been to. We have had long conversations about Egypt and Italy. She is both clever and incredibly artistic – she has examples of her paintings around the house. The first Christmas that she ever gave me a present, she gave me this needlepoint thing she had done. It wasn't the usual needlepoint, it was an almost cubist design and it was obvious that she'd put a lot of thought into it. After all the nothingness there had been, I thought she was trying to put in some effort, as though somehow she could make up for all the lost time.

On our Christmas cards they do this strange thing, they sign it 'from Alan and Joan', never 'Mum and Dad'. It's odd that people would stop calling themselves Mum and Dad. This year for the first time she wrote 'with love from', and I thought she must have forgotten that she doesn't do 'love' here. But the children always have 'lots of love' on their cards.

You hope you will be a good mother-in-law but I wonder what I would do if my son left his wife with three children under the age of five? It is nice for my children that they know James's parents but I hope that before they die James will be fully reconciled with them.

Mothers-in-law on the Web

Put the term 'mothers-in-law' into Google and nearly 300,000 results come up, almost twice as many as for 'fathers-in-law'. The web has become the place for daughters-in-law to pour out their feelings about mothers-in-law, in a mostly vituperative fashion, through discussion boards and on websites with names like 'Mother-in-law Stories', 'Quasimother', 'Disarming the Dragon', and 'The Secret Society of Tortured Daughters-in-law', in which the general editorial direction is self-evident. If there are sons-in-law with issues about their mothers-in-law they are not sharing them on the internet. Likewise, daughters-in-law who have good relationships with their mothers-in-law are not enthusing about them either. There are, as yet, no sites led by mothers-in-law but it is only a matter of time; one that promises to be launched in the UK (the others are all American) is called simply 'Mothers-in-law' and has the more even-handed premise of 'Love them or loathe them . . . You decide', giving at least the semblance of fair play. The use of the internet may be a generational issue; daughters-in-law are more familiar with the internet than their mothers-in-law, but the need that both have to share experiences is clear from the few discussion threads set up by mothers-in-law.

Communicating on the web feels safe. Daughters-in-law can both let off steam and get advice from other web users. The site 'Mother-in-law Stories' has jokes, polls, worst gift stories and a place for women to post any anecdote under the heading 'Frequent Fry Her'. What strikes you about reading these stories is how trivial are some of the slights felt by daughters-in-law, but nonetheless how bitterly they are resented. Women who have told their mothers-in-law a million times before that they are vegetarian find themselves again being served lamb stew. There are more serious stories that suggest some mothers-in-law are unable to resist interfering in the lives of their adult children, giving unwanted advice on when they should have children and who should do the childcare afterwards.

Frequent areas for battles are the question of which relatives a couple spends holidays with and the presents mothers-in-law give to their daughters-in-law. Gifts from mothers-in-law are scrutinised for any signs of favouritism. The websites 'Quasimother' and 'Disarming the Dragon' are both humorously hostile in their tone, offering advice and unflattering definitions of various types of mothers-in-law so daughters-in-law can know who they are dealing with. The intention at 'Quasimother' is to encourage daughters-in-law to release tension, while acknowledging, 'If you're a good mother-in-law and have innocently slipped into this domain (which can at times be deservingly brutal to wayward mother-in-laws [sic]) then take note that this site commends you for being a total angel.'

'Disarming the Dragon' gives eighty-eight rules for 'mollifying the obstreperous mother-in-law'. 'The Secret Society of Tortured Daughters-in-law' has the most attitude of the current sites, with pictures of slutty brides complete with bridal veils, cigarettes dangling from their mouths and blurred mascara. The emphasis is on community, sharing stories and humour, venting hardcore spleen and helping other women by offering supportive insights.

Threads from mothers-in-law on general posting sites are equally impassioned, with titles such as 'Daughter-in-law from Hell', stories about supine sons being manipulated by self-serving daughters-in-law and tales of ingratitude for money given and services rendered. This is the other side of the mother-in-law paradigm, where the daughters-in-law are culpable of the sorts of behaviour of which mothers-in-law are traditionally accused. Here are tales of daughters-in-law who are openly critical and insulting to their mothers-in-law: 'My daughter-in-law was telling one of her relatives about something my grandson had done and when she saw me within earshot said, "Do you mind, this only concerns the family."' There are daughters-in-law who deny their mothers-in-law access to their sons ('I feel as though my son has died') and grandchildren. Mothers-in-law voice concerns that certainly do not sound vindictive, about how well their grandchildren are being looked after ('My granddaughter is clearly overweight but they keep piling her plate up with food and don't encourage her to take exercise') and how much they want their daughter-in-law to be pleasant to them. They frequently sound genuinely baffled as to why their relationships with their daughters-in-law are so appalling. Some of the 'daughters-in-law' sites are routinely visited by mothers-in-law hoping both for insights and for the possibility of 'educating' the accusatory daughters-in-law. Rather than trying to educate each other it might be easier for mothers-in-law and daughters-in-law to just respect their differences.

Isabella Franklin on setting up 'The Secret Society of
Tortured Daughters-in-law'

I come from a long line of women who haven't got on with
their mothers-in-law. When my grandmother, who was
Catholic, had a set of twins alongside her other children,
her mother-in-law, who was a Baptist, scornfully said that
she was 'having them in litters like a dog'. My mother's
mother-in-law openly declared her son had married
beneath him and her cousin and aunt both had problems
with their husbands' mothers. But when it happened to me
I was completely unprepared even though it had become
almost a tradition in the family.

I'm Catholic and my husband Phoenix is Pentecostal
and Hispanic so for his parents I'm the wrong religion and
wrong colour. They just weren't going to like me. I am a
gregarious person and I have never been disliked, so it has
been a shock. I should have realised how difficult the relationship was going to be when my mother-in-law was two
hours late for our wedding because she was getting her hair
done. She had been late for our wedding rehearsal the day
before because she was shopping. I worked very hard to
put it all behind me and I had them over once a week for
dinner. The first Thanksgiving I had a party and she was
late again. For a new bride who was trying so hard it was
incredibly difficult and just as she arrived my puppy made
a mess on the floor and she and her friends just laughed at
me, they didn't do anything to help.

I don't think I'd embraced how bad things were
because I needed a job and I took one at the same non-

profit organisation as my mother-in-law worked. We were equals but I had to look over her work. I soon learnt never to have a conversation on my own with her. I would contact her by email and copy in my boss. I did this to protect myself because she would blame me as much as possible by saying in front of people, 'You should have given that piece of work back to me weeks ago.' People who I worked with used to hear what she said to me, like, 'Your hair looks terrible today,' and they would say to me, 'I can't believe she just said that.' If I mentioned an accomplishment in front of her she would say, 'That's no big deal,' and she would constantly imply I had put on a lot of weight. When I walked past her in the hall I thought I would pass out, I felt so dizzy. I was so unhappy about it that I started going

to counselling and my counsellor said, 'Why are you trying to evolve her when God chose not to?'

I had met Phoenix at school in Pittsburgh but only started seeing him after we left and he was living in Philadelphia with his parents and I was in Virginia. When he started seeing me his parents would say, 'You're only going down there to Virginia to have sex,' so I said to Phoenix, 'So they're calling me a whore.' When I first met my mother-in-law at her house (we drove up for me to meet them) it was quite good, I was nervous but she was cordial although she did-n't say much to me. It was not until the wedding planning that I thought, 'This is going to be rough.'

She said, 'We're not having alcohol,' and spoke of my family as though they were lushes. There were no congrat-ulations on our engagement. Phoenix stopped telling me what they said about me because I just got so angry. There wasn't exactly a warm welcome into the family.

My mother-in-law is a very serious Christian and she has set standards of belief and at some point she started telling people that I was not going to be saved and wouldn't go to heaven. My mother got to hear and she was furious and rang her up and said, 'You can't say this about my daughter – it insults me as well.' And so I rang my mother-in-law and said, 'Do you want to talk about this now, because if so let's deal with it.' She hung up, so I kept ringing because I was angry that she had hurt my mother and eventu-ally my mother-in-law said over the phone, 'Erase me from your memory.' I rang her back and said, 'You better mean it because if you say this you won't see your son or grandchildren,' and she did not respond. In retrospect it was the best conversation I ever had with her because it made it easier to cut her out. I had kept thinking up until that point I could make our relationship better, that by showing her what a good wife I was my mother-in-law would love me.

My husband had never stood up to his parents and he couldn't do it for me. It was only when I walked down the stairs and said I was done and that I was fed up of him not supporting me that he said we'd walk away together. I was no longer a sunny person; I was an angry, vindictive, bitter woman.

When we moved to Virginia we didn't say goodbye to his parents. I thought it would be better because we were further away but what I've learnt is that you can live on the same street or five hundred miles away from your mother-in-law and still have a problem.

I decided to set up a website for women like me because I thought only other daughters-in-law would understand, and my husband, who develops websites, did it for me because it was hard for him to listen to me complaining about his mother. He was happy with the idea that I would be able to talk to someone else other than him. The first woman that posted, I remember thinking, 'She has the same story as me and feels the same way. Wow.' This site is for women to get things off their chest – it isn't a sad place, it's a funny place – who wouldn't want to be a member of this secret society of tortured daughters-in-law? The women here are funny and smart but also they are hurt. Some women can't post straight away – they see themselves in a story and then they can tell their own story and then they start advising others. The biggest successes are the women who the site helps to move on – women who tell their stories and get on and face their mothers-in-law.

I didn't expect the site to heal me but I feel normal now, whereas I used to feel crazy. It helped to have 450 other women saying, 'Oh yeah, my mother-in-law said that too.' I think some of the mothers-in-law on this site are nasty women and there is something about a daughter-in-law that pushes her buttons. There is a power struggle between who the son goes to if he is sad or sick. I understand that must be difficult for them.

I recently saw my mother-in-law for the first time in two years. I realised I would never forgive myself if my husband didn't have a relationship with his parents for the important things that happen in his life. Friends were horrified when they heard us saying his parents would never see their grandchildren. When I walked into the room I felt in complete control and it was his parents who looked nervous. I knew I had the secret of my website and I know how terrible some of the living hell stories are on there and I thought, 'My situation is not so bad, I can see my mother-in-law for an hour or two,' and we chatted lightly for an hour. I used to say I wanted her to say sorry but I've given up on that.

I would hope that most mothers-in-law and daughters-in-law have healthy relationships and if that's the case my website isn't for them. I would hate to think that most mothers-in-law are like the ones I see on the site.

We've had mothers-in-law infiltrating the site posing as daughters-in-law; some have found their daughters-in-law on the site – I have caught them all. One looked in the history of their daughter-in-law's computer and saw she'd visited the site. If a new member shows too much interest in another member who has been on the site for longer then we get suspicious. Most new members want to talk to me first. A mother-in-law came on and wanted to educate the girls and give her perspective – she started to get angry and say nasty things about her daughter-in-law, so we booted her off. I would hope though that mothers-in-law have their own site to go to but they can't come and try to heal themselves on our site.

My husband has two younger brothers – one has married the equivalent of his mother, she is Pentecostal and my mother-in-law thinks she is the perfect woman. She is strong-headed but they go shopping together and sometimes it is upsetting – I don't know why I couldn't have had that relationship with my mother-in-law.

How to Be a Good Mother-in-law

How to be a good mother-in-law? You may as well ask how to be a good human being. As with most relationships there are few instructions and even fewer rules. But mothers-in-law are hampered by some negative stereotyping before future in-laws ever meet them. This undoubtedly influences how we all think of mothers-in-law. A study in America in the 1950s by Dr Evelyn Millis Duvall, a mother-in-law herself who recorded what over five thousand men and women thought of their relationships with their in-laws, found that mothers-in-law were deemed the trickiest. The tensions were mostly between mothers-in-law and daughters-in-law. Mothers-in-law were accused of being possessive, interfering and critical, but also aloof, distant and uninterested, thereby raising the question of whether mothers-in-law can ever get it right. Mothers-in-law in the same survey were rarely critical of their daughters-in-law and felt baffled and bitter at how they were treated. Terri Apter, a psychologist at Cambridge University and expert on the mother-in-law and daughter-in-law relationship, says that daughters-in-law have no sense of how mothers-in-law feel. 'The way that some daughters-in-law rebuff and edge her out is quite awful,' she says. 'They feel they have permission to be less kind to this particular woman. Some mothers-in-law have daughters-in-law who are immensely rude to them.'

In the absence of tips on how to be a good daughter-in-law, this chapter will provide its own. There are, however, a few guides on how to be a good mother-in-law, including one from 1937 called *Are you a mother-in-law? A useful guide for all in-laws*. This is a book of etiquette for mothers-in-law and is completely one-sided as well as deliciously dated. Mothers-in-law are advised not to offer their daughters-in-law tips on how to get food to the table still warm, or to ask their sons dramatically if they feel ill or have something on their minds. 'Now if you are a mother-in-law and want a little sound advice, never interfere with your married children, their homes or their possessions. If you do you will soon find that you are not wanted. If your opinion is sought, give it, but be circumspect how you give it. If your opinion is not sought, don't volunteer it, just because you feel you ought. Keep to these simple rules and you will be more than a welcome visitor to the new home. Break them and you will be one more mother-in-law who has added to the sum of total unhappiness in the world.'

The right sort of mother-in-law, says the guide, is welcoming to new in-laws and gets to know their preferences so she can pander to them. She makes her new daughter-in-law feel part of the family and buys small, not oppressively costly presents for the couple's new home. So far so good, but this is largely one-dimensional advice. Being a good mother-in-law is a more complex business altogether. And to be a successful one you usually need a good daughter-in-law as well.

Top tips for mothers-in-law

1. EXPECT TO FEEL a huge sense of loss when your grown-up child finds a serious partner – and you may be pleasantly surprised to find that you don't. Healthy parenting releases independent adults into the world who can have loving relationships. So well done, job done. Unfortunately the time when your grown-up child meets Mr or Ms Right coincides with the time when some mothers edge towards the menopause. There is the natural but painful reality of one family life beginning and another ending. It would be strange to be the most important person in your son or daughter's life for ever, but the transition to mother-in-law is unsettling. You are likely to have no control over whom your child chooses and when they do so. Effectively you are at the mercy of your child as to when you become a mother-in-law.

2. OPENLY GRIEVE to sympathetic friends about the loss of your child. The move from mother, at the heart of the family, to mother-in-law, on the periphery, is a clear relegation. But the wise mother-in-law prepares for this moment by having a life that is so busy she barely has time to cast anything but a benign eye over her son or daughter's new household. You have to move on because you have no choice – all mothers have to separate from their children.

3. THE FIRST MEETING is significant for both you and your son- or daughter-in-law. Try to be as welcoming as you can, ask them questions to draw them out and show your interest

in them. Daughters- and sons-in-law are usually sensitive to the impression they make on their mothers-in-law and will be grateful if you seem welcoming. If you don't they will never forget and will tell all their friends.

4. GET TO KNOW your son- or daughter-in-law as a person in her own right outside of family events. This is essential because it is much harder for misunderstandings to arise if you know each other and have an independent relationship.

5. MANY MOTHERS STRUGGLE to think that anyone is a good enough partner for their child, but even if you don't like your son- or daughter-in-law you are going to have to try. You can't dictate to your child their choice of partner, so if you can't work out why they have chosen as they have, stand back and accept that it wasn't your decision. Hope that you are wrong and say nothing. Avoid conflict as it escalates and leads to estrangement. Try to be civil.

6. THE QUALITIES that people appreciate in their mothers-in-law are, according to Duvall's and other surveys, 'friendliness', 'acceptance of them', and being 'thoughtful, kind and generous'. Does this sound like you? Would that all people were like this.

7. IF YOU WANT to help your son- or daughter-in-law ensure that they want it and use restraint as too much help can make them feel heavily obligated. Also be sensitive to what the other set of parents is doing or you may end up inadvertently in competition. It may be safer to wait to be asked for help as unasked it can be intrusive – especially if it involves throwing out any of their possessions. Couples like to do things their way, just like you did.

8. TREAT YOUR son- or daughter-in-law like a new neighbour, politely and at some distance. You wouldn't go into a stranger's house and say that you love the sofa but the curtains are hideous.

9. IF YOUR DAUGHTER-IN-LAW in particular is uninterested in any relationship with you, it is probably nothing personal. Some women only want the son, not the rest of the family. You may need to have a non-threatening talk to your son. Sons can mediate your relationship with your daughter-in-law but their loyalty should usually be to their partner.

10. YOU WILL NEED to compromise on the thorny issues of family events and holidays. Try to remember how stressful it is to please two sets of parents and be as relaxed and generous as you can. It will be appreciated.

11. IF YOU HAVE GRANDCHILDREN, rejoice but don't get carried away. Childcare fashions come and go and your way is likely to have gone, in which case you may be incapable of doing

anything right. Some mothers have become too frightened to let their children out of their sight or to feed them anything with sugar in it. Discipline has given way to stepwise negotiation. You must show interest (which you may naturally have) in your grandchildren but you are bound to do as their mother wants when it comes to babysitting duties. Remember how little you knew about bringing up children when you first had them and be compassionate.

12. IF YOU HAVE a daughter and daughter-in-law who both have children, make sure you don't show any favouritism. Be scrupulously careful with presents and the amount of time spent with grandchildren, as in-laws will feel hard done by and no one takes kindly to being the least favourite.

13. WHEN YOU VISIT, offer to help with making a meal or washing up. You occupy a precarious position of being family but not really family, so you can be damned if you do help and damned if you don't. But do offer.

14. REMEMBER your son- or daughter-in-law's birthday; it shows you are treating him or her like a member of the family. Try to do some research into what they might like – vouchers for a favourite shop are usually safe.

And a few tips relating to daughters-in-law in particular:

15. MAKE YOUR DAUGHTER-IN-LAW feel appreciated by telling her how well you think she is doing and how pleased you are that she is with your son. Tell as many people as possible and hope it gets back to her. You can also tell her in a letter.

16. AVOID doing anything helpful in terms of domestic tasks for your son, like his ironing. There are lots of surveys that show daughters-in-law hate this. Never suggest that your daughter-in-law should be looking after him more thoroughly.

17. IF YOU DON'T get on with your daughter-in-law, it is usual for the relationship to improve over time as you both mellow. Keep some distance but not too much or you will be accused of absenteeism.

Top tips for daughters-in-law

1. YOU DON'T GET TO CHOOSE your mother-in-law but she doesn't usually get to pick you either. She can only hope that you'll make her son happy and let him still see her now and then. It makes for a good relationship if you give the appearance of being able to do so.

2. YOUR MOTHER-IN-LAW is the mother of the man you love, so she deserves some credit. Don't just hold her responsible for his faults.

3. DEVELOP A RELATIONSHIP with her outside of your relationship as her son's partner. Try to understand her as a real person and get some idea of what she's done in her life and what matters to her. A lot of the issues that arise between mothers-in-law and daughters-in-law are due to perceived slights and poor communication. Take her out for lunch or phone and invite yourself for tea. If issues do arise it will be easier for you to talk to her about them.

4. MOTHERS-IN-LAW often feel they have a lot of useful things to tell their daughters-in-law, whereas their daughters-in-law think they either know most of them already or that they aren't useful at all. Your mother-in-law isn't a threat to you so you can be indulgent sometimes. You wouldn't be so hard on her if she was your mother instead of your mother-in-law. She also does have some useful things she could tell you, especially about your partner.

5. ENCOURAGE YOUR PARTNER to visit his mother on his own. However much his mother likes you, she will enjoy seeing her son on his own occasionally. This will make your mother-in-law feel more secure in her relationship with both of you and shows that you are not in competition with her.

6. INCLUDE YOUR MOTHER-IN-LAW in some of your life decisions, such as buying a house. Traditionally women get their mother involved but leave out their mother-in-law entirely. You may not need your mother-in-law's opinion but it is kind to make her feel included.

7. IF YOU NEED to complain about your partner, it may be

better to do so to your mother-in-law than your own mother. Your mother-in-law will be a good sounding board and feel flattered that you wanted to talk to her. Your mother will hear what you say about your partner and never forgive him.

8. IF YOU HAVE CHILDREN you may want to ask your mother-in-law to help you out. If she is still working her help may be limited. Some mothers-in-law are less keen than others to help out so don't take offence if she is not as enthusiastic as you'd like her to be. It may depend on her own experiences of bringing up children.

9. IF YOU CAN'T GET ON with your mother-in-law try to behave as though you do. You don't have to love her, just treat her with enough civility so that it's not difficult for your partner. If your mother-in-law really is a terrible woman, and mothers-in-law will range, like most people, from wonderful to unbearable, then you have to talk to your partner and devise a strategy.

10. WHEN YOU MEET at family gatherings, make sure you greet her warmly and talk to her. Make her feel included.

11. TELL YOUR MOTHER-IN-LAW you appreciate things she has done for you, and if you do like her, tell her. The normal rules of human behaviour apply.

Top tips for sons-in-law

1. YOU MAY FEEL that your mother-in-law is nothing to do with you, but your partner will appreciate it if you are friendly and welcoming to her.

2. DO NOT MAKE JOKES about mothers-in-law. Women do not think they are funny and, worse, they think they are jokes against themselves.

3. DO NOT SAY to your partner, 'You're just like your mother.' Unless you mean it in a complimentary way, you will in one sentence have been rude to your partner and her mother. Which you probably knew anyway.

4. AT FAMILY GATHERINGS make a point of looking pleased to see her and do not immediately look over her shoulder for someone more interesting.

Carolyn R. Young is a psychotherapist in Colorado, USA, and co-author of a research paper called 'Daughters-in-law and Mothers-in-law Seeking their Place within the Family: a qualitative study of differing viewpoints', published in the *Journal of Family Relations*.

> I have been a mother-in-law for nine years. I have one son who is an only child and when he married, it felt like I was losing him. My daughter-in-law is part of a close Italian family with three brothers and my son was pulled into that family. It was a replay of *My Big Fat Greek Wedding* except with Italians. I wanted to work out why this transition was so wounding to me and so with a friend and colleague I started doing some research into the mother-in-law and daughter-in-law relationship. I wanted to look at my inner processes and work out what was going on. This relationship is a connecting link between mothers, our sons and the grandchildren so it is important for it to be healthy.
>
> Often our research, which involved interviewing mothers-in-law and daughters-in-law, showed that they started off feeling pretty good about each other but then became disillusioned with their relationship.

There is no way to deal with an unsatisfying mother-in-law and daughter-in-law relationship. It isn't like a husband-and-wife relationship where you can go into counselling. There is competition between a daughter-in-law and mother-in-law; the son's favourite foods are no longer his favourite foods because he has learnt new foods. It is painful for mothers-in-law. You go through grief and it is very raw. Some mothers-in-law feel angry and some feel defensive. On a subtle level many mothers-in-law never feel there is a woman good enough for their son. You just hope she will be someone who is really good for him and will support him.

The mother-in-law and daughter-in-law are at different stages of their development: the daughter-in-law is moving into an exciting new beginning phase of her life, the mother-in-law can feel like she's ending one stage and doesn't know what comes next. She may have been a mother for over three decades. This difference in life stage makes for clashes. If the mother-in-law says to the daughter-in-law, 'If you put olive oil in the pasta it won't stick,' the daughter-in-law may become irritated and resentful because she wants to cook her own spaghetti. The mother-in-law wants to teach, but the daughter-in-law wants to create her own identity. They may feel that their mother-in-law is being critical when she is not. I would like daughters-in-law to look at this more honestly instead of jumping to a negative interpretation. I had to do that with my own mother-in-law.

The whole world is made up of triangles and in the triangle of mother-in-law, son and daughter-in-law someone is always on the outside. In the beginning the daughter-in-law may feel the outsider because she is coming into a family in which people will have a lot of similar values. But the daughter-in-law really has most of the power in the relationship with her mother-in-law as time goes on, even if she doesn't understand that she has.

I have worked very hard at my relationship with my daughter-in-law. We volunteered our services for the wedding, we stuffed envelopes, and we did lots of things to stay involved. Many times the mother-in-law isn't included in the wedding plans. The wedding starts you off on the whole asymmetry of the relationship.

My son travels and I'll go and spend the night with her and help get the children ready for school in the morning. I have tried to find my own unique place in their family system. She sent me a card recently saying how much she appreciated me, that she knew how many miles I had driven in an effort to spend time with them. I can tell my daughter-in-law understands this is a mutual relationship. Both she and my son spend time with each other's families although one of the conflicts for the mother-in-law is that more time is spent with the wife's family. This is a source of grief and loss for a mother-in-law.

A Chinese story

A long time ago, a girl named Li-Li got married and went to live with her husband and mother-in-law in a village far from her home. In a very short time, Li-Li found that she couldn't get along with her mother-in-law. Their personalities were very different, and Li-Li was angered by many of her mother-in-law's ways. Her mother-in-law criticised Li-Li continuously.

Days, weeks and months passed and Li-Li and her mother-in-law never stopped arguing and fighting. Chinese tradition decreed that Li-Li had to bow to her mother-in-law and obey her every wish. Finally, Li-Li could not stand her mother-in-law's bad temper and domineering ways any longer, and she decided to do something about it.

Li-Li travelled to see her father's good friend, Mr Huang, who sold herbs. She told him how terrible things were with her mother-in-law and asked if he could give her some poison to get rid of the old woman. Mr Huang thought for a while, and finally said, 'Li-Li, I will help you solve your problem, but you must listen to me and do exactly what I tell you.' Li-Li agreed.

Mr Huang went into the back room, and returned with a package of herbs. He passed them gravely to Li-Li and said, 'You can't use a quick-acting poison to get rid of your mother-in-law, because it would be obvious that you had killed her. No one must suspect you, so I have given you some herbs that will slowly poison her body.

'Every other day prepare some delicious meal and put a little of these herbs in her serving. Now, in order to make sure that nobody suspects you when she dies, you must be very careful to act in a loving way towards her. Stop arguing with her, obey her wishes and treat her beautifully.'

Li-Li was delighted. She thanked Mr Huang and ran home to embark on her plan to murder her mother-in-law. Days, weeks and months passed and Li-Li served the specially treated food to her mother-in-law. She remembered what Mr Huang had said about avoiding suspicion, so she controlled her temper, obeyed her mother-in-law and treated her like her own mother. After six months had passed, the whole household had changed.

Li-Li no longer got angry or upset. She hadn't had an argument in months with her mother-in-law, who now seemed much kinder and easier to get along with.

The mother-in-law began to love Li-Li like her own daughter. She kept telling friends and relatives that Li-Li was the best daughter-in-law anyone could ever find.

Li-Li's husband was very happy to see what was happening. Li-Li could barely remember that she was meant to be murdering her mother-in-law but the day that she did she ran to Mr Huang, begging for his help again. She cried, 'Dear Mr Huang, please stop the poison from killing my mother-in-law! She's changed into such a nice woman, and I love her like my own mother.'

Mr Huang smiled and nodded his head. 'Li-Li, there's nothing to worry about. I never gave you any poison. I gave you vitamins instead. The only poison was in your mind and your attitude toward her.'

Acknowledgements

Among those who listened and offered ideas are: my mother, my fiancé John (who also read the proofs), Maggie (my mother-in-law), Ann and Sam Robinson, Rebecca Stewart, Rebecca Snelling, Caroline Overy (a friend at the Wellcome Trust who told me about David Livingstone's mother-in-law), Karen Rose and Rachel Armitage. Thanks to three friends who let me write on what should have been a girls' weekend away, Anastasia, Heather and Janice (who I also thank for telling me about her mother-in-law Agi and for allowing me to interview the amazing Agi). Thanks to Andy Anthony for his beautiful writing and to his charming mother-in-law Von.

The Society of Authors, and staff of the British Library, were excellent. Thanks to Rupert Christiansen, whose *Complete Book of Aunts* sets the standard.

At the *Guardian* newspaper thanks to Merope Mills, Emma Cook and Simon Hattenstone. The greatest thanks go to Sam Wollaston, without whom I would not have written this book because he secured for me the column that I write which was seen by Belinda Matthews, my editor at Faber. Belinda is an inspirational editor and the joy I had in writing this book is due to her. Also at Faber Katherine Armstrong, Kate Ward, Eleanor Rees and many others were wonderful. Stephanie's illustrations are so good I bought some.

Thanks to time given by two giants of biography, D.J. Taylor and Andrew Lycett. Lynn E. Neidermeier sent me pages of detailed notes on Eliza Calvert Hall; Linda Lee sent me academic papers on fairy tales. Justine Roberts let me collect stories from her Mumsnet mothers and Esther Tyldesley told me about mothers-in-law in China. Thanks to psychologists Marsha Ross, Teri Apter and Carolyn R. Young for their wisdom. Thanks to the writer Katherine Whitehorn for talking as brilliantly as she writes.

Professor Nicholas Roe helped me with Keats's story as did staff at the Keats Museum, Hampstead, and the Keats–Shelley House in Rome. Mark Rough gave a stand up comic's view of mothers-in-law.

A final thanks to my brother, Larry, and father, Robert, who taught me to write. Any complaints will have to go to my brother. My father died on the day I started writing this book by his bedside and I'm so sorry he can't see it.

'I'm getting ready for my Mother-in-law' Words and Music by Jack Norworth, is reproduced by permission of Francis Day and Hunter Ltd, London.

'Ninga on my Palm' from A. K. Ramanujan, *A Flowering Tree and Other Oral Tales from India*, is reproduced by Berkeley London, University of California Press.

Extract from *The Letters of Mozart and His Family*, MacMillan and Co. Ltd reproduced with permission of Palgrave Macmillan.

Extract from the *Letters and Private Papers of William Makepeace Thackeray*, collected and edited by Gordon N.

Ray, Harvard University Press, reprinted by permission of the publisher from the *Letters and Private Papers of William Makepeace Thackeray*, Volume I, 1817–1840; Volume II, 1841–1851; Volume III, 1852–1856, Volume IV, 1857–1863, collected and edited by Gordon N. Ray, Cambridge, Mass: Harvard University Press, Copyright 1945 by the Presidents and Fellows of Harvard College.

Extract from *The Diary of Virginia Woolf* by Virginia Woolf, published by Hogarth Press. Used by permission of the executors of the Virginia Woolf Estates and The Random House Group Ltd.

Extract from *The Diary of Virginia Woolf*, edited by Anne Oliver Bell, published by Hogarth Press. Reprinted by permission of The Random House Group Ltd.

Extract from *Sade: A Biographical Essay* by Laurence L. Bongie, reprinted by permission of University of Chicago Press.Ltd, c. 1998 by The University of Chicago. All rights Reserved. Published 1998.

Mother-in-law translations reprinted with permission of Wikitionary

Extract from *The Collected Letters by Dylan Thomas*, published by Orion reprinted by permission of David Higham Associates Ltd.

Extract from 'The Intersection of Class and Age: Mother-in-law/Daughter-in-law Relations in Rural Taiwan from the Journal of Cross Cultural Gerontology' is reprinted by permission of its author Rita Gallin.

Extracts from Byron's 'Corbeau Blanc', by Jonathan David Gross, reprinted by permission of Liverpool University Press.

Extract from 'Sharon and my Mother-in-law' by Saud Amiry, published by Granta Books, is reprinted by permission of Granta Books.

Extract from *Good Wives?* by Margaret Forster published by Chatto and Windus. Reprinted by permission of the Random House Group Ltd

Extracts from *Somebody Else's Mama*, by David Haynes (Minneapolis: Milkweed Editions, 1995). Copyright © 1995 by David Haynes. Reprinted with permission from Milkweed Editions. www.milkweed.org

Songs from the 'Sad Lot of Women in Ukranian and Yiddish Folksongs' by Robert A. Rothstein, in *Texture and Mourning: Thirty years of Judaic Studies* at the University of Massachusetts reprinted by permission of its author Robert A. Rothstein.

Extracts from letters of Keats from *Letters of John Keats* edited by Gittings R. (1979) and excerpt from *Letters of Fanny Brawne to Fanny Keats* edited by Edgecumbe F. are both reprinted by permission of Oxford University Press.

Extract from *Makito's Diary* by Makito Nakanai is reprinted by permission of the Stanford University Press.

Extracts of Edgar Allan Poe's letters and poems are reprinted by permission of the John Hopkins University Press as they come from Edgar Allen Poe, *A Critical Biography* by Arthur

Hobson Quinn although the poems and letters are in the public domain.

Extract of letter from Mrs Brawne to Joseph Severn comes from the Keats–Shelley House in Rome.

Quotes from the letters of Lida Calvert Obenchain transcribed by Lynn E. Niedermeier, Western Kentucky University from the collection of her letters in the Calvert-Obenchain-Younglove Collection at the Kentucky Library, Western Kentucky University. Background from the biography *Eliza Calvert Hall: Kentucky Author and Suffragist*, by Lynn E. Niedermeier, published by the University of Kentucky.

Extract from *The Inner Quarters* by Patricia Buckley Ebrey is reprinted by permission of the University of California Press.

Extract from *Times to Remember: An Autobiography*, Rose Fitzgerald Kennedy, published by Collins, reprinted with permission from Random House Inc.

At the time of going to press some permissions have yet to be returned. If these and any I have missed are in copyright or need payment for use, please let either me or Faber know. The ones that we know about and have tried very hard to get permissions for are:

Quotes from letters by Mary Moffat in *Heroines of the mission field: biographical sketches of female missionaries who have laboured in various lands among the heathen* by Mrs Emma Raymond Pitman, published in 1880.
An extract from Fanny Brawne by Joanna Richardson.

'Quiet Please there's a lady on the stage' by Peter Allen.

'To my mother-in-law by Lee Sook-Jung' published in *Yisei* Magazine.

Quote from *Lord Byron's Wife*, by Malcolm Elwin, published by MacDonald and Co.

Extract from the *Mother-in-Law Diaries* by Carol Dawson, published by Simon and Schuster Inc.

Extract from *Are you a mother-in-law? A useful guide for all in-laws* by Edgar and Diana Woods, published by Universal Publications, London.